Would anywhere ever be home for us again?

Any place was safer for us than Warsaw, 1941.

We were lucky to be getting out, for the ship, for Shanghai, the last place we might be allowed to come.

I first saw Shanghai from over my father's shoulder, Papa carrying Naomi, me, and all our things. We had been traveling for over a month and now we were here. As far as I could see there were human beings, an electric mob of running, waving, shouting, on streets throbbing with heat. Out of the endless rush of people emerged a man on a bicycle. In back it was stacked with so many packages it looked like a house made of boxes. He was the first Chinese person I'd seen, and he looked the same as anyone else, but also different.

What did I look like to those who weren't me?

Harrowing, moving, and historically fascinating, *Someday We Will Fly* is an unforgettable coming-of-age story.

OTHER BOOKS YOU MAY ENJOY

SOMEDAY We Will FLY

Rachel DeWoskin

PENGUIN BOOKS

PENGUIN BOOKS
An imprint of Penguin Random House LLC, New York

First published in the United States of America by Viking,
an imprint of Penguin Random House LLC, 2019
Published by Penguin Books, an imprint of Penguin Random House LLC, 2020

Visit us online at penguinrandomhouse.com

THE LIBRARY OF CONGRESS HAS CATALOGED THE VIKING EDITION AS FOLLOWS:
Names: DeWoskin, Rachel, author. Title: Someday we will fly / by Rachel DeWoskin.
Description: New York : Viking, published by Penguin Group, [2019] | Summary: Lillia,
fifteen, flees Warsaw with her father and baby sister in 1940 to try to make a new
start in Shanghai, China, but the conflict grows more intense as America and Japan
become involved. | Identifiers: LCCN 2018018516 (print) | LCCN 2018024506 (ebook)
| ISBN 9781101617885 (ebook) | ISBN 9780670014965 (hardback) | Subjects: LCSH:
Jews—China—Shanghai—Juvenile fiction. | CYAC: Jews—China—Shanghai—Fiction.
| Emigration and immigration—Fiction. | Circus performers—Fiction. | Sino-Japanese
War, 1937–1945—Fiction. | Shanghai (China)—History—20th century—Fiction. |
China—History—1937–1945—Fiction. Classification: LCC PZ7.D537 (ebook) | LCC
PZ7.D537 Som 2019 (print) | DDC [Fic]—dc23 |
LC record available at https://lccn.loc.gov/2018018516

ISBN 9780147508911

Printed in the United States of America

Set in Kepler   Book design by Mariam Quraishi

10 9 8 7 6 5 4 3 2 1

For anyone who has ever needed to leave home.

And for Shanghai, a haven

for so many refugees in the 1930s and '40s.

May America be a sanctuary, too.

— —  — —

The Bridge

I didn't believe,

Standing on the bank of a river

Which was wide and swift,

That I would cross that bridge

Plaited from thin, fragile reeds

Fastened with bast.

I walked delicately as a butterfly

And heavily as an elephant,

I walked surely as a dancer

And wavered like a blind man.

I didn't believe that I would cross that bridge,

And now that I am standing on the other side,

I don't believe I crossed it.

—Leopold Staff (1878–1957)

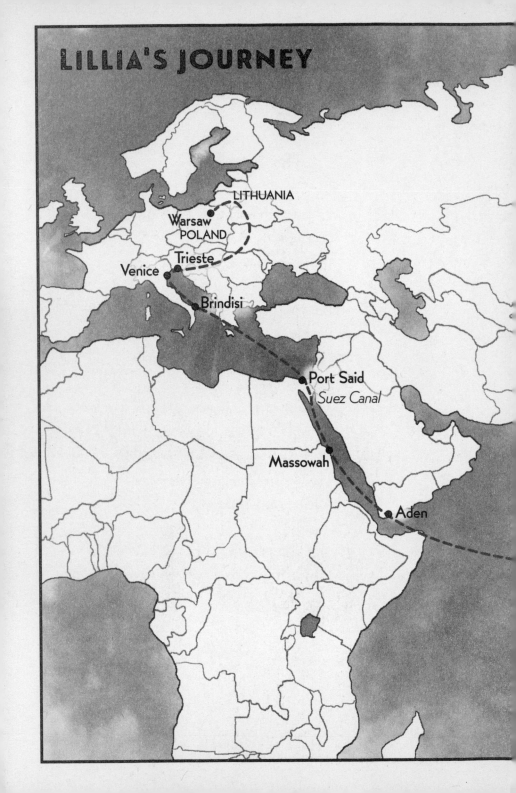

LILLIA'S JOURNEY

LITHUANIA

Warsaw
POLAND

Trieste

Venice

Brindisi

Port Said
Suez Canal

Massowah

Aden

CHAPTER ONE

Domu, *Home*

In the last act I saw my parents perform, they already looked like ghosts of the Stanislav Circus. It was spring, this spring, May 17, 1940. Alone in low light, they stared at each other for six seconds before my father bent at the knees and took my mother's hands in his. She stepped onto the bend in his arm and kicked off as he lifted and turned her upside down. He straightened slowly and she rose, her hands atop his, her hair falling into the space between their heads. They were dressed in blue and silver, like liquid or vapor, moving. They stayed, as they had my whole life and I guess even before that, in motion, attached to each other. Papa walked toward the audience, with Mama above him.

As they came forward, no one breathed. The audience was just a few of their former colleagues from the circus, my silent baby sister, Naomi, and me. Mama's face was turned away from us, but Papa smiled and in spite of the poor light, we saw his teeth flash, saw the glitter tear painted on his cheek. He lowered Mama so slowly, smiling, maybe feeling the joy they'd decided was worth risking a performance. Even though they were forbidden. They hadn't performed in so long it felt unbearable. So here they were, although there was no real ring, no antique building, no fiery spotlight. There was no music.

Their faces met, hers upside down, and then he lowered her more, until she was at his chest, his stomach, his knees. She bent and suspended herself across him, making their bodies a V before rising up again to his shoulders, where she balanced the back of her neck against the back of his. This was their most perfect act, and I waited, squeezing my sister tight, knowing next our father would flip our mother from his shoulders and catch her so surely that her body would look, even in this pitiful place, as certain as an arrow finding its bull's-eye.

But everything went black. We heard the cracking of a door kicked open, broken, something slamming across the floor my parents had taped up. There was a chorus of screaming voices, my mother's among them. I began to scream, too. Someone grabbed me so roughly I didn't know until I felt the shiny fabric of his blue-and-silver suit that it was my father. He put me on his back, and I held on as he ran into the blank night, gripping my sister under his arm so she wouldn't slip from his grasp and be lost. We flew to Zgoda Street, where he bounded into the back of our apartment, set us down, locked the door, pulled the blinds, and turned to me, no breath left in him. "She'll come. We have to wait."

I hadn't asked.

We waited all night. Naomi cried the way she does, clicking a cricket noise in the back of her throat, exhausting herself and us. There was nothing we could do. Only Mama knows what Naomi wants, and most of the time what she wants is Mama.

The sun rose and we stared through a tear in the drapes my grandmother had sewn as Warsaw came alive outside. In the day's first dim light, silhouettes of soldiers moved like shadows. Our non-Jewish neighbors, still allowed to work and study, hurried by. When Naomi finally fell asleep, I turned to my father, wild with fear I saw in his face, too. Why hadn't he gone back into the night to find her? Was he afraid of vanishing, too? Had he chosen between her and us?

"Where is she? What happened?"

He said, "I don't know."

We had tickets on a train leaving Lithuania for Italy in two days. We were to drive to Lithuania—the four of us—and then take the train to a ship that would sail in six days. Sail to Shanghai, a place we couldn't imagine. I tried to clear my mind by counting: six days was one hundred and forty-four hours, eight thousand six hundred and forty minutes. That was enough time. She might come back, meet us at home in time to drive to Lithuania, ten hours away, or in Lithuania in time for the train from there to Italy, which took two days. As long as she got to us before we drove, or met us at the train, or found us in Trieste, at the dock. Those were all possibilities, and the more I considered them, the more I felt a good one might come true. I told myself she had climbed down from my father's arms, skipping the finale intentionally, to escape. I put the screaming outside of my mind and imagined her on her way back, coming through the door, scooping Naomi up, wrapping her arms around Papa's neck, turning to wink at me. My grandmother, Babcia, would come in singing off-key, delighted. If I thought hard enough, really believed they would be home any minute, there were lots of minutes for God to make it happen.

All of her bird clocks chimed, and I jumped like a rickety puppet, shocked. It was five in the morning, but we were upside down, our day ending. Papa looked desperately at Naomi. Her cheeks were hot, dark curls stuck to her forehead, and a ribbon of drool glistened down her chin. A wooden cuckoo popped out of our best clock, and I waited for it to slide back to safety, but it stayed frozen, outside. No one else seemed to notice, so I said, "It's broken, look."

My sister didn't stir. Papa draped a red quilt over her, and then reached down to pick me up, even though I was fifteen.

We often carried each other around for fun. My father lifted, threw, spun, flipped, and caught us. I was made for the circus, small for fifteen and bendy. I had always been able to push two chairs close to each other and hold myself up over them, my hands the claws of a limber bird. Naomi was small as well, too small, and when we held her, she slid as if boneless, through our arms. My parents called her their "surprise baby," even before she behaved in surprising ways, but she wasn't like other one-and-a-half-year-olds and no one knew why, not my parents, not the doctors, not me.

But when my father picked me up from the couch, it was a different lifting, as if a switch had flipped and my weight might crack his spine. He hunched over my bed after setting me down.

"Maybe's she's found Babcia," I tried. "Maybe she found the camp, and that's why they're . . . well, they're coming back together, that's why—" There was silence until my false, looping voice started up again: "If not, we won't go. We don't have to go. We can take a different ship. We can . . ." These were questions, but he didn't answer and I felt the blood in my limbs go cold and slow, dimming from red to pink.

"Well, *I* won't go," I told him. I picked up my doll with the faded face, her yarn hair redder than my mother's or mine. And a mouse Babcia sewed for me when I was three. They were my only remaining toys, but I wished I'd kept every doll and animal, each game I'd ever played, because it came to me that I might never see my life again. Or Warsaw, our glittering Vistula River, Zgoda Park. Our city. Even after the soldiers came and I wasn't allowed at school, the streets still flashed with color. We were still from somewhere.

I tried to imagine my mother. Was she running along the river? Almost home, in the park? Was she alone? She was fearless, preferring no net at the circus, securing herself to Papa's limbs or ribbons hanging from the ceiling. They fought about this often, and he told her over and over to be more careful, but she laughed. Even angry, he stood beneath her, ready to lift her up and catch her, maybe careful for them both. After I was born, he made puppets and taught me to dance; he didn't like my contortion acts because he thought I might get hurt. But I wanted to be like my mother, brave, so I twirled as fast as a toy top, never got dizzy, bent into the wildest shapes I could make, flipped across every lovely expanse of stage I could find. I was dancing before I walked and everyone called me Wróżka, *Fairy*, because I danced like someone flying. Mama had her own name for me, though, Słodkie Lillia, Sweet Lillia. Little, silent Naomi we all called Lalka, *Doll*.

Now my father said, "Wróżka, I'm going to the circus offices to find out where your mother went. Stay here. Watch Naomi. Do not answer the door. Keep the curtains shut and don't look out the window. I'll tell Ana you girls are home."

I didn't want to stay. Or watch my sister. Some drum sounded inside me, formed more words: *What do I do with Naomi? What if you don't come back?* The worst fear filled me. Even if I asked questions forever, I could not keep him here. He hadn't even let me walk to school or Zgoda Park since the soldiers came, but now he was leaving me alone with Naomi after our mother vanished? Now he was kissing my forehead and I saw his eyes, lined with veins like red threads. Now he had become someone else over one night, someone sewn up sloppily.

I grabbed his hand, but it was cold. The glow around him, a bright clown blue he'd always had, was gone. "Don't look out the window," he reminded me. "Stay inside. Keep the lights off. There is food on the counter and some milk in the icebox. Only if there's an emergency, go get Ana."

Ana was my best friend Kassia's mother, and I didn't want to get her even though this felt like an emergency already. I listened for Naomi, angry with her for being a baby, for being so strange, for probably waking up soon and needing something I couldn't guess. Why didn't she crawl or babble like other babies? Papa used to joke that he loved me better once I learned to talk. But he hadn't said so in a long time, not since Naomi should have talked but didn't.

The clocks ticked like a chorus of clucking human tongues: *tluck, tluck, tluck, tluck.*

Our dog, Piotr, climbed up onto my stomach. We'd found him behind a rock at Zgoda Park the winter Naomi was born and even though she didn't like animals, Mama said it was because I needed someone to take care of that he'd appeared. Naomi would be her baby and Piotr, mine. Mama was fair like that, so she let me keep Piotr. He watched me now, his white eyebrows moving as they always did when he was thinking. "They'll be back," I tried to convince him, but he closed his eyes.

I tried to will it. They'd be quiet because of the soldiers, but I would hear their steps: a slight beat between Babcia's right and left, my father's even heels, Mama's skittery walking. Her bold voice, "Sorry we're late, Słodkie Lillia." She would leap on my bed and tickle me, apologizing. "Późno, *late*, przepraszam, *sorry*." She was always late. That's why my father loved buying her clocks.

The first time they met, she was late for her call at the Stanislav Circus. It's my first memory of her, even though it's not my memory but a story they loved to tell each other and me, how she came running into the Warsaw Cultural Center like a gazelle, long-limbed and elegant except when she was frantic. Then she seemed very silly. She was shedding layers, the felt coat with a wool collar, the scarf Babcia had made her, a sweater. She kicked free of one boot and was struggling with the other, unbuttoning and pulling off her pants just as Papa, not Papa yet, came out of the dressing room, in his clown outfit.

"Przepraszam!" he said, the first word he ever spoke to her, *sorry*. She was hopping furiously on her strong legs, in underpants she told me were orange.

"Nie przepraszaj! *Don't say sorry!* Just help me! I'm late!" She flung her things, inside out, all about. "Please," she gasped. "I'll be fired before I start! I need this job. . . ."

Papa stared. He knew the moment mattered, so he snapped alert and dug in the trunk for tights, tape, a leotard she pulled on. They taped up her hands, and she ran into the hallway behind the ring.

Now my sister was crying, and I snapped back into the terrible day and went to get her.

"Papa is out, but I'm here," I said in English. I'm good at English, because Babcia made me read all her books. She never said so, but I knew it was because she wanted to make sure I could do something other than be in the circus when I grew up. In the kitchen, I held Naomi on the counter and fed her some milk and noodles. I said, "Milk," when she drank, and "Noodles," while she chewed.

Then we sat in my room, where time pressed us down, spun us under. Naomi threw my two toys off the bed, and I picked them up and she threw them off again. She laughed wildly, closing her eyes and tipping her head back the way she does, like she's drinking whatever is funny and then coughing it back out: *zla, zla, zla.*

A wash of light rose outside until my ceiling and walls were bright in spite of the drapes. I stared at the review I had pinned up—of my parents' act, "intimate, dazzling." It called Mama "weightless" and Papa "a masterful anchor." In the photo, she is upside down, her hands atop his. He is looking up at her. Next to that was my poster of Zishe from Stryków, on a ladder, holding an elephant in his arms, and, in his teeth, a rope attached to a wagon full of people. Papa's hero, he was not only the strongest man in the world, but even better, a Jewish strongman. Zishe rolled into arenas in a chariot covered with Stars of David. He died the same year I was born, 1925, and Papa started wearing the glitter tear. He said I was the only thing that cured the heartbreak of Zishe dying too young. Our circus had so many Jewish acrobats, clowns, and dancers. We played festive klezmer music and our tightrope walkers were sisters whose mother recited tehillim as they walked the wire, her prayers keeping them safe. No one minded Jewishness yet.

The sun moved higher in the sky and I knew it was midday; when it sank, I knew dusk; and when it disappeared, night again. Naomi finished the milk and then there was nothing left. Despair darkened our apartment, and I began to panic. I carried my sister to the stove, set her down, got on my hands and knees, and scoured the ashes. When my fingers found the ring I'd seen our mother hide, I said out loud to Naomi, "Look. She'll be happy when she gets home." But I didn't believe it, and Naomi didn't even understand. I washed the ring's gold star, then tore open the stomach of my toy mouse and sewed the ring in. Naomi watched, the quietest audience member. I finished sewing and stood on my hands.

"A show for you," I whispered. But I was stiff and fragile, from being inside too much or from fear. I fell out of my handstand and danced, without music, until I was warmer. Then I lay on my stomach and twisted into a spider, legs over my shoulders, feet in my hands. I smiled at Naomi, but she just stared, her giant eyes unblinking.

I untangled myself, fast, and became nothing but a girl again, too afraid to move.

— ▣ —

We should have left when the soldiers came. Last fall, in 1939, armies invaded Poland—first Germany, then the Soviet Union, both in September. It was only ten days after the second invasion that we had to surrender. They took over everything, but my parents didn't want to leave. Others knew to go. First was my friend from school, Renia Antol. Even before the invasion, one day we were all outside in the courtyard, dancing. Kassia was bent in half, a laughing elephant, swinging her right-arm trunk, and I had my wings in the air beating and flapping when Renia came over with a grave face.

"Do widzenia! I am not allowed to tell you, but my family is escaping!" Renia was a dramatic girl, prone to telling lies to excite everyone, but she said good-bye in a voice that made my skin prickle and itch. I felt stupid, too, because Kassia and I were dancing animals, and now this, something serious. Kassia shouted: "Escaping? What? Where are you going?"

"Shhhhh!" Renia pulled us into the brick L where our buildings came together. She was big and spoke in a whisper, low, like a man's: "England. My father says Poland will be torn in half by Germany and Russia and all Jews should get out now."

I looked down at the riot of flowers my mother and Kassia's had planted in the courtyard, and suddenly the stems, leaves, and petals were a map. Germany and Russia, fanged giants on either side, devoured our apartment and garden with Naomi and my parents in it.

Kassia, always sweet, had begun to cry. She wasn't Jewish, and I thought she didn't mind losing Renia, but she didn't want to lose me. She put her arms around my neck. To Renia, she said, "Wróć," come back.

The joyful shouts of Kassia's handsome older brother, Janusz, and his friends became ugly in my ears and I pulled away. I turned a line of crisp cartwheels across the courtyard to my apartment so I would seem carefree, because I didn't want Renia to be right.

But at dinner that night, I asked my parents about what she had said.

Mama's jaw tightened. "Eat your dumplings, Sweet Lillia."

I'd stared at her until she spoke. "Some people in Poland hate Jews, yes, but in a different way from the Germans. Our government will never allow that sort of thing here." She was holding Naomi on her lap.

"You don't think?" Papa asked, and I knew then that he wanted to leave.

"Tolerance is in our constitution, Bercik, especially for Jews," my mother argued. "We've been here since the Middle Ages. Come." She kissed Naomi on the mouth, as if reminding my father that Naomi was too young for this conversation. Then she strapped my sister into the special chair she couldn't slip out of and Naomi tried to stuff an entire dumpling in her mouth.

"Yes, Naomi!" Mama said. "Eat your dumplings just like your big sister."

"Renia Antol's father said all Jews should get out now."

"Let's wait and see, Lillia," Papa said, moving over to Mama's side of things, as he always did. "Maybe it will get better. And leaving isn't easy."

But "it" got worse. Small horrors kept seeping in slowly, then growing. In October, Yiddish papers stopped arriving, so my mother shrugged and read the Jewish one in Polish. In November, the Jewish paper disappeared. At services in December, which Mama and I attended but Papa and Naomi avoided, the rabbi said, "My friends, things are getting worse." Now "it" was "things," too many to be contained by one small word. His voice was gentle, and pages of prayer books rustled. The cantor sang, violet notes everywhere, our temple warm with syllables we shared. My mother swallowed and looked at me with sideways eyes, but we stayed.

By winter, Jewish girls weren't allowed at school anymore. I loved school so much that this sucked the blood from inside me and I wanted to cry all the time. Kassia came every day after school and whispered lessons to me, so I could keep learning. Outside, families—including children—dug trenches. People began to wear gas masks, and soldiers drowned out the voices of my friends, Piotr's barking as we walked him to the park, any familiar sound or color, but my parents stayed. They kept me and Naomi inside. Power stations closed. Zgoda Street felt metallic and smelled like ash. Everyone said we should leave.

I repeated to Kassia what I'd heard my parents say: "Leaving is as dangerous as staying." And: "There's nowhere left to go." It was true. At first we didn't know we had to leave, and then we couldn't leave. There were no more ports. The world was a map of impossible borders.

"Where will I go?" I asked Kassia. It was March 1940, seven months since we had been invaded, and already the rest of the world had locked itself up.

"Go to England, like Renia! Or Italy. Or America. Go to America!" Kassia said.

"America sent a whole ship back," I told her, despising her for her luck, for her not needing to know about America what I knew: "A thousand people, even though they had families there, waiting for them, who said they would pay, who would take them. We don't have anyone anywhere except here. And America sent away those who do. If America wouldn't take them, America won't take us."

— ◙ —

The night of May 18 vibrated with quiet like the wings before a show, the next act about to happen. There was no sign of Papa. Naomi was asleep, hidden under the covers with me. I was shivering. I kept thinking of the date, May 18, the year, 1940, the hours themselves, broken into minutes, seconds, dust.

Now the ship to Shanghai would sail in five days, one hundred and twenty hours. This seemed suddenly like too little time for Mama and Babcia to make it back, for any of us to get anywhere. Naomi and I would stay in my bed forever, or until soldiers came to get us. Where would we hide? They would take us to a camp. Maybe the same one where they had Babcia. That would be okay. I could help, could rub her good foot at night, sing the cat song she loved. Only the week before, on May 10, Germany had invaded Western Europe. Luxembourg was occupied, and the Netherlands surrendered four days later. My mother cried, and my father consoled her that at least we had tickets. We could leave. We had waited nine months since Germany had kidnapped Poland, and one terrible month since they'd taken Babcia.

I was too afraid to turn the light on. Naomi woke and cried small yelping wails, maybe hungry, maybe as afraid as I was, maybe even more afraid. I couldn't remember what it was to have no words, to want Mama but not know how to say so. Did Naomi think if she just said "Mama" or "Papa" they would come? I had to let her cry.

When we finally heard steps outside, I couldn't tell whose they were. If it was a soldier, I wouldn't open the door. I wouldn't answer any questions. I wouldn't let him take anything. I would protect Naomi. I would—

"Lillia?"

Naomi clicked her mouth. She had been waiting, too. "Shhhh, it's just Papa," I said. I picked her up and squeezed her to me. Papa appeared in the wavering hallway, holding a candle. I saw Naomi's puffy eyes, and her curls, so matted she looked like a doll with its hair painted on. When Papa reached us, she clicked frantically. He handed me the candle and took my sister, who tried to clutch his neck and bury her face in his shoulder, safe. I envied her.

"Where's Mama?" But he shook his head. "Did she go to find Babcia?"

Nothing. In the light of the small flame, he resembled a dead person. I'd never seen one, but I knew. It was as if someone had slid the bones out of my father's body, pitted him.

He said, "We must go tomorrow. We'll leave word, and they'll follow when they can. But we can't stay."

My fear caused something inside me to turn off. It happened fast: all the lights in my mind shut down and I fell.

On April 14, the day we got the letter saying Babcia was at a camp, my mother fainted, too. She had never fainted before that, not high up, not spinning, not even the time she fell from a nine-foot swing at the circus. She just landed, bounced, opened her eyes even wider, and said, "Au," *ow*.

Papa carried her from the ring, carefully, as if she were a broken puppet he would mend in the workshop. But while he was carrying her, she swung her legs and grinned and waved to me. I knew she was fine. She always said a fall at the beginning of a show was necessary—to remind the audience of the "danger" that was part of the drama. In our bike act, six acrobats rode around the ring, dancing on their seats, standing on handlebars, leaning so close to the floor that the bikes went flat. Each time, one girl slipped off, only to pop back on. It looked like an accident but was a reminder to the audience that we were vulnerable. We made our acts look more difficult than they were. Exaggerating danger was part of the performance, but it wasn't supposed to be real danger.

The news of her mother being taken to a camp knocked Mama flat. Even once her eyes were open, my father had to hold her up. That April, Germany had invaded Denmark and Norway. Poor Denmark surrendered the day it was attacked, but Norway was still fighting. I knew at once that the German soldiers taking Babcia felt bigger to me than the German soldiers taking entire countries. I thought God might punish me for that. And maybe God did.

When Mama was upright again, she snapped into fantastic acrobatic action, running through the house as if she hadn't collapsed only moments ago, as if speed were the key to finding Babcia. I was panicked by her throwing herself into clothes and shoes, grabbing Naomi, and running out. Maybe she thought carrying a baby would remind whoever had Babcia that we were human. She told me not to come, but Papa rushed after her, afraid she would do something dangerous. I was alone. I watched the street, desperate for them or Kassia. But they didn't come for hours, and I began to lose light, to wither at the window. Eventually, I saw an old woman with a group of soldiers tightening around her. I squinted. Was it Eva Rosenbaum? My friend Max's grandmother? Eva always kissed us, leaving shiny marks on our cheeks and foreheads. She smelled like mint mothballs and carried licorice in her coat pockets. At Max's apartment, there was a picture of Eva standing with Babcia, helping give me a bath in the sink when I was a baby. I look like a naked moon, pale, with a little fuzz of hair on top of my head. Max made fun of it constantly, making me furious.

Eva's mouth out the window was an open scream, and then she was rubbing the sidewalk with her fur coat, pockets maybe full of candy. Why? What was she scrubbing? I tried to see the ground where she knelt. There were leaves on the pavement, green fingers, reaching up toward Eva. I remembered it was April, spring. All the flowers were blooming. A soldier kicked Eva and she flattened, then pushed herself up and began crawling, blood leaking from her. Her coat stayed dead on the ground behind her. I covered my eyes. What would Max hear of his grandma?

One of Babcia's legs was artificial. If someone kicked her, she would not be able to get back up without help. And she hated help anyway, was tough and bossy and beloved, maybe the reason we had waited too long to flee. My mother wouldn't leave Babcia, and Babcia would not have given up my grandfather's grave in Bródno, or her former art students, friends, or doctors. Abandon her kitchen, with a ceiling she had painted herself? The parrot she'd brought home after my grandfather died? She would never even leave the mechanical chair my grandfather built to carry her up and down the stairs. She refused to use it because she was too proud, but she showed the chair off, said, "Look what my genius husband made me!" On Friday nights, while the chicken was roasting and the challah cooled on the counter, Babcia prayed and Mama smiled and sang along. I rode the chair up and down the stairs for fun, carrying Naomi on rides.

When my parents finally returned the day I saw Eva crawl,

I was still behind the couch, flat on my stomach on the floor, my hands over my face. Mama pulled me out, her eyes wild and unrecognizable. "What happened, Słodkie Lillia?" But before I answered, she said, "You're okay, you're okay," in a voice she used for lies. I repeated this one: "Yes, I'm okay." Naomi made the strange green sound that meant she was going to cry.

"Lillia's okay," our mother said, and then, "Imagine." She always told us to imagine when we were afraid. Picture the circus, a swing, the ring, sky, river, Piotr, something or someone we loved. I saw Eva bleeding, imagined Babcia kicked and thrown.

I said what had happened to Eva and saw my mother's relief. Because it hadn't happened to me. We were less human suddenly, wanting to survive when other people didn't get to, maybe even especially when they didn't. This made me hate my parents, even though I felt it, too.

They never told me what they'd found out looking for Babcia.

Our parents used to say Naomi and I were lucky. How when they joined the circus, Papa's parents had stopped loving them and only because Babcia fought for her had Mama been forgiven by her own father. Babcia was disappointed my parents weren't religious, but she didn't mind the circus so much. Naomi and I could grow up to be whoever we wanted. We could be free. Mama often said, "Girls less lucky have no choices. Some aren't allowed to be courageous. You *get* to be, so you *have* to be. Your fortune is your responsibility." Until it wasn't.

Papa's hands looked like clay he was twisting and shaping, making each and then destroying it with the other. "Alenka, if not west, then we must—"

Even before he finished, she said, "Yes, okay, anywhere"; said, "ship"; said, "transit visa"; said, "Shanghai" because she had heard—we had all heard—that Shanghai was the last place we might be allowed to land.

But the lights went out in my parents' makeshift ring, and she was gone. We were about to sail across the entire world, leaving her behind.

CHAPTER TWO

Obcy, *Stranger*

We drove in the closed heat of a car we would leave somewhere for a stranger to retrieve. Lying in the back, I listened to my breathing as if it were a song: whisper, flutter, gasp. I tried to count, to even my terrible thinking into numbers, something sensible. Breathe in for five, hold for five, out for five. I thought, *May, the fifth month, twentieth day.* It had been three days since Mama was stolen. She had not returned in time to come with us, so it could not have been her choice. Four hundred fifty-nine point two kilometers to Lithuania. And then the train that would take us to Italy: Two thousand two hundred and forty-seven kilometers. Nine thousand one hundred and nine kilometers next, on the ship to Shanghai. Breathe in, five, hold, five. Numbers might lock me down as the places I'd known my whole life vanished. Breathe out, five.

Eventually, we were released from the car and a gray day came into focus, blurred but clearing slowly. I sipped from a thermos of water as I looked around. Papa was holding Naomi on his hip, but she slid down his side and he set her gently on the ground. She stayed like a small puddle there, didn't even try to crawl.

"You were brave," he said. Did he mean me? I did not feel brave.

The day became bright then, and unreal, as we shuffled in a crowd of endless winding lines. I stood in white sunlight, families everywhere, moving, sweating, gasping toward train tracks ahead. Papa looked smaller. His big shoulders sagged and so did the skin on his face, like a balloon days after the party. He said, "Lithuania," several times, as if he were naming the place for himself, couldn't believe we were here, even though it was only to leave immediately for the next terrifying stop in Italy. Trieste. From there, we would go straight from the station to the edge of the water where a ship to Shanghai awaited us. Papa kissed Naomi's sweaty neck, and said, "Lithuania," again. I prayed, finding only the choppiest words for what I wanted— *Mama, Babcia, home.* Lithuania! Mama had lived there as a girl while her father studied in Vilna, but we had never been back.

She said no place that changes hands so often is safe. Now it was safer than home, now any place was safer than where we came from. I held my father's hand so tight that my nails left marks.

Now Papa said, "It will be okay. This will be okay," but not to me. He was trying to believe what was impossible to imagine, to imagine what we couldn't believe. Once, I overheard Babcia and my mother arguing, Babcia pleading: "Can't you just try?" And Mama responding, "I have faith in us, our children, our traditions. But I can't believe, or pretend to believe in what I don't." She meant God, and maybe he heard. What if my parents had believed? Would she be with us?

We moved among people carrying other people, suitcases, trunks, instruments, furniture, animals. A man shoved by with a chair over his back, another with a ski across each shoulder. My family was different, I told myself. Others were performing a horror we were watching, that was all. But Papa talked the way Kassia had when I'd gone to say good-bye—a lot of fast, rocky chatter. He bounced Naomi in his grip, too quickly. She looked surprised.

"We are lucky to be getting out, Słodkie Lillia, for these train tickets, for the ship, for Shanghai," he said, using my mother's nickname for me. Would he have to be both of them? I shuddered.

I took the word *lucky* and discarded it, turned my mind off. I ate the bread Kassia's mother had given me when we'd gone to say good-bye, knowing I might never see Kassia again. I had lost Mama, Kassia, and Babcia all at once. Piotr, my puppy, too. We had given him to Kassia, which had made me feel I hated her, even though I loved her. When we went to her house for the money her father had collected and for the bread, I heard Kassia's father say it was from selling "the fourth ship ticket"— Mama's. Kassia pulled me then, toward their kitchen table, but I felt liquid and clear, as though I might dissolve and flood their house or vanish. I was shivering. I heard Kassia repeating my name: "Lillia, Lillia? Something, Lillia, something. Tea? Potatoes? Lillia. Your hands are cold. Ma, her hands are cold. We will find your mother. Don't worry. Pa says she'll go on a ship later, as soon as we—Your babcia, too. You go first. We'll take care of Piotr. We'll—"

I came back to myself only when her older brother, Janusz, said, "Hush, Kassia, enough!"

Her blonde head snapped up, and her eyes spilled tears. "*You* hush, Janusz!"

Janusz was beautiful and usually in trouble. Once he had climbed our building and waved to old Mrs. Banik on the fifth floor from outside her window. She almost had a heart attack, and his mother made him write an apology letter and wash Mrs. Banik's windows for the rest of his life. Another time he'd tied all the socks in the Kozaks' house together into a rope that stretched half the length of Zgoda Street. But our last day in Warsaw, even Janusz was quiet and his eyes looked burnt. Whispered words from the conversation between Papa and Kassia's parents floated up and then settled all over us like ash:

safe conduit, money we'll wire, London, Shanghai, Sergo, ticket, Alenka. "Lillia," Janusz said gently, taking my hand, "come." My hands were clean then, soft. I was thrilled that Janusz was holding one.

But happiness itself gave me a feeling of falling backward: Mama had been with us, and now was gone. She could have been with Kassia's mother in the kitchen, drinking kompot, pouring in splashes of vodka. Or rolling out dough, dancing to the icebox. Kassia's mother had brought us tea that sat until its cold surface glistened. I watched her. Why hadn't she been stolen instead? Kassia had looked over at me. She had heard me think it.

"Lillia!" Now Papa was shouting my name, pulling me toward the train. Since the war, everyone was always pulling me. There was screaming, a clustered rush of people pushing away from something, the crowd throbbing outward. Three soldiers burst from its center, dragging a man by his hair. The screaming was coming from the throat of a woman trying to run behind them. Blood sprung from holes in the man's scalp as if from valves. The screaming woman fell, and an older woman tried to help her back up, but couldn't, and fell, too. The soldiers shoved the man into a truck. Papa tried to push his way toward her, to help, but the crowd closed on us and he gave up, hiding Naomi in his shirt. He reached out to put a hand near my face, maybe wanting to cover my eyes, too, but I wrenched away. "What did that man do?"

My father shrugged, said nothing, because what would it

have been? Another "I don't know"; another "lucky"; maybe we were lucky not to be that man? But maybe a soldier would rip the hair from Papa's head next. Or mine. Was the bleeding man missing papers? Had he spoken rudely, carried a book, jewel, forbidden check? Maybe the soldiers resented him for an arbitrary reason, envy of his pretty, screaming wife, whose life they had just ruined.

"Take your hand out of your mouth, Lillia," Papa said. I released my bleeding fingers at the same moment I realized they were between my teeth. I watched our feet, heard someone shout, "Look up!"

Naomi was crying by then, and I realized, as if I were emerging from underwater, that the shouting voice was talking to us, to me. Papa was showing our passports, the *J* on each a dark mark. Now he was putting them back in the inside pocket of his jacket, balancing Naomi. The guard locked twin blazing eyes onto my face. "Can't you hear? Look at me, now!"

I jerked my head up and bent backward, as if I might flip away from him. But Papa, maybe feeling I was moving in the wrong direction, put a hand on my shoulder, steadying me as he bounced Naomi, trying to stop her crying. She had lost a leather slipper—I saw it on the ground and glanced at her foot, turned in, unused, never walked on. I didn't point my toe across the dirt to try to get the shoe, just stayed still and stared ahead. The guard's big, square face moved close to mine. I made my mouth a straight line and didn't breathe, lest I inhale poisonous thoughts. But my eyes stayed open, and I was surprised by his clear skin and black lashes.

Papa had warned me to pack nothing of value, but I'd gone to the stove for my mother's ring and now I could feel it as if it were moving inside the stuffed mouse. The guard grabbed me and Papa's hand fell. I thought I heard the ring pulsing, glowing, dripping. He would find it and kill us. His hands were on my back, my waist, moving down. He leaned right into me so I smelled his words, smoked meat. "What are you hiding?"

I tried not to gag, choke, or scream, just shook my head fast, *no, no.* I wanted, in my bones and teeth, to lunge forward and bite his face. But I let him yank open my sad cotton bag: four of Mama's shirts, a coat, my blue dress; two books, *Kajtuś Czarodziej* and *The Last Lithuanian Foray*; and the mouse, that was all. Please, God, I prayed wildly, let him think I'm a child. Move his hand. Don't let him look closely at the mouse, please. Another soldier shouted then, and the one holding me let go so fast I fell. He threw my bag, and I grabbed it and sprang back up, wanting him to see I was an acrobat, that he hadn't hurt me. But no one noticed. And it wasn't true anyway. If he'd wanted to kill me, he could have. I worked hard not to cry, then noticed Papa behind me. He had bent to catch me while holding Naomi.

Someone yelled, "Shut that ugly brat up!"

Naomi's small mouth had turned blue, and she was screaming a new cry. Papa flew us forward up stairs to the train. On the top step, he shoved me into the passenger car before leaning over, holding Naomi away from himself, and throwing up onto the tracks.

When the train slammed alive and rattled toward Italy, toward the ship, toward whatever Shanghai would mean, my father and sister were silent. He held her so tight they both turned white.

I looked at my hands, no longer clean or proud. My fingers were bloodied by chewing, and my nails jagged, lines of dirt beneath like ten desperate horizons. Janusz would never hold my hand again, anyway, and suddenly I wasn't a real person anymore. I was nobody's fairy or Słodkie Lillia. I had no idea who I might be next or ever.

Papa said, "Lillia, drink," so I swallowed a single sip of water, counted *one*, watched the numb world vanish out the window.

— ◘ —

On May 23, the ship called *Conte Rosso* sailed from Trieste to Shanghai without my mother, just as the car had driven to Lithuania and the train had sped us to the port and the sun had risen, relentless. To the world, she didn't matter. But to me, nothing could be beautiful, not even the ship with its elegant, impossible light and food: warm bread, meat, cheese at every meal. We ate fruit so bright it was waxy. There were no soldiers, just "lucky" families escaping our own lives. The ocean churned, brown, blue, and green, vast enough to make us feel miniature.

It was as if God moved us around the decks like dolls, in and out of cabins, organizing as I used to when I had a dollhouse. The ship itself, enormous when we boarded, was tossed about like a toy Kassia and I used to sail in her tub as children. Our cabin, which we shared with a Russian family, had six stacked bunks with individual reading lights.

I liked my spotlight, imagined if I were small enough, I'd dance in its single circle of warmth, flip and twirl. I walked the fingers on my right hand along the palm of my left, little performers on a tightrope. I tried to clean my nails by scraping under each with another, tried biting them smooth. I flicked the light on and off. But I could not read the books he'd made me bring, because my father talked as if a dam between his brain and mouth had dissolved. As if words might save us, he named each place we would pass: Venice, Brindisi, Port Said, the Suez Canal—an amazing wonder, he said. Then Massowah, Aden, Colombo, Penang, Singapore, Hong Kong, Shanghai. All I heard at first was Shanghai. In thirty-six days we'd be in Shanghai. The water was this; the ship was that; China would be beautiful; its language musical; its sea called Yellow, river, Huangpu. We would see the Yangtze delta. Everything he said stirred inside me, lost shape, made me sick. I preferred to be just a body, tried not to hear or think. Some days I stood on the deck, held the railing, and kicked my legs hard, flying. I worked on lifting both feet at once.

Naomi said, "Ah, ah, ah, ah," more sensible than Papa, who chanted endlessly: "There will be rice paddies, Lillia, and mountains! With your talent for languages, you'll learn Chinese quickly."

The Russian family in our cabin had owned a toy store in Moscow. The manager had taken it, after working for their family for seventeen years. It was all Natasha, the mother, could talk about. She seemed stunned beyond repair, even though to me they were luckier than we were, all four of them safely on the ship together. The two boys, nine-year-old Sasha and four-year-old Alexi, heard her story again and again and so did I, until I saw puzzles, blocks, the shining marble eyes of stuffed bears. I saw the manager, descending into the shop from the ceiling, taking everything, rising again like a demon with all the toys clutched in his arms. Papa translated Natasha's Russian words for me and Naomi. The boys' father didn't speak and neither did Sasha. They were all eye sockets and silence, but Alexi talked and sang, wondered about the ocean, the ship, its captain. Naomi watched Alexi until she couldn't keep her eyes open on him a moment longer, in whatever love is for a baby. She slept with me, as hot as a boiling pot, wild as a kicking beast. Each morning, when I saw her still asleep, her cheeks blushed and sweaty, I remembered she was just my little sister.

On June 2, our eleventh night on the ship, after Papa and Alexi had both finally stopped talking so the rest of us might sleep, we heard shouting from the deck. Papa forbade me to follow him out of the cabin, and when he returned, we were all awake, sitting up.

He said, "There was an accident."

"An accident?" Natasha asked.

"A woman fell."

"Fell?"

He was looking at me when he whispered, "Overboard," like an apology. I searched his face, knowing the railings were too high to fall over. She would have had to climb, dive, fling herself, leap. Like an acrobat. The ship did not reverse to retrieve her, and even Papa went quiet.

In the mornings that followed, the mist made me feel we were sailing through a cloud, and in the afternoons, we approached waves that looked like mountains of water. I couldn't stop imagining the woman, floating forever, her flesh devoured by salt or creatures. Her eyes in particular. What had she seen going over, then under? For how long had her eyes kept working? How many thoughts had her mind made while her body was thrown about? Enough to regret her choice? Was it a choice, or had her body taken over her brain? Maybe that could happen to any of us, to me. I didn't know how to turn my thoughts low enough not to perish from fear, but leave them on enough that my body couldn't throw itself off the ship without my mind's permission. The parts of me had never been so separate before.

Clusters of birds flew high above us, their bodies black *V*s against a sky so vast I wondered if they soared to avoid the terror of some giant, endless feeling. They shifted shapes, countless birds together, and I envied them, flying in a pack like that.

I danced with the ship, lurching and bending, keeping my balance on the violent sea.

— ⬚ —

We stopped in Venice for fuel and food, then sailed on. Mountains rose as if straight from the sea and days became weeks, the names of places actual places: Brindisi, a port where more food and fuel were loaded on, where passengers were allowed to disembark, but Papa forbade me. He said no place was safe for Jews, that we would get off the ship only once we reached Shanghai. I watched from the deck, envious. The ship got more fuel—and cotton and rice—in a city called Port Said, where white buildings towered and white birds dipped into the tips of waves only to launch back up. A statue of a man stood over the sea. Papa said he was called de Lesseps, had built the canal we made our narrow way through, trees on either side.

I whispered to Naomi, on our bunk, sometimes for hours, because she asked no questions and didn't talk herself. Telling her stories was as safe as talking to myself, but less lonely.

"Mama ran backstage," I said. "She was always late. Remember?" Naomi put her fingers in her mouth. She looked smaller than when we left. Was it possible for babies to shrink rather than grow? "Remember?" I went on, maybe like our father. "Then Papa went backstage, in case Sergo, their boss, fired her. He thought he might never get to see her again. But she was in the ring, dancing, flying almost." Naomi still said nothing. "I think you might be like Mama when you're older." My sister sighed and flopped a soft arm across me.

"But Sergo didn't fire her, because he liked her. Everyone liked her. And Papa didn't go home that day. He went downstairs to make a puppet. Do you remember Rosy Mischa? She had red hair and green eyes, like Mama."

Now Naomi said, "Ah, ah, ah."

Rosy Mischa and Mama were almost identical, and when my father first gave my mother the puppet, Mama raised her hand, and so did Rosy. When she pointed her toes, Rosy tried, although her feet were made of wood.

On the ship I asked Naomi, "Can you point your toes?" Naomi looked at me. "Toes," I said again. I raised my leg as high up as the bed would allow, and touched my toes, counted them for her in English: one, two, three, four, five, six, seven, eight, nine, ten. But Naomi just stared. I felt sorry for her, my sister who might never be in any circus. So I said, "You came to the circus, too, and you would have had an act when you were a little older. Mama didn't worry about you not talking. She said you would when you were ready."

Naomi said nothing.

Sergo wasn't there the day my father gave our mother her puppet. Maybe if he had been, he would have fired them and I would never have been born. But that's not what happened. What happened was that Mama kissed Papa for so long in the ring that Papa's clowning partner, Ashton, changed out of his costume and went home.

For my third birthday, my parents gave me a leotard, tights, and a monkey puppet Papa made just for me. That was my first circus: I danced into the ring, lit lavender, my favorite color at the time, and twirled until stars formed all around me. Papa put the monkey puppet on my shoulder, then spun me around. When he finished spinning me, the monkey was gone.

"Where is it?" I asked him.

He lifted me, put me on his shoulders, and whispered, "Take my hat off."

The monkey was sitting under the hat on Papa's head. I shrieked with joy and reached for the monkey, dropping Papa's hat, but he kicked his foot up fast and sent it spinning back up onto his head. The monkey and I clapped. We would have fallen, too, but Papa held my ankles, just like the review said, "a masterful anchor." In that purple room, the audience cheered with us.

— ◙ —

We docked in Massowah for fuel and food, but I wasn't even allowed to watch from the deck, because Papa said Massowah was a port that wouldn't do anything Germany didn't like. Like let a Jewish girl stand on a ship, I guess. This made me furious, and I began to explore the ship whenever I wanted. Often Papa was out of the cabin, trying to get money, so he couldn't stop me.

I danced when the air was so wet and cloudy it could hardly be distinguished from the sea, when I couldn't be seen at the ship's edge. I peeked inside the dining room, glass casting diamonds of light as if over a circus ring. I imagined hanging from chandeliers, swinging out over everyone. The second week transformed into the third. Time became a color, something swirling. It became the distance between us and my mama and Warsaw. Days felt like months, and I stopped counting.

Once I walked by a man in a suit and gloves, who stared until my skin heated with embarrassment. Had he seen me dancing? Could he tell I did not belong on a ship sailing toward safety? My clothes were thinner each day, my red hair ragged and my skin pale even though I was often in the sun. I thought he could see I had no home or mother, that I was uchodźca, a *refugee.*

Another day, a woman in an orange dress approached me. With her yellow earrings and red lipstick, she looked like a salad made of fruit. She said, "You're a beautiful girl," but I didn't thank her, because I felt she wanted something and I couldn't guess what. Then she told me, "If you want to make some money and help your family, I'd be willing to pay two American dollars for your hair."

I reached up, felt the color of my own hair as if I were seeing it with my hands, felt my mother's red hair, too. "You want to buy my hair?"

"Yes. You'll still be pretty without it."

The last time I'd looked in a mirror was at home, and I'd thought I could see through my skin to my veins and bones. I had put my face close, leaning in as if for a kiss. If I were going to kiss someone, this was what he'd see. Green eyes and pale, pointed face. I couldn't tell whether I was beautiful, or looked like Mama, or even myself. Who would love me, would anyone?

"Why do you want hair?" I asked the orange woman.

"Someone will use it to make a wig. It won't cost you, of course, as it grows back. There will always be more where it came from." She let out a laugh that sounded like coins in a pocket. "Think it over," she said, and walked away.

Papa was on deck, talking to a handsome man with a big face, maybe trying to sell something, although I couldn't imagine what. Papa had already sold the single diamond earring Kassia's mother had sewn into the waistband of his pants, and had tried to use ship coupons that came with our tickets. He wanted metal or jewelry from the ship's shop, things he might also sell when we arrived in Shanghai, but the first time he went, there was already nothing left. I did not tell him about the ring I'd hidden, lest he exchange it for a handful of withered American or British dollars. I just leaned my back against a railing and overheard snippets of his conversation: "What to sell so we won't starve . . . disease . . . has twenty pounds . . . has Chinese National Dollars . . . crime . . . a wedding ring . . . melted . . . it could be melted."

"Your ring?" I whispered, and Papa said, "She would want me to. We have to eat when we get there. She and I can always get new rings."

An old man and a younger woman began shouting. She said he had taken something. He denied it.

"Six CN and fifty wen are worth one American dollar," the

man talking to Papa said, as the fighting man raised a fist and began punching the air above the woman accusing him. Papa ignored them. "They call dollars fa bi, legal currency," the handsome man said, "CN are Chinese National Dollars. Wen are cents."

"What are those people fighting about?" I asked. Papa put his hand on my shoulder. "Don't worry. Everyone is anxious, that's all. We all need to get as much money as we can before we arrive, in case it's difficult to find work." He didn't speak about disease and crime, stealing on the ship and in the streets of Shanghai. But I'd heard others talking.

When the *Conte Rosso* docked in Colombo, Papa held on to Naomi and me, lest we disobey him and walk into the real world to buy rice or rubber or trinkets. I looked longingly at the port city with dusty buildings set against the bright blue water, but almost immediately we were sailing toward Penang. Left alone, I went to the railing, held it, and stretched backward, the sun on my face and my hair down my back. If I went over the edge of the ship, my hair would be wet red seaweed after six or sixty or six hundred seconds. I bent my body back until my hair touched the deck. The adults went upside down, their frowns smiles.

I stood and left to find the orange woman. "You can have my hair," I said. I would hand Papa American dollars, be helpful. I followed the woman to a second deck, from which traces of fish were visible to the side of the ship, the water churning less viciously there than it did behind us. I watched for whales or sharks while the fruit woman held scissors that gleamed like her laugh. I tried to shut out the metal sound closing across my hair. One, two, three, she opened those blades eighteen times. My head lightened. I reached up. Fuzzy spikes. She handed me two American dollars, and I looked at the faces of men on the bills, as if they were people I was meeting. Would I exchange them for thirteen Chinese papers, CN, and if so, with whose faces?

The woman seemed angry. "You look fine. It will grow back," she said. "No need to look at me like that."

I returned to our cabin, the dollars in my waistband. I opened the door, and Alexi shrieked in Russian. Papa was on his bed with Naomi. He stared.

"What did Alexi say?" I asked. Sasha eyed me sadly, as if I'd lost something important. It was their mother, Natasha, who said quickly: "You are beautiful, Lillia" and "It grows back."

"But what did Alexi say?" I asked again.

"Just silliness, you look like a boy. He means a compliment."

"I don't care what I look like," I lied, and lay down on my bunk. Tears ran sideways from my eyes, and I felt them on my embarrassed, ugly scalp.

I put the dollars in my copy of *The Last Lithuanian Foray*, instead of giving them to Papa. He never mentioned my hair, neither comforted nor scolded me. I thought maybe he hadn't even noticed.

Chapter Three

Heime, *Home*

I first saw Shanghai from over my father's shoulder. I was feverish the final two weeks on the ship, as if my hair had been protecting my head and once I was without it, sickness leaked in. I missed the last three ports: Penang, Singapore, Hong Kong. Of course I wouldn't have been allowed off the ship anyway, but I was sorry not to have seen them. When I woke, soaked with broken fever, we were descending the ship's gangplank, Papa carrying Naomi, me, and all of our things. So I guess it was for the best that we had so little with us.

As far as I could see there were human beings, throbbing with heat, an electric mob of running, waving, shouting. There were animals and also men pulling carts, racing, climbing onto and off of boats so rickety they looked as if they'd been made by hand from paper, people entering and exiting buildings; everywhere storefronts and signs covered with slashes and dots that made a language I couldn't understand. I reached across Papa's neck and held Naomi's hand. "What day is it?"

I heard him say, "July." We had been traveling for over a month, and now it was July and we were here, in Shanghai. Out from the endless rush of people carrying meat, lumber, bricks, passengers, giant pieces of glass, emerged a man on a bicycle. He was the first person I could see individually somehow. There were so many of us. He had brown skin and bright eyes watching the street ahead of him. How was he balancing his bicycle? Its back was stacked with so many packages it looked like a house made of boxes. A pole crossed his neck and shoulders; from each end hung pails that seemed to pull the metal down, bending it on either side and digging a groove in his flesh. He moved so slowly through the hot street. He was the first Chinese person I'd seen, and he looked the same as anyone else, but also different. I felt a wild confusion that resembled excitement. What did I look like to those who weren't me?

Another man pulled a two-wheeled cart by, fast. He was thin as a single bone. In his cart perched a woman whose white hair flew behind her. She held a fur blanket with an animal's head still attached. It had teeth. I was surprised to see a blanket in such heat. Only when the man veered around them did I notice the group of men with side-curls. Jewish men, walking toward the dock, moving and speaking as if none of the chaos around them were happening, as if it weren't a thousand degrees and impossible to breathe. As if we hadn't landed on another planet. I watched them, amazed by their calm, by the possibility that they—and we—could belong here.

An open-backed truck arrived and we climbed on, Papa lifting Naomi and me, saying it was from a Jewish service, had come to collect us. We were packed tight enough to be held up by each other's bodies. I smelled my own fear, all our sweat, a hundred broken fevers. I wished desperately for a shower. We'd washed in a small cubicle on the ship. I was hoping so much for an actual bath here. We were all, even chatty Alexi, too shocked to speak. Except Naomi, who shouted, "Ah, ah, ah," from Papa's arms.

Her eyes had begun to look green—they'd been gold before, the color of coins or a lion's mane. I was glad for this change and relieved she had no words. Even if we'd known what to say about this place, what language would we have used?

The dock was behind us, baking in the sun, crowded with men, some bearded with turbans, others in white shirts and khaki shorts, still more in military uniforms. I hoped to see the religious men again, but they were gone. I knew, in a strange and certain way, just how alike we suddenly were, those men and I. Even though all that connected us was being here, being

Jewish. In that instant of looking out at the city, I saw everyone else and also saw myself among them, another stranger.

— ◙ —

I woke in a steel bed to find Papa watching me, Naomi on his lap. I hadn't seen him sleep since Mama disappeared. Maybe he stayed awake watching me, afraid if he looked away, I would vanish, too. The way I feared he would. But I couldn't stop falling asleep, maybe because I'd been sick, or maybe because it was a way to escape my mind.

"Good morning, Sweet Lillia."

I said, "Hi." My vision cleared. On the far cement wall hung a poster: a woman smiled out from its center, her teeth oddly gleaming in spite of the withered paper. She had markings around her, the same sort I had been unable to read on the street. The woman in the poster looked luxurious, with lipstick, a lovely dress, and maybe a secret keeping her lit from inside. "Where are we?" I asked suddenly, wondering where my mother was, how far from us, how we or she would ever cross that distance.

"This is a shelter, a Heime. We'll stay just until we find rooms."

"Heime?"

"It's German for *home*."

I stared at him. "Is that supposed to be funny?"

His eyelids came down halfway. Usually when this happened, I thought he would cry, but he didn't. Not the night she didn't come back, not when they beat Eva on Zgoda Street, and not when the soldier grabbed me. The only tear I'd seen on Papa's face was the silver glitter one. I remembered suddenly his orange cap, two blue feathers sticking from its brim. Where was it? Where was my monkey puppet? Where was anything we'd ever held or had, and did our objects still exist even if we never went home again?

"Heime isn't meant to be funny, no." Some thick, real tears dripped down his cheeks. Seeing him cry slowed my thoughts, but Naomi reached up and patted Papa's cheek, warbled, "Ah, ah, ah, ah, ah, ah, ah." It was over her odd refrain that I heard shouting, then weeping, the sudden sounds of a tangle of languages. It was terribly, unbearably hot. The noise and heat came at me at once, and fear moved through me, too, fast and dizzy.

"What is all that shouting about?" I asked.

"It's a noisy place," he said. "I don't know how much you took in, but it's like nothing I've seen. Those are vendors selling breakfasts, and honey carts collecting—" He paused.

"Collecting what?" I hoped it wasn't documents, or money.

"Human waste." He stood. "There's food here. Come, you need to eat. And you can meet some of the other families."

"Where is my bag?"

Papa leaned down and reached under the cot while I struggled to free my legs from a stiff sheet. He handed me my bag and I retrieved the mouse. Naomi thrust her hand forward, but I kept the mouse, which made her cry. "I'll give it to you later," I promised.

My father took my hand, helped me rise and balance. I was wearing one of his shirts, a blue striped button-up I had no memory of putting on, and cotton pants I'd been wearing forever, so short in the legs and loose in the waist that they rode low and uncomfortably on my hips, sagged over my underpants. The pants had new holes in them and the shirt covered me like a terrible dress. I didn't know where my thread and needle were. Maybe in my room in Warsaw.

Voices came into clearer shapes, in a language I recognized but didn't understand.

"Are there Germans here?"

Papa said, "There are Jews from everywhere—like us, no one to fear. We are safe here." We looked at each other over Naomi's head, and he said, "Safer."

He pulled the curtain back and led me past it, into another curtained space with a family in it, three children lying together head to foot in the same sort of cot as ours.

"Excuse us," Papa said to the family, as we brushed by their sleeping children. An old couple in the next curtained cubby sat shuffling papers back and forth. "We're so sorry," Papa said. For what? Having walked through their tiny corner of the shelter? They nodded, acknowledged us without speaking. The next people introduced themselves: the Lipners, Micheners, Schwartzes, in the only language we shared, English. Papa said, "I'm Bercik. These are my daughters, Lillia and Naomi." His

English was accented, and I wondered whether he would have to speak it all the time now.

"I'm Taube," said a woman on a bed. She had round, lively eyes, and a thin, bent nose both delicate and too big for her face. Her sharp chin made her cheeks flare out. I tried not to stare at her. "Where did you arrive from?" she asked.

"Poland," Papa said. "And you?"

"Oh," she said. "Poland! How lucky you're here. We came from Austria." She gave Papa a knowing look. "There they are killing people! It's absolutely—"

She stopped because Papa was grimacing, shaking his head in Naomi's direction. Something rose into my throat and clogged it. I coughed, trying to dislodge whatever it was, but it was a feeling, a color, nothing I could move. "It's nice to meet you," Papa told her.

"Of course it's much better *here*," the woman named Taube said, looking at me kindly. "Despite the conditions!" She laughed, as if we were in a play. "But to find a job! Or a room! Well, we haven't managed to find work or rent rooms yet . . ."

"Maybe we can look together," Papa said. For a room? For work? With someone we met thirty-six seconds ago? The man next to her reached his hand out.

"I'm Joshua Michener," he said. "Barber extraordinaire."

"You offer haircuts?" Papa asked politely.

Mr. Michener laughed. "I'm a banker by trade, but here I will put my other talents to use." He patted a bag, which I guessed must hold scissors. I reached up and touched my hair, remembered it was gone. "Looks like you've already gotten yourself a stylish cut, young lady," Mr. Michener said. He was round and jovial. I wondered whether he might give Papa a haircut. Or if I could borrow his tools and try my own hand at it. Papa looked wild. The woman who bought my hair should have cut his, too. We could have paid the same two dollars she'd given me, traded my hair for Papa's. This idea made me laugh, and everyone looked over. Mr. Michener laughed, too, and I had the feeling that I was outside myself.

"I was a science teacher, Lillia," Taube told me. "I bet you were a good student."

"I haven't been allowed to attend school for a long time," I said.

"Well, I've heard there's a wonderful school here!" Taube told me.

"Will you teach there?"

She looked longingly at her husband, with hope so embarrassing I felt shy. "Not yet," she said, "but it would be wonderful. Good jobs are difficult to come by." Now her gaze fell helplessly from her husband's face onto his briefcase. Maybe she would have to be his hair-cutting assistant, handing him razors, sweeping dead hair. "How lovely you look with your new style," she would say to refugees.

"The Quakers are running a Heime, too, you know," she added. "I could teach English there, and then hopefully someday science at the Kadoorie School. Where you'll no doubt go!"

"Oh, I won't go to school here," I said.

"Of course you will," Papa told me.

"They're offering English classes at the Quaker Heime so it will be easier to get work," Taube told him. "The Christians have a Heime, too, but to eat there, you have to convert. The food is apparently excellent." Now she was looking at me again—was she asking if I would be willing to convert?

I said simply, "My mama isn't here yet."

At this, she put her hand on mine, but her eyes met Papa's. "I'm so sorry to hear."

"Thank you, Mrs. Michener," I said.

"You must call me Taube," she said, "if we are to be friends."

I had never had friends who were old, but in Shanghai the rules seemed to have been canceled. I thought of her name, T-a-u-b-e, of a new life in which she and I were friends, I didn't go to school, remained bald, called Mrs. Michener "Taube." I felt a surge of freedom. Who might I be here?

Another woman, Mrs. Lipner, had sent her children to Canada. She said, "I have no news of them—I don't know if they made it yet—I don't know if—" then put her hand under her chin and rested her head on it as if the hand were a shelf. As if storing her head there might prevent additional terrible thoughts. She became furniture, no longer alive. "What about you?" her wooden mouth asked. "Do you have children?" She looked at Taube.

My mother always said never to ask that, because if people have children, they'll tell you, and if they don't, they either didn't want to or couldn't and either way, they don't want to have to say no.

"No," Taube said, her voice low. She turned to me as if I'd been the one to ask that wrong question. "We weren't able, I'm afraid."

Mrs. Lipner coughed out some wet sounds. I waited for her to say something right.

When she never did, I said, "I'm sorry," to Taube, and the feeling I'd just had, of freedom, cooled and hardened. I didn't want to have to say what the adults should know to say, to fix their mistakes. I turned to Papa. "I need a shower. Can you show me where it is?"

He said, "Let's get you something to eat," and I guessed there was no shower here, either.

We wove through more people on steel cots, inhaling air so choked and sweaty it felt solid. A small line of light appeared on the floor and I looked up: a window. I went to it, pushed a dirty cloth curtain aside, and through the cloudy glass, saw a street; water, green and racing; more of the cardboard and cloth boats; more men with poles. On the street and along the edge of the water were crowds of other men in long, belted coats and black boots. Straps crisscrossed their backs and from their waists hung blades.

"That's Suzhou Road, and Suzhou Creek," Papa said. "We'll go outside after breakfast."

"Who are the men?"

"Japanese soldiers."

"Are those knives?"

"They're bayonets."

I took this English word, all eight cluttery, hideous letters of it, and stored it away in my mind while I kept looking: *bayonets, bayonets, bayonets.* Trucks stacked with people rattled by. The creek threw delicate boats about. Only the soldiers stayed still. Everything rushed, parting where those men remained like giants.

"China has been occupied for three years," Papa said, "by Japan. There's a war here, too—that's why the buildings are— well, I don't know if you noticed all that's destroyed, but people are suffering here, too."

"Why?"

"Why what?"

"Why are the Japanese soldiers here?"

"Because they want to take over China. Any country that occupies another country wants to control that place. But the Japanese were kind to let us in. Don't forget."

I planned to forget, immediately. The Germans were "kind" to some families in Poland, too. Just not us. What difference did it make if you were kind to some, if you were beating and stealing others' mothers and babcias? I suddenly understood more than my father did.

"Japan and Germany are working together?" I asked.

"Well, only partly. They don't want the same things," Papa said.

So he thought I was simple, too. I yanked the curtain back across the window, shutting out the street, the water, and all the kind soldiers with their weapons. I followed Papa first to the bathroom, which was outside. I had to crouch over and pull my pants down to my ankles, trying to make sure they—and my feet and hands—touched nothing.

From there he led me into a large rectangular concrete room. Tables were lined up, pots on top, holding chunks of black rock. There were screens over them, and women stood, fanning until flames caught. Then they set smaller pots on the screens, as if grilling water. Others began to arrive and sit. Some carried oily bags and pouches of what appeared to be newspaper.

Papa handed me Naomi and approached the women. I saw him gesture to us. I hung back against a sticky wall, pointing my hip out and balancing Naomi on the small platform of my own bone. Two women with rags on their heads scrubbed a table before placing food on it. The absolute colorlessness of the room was changed chemically by their work. The women filled it with red-and-blue motion, almost happiness.

Papa returned holding three bowls of gray soup and a tube of newspaper. "Look!" he said, as if he'd hunted something in the wilderness.

I asked, "Who are those women?"

"Relief workers. Also Jewish. Also uchodźców," he said, *refugees*. The word in his real, Polish voice made me want to flip backward from the bench. I felt wild inside, and trapped.

"They have been here longer and volunteered to help those who just arrived."

Naomi was in Papa's arms, gobbling horrible porridge. Even she seemed like a stranger. Papa removed something from the newsprint tube, an egg he handed me. Its shell was a web of tiny, intersecting lines. I squeezed it slightly between my finger and thumb, and the cracked shell slid straight off, revealing a hard-boiled inside, darkened in the same webby pattern. I turned it around. "What makes it look like that?"

"Tea. And a sauce made from soy. Taste it."

It was so strange, this stained egg, that I felt again the force of being somewhere I might never understand. But I put the egg to my lips, and immediately was ravenous. I swallowed the whole egg almost without chewing. "Thankfully there's another," Papa said. I ate the second one carefully, considering the salty, dark taste. A cold feeling came over me once I'd finished. "Where is yours?" I asked.

"I'm having this." Papa gestured toward the gray liquid.

"I ate your egg."

"You need the nutrition." He handed Naomi and me each half of a round tube of fried bread, still wrapped in newspaper. I tore mine open and devoured the bread. When it was gone, I looked hungrily at the newspaper, warm oil marking pages of the same looping language.

Papa returned to the line and this time came back with two cups. "Milk," he said. "Also made from soybeans." He tipped one back for Naomi and she gulped. I sipped mine, tasted river, looked at our father. "How will she find us here?"

He didn't look at me when he answered, "I left instructions."

"Left them where?"

"With Nacek and Ana and hidden, at our house. Anywhere I could." I thought of my puppy, Piotr, and a hot fist squeezed my heart.

"Did you leave them at the circus, too?"

His *no* sucked the hope straight out of me. What had happened that night at their last performance? Did he know? Was he refusing to tell me?

"Will she come?"

He said what I knew he would, what I dreaded: "I hope so."

In Shanghai, I began to hate hope, the way it held heartbreak and no promise that we'd see her again. Hope contained everything we didn't know, and also its own opposite, dread.

— ◧ —

I was right that there was no shower, a disappointment I felt engulfed by, and which made the future unthinkable. I prayed God wouldn't punish me for wishing selfishly not to be dirty. I tried not to think, not to want anything. I washed Naomi and myself with cold water from a bucket Papa filled, while he held a sheet up around us. Taube gave us a chip of soap, and I moved as quickly as I could, trying to cover my skinny bluish body, dipping my head into the bucket directly, rubbing some soap onto what was left of my hair. I washed my teeth with soap, too.

I dressed in one of Mama's shirts, and my second of four pairs of clean pants. I had one dress but saved it. While I was putting Naomi's socks on her, I heard Papa talking, and the voices of other men. These floating voices said that Italy had entered the war—while we were on the ship from there. I began to sweat and chatter. What if we were in Trieste now, standing at the port? What if Mama was? The British had attacked the French navy, in order to prevent Germany from taking it. Hitler had set a date to destroy Britain. His planned attack he called Operation Sea Lion. Papa said the reason Britain and France had declared war on Germany was because Germany had invaded us in Poland.

I spotted some cord on the floor and bent to pick it up just as Papa came back with a stack of paper. I peered at the forms. "What are those?" I was hopeful they had to do with Mama.

"I am registering."

"For what?"

"To be counted among the living," he said. I looked at the paper in front of him and saw *Bercik, Lillia, Naomi.* The absence of her name glowed, and I felt a furious confusion.

"Why are they calling the attack Operation Sea Lion?" He looked up at me, distressed, as if we still lived in a place where I was spared terrible news.

"I guess because it will involve a lot of barges," he proposed.

I took the stuffed mouse from Naomi, picked open the seam of its stomach, and pulled a tuft of cotton out. Then Mama's ring. Naomi watched me, crying. "We can fix it," I told her. "Operation Mouse." I returned some stuffing to the stomach, pinched the seam. "I'll sew it as soon as I find a needle and thread."

The cord I'd found I twisted into a double band, onto which I strung the ring.

"Papa, will you tie this around my neck, please?"

He looked confused. "Where is that from? Is it Alenka's?"

"She hid it at home. But I brought it for her."

He tied the string for me, did not say how dangerous it was to have carried the ring, or how much money it might be worth. I smiled with all my teeth, like the woman in the poster. In rags, skinny after weeks of illness and a single bath from a bucket, not to mention practically bald, I must have looked like a dirty puppet made of twigs, but I was wearing my mother's star ring for the first time since being Jewish became a crime. I felt powerful.

"You look lovely," Papa said. I put my arms around him and held on for so long neither of us knew what to say, or how to let go.

I began planning how to be more like my mother, to take care of my family until she arrived, Operation Brave Lillia. Naomi, maybe understanding more than we thought she could, clapped her hands.

CHAPTER FOUR

Cmentarz, *Cemetery*

Papa showed me maps: Shanghai was shaped like the rounded beak of a tropical bird, dipping into the East China Sea, drinking. The Huangpu River was its wishbone, bisecting the city into the undeveloped eastern Pudong, and west of the river, Puxi. Puxi included Hongkou, where our Heime was, and south of us, over Suzhou Creek, parts of Shanghai that Papa said had belonged to foreigners for a hundred years: Americans, British, French. But when I asked if the city was still Chinese, he said of course, it always would be. "Even where the Japanese army is occupying, Shanghai belongs to the Chinese." I asked whose the river was, and he thought for a moment, then said we all shared it.

But the river belonged to no one, and knew its power over us. It overflowed in July and then again in August, pouring through Shanghai's streets. In Europe, Operation Sea Lion was postponed for September 21, and in the meantime, Germany attacked Britain in the water and on the ground in a battle so brutal the news of it made Taube's cheerful husband, Mr. Michener, cry. He didn't even hide his tears, just gulped and wept while he and Papa and the others listened to a forbidden radio in a back room at the Heime. We were not allowed to listen to radios by order of the Japanese army. I worried they would find Papa doing so and take him away. I listened frantically for the sounds of boots. But the flooding river drowned out other noises from outside. The adults listened to the news only at night. In the mornings, newspapers were passed from person to person until the pages disintegrated. Everything was shared. We carried and fed water to one another, water boiled for hours so it wouldn't poison us. And rice, bread, whatever food the shelter kitchen offered up. Occasionally, but rarely, eggs. On the streets, we saw noodles, pancakes, meats, and fried bread, but many at the Heime said Chinese food couldn't be trusted, would make us sick, was dirty. I longed to eat it anyway but had no money except the dollars from my hair, which I was saving.

I counted the mornings. Each day I woke and bent backward off the bed, hanging my head upside down before using my hands to stand, as Mama had. She had practiced in the mornings, holding handstands endlessly, stretching in our living room, keeping her arms and legs strong, her balance precise. I imitated her, standing on my hands in Shanghai, elbows bent so I might move, working to hold myself up. Each August morning I did her exercises only to collapse back down. I couldn't stay up six seconds. While I practiced, I whispered her name. At the end of the third week of August, I stayed up ten seconds, at the foot of my cot, eyes closed so I didn't have to know who walked by or saw me.

Outside, our eyeballs bulged and exposed skin crisped. Some of the adults at the Heime, like Mrs. Lipner, whose children were elsewhere, never went out. At first I thought it was because of the sickening, cooking feeling the heat caused, like our brains were roasting in the ovens of our skulls. But then I realized it was despair that kept Mrs. Lipner lying in the dark, staring at nothing. I was more afraid of her than anything outside. Even though rumors flew, of illness, crime, even murder, so many possible deaths coming at us, I had to escape, flee the Heime's stifling air and devastated adults. I loved to watch boats, because she might be on one. Each offered a chance of my mother arriving, waving.

Taube also liked to be outside. She was always dressed and busy, often carrying Naomi around the Heime. She said how lucky she was to know us, said the community gathered at a place called Wayside Park. "You must visit," she reminded Papa each morning.

"There's a lot of community here," I said, and she laughed as if this were a wonderful joke. Then she danced out the Heime door, saying we should come find her at Wayside. And one morning, as soon as Papa and Naomi and I had sipped down our gray soup, we headed into the rush of people. The flood carried various terrors: animals once beloved, including a dog, dead but with its eyes open, as if watching the water that had drowned it. All the strange remains of objects that had mattered in some other life: a table leg, somebody's bed, a fishing net stuffed with trash.

The streets smelled hot and raw, like the insides of something alive. Chickens screamed. A naked duck hung by its neck. Hunger and excitement rose in me, a raging combination. A group of Chinese men walked by wearing hats that obscured their faces, carrying cages with birds inside, swinging them rhythmically. Naomi, trapped in Papa's arms, swung her arms.

"Why do they swing the birds like that?" I asked.

"Maybe so they feel like they're flying," Papa said.

I wanted to fly above the city on a ribbon or trapeze. But broken pavement gripped me. Yellow rickshaws rattled by on every side, driven by men made of muscle, no hats or sleeves to protect them from the sun. Some had shoes carved from blocks of wood, fastened with straps of tire rubber. Others had no shoes at all, just exposed feet and ankles dry as burnt bone. One driver hauled the corpse of a pig. Sawed in ragged halves, it looked as if it had exploded, innards twisted and sweating.

"Must be on the way to the butcher," Papa said, seeing me

stare. He held my hand past food stalls, steamers hissing ginger air, meat buns being wrapped in squares of newspaper, kabobs, vats of boiling oil into which sticks of bread were dipped before being removed, sold, and devoured. Fish struggled to flop in packed tubs, frogs and snakes writhed and tangled. I watched a woman crouched next to a bucket of eels, slicing them open lengthwise, pulling their spines out so fast it was a dance. Everything moved quickly but also felt thicker in Shanghai. When a line of walking women passed, under parasols, carrying a box, singing, I stopped. Their singing was crying. The box was a tiny coffin. Papa pulled me away, past a bakery—sugar! I opened my mouth, but the sweet air competed with a sourness rising from underneath us, something decaying. An alley appeared on the right, piled high with trash. Fear wobbled me, made me look all over, my head turning a marionette's circles. Was Warsaw destroyed, too? Had Mama come home to find our home—and us—gone? Kassia? Piotr? Was my life still there? I began to panic. The things I loved most *could* exist even if I never saw them again. They were just outside my range.

A young Chinese boy picking through the rubble stopped and looked up. He held a board shot through with nails. The rags on his body were so thin they looked like skin, but his eyes were lit with something other than hunger and heat—mischief, maybe, or curiosity. I wanted the board, wanted to build something, a stage or set or ladder, cut the wood into even pieces I'd count and hide under my cot. I stared.

The boy seemed surprised by us, and surprised me by smiling before he returned to sorting. He used his right hand, keeping the nailed board in his left. I imagined grabbing it. But Papa pulled me away again, past another cluster of soldiers standing still with patient, expressionless faces and on their backs, packs with blankets rolled on top. I thought maybe they slept by lying down exactly where they were standing.

"There are *so many* soldiers," I whispered.

"You need a lot of people to occupy someone else's city," Papa said, his voice too loud. "You must destroy it first to make it yours. Look." He gestured. Workers swarmed, sawed, and hammered at a broken building, from which debris blew. He said, "Such a waste," as if to himself, and then remembered me and added, "When you see soldiers, look away."

Naomi, pinned to Papa's side, patted his face again. Our mother used to pat her; maybe she was comforting him. I remembered my mother's idea that the Polish way of hating Jewish people was better than the German way. I wanted to tell her it made no difference with what sort of hate human beings hated each other. It ended with wreckage like in Warsaw, like here. I hated soldiers. And suddenly, sickeningly, Papa, for bringing us here, for talking calmly like a teacher, like we could talk about anything other than her. And even her, for leaving the ring, not making it here. I hated myself, too, a feeling that came from outside and inside at the same time, one I thought might melt me. Papa didn't seem to notice my crisis.

"Apparently the Japanese believe Jews are powerful," he told me, as if I were his adult friend. He laughed a sharp, bitter bark I'd never heard. "They think we're mystical, that letting us live here might help them. Imagine."

"Imagine what?" My voice was still a whisper.

"There are three separate police forces running this city. It's as if the Japanese took over for a mob. The only reason we're here is that they can't agree on who gets what control. They only enforce rules when they feel like it."

"What if they change their minds about letting us stay?"

"As long as they believe we control Western governments, we should be fine. Who knew there'd be such a silver lining to anti-Semitic conspiracy theories? Hold on to my neck."

Naomi was using both hands to pat him. She looked busy, thwacking away. I thought again that she understood everything, was clever.

"And anyway, the world won't always treat us as its enemy, Lillia," Papa said. "Someday it will turn on others, and we'll remember what this was like. We'll help whoever is next."

"What if German soldiers are next?"

He arched his eyebrows. "I hope the Jewish people will be champions of peace and tolerance no matter what."

"I don't. I could kill a German soldier if I had the chance." I showed him my hands, as if I'd need no other weapon.

He took one, held it. "Someday you'll grow out of that," he said.

We reached the metal bridge that rose over Suzhou Creek like a double sun, two arcs crisscrossed by Xs. Papa had shown me this bridge, called the Garden Bridge, on a map. Now he pointed across the creek. "There's the International Settlement. When the money from Nacek arrives, maybe we can rent rooms there."

We crossed the bridge, and Papa pointed toward the Huangpu River, churning ahead of us. "That's where we arrived," he said, "It was so calm after . . ." But he didn't finish his sentence, and I thought he was speaking to himself again, wondered calm after what, the turbulent ocean? Our ruined lives at home?

At the edge of the bridge, two Chinese adults and a little girl were bowing to soldiers outside a small hut. Other families lined up behind them. I waited to see if we would bow, but when we didn't, I didn't ask why not. What kind of human beings forced other human beings to fold before them? I didn't want to bow or be bowed to, ever.

The International Settlement side of the bridge, just south of us, just across Suzhou Creek, felt like another planet. Lining the river was a wall of magnificent buildings: the Cathay Hotel and the Peace Hotel. "That hotel is owned by a Jewish man," Papa said, and I wondered what he wanted me to feel—pride? Hope? Relief? Envy? "He was one of the first to come to Shanghai," Papa said, "decades ago."

I considered this, a wealthy Jewish man who had chosen to live here, had built a hotel on the glistening side of the bridge. I tried to imagine him arriving. The dock Papa had described as calm looked like a choppy parking lot of military ships and small crafts rocking and sloshing, smacking into each other.

Smoke rose from some boats: cooking oil, garlic, fish.

Back in Hongkou, I worked to look down so I wouldn't meet soldiers' gazes, but my eyes kept rising as if hungry. I was hungry, smelled meat, and saw signs: DELIKAT, BARCELONA, INTERNATIONAL. Restaurants. There were restaurants here? Nothing made sense to me.

"The Vienna," Papa said, and I followed his pointing finger to a sign: VIENNA. A café. Inside, people sat at tables, eating, drinking, laughing. As we passed close by, I smelled coffee and thought how much Papa loved it. I felt sick for having hated him a moment before. He closed his eyes, inhaling as if the smell might be enough. It looked cooler and quieter inside the café than anywhere I'd ever seen. Some of the tables held cakes on china plates, glasses filled with icy drinks. "Are those refugees?" I asked.

"Yes." He looked almost happy. "In fact," he said, "let's join them."

"But we—"

"It's okay, Słodkie Lillia. We need a little joy." He led me inside. We sat at a table, and he lowered Naomi onto his lap. Papa ordered two coffees, milk for Naomi, and two pastries, their outsides so flaky they melted into pure butter on our tongues, their insides a sweet paste. I had not forgotten what it felt like to hold a smooth, heavy mug, to drink something warm. But I had not been allowed to drink coffee at home and found the sharp, dark flavor scary. Why was I suddenly someone who drank coffee with Papa? I added more of the gray milk made from soy, and sugar, until my drink turned pale. Naomi cried for more pastry, but Papa only patted her. I looked out at the street as I sipped, wishing. I touched Mama's ring, tried to pass everything across the ocean—the buttery flavor, heat of the coffee, cool of the café, Papa's power at being able to treat us.

But after he paid, his mood dimmed. "Let's find Wayside Park," he said. "We must ask about rooms, jobs, and a school."

"I don't want to go to school," I said, crashing, too. "It will mean we live here."

"We are lucky to live here, Lillia. Help me make the most of it, because—" He stopped, maybe changed ideas or his mind midway: "So we have stories to tell her."

"Stories to tell her *when*?"

He took away my meaning without answering my question: "Right, Słodkie Lillia. Stories to tell her when."

— ◙ —

In the center of Wayside Park an old banyan tree rose from pavement its roots had cracked. How many years had that tree been alive? Thousands, maybe, and it would stand for thousands more. I felt too small to bear. And also relieved that something would outlast all of this. As soon as we arrived in Shanghai, every feeling I felt was suddenly met and challenged by its opposite. I was on a trapeze above my own life, dropping into moods so unpredictable I could hardly recognize, let alone control them. I often opposed myself. The banyan's branches seemed to me to twist into arms and legs, making the same shadow our acrobats used to cast on the back wall by climbing each other's bodies. The memory made me hungry, the aching absence of Mama connected to the absence of food. My whole body felt empty.

Families sat together on benches and one another's laps, talking about shops hiring, cafés opening, textile factories, bars, war at home. Some had gotten letters from Europe, delivered to the Embankment building. The women had hollow cheeks and bruised eyes, the men thick beards. We kids had limbs like kindling. A group of old Chinese women danced under the tree, moving in unison, raising and lowering their arms, turning slow circles. Their fragile skin shone in the heat, and I realized I couldn't remember Mama's face. Was she old like these dancing women? She was forty. I didn't know how old the women were. They wore shredded clothes, visible threads glistening. Their shoes were disintegrating, but they had shoes, and I was glad for that and for my own, even though they pinched and blistered my feet.

In the fractured light filtering through leaves, Papa stood talking to Mr. Michener and Taube. Taube, who had never had a baby, held Naomi. Maybe she wanted my sister for herself. I walked toward the dancers, and my hands and arms moved as if without my permission. One woman smiled, and I went closer to her, watching. I raised my arms into arcs, let my feet come off the ground, bent my knees. Lift, bend, lift.

I came alive. In spite of everything. I moved more, made

the arcs of my arms wider, lifted my knees higher, felt years of lessons underneath me as if that life—the one where I had studied dance every day—still mattered, still existed some-where. As if time were made of layers, not a line. Focusing on the power of the muscles in my legs, I closed my eyes and breathed in the heat, sweated, danced, and felt pure good hope of a sort I hadn't since she'd been gone.

When I opened my eyes again, I thought I would find myself laughing, floating, lifted, that she might even be there. But instead I saw a short man with glasses standing nearby, watching. His cheeks were stubbly, pocked, and he had a mus-tache that covered so much of his mouth he appeared lipless. I thought he was looking at me, and I immediately stopped mov-ing, ashamed, and rushed back to my father. I was angry, as if Papa were to blame for my having danced and embarrassed myself. But he was smiling, his hands in the pockets of the long, torn jacket he wore in spite of the heat. It made him look like a beggar or a rabbi. He faced Mr. Michener, who clutched his suitcase of scissors, shouting about elections, a board of direc-tors for the Jewish Communal Association, Papa should join, should this, should that, words and more words.

I glanced back at the dancing women, but they had fin-ished and were gathering to chat and laugh. Taube appeared at my side. "Lillia," she said, pointing at a round, nervous man, "that's Irvin Katz, the butcher. It's too bad he's so bald, be-cause when we first arrived, he traded Joshua a shave and a haircut for a bit of brisket! I keep checking to see if his hair has grown back, but alas." She laughed, but I was almost bald, too. Should I laugh? Naomi was watching me. I tried to laugh but barked like Piotr.

The sour man I'd seen watching me dance thrust his hand out. "I'm Gabriel Eber."

Papa shook his hand. "Bercik Kaczka." He beckoned me over. "My daughter Lillia."

"Lillia Kaczka-Varsh," I said. I stuck my hand out, too, like a man. Gabriel eyed me, and Papa gave me a strange look because I had added Varsh, Mama's name.

"Glad to make your acquaintance," Gabriel said. "We haven't seen you yet at temple."

Would Papa admit he never attended services, because religion oppressed more than it liberated, because human beings had to create our own codes, as he loved to say? He never came with us on Saturday mornings, when Mama and I dressed up and walked to temple, our rebellious red hair braided neatly, our shiny black shoes clicking against the sidewalk.

"We haven't been yet, but we're looking forward," Papa lied, clearing his throat. Or worse, maybe it was true. He would become religious. Shanghai would make it impossible for my free-thinking father to create his own code. He would be a stranger to me.

"Our temple is Ohel Moshe," Gabriel said. "And we have the Kadoorie School for Jewish children right here in Hongkou. We must stick together now. We can't lose sight of the importance of remaining Jewish no matter what the obstacles." Had he disapproved of my dancing because the women I was with were Chinese? Some at the Heime avoided all things Chinese, even though we were here in Shanghai and owed our lives to the city. Then Gabriel began telling Papa something about Salvationist intellectuals and treaties, something Baltic, something Jakob, maybe burnt-glass? A last name, a plan, money we might owe, something government, something Japanese. There were many words I didn't know. I stopped listening and walked away, the summer heat infusing me until I wobbled and my thinking bubbled. Papa followed, carrying Naomi, and led us out of Wayside Park.

We passed a row of graves. "Who's buried here?" I whispered.

"It's a Jewish cemetery," Papa said, and then, "Did you hear the news, sweet Lillia? Gabriel said there's a school for Jewish children right here in Hongkou, in our neighborhood."

But my hearing and vision had turned cloudy. I couldn't stand the tombstones or the words *our neighborhood*. Death in Shanghai seemed unbearably unfair. Because I understood, walking by those rows of Jewish graves, that we had come here to escape dying at home.

— ◙ —

In Hongkou, you could meet someone one day and find yourself living with him the next. Even if you disliked him. We rented a room in the three-story house where Gabriel Eber lived, number 54, Ward Road. Gabriel made me feel like a bad person, not religious enough, too quick to dance with Chinese strangers, unhelpful. I feared his judgment. Taube and Mr. Michener moved in, too. And the Lipners. I had no power except to call 54 Ward by its proper name, 54 Ward, never mistake it for *home*. It was one house in a line of identical houses, overflowing with sad families lucky to be alive. Even being alive was now a lucky mercy.

We moved our suitcase, cotton bag, and three selves into a single room on the first floor. It was off the front entrance, a brick archway over an iron gate hung with laundry we had to move out of the way each time we opened the door. There was just enough space at the foot of my cot to hang my head upside down in the mornings, to shift onto my hands and try to hold her handstand, to count, thirty days, forty days, fifty. Our first month in the new room, its walls blurred, my body drained to empty, blood filled my head. Papa must have seen me doing her exercises, calling her name, but he never asked.

For all of August, hot air and dust blasted through slivers in our cracked windows, and the walls and sills swelled. But old people and children crowded the alley behind us no matter how hot, chatting, laughing, playing. Those with pet crickets compared their singing. Some people squatted over an open stream of sewage. Others spread newspapers out and sold sweaters to be unraveled and reknitted, pieces of cloth, wood, brick, matches, nails, cigarettes, food. Every alley felt like its own tiny, busy city.

At night, Papa listened to Gabriel's illegal radio in the basement. Germany lost an air war with Britain and the men cheered; Italy invaded Greece and they wept and worried. In the mornings, while I tried to hold myself upside down, while I lifted my sister to keep my arms strong, Papa read news of Shanghai, of our own life although it seemed like someone else's. He told me stories of cities in China, one called Chongqing, bombed to ash by the Japanese. He said others had already been bombed, or were still being bombed, and more cities would be bombed later. I was too afraid to ask how to tell which ones.

Starving for breakfast, Papa left each day to look for work, and I watched Naomi, washed us from a bucket we all shared, cleaned, picked bugs and glass from rice before cooking it over a pot of coal. I tried to coax Naomi into speaking so I wouldn't be so alone. By September, I could hold a handstand for twenty-five seconds, whispering *Mama*, but I was afraid of becoming crazy, so I took Naomi up to Taube's room. I hoped for food, or a needle with which I might fix our mouse, even conversation. Anything not to be in our room forever, so hungry, always waiting for Papa.

Taube came to the door in a navy-blue dress and pulled us in as if from a storm. I looked around: a lit lamp, a hand-made quilt over a chair, a table. She saw me looking, and asked, "Would you like help making your room more comfortable? Why don't we sew a pillow?"

"Can we sew this?" I asked. I held out the toy mouse, its stomach still open.

She reached behind a bed propped against the wall and got a box. Inside were three needles, two spools of thread, some fabric, and a burst of stuffing. Just enough for mouse repair and one skinny pillow. Taube helped me, fixing my accidental knots, adding stitches between those I'd sewn too far apart. Naomi played at my feet, trying to prop herself up on her arms but falling, trying to climb my legs but falling. We listened to the sounds of our neighbors, six families in a house meant for one or two. Mrs. Lipner moved like a ghost in the room next door. Mr. Lipner was always out, trying to start a business printing news for Jewish people. No one, not even Mr. Lipner, could bear to be under the drenching cloud of Mrs. Lipner's sorrow. If her boys had come, she might have been energetic, like Taube. Or if she had never had children, she might have been happier, too. Might Papa? He would have stayed behind to save our mother if not for Naomi and me, I was certain.

There was the cheerful noise of the Song family, who owned the house and lived on its top floor: grandparents, Mr. and Mrs. Song; their children; and two grandchildren—Mei-Mei and Xiao Su, six and four. The girls ran by and peeked into the door, giggling, saying, "Nihao, nihao!" *Hello, hello!* Naomi was riveted. When they ran away, still laughing, Naomi stared at the door hopefully.

"Your father says you're nervous about school," Taube said. "But the Kadoorie School will be wonderful. I can help watch your sister. We all have to work together now."

My right hand slipped and pierced my left thumb with the needle. "I want to work, not study." A bead of blood rose to the surface of my skin, and I popped my thumb in my mouth.

"Well, you'll get better work eventually if you study first."

Then why did Mr. Michener carry scissors everywhere? And Taube, a teacher, sew pillows? I picked Naomi up, and she began patting me. Had she seen me stick my thumb?

"Come," Taube said, "Let's go out for some noodles. We can watch the boats."

"Oh, we don't have—" I said, my face hot, but she interrupted.

"I'll buy the noodles, of course. Please don't worry."

I was too embarrassed to thank her and too hungry to refuse. We walked into the late afternoon, as if on a regular outing, a mother and her daughters. Except I was carrying Naomi, and we had no mother. At the mouth of Chusan Road, a man stood wearing a flour sack. He had tied pieces of cloth to his feet in place of shoes, no tire rubber straps even. Taube went to him and touched his shoulder. He turned, wild-eyed, and she handed him five CN, five dollars of Chinese National Currency, enough to buy five meals, ten sausages from a cart we'd passed, fifteen days worth of noodles or soup on the street, weeks of the rice we made at 54 Ward.

His eyes revived, as if holding enough money for food, or even shoes, had transformed him. He nodded thank you, bowed slightly. "Things will get better," Taube told him. But he fled, perhaps fearful she might change her mind. "That was so much," I said, worried.

"I still have five CN left." She smiled. "Enough for something hot for us today and tomorrow and the next day. We'll be okay, and your father will find a job."

The noodle stand closest to us had no chairs, just a cauldron over which a Chinese woman was bent, furiously stirring. Her hair was tied on top of her head, and she wore so many layers of clothing she resembled the cauldron, round and gray. She fished out noodles, before ladling broth into bowls. Taube bought two portions, one for herself and one for Naomi and me. I tried to eat slowly, feeding Naomi a bite for every one I took. Gabriel had warned us never to eat what he called Chinese street food, but Taube apparently didn't agree. And the shockingly hot broth was so delicious that we finished instantly. Naomi shouted, "Ah, ah, ah!" Taube responded, "Yes, yes, yes! Delicious!" We could take *ah* and make it mean whatever we wanted. We handed our bowls back to the noodle woman, who dropped them in a bucket of dark water.

Taube walked us to the Garden Bridge, fearless, as if she either belonged in Shanghai or didn't mind not belonging. Ships, sampans, and fishermen left, arrived, docked, scattered. The river roiled and waved out to the horizon. Taube pointed across. "Pudong," she said. "We can take a ferry someday and see the wharf. It's apparently very beautiful."

I couldn't speak, because my chest and throat felt full of mud. I was too sad to know what to do or say, had no place in me big enough for the sorrow. I closed my eyes and rocked, and Taube said softly, "One day soon, a ship will carry your mother here, and Shanghai will feel more like home."

We walked back to 54 Ward. And over the next two long weeks in September, while we tried to find work, boil water, and eat enough not to starve in Shanghai, the Canadian, Soviet, and British governments collected men between the ages of twenty-one and thirty-five—boys, Papa called them—and forced them into the war. Italy, Germany, and Japan pledged that any enemy to one ally was an enemy to all allies. The American radio Papa and Gabriel loved was suddenly blocked. We heard only Japanese reports, full of hatred for America. Japan prevented an American ship full of missionaries from docking in Shanghai, sending everyone back onto the ocean. What if they had turned our ship away? On what safe ship might my mother arrive now, and to what sort of city? Maybe she had been on the one they'd forbidden entry, and was now at sea forever, like the woman who'd leapt over the *Conte Rosso*'s railing.

Maybe nowhere would ever be home for any of us again.

CHAPTER FIVE

学校, Xuexiao, *School*

By October, no money or letters had arrived. Papa had applied for fifty-seven jobs. Construction, fixing buildings, working on a new synagogue, helping translate papers at a place called the Joint Distribution Committee. He said he would take anything, do anything, be anyone they needed. But he was competing with men everyone called coolies, who had been made invincibly strong by decades of work, carrying an entire city on their backs. Some of the job advertisements said no refugees could apply. "Workers here are driven like slaves," Papa told me. "They work for so close to nothing, it's unreal. How do you compete with that?"

Still, every morning he drank boiled water, read the *Shanghai Jewish Chronicle* with Mr. Michener and Gabriel, and then set out into the cooling city to find work. We were running out of money. I washed Naomi in the bucket, trying to make a game of it. She blinked and splashed, and then we sat until we were too bored, hungry, or worried to bear it, before heading to Taube's, or outside to watch for boats.

"Mama might come at any moment," I told Naomi, because hearing my own words made them seem more real than thinking them, and made me feel less crazy. I no longer felt pleased that my sister didn't respond, as I had on the ship. Now I wished she would talk to me.

"Ah, ah, ah, ah," Naomi agreed.

"Right, Mama. Look for her! She might be walking on her hands, in which case she will be upside down! Then I'll turn you like this, and she'll be right-side up." I turned Naomi upside down, and she laughed her gobbling laugh.

Once the weather had cooled, the open-air market on Chusan Road became even livelier, glittering in the fall air with purple eggplants, bright green beans, noodle vendors stirring their steamy cauldrons. I smiled at my favorite and she smiled back, but I had no money for noodles or potatoes. I saw onions, eggs, and flour, felt a growing desperation. One afternoon, I leaned against the table and watched the vendor, in a shouting match with an old man. There were people everywhere, pressing us. I set Naomi next to the potatoes and eggs, pretending to readjust her, and slipped what I could off the table into my bag, then ran. I had never stolen before.

Naomi bounced on my hip, as the newly heavy bag banged against my side. We came upon the pile of refuse near the Heime, where I had once watched a Chinese boy pick through trash, and I slowed. People were looking at Naomi and me. Could they see I had become a thief? Had I? Did stealing once make me a criminal? Maybe. It would always have happened—I could never undo it.

"Boats," I said to Naomi. I pointed. But she watched me.

"Can you say *boats*?" I asked. Her green eyes stayed on my face. The color green had changed for me from grass to dirty water. She didn't say *ah* or pat me.

"The things I took are for you, you know," I said.

The same decay I'd smelled when we walked by with Papa rose in a choking cloud around us. But now I climbed onto the trash, holding my sister tight, and bent to collect scraps: three small sticks of wood; a metal hook; and a black, broken wheel, maybe from a cart or a child's toy. I tucked the trash into my bag, careful not to break the eggs. We went to the Embankment Building to ask if there was mail for us, but the women just gave us sad looks and shook their heads, no, nothing for you. I carried Naomi home, trying to sing to her as we passed mobs of people, shrunk from soldiers. My parents hadn't let me walk to school alone at home. Where were they now? Did they know where I was?

Back at 54 Ward, I opened my bag. All the eggs but one had been smashed, soaking everything with slime. I deserved it, but sorrow broke over me. I left Naomi on the floor, where she began trying to propel herself like a small snake. In the kitchen I started water boiling, cracked the intact egg into a cup, and tried to salvage the insides of others, picking out shattered shell. While everything boiled, I lay down in our room to face Naomi. "Why don't you talk to me? Or crawl? Or walk? Please?"

Nothing. "Look," I said, picking her up and carrying her to my cot. "I found us some new things." I showed her the wood, metal, and black plastic wheel. "We can make a person." I used the wheel for a face, wood for the body, some metal across it, arms.

"That's a soldier," I told Naomi. "When you see a soldier, look away."

I took the metal off and put a scrap of fabric I'd taken from Taube's room across the wood slats that composed the stick-figure body. "But look! Now it's a girl!" I held it out to my sister, trying to be patient, letting her look for as long as she liked.

Eventually, Naomi pulled the fabric off. "Now it's a naked girl," I said, laughing. She laughed, too, and I was so happy that I kissed her, even though I didn't know if she'd understood, if we were actually laughing with each other or not.

I made the scraps dance as if they were puppets Then I danced, too.

When Papa came home, he said, "I found some work," and

picked Naomi up without energy. It had been four months since we'd arrived, sixteen weeks of solid looking. I leapt up to hug him. "That's very good news!"

But a sound in his voice told me it was not. "Yes," he said. We waited. Finally, he sighed. "Your mama will find it funny. I'll help build the new synagogue after all. And translate paperwork for the Joint Distribution Committee. I'm the most observant I've ever been." Then he laughed the stranger's laugh again.

"I made soup with eggs and potatoes," I said, so proud, hoping this would cheer him up. But we ate in silence. Papa forgot to ask how I'd gotten food, or to thank me, just went downstairs to Gabriel's radio. I followed him into the hallway but stayed frozen between our room and the front door, holding Naomi. I didn't know where to go, down to Gabriel's to horrible news, or back into the room where Naomi and I had already been alone for hours. Outside? I went to the door and opened it onto even more noise and commotion than usual, peered through the laundry. It took my eyes a minute to tell my mind they saw two men, skeleton-thin, wrestling something from the street into a cart. The thing was naked, fat as a large carnival doll full of air. It had a human face but looked like lavender rubber, eyes and mouth matching red, open. I twisted away from the door so fast Naomi startled and cried.

So that was what it looked like to be dead. I'd known those bone men drove a cart each morning to collect bodies. I'd heard them rattling and shouting. There were carts for waste, recycled materials, garbage, and corpses. I had never seen one before, but its appearance didn't surprise me. I felt vivid and prickly, rushed back inside only because I didn't want Naomi to see.

I had overheard someone at the Heime say the cart hauled more than two hundred dead people away some days. Where did so many bodies go?

— ▨ —

Once Papa found work, he said it was time for me to go to school. Taube would watch Naomi. The night before he sent me, he boiled extra water to add to the bucket for my bath. It chilled quickly on the rag, but he'd tried hard.

The next morning, he woke me before it was light. I held my handstand in the dark for thirty seconds but couldn't make my mama's name take shape in my mouth. I just said, "Please." We had a piece of bread left from the night before, so I chewed that as we walked through the streets, already full of people heading to work, carts competing, animals barking. My arms felt light without Naomi, as if she'd anchored me to Shanghai and now I might float up over the river. By the time we got to the school, I was shivering, afraid, desperate for Mama, Warsaw, Babcia, food. "I'm not ready," I pleaded.

Papa bent down and kissed my forehead. "We'll just have a look. Let the principal know you're here. And how exceptional you are."

"You'll embarrass me."

"I intend to!" He laughed his own laugh, surprising me out of my anger. He pretended to trip by flying forward, then springing up and winking, a clown again for an instant.

We walked through a courtyard where boys kicked a ball and shouted, toward an L-shaped building Papa entered as if we belonged. Inside, kids were everywhere. Most of the refugees I had met were old people like Papa. Here, there were people my age. Two girls walked by wearing pressed dresses. Another passed in a shirt so shiny from washings I could see through it to a lumpy undershirt. The well-dressed ones didn't notice me, but the girl in the ruined shirt looked over curiously.

Kids burst from every direction and funneled into classrooms. I shrunk back. I had never been to school without Kassia. We always planned what to wear, tried to match, showed up scrubbed and lovely. I felt the warmth of her breath whispering in my ear.

Papa stopped to ask a tall boy where we could find the headmaster. The boy wore a shirt with a picture of a tiny tennis racket imprinted on the chest, next to the letters *TKS*, maybe for the Kadoorie School. It seemed amazing to me that someone had made such a shirt. Did people play tennis in Shanghai? The boy had the beginning of a faint mustache that appeared to have been smudged on with charcoal. "Down that way," he said in English that clicked and snapped.

"What's your name?" Papa asked him, using English, too.

"Benjamin," the boy pronounced.

"Hello, Benjamin. This beautiful person is Lillia Kaczka. From Warsaw."

"Papa!" I said. What was wrong with him? His eyes were glittering with delight.

"Hello, Lillia Kaczka from Warsaw," Benjamin said. I looked at the floor. All around was a rush of languages so thick and confusing I couldn't separate individual sounds: Russian, maybe, some Chinese, words that were English, but not possible for me to make out. I listened for Polish, even one familiar syllable, but none came. When I looked up, the boy named Benjamin was gone.

A cluster of girls stood laughing. Some had ribbons in their hair, fresh dresses, clean boots. One wore a Star of David around her neck. I touched my mother's ring. What would happen—had happened already—to all the dresses I'd left? When we had everything, I thought we needed it. But now we had so little that even one of my outfits would have been lovely here.

Papa pulled me into an office. The headmistress took Papa's hand, and I remembered he was handsome, tall, sharp-boned, and wild-eyed. When her gaze traveled over me, I was ashamed of my dress and my sticking-out hair.

"This is my daughter Lillia," Papa was saying in English. "We just arrived from Warsaw and would like for her to attend school. It is possible? We have heard wonderful things."

"Welcome to you both. I'm Mrs. Aarons," the headmistress said, sitting at a desk made from a door balanced across stacked cabinets.

"Sit, sit," she told us. We sat like obedient students. Around her office were boxes and framed photos: Smiling boys in tennis shirts like Benjamin's. Girls wearing rags, clutching dolls. A chorus of little ones singing, their mouths open *O*s.

"The Kadoorie School is excellent," Mrs. Aarons said, "Especially given the—"

"Yes," Papa interrupted, maybe not wanting to hear her next words. He warned her: "Lillia's mother is not with us here yet."

Mrs. Aarons just nodded, her brow furrowing deeper. She must have heard countless stories of broken lives and missing mothers. "At Kadoorie we take care of one another. We only started running full-time recently—last year, we held some classes and a fresh-air camp for Jewish children—well, at an unused tuberculosis sanatorium in Hongjiao, of all places!" She laughed. "But of course that wouldn't do long term."

Papa and I stared at her, our footing rocky. How did people talk to each other? Was this funny? Should we laugh with her? What was Hongjiao? An unused tuberculosis sanatorium? Would we get something wrong and cause her to refuse me? Now that we were refugees, we were always begging. For water, food, jobs, now for school for me. If our landlord, Mr. Song, discovered Gabriel's radio, he could turn us in to the Japanese police. We would beg him not to. Before the war, we had never pleaded. If we ever arrived at that luxurious position again, I would remember this feeling—of scalding fear and humiliation—forever.

"We realized that at the rate refugees are arriving, well, at a rate that—fortunately, Mr. Kadoorie is so generous. God bless him. Because of his support, we are able to offer Hebrew, scripture, grammar, literature, algebra, history, geometry, Chinese, geography, German . . ."

So maybe she would let me in after all? She stood, came out from behind the desk, and put her arm over my shoulder. Confusion blurred my vision. "Come, Lillia," she said. "Let's get you situated. We'd be grateful if you'd write a short essay, just so we know the level of your English. How is your English, dear? We speak English here at Kadoorie and our lessons are in English, so it's important to know at least enough to follow along at first."

I realized I hadn't spoken. "Oh, my English is okay," I said. "My grandmother speaks English. She's an art teacher. She has a library of English books she read to my mother and to me when I was small. Also, we studied some language at gymnasium—school—at home."

Mrs. Aarons clapped her hands together, reminding me of Naomi. "Mrs. Campton will be delighted to have you. Come. She can give you some placement tests to make sure you're in courses that will benefit you. But I can already tell that you'll do wonderfully here."

I wondered what Naomi was doing at 54 Ward with Taube. It was her naptime now. Was she curled up on Taube's lap? I felt burning, miserable jealousy of them.

"I will be here at four to pick you up," Papa said. "Work hard."

"I don't want—"

"I know, Lillia," Papa said. Mrs. Aarons pretended to be looking at something on her hand. He continued: "But you must. It's important. School will be—" He paused. Maybe he would say fun, or interesting, and the scream lurking in me would be unleashed. But he just said: "Useful for us both," and I was silent as he kissed my forehead, as he left without turning back, as if I were okay, could go to school, could manage. As if I were still myself.

— ◻ —

Mrs. Campton's classroom was full of people chattering, walking around, laughing. I didn't see anyone who looked like a teacher, so I silently slid into a seat in the back and waited to wake up from this fresh nightmare. When the teacher walked in, she stood in front of the blackboard and everyone scrambled into dirty desks, boys with awkward ears poking out, girls giggling. The teacher wore a navy skirt and patterned jacket. She smiled, plump and pretty, with a high, round forehead and white hair.

"Please take ten minutes to write in your journals," she said. Everyone took out pencils and began writing in composition books. I stared at my hands, flat on the desk. Maybe the composition books cost money. My skin burned. A shadow crossed my desk, and I glanced up: the teacher. "Welcome," she whispered. "I'm Mrs. Campton. What is your name?"

"Lillia." I barely managed to say it.

She put her hand on my shoulder. "Hello, Lillia. Where are you from?"

"Warsaw."

"We are very glad to have you here. I'll introduce you to everyone when we are done writing. You may take the next few minutes to write whatever you like, in English. You won't be required to read this aloud." She handed me a composition book and a pencil.

I tried to accept the gifts casually, but my heart expanded until it couldn't fit in my body. "Thank you," I whispered. Both words broke. I worried she would think I didn't speak English well and would take away my pencil and notebook. But she smiled and returned to the front of the room. I rolled the pencil in my hand, joy coursing through me. I hadn't held a pencil since before I was thrown out of school in Warsaw. It felt heavy, familiar, lovely. I raised it to my face and smelled it, then pressed its tip against the page and felt violent happiness when it made a dark dot. I pushed harder, grinding the point until the paper tore. Then, next to the small slice, I made a clean *L*, an *I*, an *L*, an *L*, an *I*, an *A*. I wrote it over, over, over: *Lillia. Lillia. Lillia.* The tear was my starting line. At the bottom of the page, I put *Kaczka-Varsh*, my new double last name.

When Mrs. Campton said, "Take a minute to finish up the sentence you're working on," I wrote *Shanghai*, and then drew a light outline of the woman I'd seen on the poster at the Heime.

It seemed like years had passed since we arrived. I set my pencil down, and my hand felt sad.

"A new student has joined us from Warsaw," Mrs. Campton said. "Let's welcome her."

The class shouted a word I didn't recognize. And someone, a girl, whispered a hiss. I looked around and saw teeth, mouths open, forming another word together: "Welcome."

"Now, who can welcome Lillia in her own language?"

One voice popped out: "Witaj!" *Welcome.*

I turned helplessly, toward a grinning girl. I felt as if we'd been caught getting in small trouble, this other Polish girl who was maybe like me and me, Lillia, who used to get in trouble sometimes at school. For passing notes, laughing, talking, drawing silly pictures of the boys. How easy my life had been when it took place in Polish.

I was afraid that this girl and I were alike. The sound of her witaj reminded me how unwelcome I was where I most wanted to be, home. She was mouse skinny with a pink face and circles outlining her eyes. I felt surprised she had neither whiskers nor triangular ears. Her hair was pulled back on one side, falling on the other. I thought maybe she was ill.

"Dziękuję Ci," I said, *thank you.*

Mrs. Campton laced her fingers together. "Lillia, this is Biata. She is also from Poland!"

The girl named Biata said, "Nihao, Lillia. That's *hello* in Chinese."

Biata watched me all morning, and I snuck looks back.

Sometimes she looked away as if I were the odd one staring. A group of girls in the front row of desks glanced at us and whispered, passed papers between them. Were Biata and I the poorest or unluckiest? Was I especially strange and awful? Or just new?

Mrs. Campton introduced three German girls, Eliza, Anna, and Nina. Nina told me, "I was called Sara in Germany, but here I am Nina." I was interested that she had changed her name. This seemed like a good idea to me. The note-passers were Sally Miller and Rebecca Rosen, Americans. Sally wore a Star of David and a pressed dress, and had beautifully braided dark hair. She was plump with baby cheeks and looked, as Mrs. Campton did, imported from a country where people still ate meat and drank cream. Rebecca was small but not in the starving way Biata and I were. Rebecca seemed weightless and shiny clean, her light hair glowing. Maybe she bathed for hours in a tub of hot water.

She waved and smiled, her eyes crinkling. "Hi, Lillia. Welcome to Shanghai." She spoke in mouthy English, as if drinking something bubbly and forming words with it.

Mrs. Campton said, "Let's ask Lillia some questions, please."

A boy made mostly of neck spoke very fast. "Where are you from? How'd you get to Shanghai? How long have you been here? What will your parents do here?"

I stared at him. His neck was the stick of a lollipop, his face shiny red candy.

"Warsaw," I managed. "I came on a ship."

Everyone waited. "Let's tell Lillia about ourselves," Mrs. Campton eventually said. "Sally, can you tell Lillia something about Shanghai?"

Sally stood up reluctantly. Did we have to stand each time we spoke?

"There's a lot to do here," she said.

"Say the things you like most," Mrs. Campton prompted.

"Dances? Concerts?" Sally asked. Whom was she asking?

"How long have you been here, Sally?" Mrs. Campton asked in the way you ask something you already know the answer to. I felt as if a performance was happening, but I was trapped both in the audience and on stage.

"Three years." Sally sighed. "We came before everyone else, because my father was teaching. He already knew all about China." She looked as if telling me this had been an exhausting favor. But I didn't want to know, didn't want to be here.

"What about you, Rebecca?" Mrs. Campton asked. Sally sent Rebecca a look I didn't understand, but Rebecca smiled. "Two years. I lead the Girl Guides, if you want to join."

She meant me. "Thank you," I whispered.

"Sometimes we meet at my place, in the International Settlement. But sometimes other places, too—like Sally's in the French Quarter. And next summer we're camping at the wharf!"

So Rebecca lived in the International Settlement and Sally in the French Quarter. I learned at Kadoorie that only the poorest of us lived in Hongkou: the Polish Jews, some unlucky Russian families who had arrived too late, and Chinese who had come from the countryside. Anyone with any money lived across the bridge. I hoped God would punish the lucky girls.

Taube had told me Shanghai's neighborhoods were like different cities, with their own police and laws. If I got in trouble, I should find a policeman who was Sikh, with a beard, wearing white clothing and a turban. He would treat a foreign girl more gently, being foreign himself. Not a Chinese policeman, who worked for the Shanghai Municipal Council, or a Russian policeman. Worst of all would be a Japanese soldier. "But aren't they all foreign, too?" I asked Taube. It was important to keep track of insiders and outsiders, who hated whom.

"Well, yes, in a way, but find a Sikh policeman if you're ever in trouble."

"What kind of trouble?"

Taube didn't say, because she was unwilling to name new possible terrors.

The school day rushed by like the Huangpu River, picking up my thoughts until they were soaked and bloated. By afternoon I felt as if I'd been carried away, too, so far from 54 Ward I wouldn't find my way back. Teachers came and went, speaking their subjects. After a grammar lesson, Biata stood at my desk and asked, "Chcesz usiąść ze mną tiffin?" Did I want to sit her with her at lunch? I nodded, mute. A pot of porridge was wheeled in on a shelved cart, bowls stacked beneath it. I had rocks in my belly. What if Papa didn't come after school, what if Mama never arrived at all? Would today be the day I became an orphan? Would Naomi talk and walk today, with Taube the only one to see? I wondered if I would faint, almost hoped so.

Instead, awake and conscious, I gulped the watery porridge, some of it dripping from the smile I tried to return to Biata, who sipped and grinned sideways. I clamped my mouth and wiped it on the side of my sleeve. The gray flavor was familiar now. I no longer remembered what milk, soup, or dumplings full of meat had tasted like in Warsaw. Papa was worried about Naomi's and my growing, so he tried each day to bring us something nutritious: an egg, a bun stuffed with bean paste, a stick of sugarcane to chew. But often he couldn't.

I was embarrassed to have finished my horrid lunch so quickly. Were the others less hungry? "Jak długo tu byłeś?" I asked Biata. This time, she answered me in English: "I've been here seven months." Maybe she agreed it was unwise to make a spectacle of being Polish. Some girls spoke German, while the Americans chattered in their big, open English. Rebecca's voice rose like a string of silver notes. How good did it feel to be her?

"Maybe I'll change my name, too, like Nina," I said.

"But that was because Sara was never her real name," Biata said. "Germany made everyone be called Sara." Then she said a garble of sounds. One of them was "Shanghai."

I thought she must want a compliment, so I asked, "How do you speak Chinese so well?"

She beamed, the shadows under her eyes creasing. "Oh, I

don't know *so much*," Biata said. "My parents don't let me talk to Chinese kids in our lane. But I have a book—it says some Shanghai phrases: *rickshaw, bank,* how to find your way around the city alone . . ."

"Where do you live?"

"In Hongkou, like you, right?" She dropped her voice to a whisper. "Right near the prison. Sometimes when I walk by, I can hear people screaming. But my parents will open a bar soon, and we'll move to the French Quarter where my aunt lives. It's safer there."

"Prison?"

"Ward Prison!" She laughed, as if she had told a joke. "Do you know why they scream?"

Ward Prison? Was it on our street? I held a hand up, didn't want to hear. But she continued, switching back to Polish whispers, maybe not wanting anyone else to overhear her hideous words. Or maybe feeling English was too refined to express ciało spalone, *flesh burned*; gwozdzie wbite palcow ludzi, *nails driven into fingers* and oczy, *eyes*; water forced into their stomachs until they rozerwanie, *burst.*

I said: "I'll look away when I walk by."

"I'm not afraid," she said.

We could not be friends. I would have no friends in Shanghai. I needed the bathroom but didn't want to ask, stand up, or leave the room, so I sat miserably and tried to will time to pass faster. After science, mathematics, and a recitation lesson on English nursery rhymes, 4 p.m. finally arrived. I was a fossil, had been in Mrs. Campton's room a thousand years, and might someday be dug up. I planned to shout at Papa as soon as I saw him. And never go to school again. But right as I despaired, we were dismissed. I ran, desperate, but when I pushed open the door I thought led to the bathroom, I saw a closet instead.

"Nihao, *hello.*" A Chinese boy was carrying an open box that teased me with its stacks of silky paper. I used to lie on the rug in my babcia's living room, drawing pictures while she and Mama made dinner and laughed in the kitchen. I had endless paper, crayons, and colored pencils then, but I'd never thought about it. The boy stood looking at me, black hair hanging over his eyes like a curtain. I had to go to the bathroom so terribly. My face filled with tears.

I used English, even though the words were floating and popping as I spoke them, "Oh, I'm sorry . . . I . . . Oh, do you know where . . ."

He blew at his circus curtain hair, opening his face like a show: dark eyes, round nose, a chipped tooth I saw when he smiled. Why was he smiling? I began to back out.

He said, "Mingzi?" But I didn't know what this was. Mingzi sounded like Moishe, the name of the man who had started the Stanislav Cyrk in Warsaw. I shook my head, and my head shook my body. I was a puppet again, and the tears came.

The boy pointed at himself, said, "Wei."

I knew this English word, how to go, how to do something. "Way?"

Now he used another English word, "Yes." He pointed at

himself again, "Wei," then at me, held his hands up. So Way was his name. Mingzi meant *name*. He was asking for mine.

I said, "Słodkie Lillia," because that's who I wanted to be, Sweet Lillia. Maybe he wouldn't notice my crying, and anyway what could Sweet Lillia mean to this strange boy in a closet?

He said, "Słodkie Lillia," and bent to pick up the box, then waved several sheets of the paper at me, offering them.

I didn't pretend to refuse, just reached my hand out. The pages felt golden, as if they'd been absorbing light. I slid them into my bag as the boy said something, maybe my name again. He reached a finger up to his own face, and wiped away a tear that wasn't there. He meant me.

I turned and ran. The real bathroom was down a hundred twisting hallways I thought would never be familiar, but when I sat on a real toilet, in private, my relief was so intense it became joy. I folded forward and exhaled. My first day of school was finished, and I was alive.

Outside the school, other students gathered in groups for sports. Rickshaws arrived, different from the yellow ones crowding Ward Road. These were black with cushions and covers, driven by men in hats and gloves. Sally and Rebecca climbed into one together. I imagined them riding across the Garden Bridge to the International Settlement, free of the terror of soldiers, met by dancing mothers. Rebecca waved. "Bye, Lillia! See you tomorrow!"

But my arm was too heavy to lift. The city spun and I closed my eyes, tried to quiet my mind. *Please, God, let Papa appear.*

One hundred seconds. I counted fifty in Polish, fifty in English, then opened my eyes. He was hurrying toward me, Naomi in his grip. I snapped my jaw shut and held my teeth together. Papa hugged me and Naomi grabbed some of my hair, now just long enough to yank. "How was it? What did you learn?" Papa asked. I couldn't speak.

That night, it rained Shanghai into a wall of water. My mind wrote to Kassia, but my hands didn't move. I saved the magical paper while the Huangpu overflowed, while the morning arrived with a sun like a bright fist, while I walked the flooded streets back to Kadoorie, clutching my bag with its composition note-book and pencil, the paper from the boy named Wei now safely beneath my cot. I dug an elbow into my stomach to quiet the growling. The hungrier I felt, the less real anything seemed. In the rush of river bleeding into the streets, dream Lillia flooded real Lillia. I saw more objects: pieces of buildings, a thousand branches, metal pipes, an empty bottle, shards.

I took as much as I could carry, the trash undeniably real. Under my cot was a world. I would make people who lived there, puppet people. I'd give them what they needed, the way Papa was trying to do for us. I would keep my puppets safe, sup-ply them with stories they would love to live. My puppets would fly, have their families nearby, be free. Someday maybe I'd do a show! In Shanghai, with my puppets, when she arrived. I would make a Shanghai circus to welcome her, would use my puppets to tell the story of what had happened, might happen—for an audience of one.

The river would bring me what I needed. I just had to collect and dry it all out, build it, figure out what the story was,
who the puppets would be. This idea made me lighter, as did
the strange thought that maybe the boy from the supply closet
could help.

His cheek had looked so smooth when he brushed away
the tear that was actually mine.

CHAPTER SIX

朋友, Pengyou, *Friend*

November became December became January. Then caught up with now and 1940 became 1941, no longer the year we were invaded or even the one in which Babcia and Mama vanished, no longer the year we left. Now, when people asked when we'd arrived—everyone in Shanghai asked this all the time—we said, "Last year." Now we didn't live in the Heime, but in our room at 54 Ward. Now Papa worked and Naomi spent her baby days with Taube and the landlord's grandchildren, Mei-mei and Xiao Su. Now Taube sewed hats and I could hold a handstand for fifty-six seconds at the foot of my cot, even hungry. Now I was almost a regular girl, cold, afraid, and hungry, always hungry, but walking to school with my book bag, trying to replace the fear in my mind with ideas and Chinese words. Now numbers were just dates that gathered behind me, moving me further from Mama, and myself.

We ate porridge for breakfast, or bread Papa lined up for at the Heime, after waking at 4 a.m. A few times he managed boiled eggs, tubes of golden fried dough, once even a Chinese pancake, thin, with egg inside. One night, he brought two sticks of sugarcane. Naomi and I sucked the sweet juice out and spit shreds into the cold courtyard. Our walls and windows shimmered with white ice. Rumors of fever, lice, typhus, and dysentery swept through the streets. I tried to find my way back to safe thoughts by way of beautiful English words I whispered to myself: *river, city, glitter, silver, Rebecca Rosen.* I recorded the strokes in Chinese characters, the tangle of noodles Taube brought us, the skin that peeled from each roasted potato. I kept track of colors: Shanghai was tan, gold, green, and sometimes red, especially at night. Water was every shade but blue. Japanese planes turned the air metallic, chopped clouds into patches intersected by lines. I sneaked to Wayside Park on days when Papa worked and Naomi was with Taube and the Song girls. There, I danced, hiding myself—on good days losing myself—among the old Chinese women and the music.

At school I watched Rebecca, hoping we would speak.

After school I passed the supply closet, slowing, hoping to see the boy named Wei, but too shy to knock. I was terribly lonely but even more embarrassed and afraid. Only Biata seemed to want to be my friend, but I feared the things she said, feared we were alike.

I collected Naomi each afternoon, washed us with cold water, used a small rock to sand down my broken, dirty fingernails, then boiled everything—what we ate, what we wore. While I worked, I set Naomi on her stomach and watched her try to lift herself up, to move, to crawl. Once, I had just washed Naomi and was washing myself when the door opened. Papa.

"Oh!" he said. "Lillia. I'm sorry—"

A scrambling feeling of bugs or mice came to life in my stomach. I wanted to grab the blanket and cover myself, or hide behind my cot, but I froze, meeting Papa's gaze as he backed out of the door fast and pulled it closed. I put my clothes on immediately, and it was half an hour before he returned. This time he knocked. We never spoke of it. But I wondered sometimes what I had seen in his eyes—fright? We had no privacy, nothing safe or hidden.

Shanghai—or maybe just the war—made me consider my body. I was growing but also felt shrunk. It was impossible to smell lovely, or be clean and proud. My hands and feet were wounded and dirty. In my composition book for our anatomy course at Kadoorie, I wrote about bodies. We had to make a list of the organs of respiration: mouth, nose, larynx, trachea. The trachea divides into tubes. Air sacs and lungs let us stay alive. I studied blood: capillaries; veins; the heart, a pumping, tired muscle. We learned the science of our bodies at school, while I worked at home to keep Naomi and me alive and as human as we could be.

I recorded Chinese words for nouns I needed: *tram, street, sun, river, rickshaw, noodle.* We learned to write the character for *person*, its two strokes running legs. Chinese was logical: *person* was a skinny symbol, little pencil-line limbs like mine; *mouth* was a mouth; *sun* a sun; *moon* a ladder I might climb or push a puppet up. Chinese words became what numbers used to be for me, sensible and comforting. I imagined them in the shapes our floor made as I scrubbed. I assigned my treasures from the streets Chinese characters: *girl, boy, eye, mouth, arm.* I worked on making them into puppets, using pens from Kadoorie to draw faces on stone heads. Wheels and sticks became bodies.

Once, I stole string from Mrs. Campton's classroom and made a tiny tightrope. Another time, I took a pair of broken chopsticks and gave my best girl puppet stilts. I made her walk across the cot on them, and Naomi laughed and raised her arms. She wanted the girl to walk high up again, so I made that happen. I said we were rehearsing a show for Mama, almost believed it.

One night I had finished my schoolwork and cleaning, and Naomi and I had eaten rice, when Taube came to our room with pieces of eggplant in soy sauce. We ate like dogs thrown scraps and then Naomi, as if powered by the first taste in months of anything fresh, pulled herself on her stomach, forward, forward, forward. She moved toward me, like a tiny worker, so focused, pulling, struggling, falling, stopping, crying a little, starting up again, and finally arriving. She made it all the way over, and I was shouting, "Crawling! That was crawling!" I clapped until orange sparks filled our drab room. She looked up at me, smiled, and said, "Lee."

"Let's celebrate." I remembered Papa taking us to the Vienna when we needed joy. I slid one of my two dollars out of *The Last Lithuanian Foray* and took my slithering little sister out into the crowds of soldiers and drunks. We saw women teetering in shoes with heels like the stilts I'd made for my puppet, their lips so red they glowed. Some sat in rickshaws; others walked back and forth on the Garden Bridge. At Kadoorie, the girls called these women bridge walkers. Sally and Biata both liked to whisper about them.

I kissed Naomi's head. "They're beautiful but scary, right?" She stared and said it again, this time three times: "Lee. Lee. Lee."

What was it like to sit perched in a shiny rickshaw paid for by a man or men? I imagined tripping across the bridge in heels myself, feeling powerful. Or powerless. Or both. I whispered to my sister, "For boys they're not as scary, I don't think."

"Lee?"

"Look at all the lights. Isn't Shanghai strange?"

I used some of the precious American dollar to buy two

fat sticks of sugarcane and got stacks of CN bills and heavy coins for change. I felt rich. Naomi laughed as we chewed away the stringy sugarcane outsides and ate the sugar. I smacked my mouth noisily, which made her laugh more. We watched the night go by, the leftover money in my pocket popping and shimmering with possibility, the moon high above us like a giant Chinese coin. My sister was happy, sweetly heavy on my hip. As we walked, she made a sound and I held her close to my ear. "What did you say?" I asked. She made it again, a three-part sound that didn't have meaning. It sounded like "Lee, Ang, Jeh."

"Are you talking?" I asked.

"Leeangjeh," she said.

I squeezed her to me. "What is Lee Ang Jeh? What are you saying?"

— ▣ —

Only when the city began to thaw in late February did I take out the paper I'd been saving. Seven weeks had passed, and I had spent the change from both dollars, gone so fast it made my stomach hurt. We had needed the rice, vegetables, potatoes, and bread. There wasn't any money left for luxuries like paper, so I used what Wei had given me only when it became unbearable not to. I drew dozens of busy human beings, just as I was making the puppets under my cot, for company.

I smiled as I gave my drawings smiles. Then I made them

arms and legs. Here was Chusan market: tricky rickshaws flickering by, wheels sparking, plump refugees trading meat, tea, eggs and eggplants, lumber, fried bread, sugar, puppets, fresh black coal, new clothing, antique trinkets. In the left corner, so small she was almost invisible, I drew a woman taking off her wedding ring and next to her, a girl selling her hair. A baby stood on her own, head tipped back with laughter, a stick of sugarcane tied to her belt like a tasty bayonet. I made the baby walk, little motion lines behind her, and showed Naomi. She studied it like a scholar.

I twisted my way through the crowded streets especially fast the next day, and when I arrived at Kadoorie, I put the picture on my desk, hoping for notice. Rebecca came over right away. "Did you draw that?" I nodded. She held it up for everyone to see, and I felt such happiness that I told myself I'd brought it for that reason, to show Rebecca I was capable of something good, wasn't just someone poor and ragged. Maybe she would want to be my friend.

"At my old school, we did amazing art projects," Rebecca said, and I nodded, tears rising into my eyes. "Us, too." I looked away.

I held the paper for the rest of the day, knowing it was magic, had brought Rebecca close. When we were dismissed, I slowed as I went by the supply closet, stopped, breathed, and made myself knock. The sound was so soft I was ashamed. I was such a ghosty, scared person. At home I had been fun and funny, maybe even brave. Now I knocked hard, hurting my knuckles, holding my breath. He came to the door.

"Nihao," I said, *hello*. I smiled.

"Nihao," he said, turning his head sideways. A question. What was I doing there?

I had practiced the words: "Gongzuo? *Work?* Wo? *Me?* Ni? *You?*"

He looked me over. "Ni shi xuesheng," *you're a student*. I was thrilled he had understood enough of what I'd said to respond at all. And that I knew his three words: *you, are, student*.

I picked up an imaginary rag, wrung it out, and acted like I was wiping something, showing what a good worker I was. I pointed at myself. He didn't respond. Maybe he didn't want to share his work. I reached into my bag and handed him the drawing. He studied it for so long I wondered what was wrong. But he didn't give it back, just looked up at me.

"Gei ni," I said, *give you*.

He said, "Xiexie," *thank you*, then his name again, "Wei."

I said, "Li-li-ah," and took a pen from behind my ear. I drew on my left hand a flower "Lillia, hua, *flower*." Because my name means lily, and I wanted to tell someone—Wei—something true about me.

"Hua," he said. He took my drawing to the back of the supply closet and put it away.

I stayed and followed him around the school after that, watching him empty the waste bins, wash the floors, move chairs, restore order to the rooms we studied in. He paused for a moment near Mrs. Campton's shelves to pick up and open one of the few books we had.

"Can you read it?" I used English, curious how much he understood.

He answered slowly, half in each language. "Wo xihuan," he said, *I like.* Then he stopped, maybe getting ready for the English part: "to be student." He pointed at me.

He wanted to be a student, like me, like the rest of us in the school. Maybe working here made him feel more like one.

I pointed at him. "Wo xihuan," *I like*, I said, "to gongzuo." I like to work. We both laughed at the mess of languages, but while he was laughing, he shook his head. "No, no," he said. "Xuexi hao," *studying is better.*

I wanted to spend every afternoon with him, like this, working, talking, watching. He made me feel less alone, and somehow, less strange. "You can study English here," I said.

"No," he said. "Gongzuo." *Work.*

"I'll teach you," I said, my face turning a red so dark I felt the color come up as if it were cooking me. I talked faster. "I can work with you? And teach you English? You can teach me Chinese?"

He smiled. And my heart climbed straight to the rafters, swung across my mind like a happy acrobat.

— ◈ —

But the next few days he wasn't in the supply closet after school, and I didn't know anyone I could ask where he might be. Rebecca had begun to stand next to me during exercises in the courtyard.

She liked to talk about books, about being Jewish, about Shanghai, what she called "our lives." Even though I thought my life was too different from hers to explain. She mainly loved the Kadoorie exercises and the boy who led them, Abraham. He already had a beard, unlike Benjamin of the big ears, frozen smile, and table tennis shirt. Rebecca looked over at me after each move Abraham made. Her laugh sounded the way his muscles looked moving in his thin arms, a ripple. I tried to giggle back, but I sounded like someone drowning. One day after exercises, Rebecca came up to me. "Hey," she said. "Do you want to borrow some lipstick? You could be so pretty. Here." She held a tube of lipstick, and I smelled cherries, saw a spot of freckles on her cheek, a dimple below her smile. I held still. When she came so close she blurred, I closed my eyes, imagined the circus. Rebecca became Kassia, touching the gloss to my lips.

"Doesn't she look pretty?" Rebecca put her arm around Sally, who had appeared behind her like a shadow.

She meant me, that I looked pretty, but Sally didn't respond. Rebecca said, "Just like Vivian Leigh. Here! You keep this!"

I wanted that shiny tube as much as food. As much as—what? More than being proud, even in front of Sally, who loved to know I was poor. I tried not to grab the lipstick, just took it like it didn't really matter, and said thank you in an even voice I liked.

I kept that gift in my pocket and touched it all day, lucky stone. Each time I thought it might be gone, I found it there. I held it as we presented about our journeys to Shanghai for

Mrs. Campton, as the German girl called Nina said they had made her change her name to Sara in Germany. As Biata looked over because she'd told me so. Nina looked at us all angrily and I liked her anger, the way her face asked could we believe such a thing, eyes sharp, brows arched, thin, furious mouth twitching. She said her ship was called the *Kashima Maru*, that it crossed the Mediterranean, a bright blue sea. They had stopped in India, where everything sparkled.

"When I'm free," she told the class, "I will live in India."

But Sally asked, "Don't you want to go home to Germany? What about your family?"

Nina reeled back. "No one in my family will go near Germany! What kind of a *home* is it? Germany? I hope it dies!"

Mrs. Campton said nothing. She let us have whatever vocabulary we needed. I whispered to myself, "I hope it dies," imagining Warsaw, trying out the words. But maybe my mother was still there, and Babcia, Piotr, Kassia, Janusz.

My turn. I said, "We took a train from Lithuania and a ship from Italy. Called *Conte Rosso*." This seemed too little, so I added, "My father told stories about China on the way."

Rebecca asked: "Did Shanghai turn out like the stories?"

I said, "No." And she laughed, though I hadn't meant to be funny. Once she saw that Rebecca was laughing, Sally laughed, too, and the other girls followed. But not Biata.

Then Sally asked me, "What happened to your hair?"

"Nothing," I said.

"Did you cut it yourself?" There was a moment of quiet

and I shook my head no, but not before Biata interrupted in a sharp voice: "It's a style in Poland right now, so modern. All the girls have hair like that." She smiled, lots of small crowded teeth fighting for space in her mouth. Then she turned a fierce face toward Sally. "I came on a train across Siberia," Biata said in a loud voice. "We saw many lumpy camels and hairy men." Everyone laughed and stopped thinking about my monstrous hair, growing back uneven and clumpy.

When we were dismissed that afternoon, I headed to the supply closet.

"Do you want to come over?" Rebecca was behind me. "We'll have a Girl Guides meeting Saturday. I live across the bridge. We can send a rickshaw for you, or—" She stopped.

Wei was standing in the hallway. He looked dusty, as if he'd been in a cave. I thought he might notice the lipstick I'd put on. It felt pretty. Warm.

"Is that Chinese boy waiting for you?" Rebecca whispered. I tried to think of the right answer. But Sally had begun to pull Rebecca away, out the door, and I was grateful.

"Rebecca, come on!" Sally said. Rebecca turned to me. "Well, I hope you'll join the Girl Guides and come to my place sometime. I'd love to have you."

"Thank you," I said softly. I was looking at Wei, hoping he wouldn't notice that I hadn't answered the question about him, or offered to introduce him, or even acknowledged that I knew him. I wanted to stay again, help him work, hear his English. We weren't supposed to talk to Chinese people about anything other than rides or noodles or business. I didn't know how I knew or even why this was, but it was another sad fact, like war. I was tired of other people's facts. I waited until Rebecca and Sally had disappeared out the front doors and said, "Nihao, Wei."

But Wei was looking past me. I turned and saw a Chinese girl walking toward us. Bangs hung straight across her forehead and her eyes were too big for her face, frog-like. She was sharp cut as if from precious material, her cheekbones high. He hadn't been waiting for me, but for her. He hadn't noticed me ignore him in front of Rebecca and Sally. Envy corroded my bones. Why couldn't I be the one Wei—or Rebecca or even Papa or Naomi— was waiting for? I wished to be someone, anyone, else. The girl I wasn't spoke to Wei fast, in Chinese, turning to look at me only when she'd finished. I was still staring at her. Our eyes met, and then I lowered mine. She wore a round, almost clear green stone on a string around her neck and a matching bracelet.

"Li-li-ah, Hua," he said, Lillia, *Flower*, my names. He pointed at her. "Aili." Then he said, "Zai jian, Hua," *good-bye, Flower*, and they left. The supply closet was open. Students rushed by me, into the courtyard, shouting soccer, homework, marks, temple. I slipped into the supply closet and took paper, pens, soap, nails, rope, and an empty box.

— ▨ —

The next day, Rebecca found me reading in the back of the classroom—a book of maps. She flipped the pages to New York and pointed at a picture of a statue she said the French had given the Americans, celebrating freedom. I thought about freedom, how I had more of it here than I had at home but wasn't free at all. I didn't know how to say this to Rebecca, or how to keep her close, not ruin her idea of me with the truth of how scared and desperate I was.

"There's a song I'd like to play for you," she said. "From America. Called 'Somewhere Over the Rainbow.' Come to our next Girl Guides meeting and we'll play it, okay?"

I promised to come, wondering why she liked me, and how to avoid losing whatever made her talk to me. After school, I waited until she and Sally drove off in their rickshaw.

I found Wei touching up a pipe in the hallway with paint. A second brush rested in the pan of paint next to him, and I dipped forward and picked it up. When I swirled its bristles in the paint and then lifted it to the chipped pipe, I felt a shiver of something good.

Wei didn't tell me not to help, just asked, "Ni shi youtai ren, yes?"

Youtai ren meant *Jewish*, Biata had taught me. Sometimes people said, "Youtai ren!" as we walked by on the streets, not unkindly, it didn't seem, but as a statement of fact. We were all trying to understand each other and our places here.

But why would Wei ask me if I was Jewish, and what else would I have been? So I asked him, "Wei shenma?" *Why?*

We looked at each other, but he didn't answer, so I asked, "Ni shi youtai ren?" *Are you Jewish?*

Then he laughed, showing his chipped tooth, making me think of the broken puppets under my cot. "Bu," he said, *no*. "But"—he tapped his chest again—"youtai ren he Zhongguo ren yiyang." Yiyang meant *the same. Jewish people and Chinese were the same?*

I thought he meant we were poor, despised by others, cast out. But he said, "Youtai ren he Zhongguo ren ai xuexi, ai jia ting." He spoke slowly, hoping I might understand, but I didn't, so he added some English words: *love study, love home.* He made an arc with his arm, indicating Kadoorie. "Love school. Love here."

A thick drop of paint was sliding slowly down my brush's side. "I don't love it here," I said. "At school, I mean. At Kadoorie."

"I love here," Wei said. Then he stood and returned to the closet. I followed him, found a piece of paper I used to wipe some paint off, before wrapping the brush up and tucking it in my bag.

Maybe to distract Wei or maybe because I was too curious to resist, I said, "Zuotian? Pengyou?" *Yesterday? Friend?*

"Aili," he said, and added, in English, "Sister."

The beautiful girl was his sister. I felt unreasonable surprise, that he had a sister, that anyone other than Naomi or me had a sister. Also happiness that she wasn't his girlfriend.

"Oh," I said, in English. "Sister." I didn't know how to say the word in Chinese.

"Meimei," Wei said. "Wode meimei."*My sister.*

I felt wildly happy. "Wode meimei Naomi," I told him. Then, just in case, I said, "My sister is Naomi."

"Li-li-ah sister, Wei sister," he said. "Women dou you mei-mei," *we both have sisters.*

I had already learned more from Wei than I had in the weeks I'd spent at Kadoorie. Maybe I'd start to "love here," like he did.

— ◙ —

I taught Wei to ask questions in English, finding out as much as I could about him as I went: Where do you live? Where are you from?

He said, "Six-eighty Chusan Lu," his address. It was nearby, in Hongkou. "But I'm from Zhabei." I didn't know where this was.

"You live where?" he asked me.

I said, "Hongkou, like you. We are neighbors."

"You come from?" he asked.

But I shook my head. "Nowhere."

"Wo dong," he said, *I understand.* I didn't know how he, a Chinese person living here, could understand what I meant, but I didn't argue. Wei said, "Hongkou," our neighborhood's name, and drew a rainbow over hong, a mouth over kou. He taught me that we lived in the mouth of the rainbow.

Watching Wei hammer a shelf back together, I felt less lonely. When the sun set and he finished, he began to lock the supply closet up. I grabbed a few more nails, wrapped a rag around them, and pressed them into the bottom of my bag. I didn't think he noticed and didn't think he would mind anyway.

He came over to me, holding out his hand with a coin in it. He was offering me some of his money. Embarrassment drenched me, but I took it, whispered, "Xiexie."

The coin was a magical engine, powering me to the Chusan market, letting me buy three roasted potatoes, one for Papa, one for Naomi, and one for me. They were our first since I'd run out of money from my hair. Once the potatoes were in my bag, I played a game. I was God, and my potato was a country. If I ate it on the way home, it was Poland. If I waited, Germany. One bite now and Warsaw ceased to exist. This way I made myself wait, so I could eat with my family. Farmers were selling sacks of rice, and I wondered where the families in the marketplace came from. The countryside? Could they go home? Or were they here to escape, too? Was Wei?

I ran by Ward Prison and looked up at its roof, designed to slice flesh, its metal bars transforming windows into cages. I listened for screams but heard only automobiles honking through the narrow streets and crowds of people shouting, the usual music of the Shanghai streets. Maybe Biata had been lying about prisoners screaming.

I ran past a blur of pawnshops, workshops where men hammered wood into coffins, medicine shops with herbs and roots hanging from their awnings like vines. All the way to 54 Ward, where I bent and held my knees, evening my breathing before I went upstairs to collect my sister. Taube kissed us both, said, "Didn't we have a lovely day, baby?" to Naomi and "How was school?" to me.

I said, "Okay," guilty because I had only three potatoes. I carried Naomi down the stairs quickly and showed her the roasted potatoes. They melted on our tongues, their crispy skin, even no longer hot, was so delicious I tried to keep each bite in my mouth until it disappeared without any chewing. We were so sad to finish that I sang Naomi the song Babcia loved: "Wlazł kotek na płotek" about the kitten who climbs a fence and winks, and a grandma who pours the milk he drinks. If Rebecca ever taught me the song she'd mentioned at school, maybe I would teach her the kitty song. When we'd finished singing, I told Naomi the Chinese words from Wei: hua, *flower*; mian, *noodle*; Chusan Lu, the street he lived on, where our favorite market was.

Before bed, I gave Naomi the word I'd saved for last for her, one I had asked Wei to teach me because I knew Naomi needed it: laoshu, *mouse*. Each time I said it, I made the toy mouse dance. As if Papa had been right on the ship that we would love learning Chinese, as if Chinese were a song.

— ▣ —

In one of my parents' acts, Papa used to start asleep on a bed in the ring. He turned and kicked the blankets into a billowing tent, until a light came on high above him. Mama swung across the lit circle, attached to the rafters by silks so much stronger than they looked that the strength was itself invisible magic. She was Papa's dream, singing as she twisted her way down into the bed. And after she arrived, he snored and slept beautifully, making the audience laugh. Then she woke him and swept him away by tying him in with her. They held each other above the ring, twisting together until she rose and he lowered. On the floor, he held the silk and spun her into a blur, around and around the ring wide enough to fly out over the audience, so fast we gasped, and while she was spinning, she released handfuls of paper flakes, beautiful, sudden snow. I could always feel in that act, maybe everyone could, her sacrifice. The danger she risked, spinning just to send beauty out over us. When she flipped down the rope to the ground, Papa was there, head tipped back watching, arms up, waiting to catch her.

But in my Shanghai dream, Papa was gone, and I was the one above Mama, shouting words that arrived in the wrong languages, failing to wake her, spinning on ribbons made of water and then falling, finding the water full of human teeth, thousands of them, rushing together, clacking.

I stopped sleeping, because I was so afraid of the dream. March came and melted Shanghai into a wet mess, making my tired nightmares indistinguishable from the regular daytime flood of gossip: Germany invaded Greece, to "help the Italians kill more people," as Sally put it. Germany, Italy, and Hungary tore Yugoslavia to pieces like a roasted chicken, just as Germany and Russia had shredded and devoured Poland. Even Biata seemed too afraid to speak, and in my loneliness, I began to walk home from school with her on days when I couldn't find Wei.

Once, Biata and I sneaked to the International Settle-ment, walking by the clubs and gambling dens, orange heat pouring from doorways. Papa never made it home until too late to know or ask where I'd been, and Taube believed I stayed at school late. After nine months in Shanghai, I couldn't imagine I had ever been Słodkie Lillia, not allowed to take Piotr to Zgoda Park. What would Kassia think if she could see me now? What would Warsaw me think if she could see Shanghai me?

The afternoon Biata and I crossed the bridge, we slowed to watch a group of women in silk, mismatched furs, and sleek heels. They sat in black rickshaws, perched like nervous birds, men standing over and around them. One man, with lion shoulders and a face like poured cement, began shouting. Even Biata, so proud of her Chinese, couldn't understand the words he said, but we both knew he was shouting at us, and then he laughed like an animal when we ran. I followed Biata in the wrong direction, away from Hongkou, toward Avenue Foch, into streets of iron gates and trees. One gate slid open as we passed and I saw a yard. A swimming pool! I stopped to stare. A car pulled into the driveway of that palace, and a little girl in its backseat turned to look out the window as the gate shut. Her hair was so bright yellow she looked porcelain, a princess on a playroom shelf. She lifted her hand in a wave. At Biata and me. I couldn't tell if she was friendly or mocking. What would it be like to live in a house, ride in a car, swim in a pool again? I had never felt so poor.

Maybe Biata was sad, too, because we returned to Hongkou silent. On the bridge, two young Chinese women were bowing to soldiers who looked at each other, laughing over the women's heads. One reached out and touched the face of the woman on the left, dragged his hand down her cheek. Biata turned to me and whispered, "Do you think they have enough water to fill it and swim in summer?"

The cold blue feeling of swimming came back to me, a park next to the circus building in Warsaw, Papa lifting me up and throwing me into water, scanning comically, his hand shading his eyes, as if watching for me to resurface in an ocean. I bobbed back up and spun, leaving a ring of waves in my wake. Or stood on Papa's shoulders and dove. Sunlight was glittering and precious, Polish sunlight, different from Shanghai's no matter what the season. Soon it would be summer again; we would have been here for a year.

I could not say anything to Biata about the pool or the girl, because I would never risk crying in front of her.

On another afternoon, we went to the Embankment Building, to watch new refugees arrive, line up, look around, as afraid as we—or maybe just I—had been at first. How much older I felt already. I watched for Mama while Biata checked for mail from the boyfriend she told me was waiting for her at home in Mazur. There wasn't any. As we walked outside, Biata said, "Look back. The building's an S from above."

I couldn't see what she meant.

"Because the Sassoons built it," she added. "If you flew above it, you would see the S shape."

There were families wealthy enough to build buildings in the shapes of their names, powerful enough to save themselves and each other. There were rooms full of letters! How could so much mail arrive in Shanghai and not one piece of it bear our names?

CHAPTER SEVEN

随跟, Suigen, *Fitting In*

Biata's parents worked at a textile factory and went straight from work to a bar they were trying to open. Weeks passed, and in Biata's room, we had complete, horrifying freedom. It was small and cold and stuffed from the floor up with boxes, suitcases, bottles, and bolts of cloth, but her place was quieter than 54 Ward. We sat on her cot and talked about the other girls. Biata didn't like Rebecca and Sally because she thought they were full of themselves.

"I think Rebecca's okay," I said.

"Of course you do. You want to be just like her."

I ignored this. We said what we would do when we left Shanghai—rush back to Mazur to her boyfriend, in Biata's case. I said everything depended on what my mama said when she arrived, whether she wanted to return to Poland or go somewhere else. Neither Biata nor I believed what we said, but we kept saying it, hoping to trick ourselves or at least each other. Biata took her mother's face powder and dusted our foreheads and noses with it, then pinched our cheeks hard red. We tried to see our faces in the reflection of the window, but it was too bright outside. "I wish I had a mirror." She sighed.

"Who's going to see you? Me? Mrs. Campton? Soldiers? Bridge walkers?" Then we both laughed, nervously.

At school, Sally warned us that the Americans might leave soon, and then there would be no one to protect the Jews anymore. I asked, "Who are Americans protecting us from?"

She stared at me like I was slow. "The Germans, obviously."

"But the only Germans here are refugees, like us," I said.

Sally narrowed her eyes and twisted her lips. She didn't like to be called a refugee, to be reminded of any way in which she might resemble me. "How do you know, Lillia?" she hissed. "And even if you're right, how do you know the soldiers and spies aren't coming?"

Rebecca took my hand. "Come with me. I have something I want to show you."

"What is it?" I had not gone to her house, even though I'd promised. I was too embarrassed to be friends with anyone other than Biata and Wei. I knew I could never let Rebecca see our terrible room. I didn't belong and could only be with other outsiders.

Rebecca pulled a dress from her bag. "This doesn't fit me anymore," she said quietly. "I think it'll look good on you. If you want it. Don't worry if not. I won't mind." She handed it to me in the most casual way, as if it were nothing—as if I might turn down a soft, light pink dress, lovelier than anything I had or could have hoped to have. I tried to thank her, but so many tears came up inside me that I could only swallow again and again.

Rebecca took my hand awkwardly. "Don't worry about the dress, please. It's nothing, really. I still hope you'll join the Girl Guides, and I'm glad we're friends."

We were friends. Were we friends? I felt I'd won something. The voice I squeaked out might have belonged to Naomi's toy mouse: "So am I."

— ⊠ —

All spring, I whirled through our damp room at 54 Ward as if I might keep us safe by boiling and bleaching, until so much skin peeled from my hands that I had to wrap them at night. In a shirt, because we had no bandages. I mopped with hard chemicals from the supply closet at school, using a jar I'd found there, too. Every few weeks, I took our blankets and clothing into the courtyard and scraped them along a washboard with water in the cement sink.

And yet, one blue morning, when I hung my head off the end of my cot, starting Mama's exercises, breathing for the handstand, peeking at my puppets, and thinking about what I'd assemble next, I saw a slow gray blur out of my sideways eye. My body knew what it was first. There'd been warnings at the Heime that rats could carry the black plague. We ate nothing raw, not only because it might have been grown in human waste, but also because rats might have crawled over it. We tried not to walk outside with any part of our feet exposed, although many had no shoes. This rat had probably slept with me and Naomi and our toy mouse.

I didn't scream. A slow, strange revulsion moved through me, infusing my blood. The rat's bones were visible through his bent back, and he seemed barely able to move. I felt so sad for him. I stood and opened the door and released the rat into our hallway as if I were letting a prince outside for a stroll. Then I got back in bed and watched him make his injured way out. I did not try my exercises again, did not hold my handstand or count, just put on the scraps that remained of my shoes, and headed to the kitchen, where the flame had already caught and offered the only colors in the room: a spot of orange with blue at its center. Everything but that was colorless, even Naomi, in a still pool at Papa's feet.

A pot of half-boiled water gurgled on the stove. Papa worked on the water, looking like a shadow. I was wearing Rebecca's pink dress and tried to float above our lives, above the last hunk of bread Papa had collected at the Ward Road Community Center and was putting in my bag. Above my sister, now looking at me, above Papa, who didn't notice I had a new dress.

"Zaijian," I said to him and Naomi, *bye*. She reached up.

"Yao!" Naomi said. *Want*, pronounced perfectly, as if she'd been storing up the syllable all along, as if Polish and English hadn't been worth her time, but Chinese was useful to her.

"Say it again!" I shouted. "Papa, did you hear her?"

"What?" He turned from the water to look at us, as if he'd never seen us before.

"Naomi said, 'Yao,'" I told him. "She said it perfectly."

"Say it again," he told her.

But she said nothing. I said, "Yao!" And she smiled at me. "Yao."

Papa picked her up off the floor and swung her around.

"Are you talking, Lalka? Are you saying something to us?" There was joy in his voice.

Now my sister said, "Leeangjeh!"

Papa turned to me. "What's that word?" he asked, dancing a bit. I hadn't seen him move like an acrobat since he play tripped at Kadoorie, almost never saw him happy. My Chinese was much better than Papa's, but I didn't know what leeangjeh meant, if anything.

As I walked out of the house, Naomi called, "Hoo! Hoo!" Small owl.

I walked along Ward Road in Rebecca's pink dress, full of hope. Naomi had spoken a whole real word, Papa had danced! A voice said: "Miss, no mama, no papa, no whiskey soda"—the song of small children who begged in the streets. The refrain was "Give money, give money."

A tiny, dirty girl stood in front of me, an even smaller boy behind her. My hope flattened as she sang her grim chorus again, the boy mimicking: "No mama, no papa, no whiskey soda." He reminded me of Naomi, and she of the Song girls. Or of me. Except we were luckier. Having parents—even one parent—was lucky. I had no money, just bread. But I had Rebecca's dress, a book bag, Papa, Mama maybe on her way, a sister who could say *want*. I held my bread out to the girl, and she snatched and hid it in her shirt. Then she reached into her waistband and pulled something out, thrust it at me: a shard of pencil the size of a fingernail. Something in return for the bread. Before I could say xiexie, she grabbed the boy's hand and disappeared into an avalanche of people.

At school I went straight to find Wei. The closet was unlocked, so I slipped in but he wasn't there. I opened all the cabinets, found rags, buckets, mops, sponges, paints, pencils, composition books, toilet paper. And some glue, which I needed. I would bring the supplies back, I told myself, I was just borrowing. Mrs. Campton would forgive me if she knew, and I was sure Wei must know, didn't mind. I needed all the small things I took.

— ◧ —

Rebecca's voice floated over me. "What book is that?" She was standing behind my chair, her hands on my shoulders.

"Oh, um, an artist." I showed her the painting called *Time Flies*, the woman in it totally still, a clock behind and an airplane above her. "That's her," I told Rebecca. "The artist."

She said, "It's really weird. But beautiful, too."

"She painted it ten years ago," I said, and since she had said we were friends, I confided, "It makes me feel like time will move even if we stay still, that things will change." I didn't know what else to say, but wanted her to stay. "And—"

"And we can go home," Rebecca said, finishing my sentence. "And you can see your mom." Now she bent down and leaned her chin on my shoulder. "I like her necklace," she said.

"Me, too." I wanted her face next to mine forever, for Rebecca to be my sister. I liked how she had said *mom*, so casually, like all it would take was some time and there she'd be, my mom, waiting. Rebecca sounded like she believed the things she said, even though Biata and I didn't. Sally believed the things she said, too, but they were mean things, so where was the good in that?

"Isn't it funny that if that artist were Jewish, she'd be here—or at a camp?" Rebecca said.

"What do you mean?" I asked.

"Just that it's arbitrary that we're in danger just because of our Jewishness."

I didn't think Jewishness was arbitrary, or even something that could be separated from any other quality making a person who she was. I began to consider this, thought of what Taube had said at the Heime—that you could eat better food if you converted. But that was a performance, I thought, you couldn't become unJewish, could you? And if you could, would I have been weak enough to want that? Would Rebecca?

"Everyone find a partner," Mrs. Campton said. "You are going to work in pairs today to create timelines of Jewish arrivals in China."

"Come," Rebecca said, and I saw Biata and Sally shrug at each other and sit down. Biata had lately turned more red than pink and looked old. I felt guilty, as if I should be her partner because we were Polish and poor.

"Work on the project in Chinese and English," Mrs. Campton said, "and illustrate it to show the history of the relationship between the Jewish people and Shanghai."

Rebecca and I started our timeline a hundred years ago: the Jews who arrived then were kings. She drew jewels on them, using a red pencil to flush their cheeks with health. She turned to me. "Fatter! They were rich, not skinny." She added bellies to the stick figures, and I laughed.

We drew 1854: British, French, and Americans holding a scroll meant to represent their arrangement for how they'd run "Frenchtown." Rebecca made a little Frenchtown sign, and she drew an address: #3 The Bund. "What is that?" I asked.

"It's the Shanghai Club, where rich men drink and eat, even now. My mom says it's appalling that people would spend money on entertainment when others don't have food."

I looked Rebecca over for a moment, wondering, Did she pity me? "My papa says so, too," I said, feeling that since we were both poor and entertainers, we might be wrong in every way. I drew a fur store like the one on Nanjing Road, owned by a Jewish family. "Do you think rich people are selfish or bad?" I asked.

"Not as long as they share." The dress she'd given me swung like laundry in my mind.

We used little circles and dollar signs to represent the seven hundred Sephardic Jews whose fathers and grandfathers arrived from Iraq as traders in the mid-1800s and became tycoons. More circles were the Ashkenazi Jews who came from Russia in 1917 because of the revolution. They didn't get dollar signs, because so many were poor, too. I knew the foreign bridge walkers in Shanghai were mostly Russian girls. "Should we put in some dead people?" I asked. This came out badly.

"What?" Rebecca looked shocked. "Who do you mean?"

"I just meant maybe some soldiers?"

"Where, here? Japanese soldiers?"

"Or Chinese ones?" I knew from the radio that in a place called Jiangxi, two hundred Chinese soldiers had just died fighting. Papa had said probably even more Japanese lives had been lost. I told Rebecca this, and she stared the way I did when Biata told me hideous things.

"Uh, let's leave that out," she said.

"Okay." I looked down, burning, and drew myself at the end of our timeline, with bare feet sticking out. But I made my face smiling.

Rebecca was laughing. "Nice feet! What about me?" she asked.

"Do you want to draw yourself?" I held the red out to her, but she was writing dates.

"You can do it," she said, but the red pencil froze in my hand. I wished I hadn't made myself barefoot. I decided to draw Rebecca as a dancer, to make her feet bare, too, but her legs like a ballerina's.

"Ooh! I'm a dancer," she said. "Oo-la-la!" She stood, pointing her right foot and standing on the toes of her left until she toppled forward and grabbed the desk.

This brought Mrs. Campton over, but instead of scolding us, she looked at our work, nodded. She put her hand on my shoulder. "Most timelines end with the present," she said. "People by their natures draw what has already happened, but your next assignment will be to make a timeline of the future. What would you like to happen?"

I wished we had thought to draw Germany losing the war, ships sailing us home. That I had put Mama on our timeline, here. It felt too late, as if adding it because Mrs. Campton had asked would be cheating. Why had I thought of drawing more horror, rather than hope?

That afternoon as I knocked on Wei's supply closet, I heard Biata behind me. "Maybe next time we can work together?" she asked in a sad and soft voice.

"Oh, of course," I began, "I—" Our gym teacher, Mr. Myer, walked by and stopped.

"Who are you girls waiting for?" he asked.

I backed away from the door and lied quickly, "Just each other."

He nodded and kept moving down the hallway before Wei came to the door. I pushed inside, shaking my head no at Biata. She couldn't come in, because I was mean, angry that she'd seen me lie to Mr. Myer, and unwilling to share Wei—or Rebecca—with her.

Wei was collapsing and stacking cardboard boxes, so I folded a box flat, too, then another. Another. I felt we were dancing, the boxes our props, their cracking seams music. When we had finished, Wei handed me a wet mop and pointed out into the hallway. I paused, clutching the neck of the mop, knowing I would be seen with it—by all the students who stayed for activities. Wei saw me hesitate and reached to take the mop back. Had he been testing me?

"Bu," I said, *no*, and headed into the hallway, imagining the mop was my dance partner. I held it straight up and down and tried to move its filthy yarn hair in a graceful circle. Wet dirt spread on the floor, and I continued to push it around. Abraham, the boy Rebecca giggled about during exercises, walked by with Benjamin. I heard, "Hi, Lillia Kaczka from Warsaw," felt flames lick the edges of my neck and face. I did not look up or say hello, just inched back to the closet with the mop and made a show of dipping it in the sink so if Wei was watching, he would think I'd returned to rinse the mop, and not guess how ashamed I was to do the work he did all day, work he had no choice but to do. He looked like he had known all along.

I rushed back into the hallway and mopped as hard as I could, trying to make the floor sparkle, trying to make it up to Wei. When I had done the best I could, I found him wiping desks upstairs. I tried to start a conversation, hoping to change his mind about me, to distract him from my humiliated mopping. "Ni de meimei?" I asked. *Your sister?*

He looked up from the desk he was dusting. "Ta hai hao," he said. I got *she* and *good*, but not the word in the middle.

I said: "Mama? Baba?"

But now he shook his head. I'd made a mistake, but was it a language one? Or some other worse slip? I was getting so much wrong with Wei today. I tried again, put together *sister* and *work*. "Meimei gongzuo, ma?" *Sister works?*

"Ta tiaowu," he said. I didn't understand this. We looked at each other.

He raised his arms above his head then, flickered his fingers, then turned a circle, kicking his legs out and— What was he doing, twirling? When he was facing me again, he was grinning. He waved his hands some more. Was this a dance? Did tiaowu mean *dance*?

"Dancer?" I asked. I danced back at him. He nodded. She danced? For work? I hoped she was a better dancer than he was! "Nali?" I asked, an easy word: *where?* But his face stayed square and straight, and he did not answer. I didn't know why, whether he couldn't understand me, or didn't want to tell me.

When Wei didn't give me a coin, I went weak with disappointment, even though I could hardly expect him to pay me at all, let alone every day. I didn't even think I could expect him to be my friend or let me stay after school with him. I was so afraid he might ask me to go, might hold a hand up at me the way I'd held my hand up at Biata.

Walking home, I squeezed into the narrowest spaces, between people and colors and smells, my heart pounding, echoing in my empty stomach. I veered away, off my route, and headed instead to 680 Chusan Road, where Wei had said he lived. I wanted to see him, see his house, his life. But he never came. I don't know how much time passed before I saw Wei's sister, Aili, emerge from the doorway. So they did live here! I ducked into the crowd, as she wove effortlessly, as if designed or trained to float through mobs. I followed her.

Aili headed onto Seymour Road, and I stayed behind her, at first casually, as if I happened to be going that direction, and then hiding like a spy, limber and twisting. As always, I avoided looking at the uniformed men clustered in hard groups. Aili did not look at the ground. She walked purposefully to the Garden Bridge, bowed coldly before the men at the far end.

I crossed behind her, my eyes pinned to her thin back as she approached an enormous building on the Bund side. She looked small all of a sudden, as if the wind had swept her up and deposited her near the building's mouth. She checked in both directions—for what?—before disappearing into an entrance. I walked up a circular drive lined with trees, and squinted at the engraved letters of a small sign: MAGNIFIQUE. The stone building had a heavy set of red double doors where Aili had gone in, and windows hung with curtains that obscured the inside.

A black car pulled up and I hid in the trees, watching a man in a suit approach the giant doors. They opened long enough for me to glimpse the building's interior: everything was bathed in red light. At a mahogany podium stood a woman who looked both Chinese and like my mother, like the woman from the poster in the Heime. Her lips were wet with gloss, her hair swept off her neck into a pile of curls. The door closed. I watched more men in suits open it and enter, some women inside who looked young. Some were foreigners, like me.

It was completely dark by the time I walked back past the public gardens, between the Astor House Hotel and the Russian and German consulates. I crossed back to Hongkou in a sizzling rush of bridge walkers, passing men whose eyes prickled my skin. Were the bridge walkers carried toward the French Quarter, poor empresses landing in warmly lit rooms? And if so, what happened to them there? Who were the women at the place Aili had gone?

Back in Hongkou, I ran. Hongkou, mouth of the rainbow, neighborhood of roaming pickpockets, desperate families, devastated refugees, drunks, soldiers, Wei, Biata, Aili, and me. I ran to the banging noise of carts, trams, rickshaws, and other people's feet. Along Suzhou Creek, I smelled water and pavement, frying fish and engine oil. I never once looked back at the lights of the Bund or at the place called

Magnifique. Not because I was above my own longing or curiosity. I knew I would be back and didn't bother to pretend otherwise, not even to myself.

— ◉ —

A knock at the front door of 54 Ward startled me out of gluing pieces of the person I was making, a puppet of Biata. I was going to tell the story of our year so far, as soon as Mama arrived, so I had decided I needed a Wei, a Biata, a Rebecca, and an Aili. Naomi and I could play ourselves, I thought, whoever we might be by the time she came.

Usually nobody knocked, since only those who lived here came to the house at all. Even the vegetable man just shouted, "Tou-bah!" up toward the second-floor windows.

I opened our door, curious, to a man I didn't recognize, someone dirty, with hair like dried grass and an eye so bruised it appeared to be leaking paint. He was sweating and his shirt was torn.

"Papa!" The fear in my voice made my father run. He stood in front of me, saying hello to the stranger who came forward and reached out. He and Papa shook like dignified human beings, even though the man looked like a ghost or monster, enormous bones in his forehead. I remembered our rabbi telling us always to give what we had, to let anyone in need into our homes. I wanted to hide instead.

"Nazywam się Leopold. Proszę pomóż mi," the man said.

My name is Leopold. Please help me. He was Polish, and Papa smiled a wide, real smile. "Lillia, go get Leopold a towel."

I fetched the rag we all washed with, dunked it in the bucket's bit of used water, and handed it to Leopold, who had come inside. I was embarrassed for us, but he wiped his face and hands energetically, as if the horrible rag were a clean, fluffy towel, said, "Thank you so much."

A smile lit his face, shocking me. He had the square teeth of a healthy horse and the crinkly eyes of someone who, like Papa, had smiled all the time until the war. Once Leo had washed, Papa fed him rice and tea, and when Gabriel got home we went to sit in his room. Gabriel was especially animated, listening to Leo instead of the radio, asking questions.

Leo said he had made it to Vilna but lost contact with his family, and Papa asked, "When did you leave Vilna?" because he was wondering if she might be there, in Vilna. His voice was desperate.

"Three months ago, in January," Leo said. "By train. I took a train from Moscow to Dalian, and then a ship—the *Dairen Kisen Kaisha*—from Dalian here. An entire Yeshiva from Vilna has now come through Kobe. But there are many who still haven't made it out of Vilna." When he said this, he began crying, and I thought maybe I had imagined his smile. In Shanghai, all the strongest, proudest men cried. Gabriel put an arm around Leo, and I stared. I had never seen Gabriel comfort anyone.

"No one believes what is coming," Leo said. "But it's clear.

Those who know are fleeing, and it's getting more and more difficult to leave."

I asked, "What's coming?" But no one answered me.

"More people will get out," Leo said instead. "The Japanese counsul, Chiune Sugihara, is stamping papers as fast as his hands can stamp. He will save more lives. Anyone who is—"

I interrupted, insulted that they were ignoring me. "Who?"

"The Japanese consul in Vilna. He is giving transit visas so Jews can get out by traveling through Japan. He saved all the Yeshiva boys. And me. Others, too. My papers were forged, like so many. He is getting people out."

"Do you know the Kozak family? Nacek and Ana? They helped us get tickets here, and they were supposed to send money and to write with news of—" I couldn't say Mama or Babcia. Kassia's parents' names had turned my lips numb.

Leopold shook his head sadly. "Are they your family? I'm afraid I don't know them."

I rubbed my eyes and in the circles of light that formed, animated figures emerged as if from a book, Papa and Naomi and me, then Leo, running along a flat map, from Warsaw to Vilna, Vilna to Italy or Moscow, there to Dalian or Kobe, then on to Shanghai. Leo had traveled through Japan, not able to stay there, even though it was a Japanese hero who had let him leave at all. I saw Mr. Sugihara, stamping a fast dance with his hands, one man empowered to save the lives of those who had no power, making the choice to do so over and over. Stamp, stamp stamp. I saw ink, *Alenka Varsh*, the consul's hands, please God, just one more stamp, eleven letters, please.

Leo was talking. "... dangerously unrealistic. They will pay for such stubborn complacency! The middle class? They have money, they have had power for years. They feel they have God's will on their side, so they can sehv ve'al taase."

Gabriel turned to me and translated, even though I knew sehv ve'al taase meant *to stay still, do nothing*. He began dividing his bedding, two thin blankets and one pillow, into two beds: one the cot he had been sleeping on for the last year and the other, a bed on the floor. "You need a cot, my friend," he told Leo. "Take mine."

Upstairs, I tucked Naomi in. "Yao, ah, ah," she said to me. "Lee. Ang. Jeh."

"Good night, Naomi." I collected the pillow I had sewn with Taube, returned to Gabriel's room, and handed it to Leopold, who kissed the top of my head.

"I can't thank you enough for everything," Leo said. "It's a mitzvah."

But in bed with my thrashing sister, I was gripped by selfishness, found a stone sewn into my heart: the more lovable I found Leopold, the more I hated him. If a Polish Jew knocked on our door and asked to live with us, if someone so desperate—and an entire Yeshiva of four hundred men!—had made it safely from Vilna to Japan and arrived here, clutching fake passports, couldn't one of them be her? This thought heated into a bubbling, feverish wish that Leopold were dead.

I'd have killed him myself if it would have brought my mother through our door instead.

⬛

Not long after Leo arrived, in late April, the butcher, Irvin Katz, grew enough hair that he asked Mr. Michener to cut it. One warm day, just like that, I smelled meat. My mind turned red and ravenous; I imagined stalking an animal, digging my teeth into its raw flesh. My jaw snapped, and I swallowed and went upstairs to get Naomi. Taube had set a cot as if it were a table. Two candles flickered on the windowsill, and Naomi was staring at their light. "Hi," I said.

"We got meat!" Taube cried. "Brisket, from Irvin Katz. As soon as Joshua and Bercik get home, we'll eat as if it's a proper dinner." She was the happiest I'd ever seen her, as if she were at home, in some sane city, hosting a party. As if it wasn't April in Shanghai, but spring of some better year in a better elsewhere. I stayed in her room while Taube flittered around like the hostess of a grand party. I stood Naomi on my feet and walked as if she were walking, stalk, stalk, moving her legs, pretending, praying.

When Gabriel, Leo, and a friend of Leo's named Talia appeared, they were like real guests, carrying a loaf of shelter bread that could have come from a bakery. If we'd been elsewhere. My parents' friends used to arrive with vodka and flowers, Babcia with fresh-baked racuchy full of apples, sprinkled with powdered sugar. I closed my eyes. When I opened them, Leo's friend Talia was standing close to Naomi and me. "Leo says lovely things about you."

She had soft curls, dark eyes like wells of paint. I picked my sister up and held her close, said to Talia, "Thank you. You, too." She laughed a wind chime sound, and I blushed because Leo had not mentioned her. Talia looked even cleaner than Rebecca and Sally. She must have had extra soap, better rice, someone else to pick the glass out of whatever she ate.

Taube cried when she served us, and Mr. Michener, no longer fat or cheerful, put his withered arm around her. I didn't know if she was happy or sad until she looked at me and said, "I miss my mother, too." I was too afraid to ask where her mother was.

Taube gave us each a coin-sized piece of brisket. Mine was the largest, almost the size of my thumb. I pulled it into tiny strings, ribbons that might last. When I put the first shred into my mouth, hunger and joy and the warmth of the fire that had roasted the meat came into my body. I felt Mama would come to Shanghai, the war would end, my hair would grow back silky like Talia's. Someone would kiss me, maybe Wei. Or if not Wei, then Benjamin. Food and hope were the same, and either could fill me for a moment or two.

"Where are you from?" I asked Talia, feeling suddenly friendly.

"Germany," she said, and Naomi started to cry. She seemed to be protesting the mention, which made the adults laugh, but actually she had eaten her meat and wanted more. Knowing she was as hungry as I was made something turn sharp inside me. The happiness and friendliness evaporated, and I collected my strings of meat into a second bite I gulped without tasting. Papa pulled Naomi onto his lap, fed her his rice and some hard bread from the Heime.

"Not a single member!" Gabriel was saying, "Every single one is here. Four hundred. Incredible!" Talia winked at me, as if we shared a joke, her long eyelashes brushing over her cheek. I didn't know what the joke was or even could be, just wanted to be Talia. Even more than Rebecca or Sally or any of the girls. I had never felt such poisonous envy ringing in me before, but here in Shanghai it was a taste, sound, and feeling all at once. Talia seemed above the suffering, safe not only from sorrow but also from ever feeling envy.

Naomi had stopped crying and was stuffing Papa's rice into her mouth. Taube spoke in a low voice: "They refused to stay in a Heime. They've all survived not because God chose them, but because it's safer at the synagogue, easy not to lose anyone when no one makes a single sacrifice. They study all day long, just as they always did. They help no one but themselves."

"Well," Gabriel said, "everyone is doing the best they can."

"No," Taube argued, "not everyone is. And some are only helping so that the poor Jews won't embarrass or discredit the rich ones."

Gabriel clicked disapprovingly, but Taube was undeterred. "It's the truth. The reason those selfish boys are all here is because the Japanese moved them. They're consolidating us."

"Maybe we should save this talk for later," Talia said gently. Was she protecting me?

"Why *consolidate*?" I asked, suddenly furious.

"It means gather," Papa said in a tired voice. They all looked at one another, an adult warning passing between them.

"I know what it means," I said. "Why are they gathering us?"

"Tell me about your school, Lillia," Talia said. "Leo says you have a Polish friend, and some American friends, even a Chinese friend?"

I didn't want to be her anymore, or anyone. "Why do the Japanese want to gather us?"

Papa spoke so gently I felt he was imitating Talia the way he used to imitate Mama, when she had been in charge of Naomi and me. "The Japanese want to gather us so it's easier to control our whereabouts and activities."

I asked, "So they can kill us, you mean?"

Papa almost shouted, "Of course not." Talia reached over and took Leo's hand.

"How do you know?" I asked. But he didn't. No one knew.

"The Japanese are on our side, Lillia," Leo said. "They consider us friends, future allies." He turned to Talia, lovely Talia still holding his hand with her clean, soft one. "Let's play some music. Do you have the violin?"

I turned to Talia then, too, my face fiery, words unstoppable. "My Polish friend, the one you asked about? She likes to walk close enough to Ward Prison to hear them torturing people. She says you can hear the prisoners screaming."

The adults stared. I stood and felt myself moving away from the table. Someone would kill us before my hair grew, before I kissed anyone, before Naomi said anything but *yao*. Want. If our futures vanished, did our pasts, too? Maybe they were already gone, and I had never had a mother. Or a dog named Piotr, or Babcia, or Kassia, a circus, a home. Thick, cold fear poured all over. I couldn't tell if it came from in or outside of me. My teeth began to chatter.

"Lillia, honey?" Taube asked. "Are you okay?"

Naomi said, "Ah! Ah!" I started toward the door, toward my cot, wanting to be alone, to shut this feeling out, to count my breaths, handstand, escape.

Naomi shouted: "Li-ah, ah, ah. Li-li-ah!" I turned back to the table.

"Say it again!" Papa said. "She said *Lillia*! Say it again!" He was clapping.

Naomi looked up and smiled. "Lillia!" She reached her arms out to me.

CHAPTER EIGHT

女孩导游, Nuhai Daoyou, *Girl Guides*

School ended in a blazing wave of heat. The possibility of not seeing Rebecca all summer was terrible enough that I agreed to go to a Girl Guides meeting at her house on June 8.

"I'm joining the Girl Guides, and I'm going to learn survival skills," I said in the kitchen, knowing it would please Taube. "Today I'll go to Rebecca Rosen's house—she's American."

"It's lovely that you're making girl friends," Taube said. "Let me get you something from upstairs. You come with me," She gestured to Naomi, who stood for a moment on her wobbly legs before toppling. The sight of her upright for an instant made me wonder whether enough food and less fear and sorrow would have allowed her to walk and dance already. When I was her age, I had tap shoes, ballet slippers, and play shoes for jumping outside. My childhood was over, but I'd had one, had Mama, the circus. Naomi would have nothing so beautiful.

Papa was reading from the *Shanghai Jewish Chronicle*: three days before, on June 5, four thousand Chinese citizens had tried to hide in a tunnel because their city was being bombed. They had all suffocated, four thousand people. I tried to imagine each of them, a whole person with a life, family, favorite book, way of sleeping, a small and troubled sister, maybe. What might it feel like to hide in a tunnel, as afraid as they were, and die anyway?

Now Papa put the paper down and grumbled. "Parties at this moment are inappropriate. No one who is indifferent to the suffering of those around them is a suitable friend for you."

"What? Are you talking about Rebecca? How do you know she's indifferent?"

He slapped the paper down. "I don't want you at parties in the Settlement. Anyone who remains wealthy when people are starving is, well, I don't have to know them to know."

"It's not a *party*. It's the meeting of a Girl Guides group where I'll learn skills to survive."

Papa looked back at the paper, and an angry engine revved inside me. "And anyway if we could live in the International Settlement, we would. We just can't," I pointed out.

"No," Papa said. "We would not."

"You said we'd move across the bridge if the money came. Rebecca is the only one who's kind to me at the stupid school *you* make me go to! Instead of working, or helping. That's *your* choice." Did he think he could just revert back to being protective whenever it suited him, even though I'd been alone on the streets of Shanghai all winter and spring? It had been a year since Mama disappeared. Here was another June, another summer. Naomi would be three in August. I was sixteen. No one had noticed my birthday, falling in March like more rain or debris.

When he didn't respond, I was even angrier. "Rebecca can't help being more fortunate than others. Just like we can't help our awful situation. And even though you have chosen everything else, including leaving without Mama, you can't stop me from going to this meeting."

He shivered. "I didn't intend to prevent you, Lillia. I will take you there." This he said with his old man voice, the one we heard most nights when he had come back from working for fifteen or sixteen hours and was listening to chilling news on Gabriel's radio.

I wanted to scream, with horror and sorrow for what I'd said, for making Papa suffer, but I stood like a pillar as the unscreamed feeling moved into my bones and settled there.

Taube returned with a long band of blue cloth, bits of lace sewn all over: a night sky full of stars. "It's a sash. I was working on it for later, but maybe you want to wear it today for the meeting? Come, I'll put it on you."

She set my sister down and pulled me close, tied the sash around my waist. Taube smelled like soap—how? I moved Mama's ring out of my collar, imagining the ring and the sash taking stock of each other, meeting like Biata and me, reluctant but familiar. Naomi dragged herself over on her stomach and pulled herself up my legs.

"Brawo!" I said, "Wstań, *stand up*."

She held my knees, trying to stand for so long I couldn't bear it and lifted her, put her feet on top of my feet, held her hands and walked her across the room.

"Look at you walking, Lalka!" Taube sang out.

I stopped and stared. "How did you learn that nickname?"

"Oh! Your father said you all used to— That it means doll. It's such a good fit for her."

I didn't speak.

"Lillia? Are you ready?" Papa was waiting for me. I smiled at Taube, to show I understood, that I forgave her for whatever that was, trying to be Naomi's mother, or something more? Something less? I needed to ask Mama. I couldn't understand anything.

"Thank you for the sash, Taube," I said, and she smiled at me sadly. I knew she would never use Naomi's nickname again.

Outside, the sun was violently bright. Papa and I took a tram solid with people. By the time we arrived in the International Settlement and began walking, I was soaked, my blue dress ruined like disintegrating paper against my skin. The sash felt suffocating.

Rebecca lived on Bubbling Well Road, two blocks from Elly Kadoorie's home. Sally had made sure I knew that Elly Kadoorie, rich enough to have founded our school, lived in a house made of marble, one with running water, tennis courts, horses, and a pool. He was from Iraq, rich like some of the Russian Jewish families—those who owned the fur stores where Taube bought scraps for her hats. Biata said the Russians came to China because they weren't allowed to be rich in Russia anymore. Here, they built a railroad in Manchuria, our synagogue, marble homes for their families, Heimes for ours. If we had known to come earlier, maybe we would have been the ones helping, rather than begging for help. Maybe we wouldn't have been so poor. Babcia and Mama might have arrived with us. I could have been like Rebecca.

"Do you think Elly Kadoorie loves it here?" I asked Papa.

He looked at me sideways. "Maybe. He lives a very regal life. But it's hard to know what someone like that thinks or feels." I thought *someone like that* was part of the new, unkind Papa, and that it was harder than ever to know what anyone else thought or felt.

"Do you think he misses Iraq?" I asked.

Papa was shading his eyes, and I remembered he'd had sunglasses. They were somewhere in the world. They still existed, like Mama. I could feel her, alive, just outside the range of what I saw or heard.

"Are you missing home?" he asked me.

I blinked at him, my eyes hurting, too. "I don't have a home."

He sighed, maybe tired of me. Or maybe just tired. "We had to come here, Lillia."

"*I* didn't."

"Yes, Wróżka, you did. We had to survive."

"If it weren't for me, you would have stayed and saved Mama—"

"Lillia, stop!" He almost shouted at me, and we were close to Rebecca's.

I lowered my voice, unwilling to stop but not wanting to be overheard. "You could have found her if you hadn't had to bring us here. You would have stayed if you didn't have us. So I'm sorry."

He said, "Don't apologize for being my child," and then there was nothing for us to say. I couldn't repent for costing him Alenka, and he couldn't for costing me my mother.

In front of Rebecca's house was an iron gate decorated with ribbons. I looked down at my old, damp dress, covered slightly by Taube's wishful sash. Not a single thread on my body was as elegant as the ribbons the Rosens had used—so casually, it seemed—to mark a Girl Guides meeting. I thought of the sad rat scuttling across our room and smoothed down my dress.

Walking up the driveway, we saw the rickshaw Rebecca rode to school, shiny black with an umbrella to protect her from sun and rain. The front door opened, and Rebecca and Sally appeared, other girls behind them, all waving like a many-armed creature. "Come in!" Rebecca said. She curtsied toward Papa. "Thank you for bringing Lillia, Mr. Kaczka! Shall we return her to you or will you come back for her?" My heart triple flipped—Rebecca was happy to see me.

But Papa smiled tightly. He found Rebecca frivolous, giggling girls in a lavish doorway evidence of his original suspicion. "I will come at two to pick Lillia up," he said. "Thank you for having her." I had asked to be allowed to stay until 3 p.m., when the meeting ended, but I didn't want to argue with him in front of Rebecca.

"Okay, bye," I said, trying to sound like Rebecca and Sally. They spoke English like it belonged to them. A Chinese maid appeared and handed me a damp towel. Had she done so for all the girls? The towel smelled and felt so good I wanted to steal it, but she collected it once I had wiped my face and hands. If Rebecca came to 54 Ward, would I hand her the rag I'd given Leo? Shame lapped at my edges, threatening to drag me under.

"Your dad looks like a film star," Rebecca said, and there was a murmur from the girls I didn't know, some laughter.

I said, "He was in the circus at home."

I felt Sally looking at me, so I added, "He and my mother were famous."

"Have you ever seen the circus here?" Sally asked. "The Chinese acrobats can fly."

I tried to hide my surprise—that there were acrobats here, that anyone could be lucky enough to be or watch them. But I wouldn't give Sally the pleasure of seeing me wish or suffer.

"Come, come, Lillia," Rebecca said. "This is Jeanne, and this is Katarine. And my mother has put out tea and snacks." I lifted my fingers in a wave to the other girls and followed them down a long hallway covered with a rug woven of the brightest colors I'd seen in Shanghai, an entire rainbow. It was a pity to put our feet on it, but none of the other girls noticed. The hallway opened into an enormous room, sunlight pouring in, furniture, glass, and a piano gleaming. A bookcase sat stuffed with books, chandeliers hung gracefully from the yellow ceiling. A velvet couch was strewn with pillows. "Have you been to the bookstore on Henan Road?" Rebecca asked, seeing me looking, knowing we both loved to read. "Or the—"

But she thought better of finishing. I hadn't been to a bookstore. Or any store.

She said, "You can borrow anything from here, if you want. Help yourself. My mother won't mind—she calls it a lending library, because so few people have their books with them here. Are your books still at home in Warsaw?"

I wished I could say no thank you, say my mother had her library here, too, or that I would just go to the bookstore, but my body propelled me toward the shelf: *The Great Gatsby*, *The Sound and the Fury*, *The Good Earth*. American books. I was dizzy with longing to live in Rebecca's life, or in any of the stories her books held.

"My mother's friend sends them," Rebecca said. "If we ever

leave, I'll donate them to Kadoorie so there'll be a real library there."

I planned to mention this generous idea to Papa later. How good it would feel to have something to give Kadoorie, rather than to be always taking things.

"Have you heard the news?" Sally appeared next to us, a note of impatience in her voice.

I shook my head. It would be something meaningless. What could a girl like Sally Miller know? The crackling voice of Gabriel's radio knew real news. His hands shook on the dial as he shut it off. Bad news was our bedtime story in Hongkou. Not here, I thought.

"America *is* going to move us out of Shanghai. I was right— the war is coming here!"

"The war is already here," I said.

"Not *that* war, *the* war—*our* war, in Europe."

"My parents will stay," Rebecca said. "My dad is working at the hospital. He said we won't go, even if— Well, not everyone will leave. They just sent my mother's friend to help get money from the New York JDC to help feed people. She's not leaving. It'll be okay, Lillia."

"My papa works for the JDC, too," I said proudly.

"I thought he was famous in the circus," Sally said.

I turned to meet her gaze. "Yes. Well, obviously Shanghai has nothing to do with our actual life. This"—I swung my hand meanly—"is a nightmare I'm going to wake up from soon."

Sally looked away. It was her nightmare, too. She was, as I

had pointed out at school, also a refugee, no matter how much better off than I was. Rebecca led us to her dining room, where her mother sat, all carved out with a beak nose and thin lips shaped by a sharp dark color. I imagined her kissing Rebecca good night: peck peck, leaving kiss marks on Rebecca's smooth forehead. I wished I had not come.

Rebecca used a pair of silver tongs to collect cubes of sugar and drop them in her tea, one by one until she'd added five. I was counting, my stomach howling. I pushed my elbow into it. Rebecca stirred the tea with a little spoon, clinking it against the sides of the teacup.

Mrs. Rosen said, "Thank you girls for coming over today. I am so grateful that Rebecca has friends in this godforsaken city." If Shanghai was godforsaken, then why had Rebecca said they'd stay? Maybe her parents fought. *Ding, ding, ding*, went the teaspoon. Katarine passed the sugar bowl. I carefully lifted one glistening cube with the tongs and dropped it into my tea, making sure not to splash. When I stirred, the sugar melted and my sorrow rose like steam. I took another cube. The maid brought a tray of sandwiches and cakes, and my mouth flooded. I tried not to stare at the food.

Rebecca's mother said, "Our friend owns a deli, so we're able to get sandwiches sometimes. Help yourselves, girls." Was she looking especially at me? Was I the only hungry one?

I took a single sandwich, but my mind buzzed, swarming with plans to fill my pockets, to pour tea into my clothes and squeeze it back out for Naomi at 54 Ward.

"Rebecca tells me you like books and poems, Lillia," Mrs. Rosen was saying. "Do you remember any poetry? Maybe you could recite a poem?"

I made my mouth work around the memory of the sandwich, which I had already swallowed. It said, in English, "Okay."

I spoke the first few lines of a poem my mama liked, by a poet named Antoni Lange, who was also a philosopher. She had read it to me in Polish and also given me the English words. I was glad for them now. "Where are you sorceress, goddess, queen? Life-making, crazy, homicidal water spirit . . ." Here, I stopped, remembering the rest of it, the graves where it ends. Why had I picked this? Why had Mama liked it? I took a sip of tea to push back the black feeling coming up my throat.

"Well, that was . . . that was lovely, thank you, Lillia," Rebecca's mother said. Rebecca's little brother and sister were standing in the doorway, a Chinese nanny holding their hands. Biata's Chinese phrase book said nannies were called *amahs*, and I'd wondered what if Naomi had an amah? The phrase book also said the Chinese "mode of thought" was different from ours, but I didn't think the amah's mode of thought was different from mine, just that her language was. I didn't think Wei's mode of thought was different from mine, either. Sally's was.

"We go walk," the amah said.

"Bye, Jacob. Bye, Ruthie," Mrs. Rosen said, blowing kisses. "Don't forget your sun hats." Ruthie looked like a mini-Rebecca, slight with a wide smile. Jacob had a short shock of hair.

As they left, I said, "Excuse me," to Rebecca's mother,

whose eyes became cubes of sugar dissolving in dark tea. "I have a different poem, a better one."

I wanted to show there was beauty where I came from, not just despair. I wasn't always poor. So I spoke the poem my mother had taught me about a bridge, another she'd given me English words for. Now the poem and its bridge seemed to lead to Shanghai:

> "I didn't believe,
> Standing on the bank of a river
> Which was wide and swift,
> That I would cross that bridge
> Plaited from thin, fragile reeds
> Fastened with bast.
> I walked delicately as a butterfly
> And heavily as an elephant,
> I walked surely as a dancer
> And wavered like a blind man.
> I didn't believe that I would cross that bridge,
> And now that I am standing on the other side,
> I don't believe I crossed it."

Rebecca's mother was wiping her eyes. She said, "Rebecca told me about your mother, Lillia. I'm so sorry."

I went cold. What had Rebecca told her mother about mine? What did they know? More or less than I did? Rebecca interrupted. "Mrs. Campton says when we read we should feel it not only in our minds but also in our bodies, that books—and poems—should matter for our actual lives."

Sally said, "I *love* Mrs. Campton," and I felt as if she'd taken something from me.

Mrs. Rosen, maybe realizing her mistake, or maybe just trying to say something to each of us, had turned to the French and British girls. "Tell us about school, dears."

"We go to the Western District School," Jeanne said. Her English was lovely, the edges of her words sanded soft. "It's okay for me. But they like the British students best." She poked her friend, Katarine, who nodded and giggled, because she was British, I guessed.

"Their school is expensive," Sally said admiringly. I quietly reclaimed the sugar bowl and filled the tongs with a fistful of cubes for my saucer. I ate two more sandwiches, the bread sticking deliciously to the roof of my mouth, dissolving slowly, thin strips of corned beef so salty that the taste lingered on my lips and I delayed swallowing as long as I could to keep the flavor. When I had finished my third one, I couldn't look away from the plate that held the rest. Rebecca had eaten only one sandwich and was chattering happily. Sally had had two, Jeanne, two as well, and Katarine, three. So three was the most anyone could have, I thought, and I had already had three. I felt Sally watching me.

"Rebecca," Mrs. Rosen said, as a maid appeared to take away our teacups, spoons, and, I feared, the remaining food, "why don't you play something, and then you girls can go up-stairs to your room and relax?" The maid was a Chinese girl even younger than the amah. I thought maybe she was our age, thought how strange it was that the Rosens had servants. My parents had done whatever work our apartment required, even at home, before we were poor. Now I was more likely to be a maid than to have one. Was that why I felt bad for the Chinese girl?

While everyone else stood, I took the sugar cubes from the saucer and put them in the pocket of my dress. I took a fourth sandwich and shoved it in my mouth. Only the Chinese maid saw me. Our eyes flickered over each other and then away. Would she tell Mrs. Rosen? And if I cared more whether Mrs. Rosen knew than the Chinese maid did, why was that?

In the drawing room, Rebecca sat at the piano. I was sur-prised when her thin fingers made music rise and hover above us. My blood moved faster through my body and my own hands throbbed with the notes. The scales felt like running through the streets, the light chords Warsaw before, the heavy music water smacking the belly of the *Conte Rosso*, the woman going over its rails, my mama's shadow.

When Rebecca finished, I was light-headed. "What piece was that?"

"Oh, Mozart piano concerto twenty-one in C." She spoke as if it were nothing to have that music in her. She stood and smoothed her skirt. "Mom! Can we please go up for our meeting now?"

"You may," her mother said, turning a radio dial without having to hide it. Were they allowed to have radios here, across the bridge? Or just fearless because they could fight back? English filled the living room: the resistance in Greece was ending. Invaded in April, Greece was now completely occupied, two and a half months later. Good countries were being devoured as we climbed the stairs to Rebecca's room.

She had a real bed with a canopy and a stack of blankets at the foot. I stared, longing to climb under the covers and sleep, to have my mother downstairs, to be safe.

"Let's start," Rebecca said joyfully. "We'll do Captain Says after the pledge, then singsong, okay? Lillia, sit with me!"

She recited a "threefold promise pledge," to God, our countries, and the Guide Law. I didn't know what the Guide Law was, but I liked our voices saying together: "I pledge loyalty to my country." I thought about whether I meant China or Poland, what it meant to have a country, one that would or wouldn't have me.

"Now, for Captain Says. Lillia, stand with me since you don't know the orders yet." Rebecca turned to the other girls. "Rise!" They stood tall. "Raise the flag!" They pretended to raise a flag. When she said "At ease," we relaxed. "Organize for reef knots!" Rebecca smiled my way. "Now we tie square knots above our heads one at a time. We untie each other's knots and then retie them."

Confused, I asked why.

"Um, it's a survival skill," Sally said. But tying and untying imaginary square knots above my head, I felt suddenly that our lives were a show, and I wanted to control it, make it beautiful instead of terrifying. I wanted a circus, no matter how small. There would be no klezmer, no tightrope-walking sisters Leah and Pese, no one swaying with prayer, no Mama ready to fly, her face full of love and focus. But I wanted whatever circus I could make here, with my puppets and sister and friends. Maybe this was what my parents had felt the night they decided to perform in Poland. Maybe they'd wanted to control something again, so much that it felt worth everything. If I made a circus, I would get—at least once—to say what my story was. My ideas about my own life might matter again.

My hope boiled over. I would ask the Girl Guides for help. We would make a show together, practice until she arrived, maybe even sell tickets, make money while making something of our own.

"If you want to pass your tenderfoot test," Rebecca was saying, "you have to be able to tie three knots. You can pick from reef, sheet, fisherman's, overhand . . ." She looked around.

Sally said, "Clove-hitch. And it's double overhand, not just overhand, it's—"

"What if we made a show?" I interrupted. "A performance—dancing, acrobatics—I've been working on puppets. We could sell tickets and—"

But they all stared at me, the energy of the room draining in a strange way.

"We could practice dance moves to start, like this—like

the knot tying, but . . ." I kept on, waiting for them to help, to understand, to feel the way I did.

Rebecca shrugged. "Sure, why not? Dance would be good. There's a dance at the Girls Hen'nai Club July third." I felt my whole self flatten.

Sally went to Rebecca's desk. "There's this dance, too. You should come." Sally held out a printed ticket: ENCHANTED PAL-ETTE, CARNIVAL OF THE 6 ARTIST PAINTERS, TO BE HELD AT THE TABARIN, 1124 BROADWAY, E. The party began at 9 p.m., and the ticket said "no curfew," said four dollars, said evening dress. These were elegant words: *enchanted* was green, *carnival*, gold, *9 p.m.* turned purple in my mind's tired eye. Four dollars was unthinkable.

Rebecca turned on a record, a warbling voice sang, "Some-where over the rainbow . . ." and she began to dance, pulling us into a line, kicking as she sang along: "There's a land that I heard of, once in a lullaby." I thought the land was Shanghai, the lul-laby my kitten song from Warsaw. The rainbow was Hongkou. I felt slightly happier, listening, until the song stopped and Sally suddenly asked, "So what's with you and that Chinese worker?"

I realized with an unpleasant burning sensation that she was speaking to me. "What?"

"The Chinese boy you're always with?" She flopped back on Rebecca's bed and stretched her legs. She could do anything she wanted. I envied her as much as I hated her. Could I ever be so comfortable?

"Um, his name is Wei."

Sally laughed, because this meant I agreed I was always with him. I wanted to push her off Rebecca's bed.

"What's it like to be in love with a Chinese boy?"

"Leave her be, Sally," Rebecca said. "He's cute, is all. The best-looking Chinese boy."

I asked, "Do you know other Chinese boys?"

I wasn't joking, but they all laughed again.

Sally said, "Do you work for him?"

"What? No!" I tried to calm down.

"Do you get paid to help him work at school? Do you eat Chinese food with him?" Sally asked. "Or do you do it for love?"

"Hey, Lillia, look," Rebecca said. "I'll show you our log book from last year's meetings." She grabbed a notebook from above her bed and handed it to me. On the cover it said, "13th Girl Guide Company, Log Book, Kept by Rebecca Rosen." The first page was a description of the company meeting. It said the guides were in clean and neat uniform, that they had tied reef knots and completed a drill about burns.

"It sounds nice," I whispered, grateful that she'd saved me from Sally. But what uniforms? Would I be asked to buy one?

Rebecca put her hand on my arm. "We'll go to Pudong and camp at the wharf in the summer. We do survival drills there— it's amazing. You can invite your friend Biata if you'd like."

I didn't want Rebecca to consider Biata my friend, but I nodded, as if considering it.

The girl named Jeanne said, "The White Stars are playing a football match this weekend. Should we go?"

Sally hopped off the bed. "I wish we could go to the British school or Western District." She sighed. "Seymour Road is much better than having to go to Hongkou! And the boys are better, too . . ."

I imagined Sally in our room at 54 Ward, my cot with Shanghai trash under it, our stove, our rat. She would sit on the overturned bucket we washed our bony bodies in, have to use the outdoor toilet we shared. I felt as if I were Sally, seeing my own life, and suddenly it was worse than it ever seemed when I was just me, living it.

Rebecca turned on another song, one with a watery sound in its voice, singing about magic in the air. She stood and began to dance with Sally, cheeks touching, clumsy and funny, hopping and loping. The British girl, Katarine, nodded over at me, "Dance?" I stood, heard the music, let it seep into my body, and started to dance with Katarine across Rebecca's carpeted floor, feeling the circus's taped one underneath me. I sped up, enjoying myself. The song ended and Sally was staring, her eyes like beads. "You should get a job as a dancer. You can make *so much* money here that way if you're a pretty foreign girl." She did not say that my dancing was good.

I felt strange anger then, remembering the woman who wanted my hair calling me pretty, as if that word stood for something I either couldn't or didn't want to give.

"We could put on a show ourselves," I said again. "We could make—"

"My parents would never let me. Circuses are for freaks and prostitutes," Sally said.

"I didn't say *circus*," I told her. "And you wouldn't be in it. You need talent. And trust."

The room chilled. And Sally's face fell, surprising me. Why did she care what I thought? But I couldn't make a circus myself. People needed each other for acts that mattered, needed affection. And something to say, some meaning. Maybe even love. I tried to stop wishing.

Papa arrived before 2 p.m., and I asked Rebecca to play him the Mozart, knowing no silly girl has such serious music in her. I was right, too. Papa's face changed in the wash of the concerto as if the notes were light. He said, "Thank you for that concert," and Rebecca blushed. Her mother handed me a book, *The Great Gatsby*. "Come back for more as soon as you've read it." She turned to Papa. "Your daughter is lovely. Thank you for sharing her this afternoon."

Outside, I untied the ribbons from the gate. "Rebecca told me to take these," I told him, as I tucked them into the pocket of my dress. "They're for a school project."

"I'm glad you went, after all, Lillia," he apologized. "I was wrong to judge them."

"I was wrong, too," I said, and held his hand like I had when I was small in Warsaw.

We passed Nanking and Bubbling Well Road, the department stores, Sincere and Wing-On, fans and radios displayed in bright windows. *Sincere* sounded like truth, and *Wing-On*, flying. They were hopeful, circus words in the city that was letting us live, giving me afternoons with Rebecca. Back at 54 Ward, I reached into my pocket and gave Naomi the sugar cubes from Rebecca's, broken and scattering grains. Naomi's eyes widened as she popped them in her mouth, laughing and crunching with her baby teeth, ruined before they'd even fully come in.

CHAPTER NINE

天空音乐, Tiankong Yinyue, *Sky Music*

I walked to Kadoorie on a late June day so hot I thought Wei might mistake me for a roasted potato when I arrived. School was finished and the sun was so violent that no one who had any choice in the matter was out. Except me. I missed Wei so much it was worth it, and I wanted to walk by the river, to check the boats. And I knew Wei had to work, prayed he'd be in the building. I found him in a classroom, packing boxes.

"Hua," he said, *Flower*, "hello." In that order, first his Chinese version of my name, then hello.

I was so happy to see him, to hear his voice, that I laughed. "Hi, Wei," I said. "What are you doing?"

He used English to say, "I work because the school moves."

"Moves?" I asked. "Where?"

"Yuheng Lu," he answered. *Yuheng Street*. I didn't know where that was.

"More work." He pointed to himself, smiling. The move meant more work for him. "More study." His eyes were glittering—he would get to be in the building all summer, maybe looking at books when he wasn't working, improving his English. He seemed joyful.

"That's wonderful," I said. We looked at each other until it began to feel funny, and then we both laughed again. I didn't want to ask him if I could work with him, even though I wanted to stay for a hundred years.

He said, "Ni yao gen wo gongzuo, ma?" *You want to work with me?*

"Yes!" I said. "I really do."

I stayed all afternoon, sweating, packing boxes, exchanging English words for Chinese ones: *summer*, xiatian; *box*, hezi; *books*, shu; *sun*, taiyang; *sleep*, shuijiao; *dream*, meng; *river*, he. We were making each other better. I told him that the Girl Guides were going camping, and he asked, "Ruguo ni you jia," *if you have a home*, "why sleep in dirt?"

Because sleeping outside with Rebecca was a dream. "We'll see nature," I said. "And breathe fresh air." I did a little dance, walking among trees, and breathed deeply to show *fresh air*. He watched me patiently. I said we would sing, by singing. I danced a little, laughing, said, "We'll tiaowu," *dance*, a word he'd taught me.

I hoped I could teach Rebecca dance moves, maybe convince her we should do a show together. Biata had asked what I was doing over the summer, whether I'd see Rebecca and Sally, but I hadn't answered or invited her to join the Girl Guides, had only said I going to try to find work. I didn't think there was room for both of us.

But at Kadoorie, packing boxes, full of joy at seeing Wei and at the camping trip, I told Wei about my idea for a show. I said *circus*, tried to show him what I meant, pointed at him and me, I hoped he might help.

He smiled but didn't speak, and I couldn't tell whether he'd understood. I was still dizzy with the thrill of having spent an afternoon with him, and of knowing I would ask him about the show again the next time we were together. Wei was the only part of Shanghai that could make the words *next time* feel like a promise.

— ▣ —

The night before camping, Rebecca took me to a concert at the Mascot Gardens. Crowds of refugees had assembled at the base of the building to hear the music for free, notes pouring down from the roof where the orchestra sat. Anyone willing to stand could hear the music under the stars, but Rebecca said, "Thank

God we have tickets." I didn't even nod. As much as I wanted Rebecca to like me, I couldn't thank God until I knew Mama was safe. We rode an elevator to the roof and sat with Shanghai glowing around us, our real lives far below. The notes of four songs played over us, landing on neon signs and people in fine clothes. There was too much beauty to take in at once, so I lost some. I wished I could spread that night over a year—live a little bit of it each day.

"Thank you for the ticket," I whispered to Rebecca when it was over.

She shrugged and spoke sweet fizzy words: "Don't worry! See you at the ferry. Oh! I almost forgot." She reached into her bag and handed me something wrapped in paper. I opened it, a book. *The Good Earth*. She said it was about China, but better than this China, and waved her beautiful hand out at the nighttime around us. Then she rode off, a princess to whom music came easily, who gave me dresses, books, a ticket to beauty, music, new views of Shanghai. I walked to Ward Road among those listening for free, clutching *The Good Earth*, so many pages of escape from the war, my own life, and the responsibility of Papa and Naomi. I walked like a weightless girl, wróżka, a fairy.

Next time, I thought. Next time there was a concert, I would bring Wei and Naomi, without tickets. We would stand under the falling, shooting notes, not hiding that we were poor. Because the music, just like the book I was carrying, would still be beautiful for us, too.

The air was hot cotton at the ferry dock. My shirt stuck to my back as I checked my bag: bread, a canteen of boiled water, and one hard-boiled egg. We were to have breakfast at Holt's Wharf, but cook dinner for ourselves at the campsite. Rebecca stood with Mrs. Campton, who was smiling and holding a pot. They waved and I ran to meet them.

Sometimes during the school year, Mrs. Campton took students home for a weekend, the poorest and saddest, so they could have warmth and food with her and her husband for a few days. She never invited me, and I knew I should be glad. Once, I heard Sally call a girl "one of the Campton kids," meaning a hungry girl who had to visit Mrs. Campton just to eat and sleep in a bed. I wondered why anyone considered me anything other than a Campton kid.

Everyone arrived shouting with excitement. We boarded the ferry like a gaggle of ecstatic ducks. Sally was singing a French song she said was by Edith Piaf, and I pretended to know who that was, tried to sing along with the other girls.

The boat banged against the dock, water sloshing onto the ramp, and we were moving. The ride felt wild, reviving inside me the terrible sense I'd had on the *Conte Rosso* that I might become somebody else, leap overboard. Rebecca began singing the American song about rainbows: "Why, oh, why can't I?" And I tried to drown out my mind with her beautiful voice, to hear only the notes. Sally stood between us, and I wanted to be closer to Rebecca, not just to hear her, but because she would try to save me if I suddenly scrambled overboard. Sally seemed not as likely. The water tipped and pivoted us, and I saw that Sally's skin had gone green. Maybe she was standing close to Rebecca because she was scared, too. Just because we weren't afraid of the same things didn't mean we weren't both afraid. I wished suddenly that I had invited Biata.

"Do you want a drink?" I held my thermos out, but Sally was bent at the waist, clutching the ferry's guardrail. "Try looking up," I suggested. "That helped me on the ship here, when I was sick." We both looked at the sky over Shanghai, blue heat making the air blur and waver. A Japanese plane flew by so low I thought I could feel it, that it might land on us.

"Thank you, Lillia," Sally said, and she sounded like she meant it, but then she added, "Oh, and just so I don't forget, as treasurer—we'll need to collect your Girl Guide dues? Anytime is fine," and a hard hand clenched my heart.

"No problem," I lied. I coughed a little. "How much is it again?"

"Just ten dollars for the year," she said, and I saw Rebecca look over. She had stopped singing, and her eyes were warm on me. I could feel her hoping this would be okay.

I arranged my face into an okay shape. "No problem," I said, an expression I'd heard Sally use. "Um, do you mean American dollars?"

"Oh, Lillia," Rebecca said, then, "You don't have to—"

I didn't let her finish. "That's fine. Dollars are fine. I'll get it to you right away."

At Holt's Wharf, land reeled out in front of us, no storefronts, rickshaws, or crowds. Just warehouses with short smoke stacks, and at their bases and the edge of the river, grass. Green. It moved in the wind like silky hair on the back of a neck, rising, breezing, settling. My eyes could not adjust. It had been months since I'd seen space or nature other than the Huangpu River. Here were colors I'd never noticed although they'd been everywhere in Warsaw: delicious grass, blue stretches of sky, perfect dirt. There was no concrete. I longed to spin across the first field, roll on the ground like Piotr. The memory of my lost puppy with his thoughtful eyebrows, combined with the ten dollars I could never pay, collapsed my happiness.

Off the ferry, Rebecca divided us into teams, the Swallows and the Doves, for a drill. I was a Dove. I vowed to tie my knots quick and straight so we'd win. I knew this would be my last moment of being a Girl Guide, friends with anyone other than my strange sister and maybe Wei. His name gave me back a small burst of joy, and I turned cartwheels across the grass, my hands as firm as ever, my balance sound. I landed fifteen and heard Rebecca clapping.

We ate a fast breakfast of porridge from a tin vat. I was too embarrassed to take my egg out, although I wanted it. We recited our pledge and then attempted to set up tents from pieces of gray-green canvas and a pile of poles whose order was mysterious. We held them up, tried to make them stand, dropped them, and tangled cloth around them. I laughed so much my stomach ached, watching Katarine and Jeanne fall over into the canvas. Sally laughed, too. Only Rebecca was capable of leaning the poles onto each other so they didn't fall, draping canvas over their tops into roofs. "It's a good thing you aren't soldiers," she said, folding a flap over the front of the tent, into a makeshift door. I dove in, sliding along the cloth floor, happy.

"Come in, men! I'm your platoon leader!" I called. Sally, Rebecca, Jeanne, and Katarine crawled in. The greenish light of the canvas made them forest fairies.

"You're all green," I said.

"Not as green as Sally was on the ferry," Rebecca pointed out.

"Where did you learn to put a tent together?" I asked Rebecca.

"At a camp in New York when I was small." She laughed.

The words came out of my mouth: "My grandmother is in a camp in Poland." Everyone went silent. I had ruined the old, fun, funny Lillia, even though I had just loved being her/me for a moment. Rebecca's face darkened, and fear pounded through me. I tried to fix it: "She has a parrot named Pippin who can speak English."

"Come," Rebecca said. "Let's do our drills." She stood, bending her back so she wouldn't hit the roof of the tent. We crawled after her and began a new drill: saving each other from injury. We made a stretcher from a sleeping bag, and the other girls hauled me on it because I was smallest. Jeanne and I carried Katarine, who giggled on the stretcher. Then we bandaged each other. Jeanne leaned over Rebecca, securing a bandage on Rebecca's arm, and said, "We love Americans! You know we gave you the beautiful gift! The statue of freedom?"

Rebecca held her hand above her. "With the torch," she said. Jeanne put her hand in the air, too. Everyone loved Rebecca most, wanted to be closest to her.

As night began to creep up, Mrs. Campton helped us build a fire. Its flames flashed and popped, and she balanced a pot of water on a screen above it, adding potatoes, onions, and a carrot—fresh, bright things. I wanted to watch Mrs. Campton cook for the rest of my life, never return to 54 Ward or anywhere real. It got late, and we drank the soup and ate bread. As the sky went completely black, our Shanghai appeared across the water, its lights far away. I felt safe. Rebecca suggested we dance, and I watched the silhouettes of the other girls flicker until I stood, closed my eyes, and inhaled the fire's heat. I danced, too, my feet landing on soft ground a surprise to me each time.

When the other girls were asleep, I slipped from the tent and walked until I thought I couldn't be seen, then lay back on the grass. The sky was bigger than the Huangpu, bigger than the ocean we'd crossed. It was so full of stars they seemed to be shooting toward me, brighter and more mobile than they should have been. I used to think the sky was a dark quilt, and stars were holes poked in it, revealing another brilliant layer of sky behind the night one. Now I tried to count the points of light, and to imagine Mama, safe somewhere, anywhere, looking at stars, too. Were these stars visible in Poland? Maybe we were all part of one endless stretch of sky.

I crouched in the dirt and ate my egg, was scratching a bit of ground away to bury the shell when I heard something and turned, terrified, to see Mrs. Campton. She had seen me, but she just nodded and backed away, returned to her tent. Had she decided I was safe?

In the morning I was awake before anyone else, doing my stretches and handstands in the grass alone. Upside down, I found two smooth rocks, flipped over, and collected them. Later, I carefully pulled up nettles, sixteen small sticks, and an empty bullet casing. I clutched my bag, planning, working to keep the green of the waving grass in my mind, to imagine a story in which my puppets saw nature and beauty again. I rode the ferry back with my eyes closed, but Rebecca came and stood beside me, said "Hey," in her bubbly way. "Do you know the fairy tale 'The Eagles'? The one about the dove-girl?" She told me a story about a king losing his wife, weeping for years, then falling in love. His new love turns out to be a witch, who transforms the king's twelve sons into eagles, his daughter into a dove. The dove-girl saves the eagles, changing them with her tears back into human princes.

When Rebecca finished, I said, "But the mother is still gone."

She shrunk back, her face cracking. "I didn't think of that, Lillia, I'm so sorry. My sister Ruthie loves that story. I thought your sister might, that the dove-girl was, well—I know you love to read, so—"

"It's fine," I said, working not to cry. We couldn't be friends. I couldn't pay dues, couldn't be a Girl Guide, couldn't bear for Rebecca or Sally to see inside my life. I cried as I walked home, no one I knew there to see me. The only person who looked curious was a woman passing with a dozen headless chickens hung from a pole across the back of her neck.

Taube was out in front of 54 Ward with Naomi, who wore a hat Taube had made, pink with a square of lace and a feather. When they saw me, Naomi screamed and waved her hands, and I stopped crying and smiled. To Naomi, it didn't matter whether I was a Girl Guide, a starving Campton kid, friendless, or even a good person.

"Lillia! Yao!" she shouted. She wanted me, used both her words to say she had been waiting for me to get home. I held her tight, smelled the fabric of the hat and her sweaty curls.

"How was your trip, darling?" Taube asked, wrapping her arms around me, too. "Did you have fun? Did you learn survival skills? You have to tell us everything."

They had both been waiting for me. I held onto Taube for a long time. Inside, I told Naomi about the grass, the fire, the stars. I showed her the sticks and rocks I'd found, told her, "Arms, legs, eyes." I pulled out a Taube puppet I'd been working on. "This is Taube," I told her.

She clapped. "Li-li-ah," she said.

"Not Lillia, Taube." I pointed to the puppet's face, made of a broken white bowl, onto which I had drawn eyes and a delicate nose. "That's Taube's nose. Where's Naomi's nose?"

She pointed to her nose and I clapped. "Can you say nose?" I asked.

"Li-li-ah." The day swelled and slowed. I wondered what the Girl Guides were doing in their rooms, as I passed hot hours with Naomi in ours. When she seemed sleepy, I sang: A, a, kotki dwa. "Aaa, kotki dwa, szarobure obydwa, nic nie będą robiły, tylko ciebie bawiły. *Ah, ah, two small cats. Ah, ah, two small cats. Both are gray, both are sad. They haven't a thing to do, just want to play with you.*"

Papa came home after dark and kissed the tops of our heads. He forgot to ask about camping. I was feeding Naomi, who had woken crying, and now I bent to pick up grains of rice she'd dropped and put them from the floor into my mouth. I kept my eyes on my father. I'd become this animal, eggs in the dark dirt, rice from the floor; he should know. But he didn't acknowledge it, seemed to find nothing objectionable in my gobbling food from the ground. I missed him so much it was as if he had vanished with my mother.

Scared to let him go, I followed Papa downstairs to listen to Gabriel's radio say that after the German invasion of the Soviet Union in late June, Soviet forces had left Kaunas, in Lithuania. That was where we had boarded our train to Italy. Gabriel and Papa had followed the news about resistance fighters in

Kaunas, cheering, waiting each night as if for a bedtime story, but now we learned that the temporary government had set up a camp and was rounding up Jewish citizens. They had tried to be independent but lost, and now they would have to answer to the Nazis. No wonder Papa didn't care from what surface I ate my rice.

My lovely memory of camping went blank, even though I tried to find my way back to it. Here at 54 Ward, there were no American girls, no Sally turning green, no Rebecca singing of bluebirds flying, no giggling, no stars, not even in my mind. I could keep almost nothing. I clutched Naomi in my cot every night. All we had was each other, some trash I'd collected for puppets, and memories of our mother, elsewhere.

Hopefully not in Kaunas. What if she had gotten that far, and would wait forever for a train that never came?

— ▣ —

Ten days after the Girl Guide camping trip, it was July again. I remembered arriving. Now a year had passed, and in the first week of this new July, I finished my most beautiful puppet: Wei. I had used the broken wheel for its head, covered it with paper, and painted big dark eyes and a mouth just like Wei's. I glued a small stone tooth to the mouth, chipped. Ink spokes flared out from the centers of the puppet's eyes, and two of the sticks from Pudong were its limbs. I even wove strands of Taube's thread together with some grass for hair.

I packed the puppet in my cotton bag and left for East Yu-hung Road, where the new building would be, where Wei would be working, where soon I would get to go to school again. I couldn't wait to see him, to hear his voice, spend an afternoon working by his side, present the puppet to him, as Papa had once given Mama Rosy Mischa. I arrived at the new building feeling shy and almost feverish with the roasting heat from out-side and the anticipation of seeing Wei after so many days. But I didn't know the hallways or belong to any of the classrooms, and I couldn't find him. I was wandering when Mrs. Aarons, the principal, broke off from a group of workers and rushed up. She looked like she might hug me, but she patted my arm awk-wardly instead.

"Lillia, how nice to see you! How is your summer? How is your father?"

"Fine, thank you."

"Are you stopping by to say hello? How can I help you?"

"I'm um, I'm looking for Wei, the Chinese boy who works in the—"

Her face changed, wrinkles I hadn't seen before radiating out from her mouth and eyes. "Oh," she said. "I'm sorry to say that we had to let him go, I'm afraid."

"Let him go?" I didn't know what this meant.

"He doesn't work here anymore, Lillia. Things were going missing. Supplies. We can't have that, no matter how much we like somebody personally." She cleared her throat and bright-ened again. "Will we see you when school starts up? Tell your father it will likely be winter. It doesn't look like we'll be quite ready by fall." She gestured toward the workers.

"Mrs. Aarons!" I said. "It wasn't Wei who took those things, it was—"

She looked at me, but my voice faded out. "Yes, Lillia?"

Would I be allowed back at Kadoorie? Would she tell Papa? He would be desperate with disappointment if I were forbidden from school again, like in Warsaw. I would wither. But would they take Wei back if I promised it hadn't been him?

I started, "It wasn't Wei . . . We shouldn't have let him go, Mrs. Aarons."

"Well, let's not guess at things we can't know the truth of, Lillia. Let's—"

"Mrs. Aarons. He didn't take . . . It was . . . me?" It came out a question, because I wasn't brave enough to say it for real, to shake Mrs. Aarons by the shoulders, tell her to let me go, not Wei, to let him work again, please. I didn't beg or plead.

"It's noble of you to try to say so, Lillia, but we've already worked this matter out, and we're not able to revisit it." And then someone was calling her name, and she was gone down the hall. I stood, stunned sick and unable to speak.

In bed with Naomi that night, I read the first chapters of *The Good Earth*, rationing so I wouldn't finish too quickly and be cast back into my own life. In the story, a Chinese farmer named Wang Lung, whose mother had died, is getting married. He fights with his father about water, tea, everything, because they have so little. He hasn't had a bath since New Year's.

Should I have been more grateful for our bucket of cold water and our single towel?

When I closed the book, I had to be my terrible self again. I stayed awake forever, promising God or anyone who would listen—maybe only myself—that I would make up for my mistake with Wei.

CHAPTER TEN

热病, Rebing, *Fever*

I opened my eyes into dark, a moment of hot nothing and I couldn't remember where I was. Papa's voice rose close by, tight and frantic. I sat up, found my room gone, Mama gone again, as she always was, but sometimes the middle of a single night could shock me with it. Our life in Shanghai crashed down and spun me under. It was August. Late summer, 1941, a year and two months since we'd lost her, a year and a month since Shanghai. We were still here! Something was terribly wrong, and I tried to come up from under whatever was crushing me, tried to understand.

"Papa! What's happening?"

But it was Taube who emerged as my eyes adjusted. "Your sister has a fever, Lillia," she said calmly. "Can you please take these and go get water. We can't boil enough."

She held out a handful of bamboo tokens. I kicked out of my cot, furiously awake, grabbed the tokens, and ran out into still-dark Ward Road, knocking into two women. I didn't apologize, just wove even faster through the street past carts howling for bodies, past a hundred predawn rickshaws. I made it to the water coolies, panting, my throat wracked raw. The line was short. I traded tokens for two jarfuls of hot water, turned the caps to seal them, and ran again, my hips grinding and knees popping, too little flesh to protect my bones from each other.

It was light out now, the day filtering into our room. Taube was gone, but Papa knelt by the side of the cot, holding a cloth on Naomi's forehead. I knelt, too, and touched my sister, who reached out dizzily. "Moh. No-mi yao moh." *Naomi wants the mouse.* A whole, feverish sentence. Her eyes were glittering, her skin so hot I felt it might burn mine. I fetched the ratty mouse, which she wrapped in her arms and patted. The only toy she had. She said my name, then "mouse," then "Naomi," then "yao, yao, yao," *want, want, want.* She could speak, knew us, could move across a room to reach me, was on her way to walking. Had these answers to some of my prayers come at the cost of others? Please God. Please. I thought in all my languages: proszę, qing, *please*. I promised to be better, to accept being hungry, not even to feel hunger, not to care whether I had friends, certainly to stop stealing and thinking I could murder Leo or anyone else to get my mother back, please, anything. I would do anything to prevent God from taking Naomi.

But God didn't believe me, and two days later, Papa's breath came rattling from his lungs, too. He couldn't stand. He became a tangle of sick, burning limbs. I was frantic with fear. I begged Taube to help me take them to a doctor, but she looked at me gently and whispered, "It's four dollars a day." She didn't have nearly enough money, either.

I willed myself not to faint. We couldn't pay, not even for a rickshaw to take them. The hospital itself? Impossible, even though four dollars was a reduced rate—Rebecca had told us her father was on the Shanghai Municipal Council and they'd vowed to take care of Jewish refugees "for less." But for us, less was still too much. If Papa and Naomi died, I couldn't pay even then. I would send their bodies out onto the Huangpu the way the poorest people did, scattering flowers as my family floated away, the river their only funeral, its nothingness their grave.

I fled as soon as Taube returned. I went straight to the station, where I handed the ticket taker six wen and took a tram to the International Settlement, packed as tightly as I'd been on the open backed truck that first delivered us to the Heime. When the tram released me, I breathed wildly, tried to calm down even as I ran to Bubbling Well Road, past policemen in turbans, along sidewalks with houses spread out across patches of land, automobiles sliding in and out of the gates that kept safe families in and hopeless families out.

I rang Rebecca's bell, sweating, trying not to cry. Her maid came outside.

"Um, nihao," I squeaked from the top of my throat, realizing only when I tried to form words how thirsty I was. "Rebecca?"

I would ask for her help, would beg. But the maid shook her head. "Bu zai," *not here.*

"Oh!" I said. I pointed at myself, "Lillia." I crossed my arms over my chest and pumped, tried to say, "help." The maid stared. I took a piece of paper from my bag and wrote to Rebecca: *My father and sister are sick. Please help! 54 Ward Road.* I handed the paper to the maid.

— ◙ —

The next day, they were worse. I put our towel on Naomi's forehead only to feel the cloth turn instantly hot. Papa was delirious, shouting: "Sergo! Sergo!" Their boss from the circus, not Jewish, not in danger, nowhere near. Why his name?

"Papa! It's okay. You're here, in Shanghai. Sergo is—" I didn't know what to say, didn't know where Sergo was or why Papa would be calling his name. But he didn't respond. Was he shouting in his sleep? Naomi twisted in pain. Papa opened his eyes and looked at me suddenly. "I can't stay. I'll miss work! We need—" His face was lit with fever.

"It's okay," I lied, sounding like a baby, trying to grow up right that instant. "Rest, Papa. You have to get well. I'll work. I'm going to get medicine.... I'm going to help, going to—"

I tried to make soup but had no vegetables, meat, potatoes, or salt. I put Naomi on Papa's cot while I washed and hung her sweat-soaked sheets. Taube and Mr. Michener brought rice and three potatoes. Later, Gabriel brought bread and boiled water. Papa was asleep again. I tried to get Naomi to drink, but she cried, wanted only the mouse and me.

I went to ask Gabriel and Leo for more help, and found Talia alone in their room. Desperate, I asked, "Can you please sit with my father and sister for a bit so I can get water?"

She rose and put her arms around me before sitting outside our door. "Of course. I'll stay until you're back. Unless I should go get water so you can stay."

I shook my head no. I had to be the one to go. On Chusan Road, there were entrances and exits on both sides of the shop I was actually headed to, a small concession to dignity that seemed worthless now. I walked in the front door and went straight to the desk, where a man stood, gnarled behind wire-rimmed glasses with a single lens. I pulled the string around my neck, felt it snap.

I handed the man my mother's ring, and he looked at me through the lens, closing his left eye and turning the star over carelessly in his palm. The string I'd found he dropped. I picked it up. The ring no longer shone, and so looked small and value-less. I wanted to smash the old man's hand down on the counter, take my ring and run. "I need money," I told him.

He laughed, and even though I had promised God, I thought, *I want to kill him*.

"Don't we all!"

"How much will you give me for the ring—it's gold."

"Twenty CN," he said.

"It's worth ten times that much, please."

"Not to me."

"Give me fifty. Please." A beggar. I was a beggar even selling my mother's ring.

"Twenty-five."

I was as determined not to cry as I was to save my family. I took the fistful of filthy bills and didn't look at the ring again, didn't want to see it in his hand. Outside, I passed a paper sign that read, ROYAL NIGHT CLUB BAR & CAFÉ. BEST MUSIC, GIRLS & DRINKS, 689 JOFFRE AVE., TEL: 72533. Music, girls, and drinks! All things people sold and bought. What was my—or any girl's—life worth? How much? I went to my favorite noodle stand, where Taube had taken us, owned by Miss Li, who smiled at me even when I could buy nothing. I spent twenty wen on two bowls and ate the first one standing, pushing my hair away. The other bowl I took home, trying not to waste a single splash. Papa woke only long enough to eat three bites, and I couldn't get Naomi to eat any, so I ate the rest of theirs, too, so hungry I'd risk any sickness for more soup.

Later, Taube sat with them and I went to Wei's and waited in the street. I thought I might be there forever, but eventually I looked up to find Wei standing over me. I didn't know how long I'd been sitting. I could have been holding a metal cup in my hand, banging it, begging, could have been Naomi, shouting, "Yao, yao," *want, want*. I'd taken such meaningless things, to make puppets! Had they told him why they were firing him? Did he know?

He helped me stand, and I thought maybe he didn't know I'd cost his job. Would I be courageous enough to tell him? To apologize? Later. I would say I was sorry later. Now I said only, "Please help. Wode baba he meimei!" *My father and sister!* "Fever." I put the back of my hand on my forehead.

He just watched me. I was in an agony of wonder over whether he knew. If I apologized and he hadn't known, he might be too angry to help me. What danger was there in hoping, praying even, that he didn't know? That he'd never know? But when he still didn't speak, I began to cry. He beckoned then and turned. I followed him, unsure where he was going, whether he wanted to help or punish me. But what choice did I have but to walk behind him, hoping?

The city smelled of open fire, everything dangerous now that Papa and Naomi might die, now that Wei was silent with me, now that I had hurt him. Merchants hovered under cardboard, trying to hide their broiling skin from the sun. Wei led me to Hainan Road, past the Siberian Fur Store, its windows a horrible curtain of animal skins, and into a building where we climbed narrow, decaying stairs, the smells of cooking oil and honey pots rising. Thick air clung to the walls, and sweat attached my hair to my neck. Wei opened a door at the top of three flights, where the deadly human smells of the stairwell were overtaken by a mix of herbs so thick it became a taste. My mouth was pasty with it, and with thirst. Chests of drawers lined the walls. A man sat at a desk covered with bags and bottles in baskets on either side of a stack of paper. He appeared as old as the dried roots hanging over him. On top of one of the chests were jars of all sizes, one filled with a coiled snake and oily yellow liquid, another several frogs suspended in gray. Next to those stood twin racks of antlers. Wei spoke confidently, sounded like music and seemed different, louder, stronger. What did I seem like to him? He knew me only in bits of Chinese and English. No Polish. I was never loud around him, or funny. How little of a person can be left and still allow her to be herself? If Wei never forgave me, there would be no more language lessons, no more of what our talking had given me: the opposite of loneliness. This would be fair, given what I had taken from him, but I didn't think I could bear it.

The old man came out from behind his desk and moved to the farthest chest of drawers, slid one open, removed some powder and a bulb, and began to grind them together in a stone bowl. He deposited their dust in a pouch of paper, which he tied and pushed across his desk. He was a doctor, I understood, and this was medicine.

"How much?" I whispered in English. But he didn't understand me, and Wei, looking away angrily, didn't help. I held up fingers and then shrugged at the doctor, a question. He waved the fingers of one hand: five. The powder would cost me five CN, a fifth of what I'd gotten for Mama's star ring. I paid, measuring the remaining twenty CN in my mind: oil, rice, bread, eggs, potatoes, tokens for extra boiled water.

The doctor pointed at the pouch, then made bubbles with his hands, poured imaginary water, pointed again. Boil. "Boil?" I asked, but he shrugged. Wei did not translate. The doctor mimed drinking. I should boil the powder and have them drink it. I said this, into silence. When the doctor shook my hand, his felt like bones wrapped in paper. He said his name then, and the English word: *doctor*. He said, "Doctor Hao," and kept shaking my hand. I said "Lillia, Hua," and held on, even though I wanted to recoil. His skin ignited my fear and also the memory of a sound: opening sandwiches Mama used to pack. Each school day I'd unwrap one to discover what she'd made me. I let go of Dr. Hao's hand as I whispered, "Xiexie," *thank you*.

Then I followed Wei down the stairs and outside. He walked away.

"Wei! Please wait," I called.

He turned without speaking, and I held out ten CN of the money from her ring. I closed my eyes, praying he would refuse. But Wei took the money from my hand, still without words. So he knew. He took the ten CN, as I had taken everything from him, including his job. I whispered, "I'm sorry, I'm sorry." But he was gone, down the street in a crush of people.

At 54 Ward, Taube went upstairs and I flung myself onto Papa's cot, half breathing. The triple pain—of having sold Mama's ring, betrayed Wei, and spent money we needed desperately— vibrated through me. Papa looked at me with eyes so sick the whites were webbed with red. I expected a spider to crawl from inside, dangle down his cheek like an eight-legged tear.

"Słodkie Lillia," he wheezed. Naomi was breathing loudly.

"Shhh. I got medicine from Wei's doctor," I said. "I'm going to boil it for you, okay?"

I hunched over the kitchen bucket and lit a fire. The water boiled, and I added some of Dr. Hao's powder. A new smell rose, of forest, bone, and ground, the whole dirty earth coming at me. I woke Naomi and forced her to drink two sips, even though she shook her head, even though she cried.

Papa was awake still, watching us, coated with sweat when I came over and handed him the cup. "It doesn't smell so good," I said.

But he propped himself up on an arm and drank the whole mug in a long swallow before lying down again. He looked like Dr. Hao, ancient, and I was terrified watching his eyes close, but also relieved when he and Naomi were asleep. Because I could wash in the leftover water, put on Rebecca's pink dress, and slip out again, this time into the night.

CHAPTER ELEVEN

华丽宫, Huali Gong, *Magnifique*

I held a pinch of the fabric of Rebecca's dress between my fingers as I crossed the bridge and found the building in the shadow of the Cathay Hotel. This time, I knocked the solid head of a brass lion against the red doors. Magnifique. A woman in a black dress appeared, her face a brick stacked on almost no neck. Two men in military uniforms stood behind her, human giraffes, her opposites, made of almost all neck. They held no bayonets and wore pale beige jackets, not the darker ones worn by Japanese soldiers.

"May I help you?" the woman asked. She looked Chinese. Her English sounded British, and the men, I realized, were Chinese soldiers. They seemed like boys in the costumed bodies of men. Maybe I looked like a child to them, too, maybe I was one. But what did it mean to be a child here? Being a child at all seemed like a dream adults had come up with, a wish to hide the world's hideousness from themselves by pretending it could be concealed from us.

We had all given up on that possibility now. I pronounced in my best English, "I am looking for work, please, whatever jobs you may have for someone? I am very hard working."

She looked me over so slowly it felt like she was touching me. I thought she might open my mouth and inspect my teeth. But she just crooked a finger and gestured toward herself, led me to a dining room with a stage at the far end, velvet curtains hugging its sides. Tables were set with linens, tucked into booths, also velvet, holding faint imprints of last night's men. I knew without being told that men were the ones who sat at this restaurant, watching whatever happened on its stage. Tabletops bloomed with tangled stems, rising into flowers that almost reached low-hanging lanterns. Music played evenly from somewhere. How different this sound was from the notes shivering out of Leo and Talia's violin. These were lush, plump chords, but also artificial, mechanically made.

I knew with sudden and excruciating certainty that there were those whom the war hadn't touched. Some it had benefitted. And that they came here to enjoy themselves, to trade stories not about what came next for those they loved, not about life, death, or the horrible combination created by the disappearance of human beings. Not about fever or medicine or water. People sat here drinking and eating, those whose papas and sisters weren't aflame with fever in soiled cots, whose mothers weren't lost. Those who weren't refugees, weren't Jewish.

"Do you have work experience?" the woman asked, her high voice almost musical. She didn't turn, so the words came from the back of her, as if she were hiding a mouth underneath her hair.

"Experience working? Oh, yes."

"Where? What experience?"

My head was nodding. "I worked in Warsaw, where I am from."

"What work?"

"I was a performer in the Stanislav Cyrk," I said, and when she didn't respond, added, "A circus? I am a trained dancer. And an acrobat." *Please, God,* I thought, *let this work. Please.*

"What sort of dance?" Now she turned, eating me with her eyes again.

"Acrobatics, ballet, jazz." As I said it, I couldn't remember whether it was a lie or something true. Either way, it felt like a dangerous confession. I remembered my lessons.

"What's your name?"

"Alenka."

"Alenka. You will call me Madame Su. How old are you?"

I said, "Nineteen," and we looked at each other. I was sixteen, although my birthday had gone unmarked, so I felt still fifteen. Would she challenge me?

"How is your Chinese?"

"It's okay," I said. And then I added. "It's yue lai yue hao," *getting better*.

She didn't smile. "Come a week from tomorrow. Next Saturday. At eight. You will stay until midnight. Better money than anywhere else."

"Oh, I—"

She looked at me like a body to step over in the street. "Or don't. Up to you," she said.

— ◙ —

Papa and Naomi drank the medicine from Wei's doctor. They sweated and called out, Naomi for me, and Papa for Sergo. This confused and frightened me, but I had no time to think. We were out of money, medicine, rice. A week had passed when I heard a knock on the door and a voice calling my name, thought I was hallucinating, that I had fever, and we would all perish. But I staggered to the door and opened it to find Rebecca.

"Lillia! What happened? Are you okay? The maid—I got your note. I'm sorry it took so long—but I brought my father." It had been seven days since I'd run to her house. It felt like years has passed.

A man stood behind Rebecca, bald with a beard, as if his hair had slid down and remained on the wrong side. He carried a leather bag, and the hand he reached out to shake mine was missing a finger. I looked down at the ground, worried I would follow his lost finger with my eye. "I'm Dr. Rosen," he said. "Your father is ill?" His shoes were enormous, gleaming black beetles.

I kept staring down. "My father and my sister both—please come in."

"But you and your mother are still healthy, yes?" Dr. Rosen asked.

"Dad!" Rebecca said.

We walked in, and Rebecca passed me something. A book. "This one's British," she said. "It's a little sad, but very good. And well, I thought you might need something to do while your father and sister recover." I looked at the cover, *Oliver Twist*.

"Thank you," I said. "I haven't even finished *The Good Earth* yet," I lied, because I didn't want to return it.

"Don't worry," Rebecca told me. "Take your time."

Dr. Rosen sat on Papa's cot and spoke quietly. Papa seemed to know he was a doctor and to be able to respond. He did not scream Sergo's name, or writhe and tangle his legs in the blanket as he'd been doing. Naomi lay still, drenched with sweat. Dr. Rosen took a needle and a vial from his bag. He pushed the needle into Papa's arm. "What is it?" I begged.

"Medicine."

"Please. Can you give Naomi some, too?"

"I'm afraid she's too small. It's not safe." He talked to Papa quietly for a while, but when he stood to go, I was desperate.

"What can I do?" I asked. He put a cool hand on my shoulder, and I imagined the absent finger, wondered how he'd lost it. He seemed a person to whom nothing tragic could happen.

"You're doing a good job caring for your family," he said. "Just continue to keep your sister hydrated and try to break her fever with water, with baths."

"Will they . . ."

"Their fevers will peak in a week or so, and you have to get them through the worst night of it. I am leaving you with medicine for your father. He can drink it with water."

I did not tell him we had no way to bathe, couldn't even keep our hands clean, could barely manage to protect the skin from rotting off of our bodies. I just thanked him.

"We'll come back," Rebecca promised. I remembered then to ask how she was. We were standing outside and Dr. Rosen had beckoned their rickshaw driver over. Soon they'd leave.

"I'm good," she said. "I went to a dance, and Abraham was there and—" She stopped, maybe thinking that given my life, she shouldn't tell me about the dance. But I wanted to hear.

"What happened? Did you dance with him?"

"I did," she said. Then she dropped her voice to a whisper so that her father, who was ahead of her on the street, climbing into their rickshaw, wouldn't hear. "He kissed me."

"Really?" I asked, pleased that she would confide in me, curious whether she had told Sally, too. "How did it happen?"

"We were dancing, is all, and then he turned me quickly and his lips brushed my face."

I did not say that this sounded like an accident. Envy

scalded me. I tried to move it out of myself but could not. Maybe she heard it sizzle, because she said, "I hope you'll come with us next time. Benjamin asked after you."

"He did?"

"Rebecca!" Her father was calling from the rickshaw. She leaned in and kissed me on the cheek, maybe wanting to make it up to me. Would she be the only person to kiss me in Shanghai? Rebecca hopped into the rickshaw with Dr. Rosen, her lucky, healthy father, in charge of saving poor papas like mine. She called out: "I hope they get well soon" and "I miss you. I can't wait for Kadoorie to start up again."

They rattled off down Ward Road, Rebecca's kindness and good fortune leaving me so lonely and empty I had to remind myself to move, to breathe, to keep living at all.

— ◙ —

The next day was Saturday, and I went straight to Magnifique before 8 p.m., terrified. I told Taube I was seeing Rebecca and promised God I would make up for this lie, too, when I made up for all the stealing.

Madame Su gave me two silk dresses, said they were my uniform, that she never wanted to see me in anything else again, especially that horrible pink rag. I was to change the moment I arrived through the back door. A foreign girl had been sent to collect me and show me where to go. But when the girl turned around, I saw she wasn't a girl at all but Natasha, from the *Conte Rosso*, Alexi and Sasha's mother, who had shared our cabin. We stared. She took my hand and pulled me to the dressing room, whispering only when she had shut the door behind us. We were in a tight row of cabinets, girls nearby in various states of nakedness.

"Lillia, Lillia!" She put her arms around me, and I smelled her, a confusion of mother and bridge walker, milk, sweat, and something winter, a sweet perfume that made me feel I'd inhaled freezing air. "Lillia, no. This . . . " I hoped she would stop repeating my name, and not only because I had lied to Madame Su. Natasha lowered her voice. "This is no place for you. Where is your father? How's your beautiful sister? Has she spoken?"

"They're sick," I said, thinking suddenly maybe she could help us. "We need money for medicine—and food—and I . . ."

"Of course," she said. "But not— There are other jobs, other ways to . . ."

I was trying to look away from the girls with nothing on, who moved about the room slowly, as if underwater, unembarrassed to be naked. Maybe they weren't strangers but friends.

Natasha didn't finish. She opened a cabinet. A sharp smell met me, mothballs or alcohol. "Leave your clothes here." Her voice went mechanical now, in need of oil or hope. Some girls looked over at us, laughing. I thought of the circus, where everyone had dressed and undressed together, but this was different. It was too hopeful to think these girls were friends. They were naked and laughing because we were performing our own private tragedies, so cut off we couldn't care. I untied Taube's sash, hung it on a hook, and pulled Rebecca's dress over my head. I kept my shoes on, afraid if I lost them I'd never have shoes again. But Natasha pointed. Here were other shoes, high and shiny. "You'll have to wear those, I'm afraid."

I asked, "How are Sasha and Alexi and—and their father?"

"Their father isn't with us anymore." I didn't know whether this meant he was dead or had vanished. Madame Su suddenly screamed, "Hurry! No loitering—this isn't a shelter!"

We sped as if wound up and released by her voice. Natasha helped me choke myself into the luxurious but dirty red dress. An oily sheen weighed down the silk. I had to work my body into it, and stuff my feet into shoes at once too big and too small. The fronts squeezed my toes, while the heels slipped off and tore my skin. I sensed the other girls who had worn the dress as if they were still struggling inside its fabric. The bottom was cut so far up the side of my right leg that I could neither sit nor bend without baring my thigh. My underpants were visible if I took a step. My right shoe slipped off, and I jammed my foot back in. I felt I deserved the stab of pain up my leg. To Natasha I said, "Um, I think maybe this dress is too small, because my, well—my underpants show." I turned to show her my hip.

Natasha said, "If they show you mustn't wear any. This is one of the rules, one of the—"

Part of the job would be to ask nothing, refuse nothing. I slid my underpants off and left them in my locker. What I looked like here would be about those watching me, rather than about me watching myself or looking out at anything at all. This place would be my worst secret, one I'd keep forever from everyone, Papa, Taube, Wei, Biata, Rebecca. I longed to see Rebecca. Just changing my clothing at Magnifique had made me older than her. And Kassia! She could never know me again, couldn't imagine this Lillia. No one knew me anymore, a thought that gave me an immediate, double feeling—of loneliness so absolute it resembled death, and freedom as thrilling as flying above my own life. It was hard to believe both feelings could be inside the same me.

"Put this in the back of your shoes," Natasha said, handing me some stuffing, which I used to pad my feet and planned to take home later and sew into something. As if she'd heard me thinking this, Natasha added, "I sew during the day." She would need it back.

"Are Sasha and Alexi okay?" I asked.

"They're surviving," she said.

"Do they go to school?"

"I'm afraid not," she said.

"There's a good school in my neighborhood," I said, fast, so glad to be able to help. Someday I would be like Taube or Rebecca, someone who took care of others, rather than demanding care all the time. "Kadoorie? It's free, so they can—"

But Natasha's mouth folded in on itself. She looked toothless and her eyes watered. "I've heard of it. But Sasha must work, and when I'm working, he helps look after Alexi, who also works—with Sasha—during the day. They earn money, but just for now, I hope. I hope they will get to study again, so much. I pray for this."

"I'll pray, too," I promised, hollow.

"Lillia—I don't think this is the right place for you."

"Is it dangerous?"

"It can be. It doesn't have to be, perhaps. Remind those you can that you're a child. Tell Madame Su what your talents are so she will keep you on even if—"

She stopped talking and I turned. Madame Su stood behind me. "You will wait at the door and welcome our guests," Madame Su told me. "If you can perform this simple task without errors, eventually you will be allowed to perform. On stage."

"She's an incredible dancer," Natasha said, although she couldn't have known whether this was true. She was protecting me, but I wasn't sure from what, and Madame Su ignored her.

I stood at the stand I had glimpsed from outside and sang a refrain a thousand times: "Hello, sir, welcome, sir. May I lead you to your table?"

A man with a thick beard asked me when I led him to his table if I would sit with him. I blinked, not knowing the right answer. If I said yes, would I be in trouble with Madame Su? If I said no? I looked around fearfully, and on the far side of the room saw Wei's sister, Aili. Also in a red dress, she was trying to move little enough that she showed nothing of her leg. I could tell by the way she walked. She had seen me, and I tried to get her attention again, wanting to ask, wanting help, wanting anything.

"You are beautiful," he said, his accent thick, maybe Russian. "Where are you from?"

"Thank you," I said, sitting hesitantly in a chair next to him. "I am from Warsaw."

"Ah." Some disgust was in his voice, "A Polish girl." What could this mean to him? He looked away from me for so long that I finally stood. "Nice to meet you, sir," I whispered, returning to the front door to welcome more men. I didn't see Aili again, although I looked.

Girls disappeared into the smoke at Magnifique the way people disappeared into the war. I felt I was in a movie, something blurry I couldn't understand. When I was little and watched movies, I talked a lot during them, asking Mama and Papa questions. Here there was no one left to ask anything.

The smoke was so thick we could almost hide. But not quite. Eyes found us everywhere, and hands. My job was to be a magnet, drawing men toward me, but once they were close, I didn't know what was meant to happen. Was I supposed to know them? To speak as if we were becoming friends? Instead of a real person at Magnifique, I had to appear like a dream. And not one person's, but a dream that could belong to anyone, a fogged mirror, in which whoever looked could see what he wanted. We were, I understood, to be cloudy and insignificant. My parents hated performers like this, with no core idea of who we were.

But at Magnifique we had no choice. We made a strange, skinny army in our huge shoes and suffocating dresses. Some of the girls were beautiful, others plain. We all had bones showing through our skin. We moved tightly, taking men from place to place, letting them stand, sit, laugh, and watch those lucky enough to be asked to dance on stage and therefore make the most money. I understood that to dance here was an honor and a humiliation. But the money mattered more than anything else, and I couldn't wait. Aili was beautiful and got many requests to dance. Everyone knew her name.

After midnight, Madame Su told me to go home, to come back in a week. I was only needed on Saturdays, when they were busiest. She handed me three withered bills, three CN, more than I could possibly have made anywhere, more than I had dreamed she'd pay me, enough for a full week of noodles; a bag of rice not from the shelter, so less glass and dirt; two cubes of bean curd; an eggplant. I could make soup that was more than salt water. I thought of my mornings, walking to school, so hungry that rocks began to take the shape of food. I immediately wished for more nights of Magnifique, planned to make Madame Su love or need me, offer me more work.

When I slipped Rebecca's pink dress back on, it felt like home, warm and safe. I hung the hard dress I'd worn all night, lined the excruciating shoes up and strapped my own broken ones back on. The three CN filled me like light. I could go back to Dr. Hao's for a pinch of powder to boil for Papa and Naomi. Next week I would use the three CN for better food if we didn't need medicine. Next week maybe they'd be better. I felt strong, proud.

"You feel you're pretty?" someone asked in English. I

turned to face a girl who stood next to me, naked. She had a wide face on a thin neck, like a delicate puppet. Her black hair was brushed bright and so long it hung halfway down her back. She wore red lipstick and her eyes flickered as if furious.

I shook my head no, looked away, looked down. Pretty? I had the unruly thought that parts of me were separating, my hair an animal I had killed by cutting it off, one who feared me since I might chop and trade it again. My arms and legs had been brought here against their will, my mouth made to say words it didn't want: *Welcome, sir. Thank you, sir.*

The girl dropped her voice. "Double money for dance," she said. "Plus extra if—" She held moving fingers up. "More for more. For private. For *love*." She said *love* as if it were something vile, then touched her own face and pointed, indicating mine. "You can. Because so white."

I wrapped Taube's sash around my neck like a scarf. Or a noose. And walked away from the girl, straight into the night, toward Ward Road, through the heat, the leering soldiers and bridge walkers, the only city that was mine. Once home, I boiled water, made rice, waited for the sun and at the first wash of light, tried to feed Naomi and Papa. When the Song girls came down dressed for an outing with their mother, I was so ashamed of our misfortune that I hid in the room until they had left. I returned to Dr. Hao's, desperate and determined. Because maybe his medicine was what had kept the fever from killing them already, as much as or more than Dr.

Rosen's. I had no way of knowing. Dr. Hao was at his desk.

I said, "Wei's friend. My father, my sister, more medicine?" I showed him two CN, and he gave me a pinch of the same powder wrapped in paper I would later fold into a shirt for one of my puppets. I used the other one CN for oil, rice, and a small bag of flour.

Naomi and Papa slept through my first nights at Magnifique. I considered this permission from God and so tried to keep my promises—not to steal, not to hate others, not to inhabit the Magnifique dress for real as I moved men from place to place. The silk smelled like me, like others, sweat, smoke and nighttime. I remembered smelling good in Warsaw, soapy, powdery, like a child, and longed to go back. I hoped God could forgive me since I was trying to save my family. But maybe to God all that mattered was what people did, not why we did it.

I told myself it made a difference why I led men to tables, let eyes linger on me all the time, the thousand insect eyes of men for whom looking meant pleasure. Girls who weren't good enough dancers—or exciting enough "company"—had to promise other entertainment or lose their jobs. This was something I would have understood even if Natasha hadn't explained it to me. I held my spine straight, worked to seem beautiful, to suggest I was a talented dancer. I thought of all the classes I'd had as a child, wanted so much to be asked to dance. I tried to find Aili, but she avoided me. I didn't know why. She couldn't have been as embarrassed as I was, since she had worked here first, had led me here, even if unknowingly.

Dr. Rosen returned ten days after his first visit. This time, he brought two clean towels, three loaves of bread, rice, and tea. I accepted the gifts, shame seizing my insides. He had seen how poor we were and knew we needed more than just medicine. But Papa and Naomi were already cooler, better. Hoping for dignity, I asked after Rebecca, who was not with him.

"Rebecca is helping her mother organize food for a shelter," Dr. Rosen said. "She told me to give you a hug." He hugged me then, as if I were his daughter, too. "You did a wonderful job taking care of your father and sister. You're a good girl, Lillia."

I prayed God might hear him, even if Dr. Rosen was wrong, didn't know the truth about me.

— ⊠ —

By my third Saturday at Magnifique, my father and sister had made it through their worst nights, under Taube's watch, and now their fevers were broken. They were awake more, sitting, drinking water and soup, healing. I fractured into even more Lillias, all lying: the girl I was during the days, with Papa, Naomi, and Taube, the one who dreamed she was her own mama. I was the Lillia from Kadoorie, waiting to return to school, read books, make timelines and friends. The Lillia who had cost Wei—my favorite boy—his job.

All those Lillias hid the one who now existed only on Saturday nights at Magnifique. I didn't know who she'd be, who I'd grow up to be, which thief, wretched friend, pawner of her mama's ring, beggar of help from anyone who came near enough to be asked. As long as the versions of me never met one another, and no one who cherished one met the others, I thought I could survive. I lied to my father and Naomi and Taube about school dances so I could return to Magnifique again and again once they were well.

— ▨ —

In September, the weather cooled at night. Soon ice would line our windows again. People would walk the streets with frenzied purpose because our skin was freezing. We would pitch forward on our cold toes toward warmth. I read *The Good Earth* over and over. When Wang Lung's wife, O-lan, gets pregnant, she delivers the baby herself, cutting the cord with a split reed and then returning immediately to the fields to work. I didn't know what Rebecca had meant by the book showing a better China, but I guessed maybe she thought it would make my situation seem less difficult. Or maybe she knew more than that, because the baby in the book goes hungry and the starvation damages her mind. She never learns to talk, but is Wang Lung's favorite anyway. Had Rebecca seen me in the book? Cleverly guessed about Naomi? I stayed awake in the dark, wondering how I might make myself more like O-lan, hardworking and uncomplaining. And fix my ruined friendship with Wei.

The second week of September, Papa managed to stand up, wash himself, and head to his jobs, to ask if they still existed. While he was in the courtyard getting water from our concrete sink, I stripped his cot to scrub and hang its devastated blanket. Next to his suitcase from Warsaw, I noticed something else. I dropped the bedding and bent down to find a small, dirty, cardboard box. Papa never intruded on my cot. He left the pile underneath it alone, but I reached without hesitation or guilt for the box. The smell was of a root pulled freshly from the ground. Maybe it contained something dangerous, a creature that would leap or some substance that would pour out, maybe even toxic light. The dead smell made me extra awake, as fear can. But with my heart flapping upside down in my chest, I reached inside: Rosy Mischa, my mother's first puppet.

He had brought Rosy Mischa. I draped the dirty blanket over her body and studied her face as if I were seeing Mama herself, her mane of fiery hair, green eyes painted with silver spokes that used to twinkle. The puppet's color had dulled. I licked my finger and wiped dust from her mouth and eyes. "Ni-hao, Rosy."

I lifted the wooden cross attached to her strings and her face tilted as she peered at me. She kicked one leg out, forward, up. She raised an arm, said, "I don't speak Chinese."

"It's just *hello*," I told her, but added, "Witaj," *welcome*, so she'd feel at home. Then I set Rosy down on the cot and reached back into the box for my mother's costume, a leotard and a pair of ragged, woolen tights that smelled like decay. I stripped my ratty pants off and pulled the tights and leotard on. Then I picked the puppet up and carried her to my cot, where Naomi was sleeping. I took out the makeshift puppets I'd made: Wei, Biata, Taube, and the Girl Guides, except for Sally, all with banyan leaves for their hair.

"Meet the Shanghai troupe," I told Rosy Mischa. "Wei, Biata, Rebecca, Taube, Aili, and O-lan from *The Good Earth*. And, Naomi, of course, not a puppet but a girl." Then I whispered, "And I'm Słodkie Lillia, do you remember me?"

The sound of our names woke Naomi. "Li-li-ah! Wo yao moh!" *I want mouse.* She was so tiny and pale it was as if the fever had burned her features away, but her face was cool. I put a hand on her out of habit, and relief drenched me each time at finding her no longer on fire.

"Hi, Naomi," I said, "Do you want to see a show?"

"Yao!" she said.

"Okay. I'll put one on for you."

One Hanukkah in Warsaw, Mama and I wrote a short act for three: Mama, Rosy Mischa, and me, all of us in red. We sang a song about clouds that make magical shapes in the sky. At the end of the song, the clouds joined together to make an acrobatic clown named Bercik. We danced synchronized moves Alenka had choreographed, and Papa laughed when it was over, clapping and dancing tiny Naomi over to kiss us. She was only a baby then—no one expected her to crawl or talk yet. My parents had been full of undiminished joy, and they both preferred presents that didn't last, performances, what they called experiences of beauty.

I held the Rosy puppet and the Wei one. "What's your name?" I said in a boy voice.

"Flower," Rosy Mischa said, "Lillia. Hua." A puppet could learn Chinese right away.

"Oh," said the Wei puppet. "You're the one who ruined my life."

"I'm sorry. I tried to make it better," Rosy Mischa said. "And those things I took were for a baby. For Naomi."

At this, Naomi said, "No-mi!"

"That's right," I said, "Those things were for you. And for our family."

But the Wei puppet said, "Why is your family more important than everyone else's?"

Papa came in then, so skinny I saw ribs through his ragged shirt. He looked just like the puppet I was making of him. He saw me in Mama's leotard, saw my puppets. "What are those?"

"Oh, just some things I made," I said.

He walked over, a slight blue glow collecting around him. "Lillia! You made these?"

I felt shy. He was staring, not at Rosy Mischa, but at my puppets. "They're beautiful, Lillia. They're . . . How did you . . ."

"Just with things I found."

He turned the Wei puppet over in his hand, studying it. I loved him very much then, so much my bones filled with fear. I didn't want to need or love anything. I put one of my fingers in my mouth and bit down on it, hard, pinching the skin with my teeth until it snagged and then tearing it back. The pain made me cry out, and Papa snatched my hand. "Lillia!"

"Why did you hide Rosy Mischa?" I asked, holding my hurt finger.

"I didn't hide it. It was always right here. Did you hide your puppets?"

"No," I said, feeling anger, unsure why, but glad. It was easier than love. My finger ached. "My puppets were right here, too. Why did you bring Rosy Mischa?"

"Oh, Lillia. Because my heart is broken and it reminds me of Alenka. That's why."

This was too painful to tolerate. I sat on the floor, collapsed. "That's why I made mine," I said, looking up. "Because they remind me of what it felt like when I didn't miss you both."

The tears poured from Papa's eyes this time, pure lines like rain down a window, each tear meeting, joining, becoming the next. He didn't even reach up to try to dry them. I bent over myself on the floor, collapsed like a puppet cut from its own strings.

"Yao! Yao!" I looked up at my shouting sister and saw her standing.

"You're standing!" I said, "Keep standing!"

She had seen that Papa was crying and was trying to get to him, waving her arms and staggering toward him until he picked her up and they patted each other. Only she could comfort him, my struggling baby sister, working as hard as I was.

Both of Papa's jobs were gone, and he began looking again, with half his strength and less than half his hope. I, with my ugly secrets, longing, and guilt, began to wear my mother's leotard and tights and plan a Magnifique act. Late at night, before I slept, I touched up Rosy Mischa puppet's face with anything I could find that didn't require stealing.

For her lips, I bit my finger and used a drop of blood.

CHAPTER TWELVE

跳舞起来, Tiaowu Qilai, *Beginning to Dance*

On my sixth Saturday at Magnifique, Madame Su led me to the changing room and handed me a new silk dress, also red, but darker and tighter than the first. A dragon of yellow embroidery thread writhed accusingly up its side. Madame Su stood close to me as I dressed, making my flesh bubble.

"You have been polite at the podium. Tonight we'll see whether you can actually dance."

"Thank you, Madame Su."

I remembered the ticket for the four-dollar Tabarin

Dance, the one Sally had shown us at Rebecca's Girl Guide meeting. Biata had heard about another dance they'd been talking about at school once, and asked with a wide-open, jealous face: "You went to a dance?" Then she had looked at me, her hopeless mirror, our eyes and mouths crumpled by envious sorrow. But Taube had told me this summer that Biata's parents' bar was doing well—she thought this would make me happy, that I was generous! And I hadn't seen Biata since school ended, so maybe she had moved across the bridge and went dancing now with Rebecca and Sally every night. Maybe her parents had prospered right when Papa was sickest. I knew I would never be able to do any childish thing again, any girl thing. I wore my mama's leotard under my dress and walked to the Magnifique stage, the *never* of my childhood life forming above me, wet and dark.

There were stairs, taunting and steep. Madame Su made a pushing motion, gesturing me up as music piped through the room, watery notes that matched the smoke, substanceless yet everywhere, with a beat underneath that made it impossible to think. I was alone on stage. No one had told me what dance to do here and I didn't want to use what I actually felt in my body, had learned as a child, or had imagined would be my Magnifique act. I had to keep everything true about me secret, or I wouldn't be a person anymore. But I also had to prove I was who I'd said I was, Alenka, a dancer so talented they would want to keep me here. I began to shiver, my dress choking me like a snake.

Madame Su waved her arms from the side of the dining room, mimicking and admonishing me: dance. I wove across the stage fast, as if I were drunk or mad. A man in the audience laughed, then another began to clap, slow and mocking. I kept moving, burning under strangers' eyes. My mother controlled the audience when she danced or flew, when she hung suspended by silks, ropes, or trapeze, and then, when she decided to, she could slip back to safety in the wings, back to Papa. But I was at the ugly mercy of those watching, a puppet controlled by Madame Su and men. I fled down the stairs, away from the stage, back toward the room of evil-smelling cabinets and naked girls, where Rebecca's pink dress and Taube's sash awaited, but before I had pushed the door open, Madame Su intercepted me. She took my arm and pulled me toward her. "Get back on stage or don't come back at all." She held my hand almost gently then, as if she were my mother, walking me to school. But we ended up at the stairs to the glaring stage. She gave me a push. "You want this job," she reminded me.

I returned to the stage with my face lifted too high to see anyone in the audience, or for them to see my eyes, leaking. I danced this way, looking up, drinking the light from above me, moving my body as I'd been taught my entire childhood, trying not to think about who was watching or who I was, just imagining I could be both puppet and puppeteer. My mind could make my body dance, my body having no mind of its own. I lifted my right leg straight up and held it, tearing the rest of the dress' side seam, turning a full circle, the music seeping into me as the audience went silent. I felt the heat of their watching and told myself I didn't mind, that the ruined dress didn't matter, I had her leotard under it, was dancing for my family. I moved down the stairs on my toes, but this time instead of escaping, I carried two chairs back with me onto the stage. Everyone waited as I pushed the two chairs just close enough to each other. Then I stood behind them and put my hands on their backs, lifted myself so slowly I almost wasn't moving, time wasn't moving. Everything became un-real. The room was still except for the music and the vibra-tion of so many watching eyes. I felt the collective breathing of the men, too, waiting to see—would I fall, could I stay up, could I bend my body into something other than my body? I imagined Madame Su's heartbeat and breath, distinct from the rest. If I did well enough, I would save myself from having to visit the back rooms with elaborately carved beds, draping canopies. We all knew, without having to be told, what hap-pened in those rooms.

I held myself above the chairs in a handstand and then began extending my legs over my back. When they were at my shoulders, I looked out straight at the audience. I bent my knees until my feet were on either side of my face, and I was a circle. I could go back this way, I thought, to the beginning, to some time before I'd performed here. I untwisted as slowly as I had twisted, lifted back into a straight line, legs up. With as much control as I'd ever had, I lowered my feet onto the floor and stood, my dress torn, but still on me like a second skin. I curtsied. Small, shocked applause lit like the flame in our metal bucket and built into violent clapping.

As they clapped, I told myself I had given them nothing, that this act was something I had given myself. I couldn't tell if I was lying. The girl who had asked me if I thought I was pretty approached the stage, and I passed her as I descended the stairs. I saw Aili among the tables of men, where she met my eyes for the first time, clapping deliberately, nodding as if she knew something. She crossed her hands over her chest. What gesture was it?

At the joyful Stanislav Cyrk, my mama and Kassia's used to dance a fight sequence, wearing silver armor, scaled and tough. They spun and fought until both were lying on the mat, only to rise wearing wings. Protected by invisible strings, they rose holding on, not for life anymore but for whatever might come after. And as they flew over the ring, people gasped at their beauty, two women winged and magical, red hair pouring over Mama's shoulders, Ana's black hair a sleek helmet. They danced in the air, free of human pettiness and vulnerability.

I crossed my hands over my heart at Aili. It didn't matter whether I knew what it meant. I vowed to double my efforts to make my own puppets beautiful, to create my circus, to ask Aili to join me for a different kind of dance, a different audience. Maybe someday we could make an act that freed us. For now, Madame Su came to collect me. She handed me six CN, twice the usual, because I had danced. She said, "I will introduce you to Mr. Takati. He has requested that you join him and his friends at their table."

I wondered about what the girl in the dressing room had said about extra money. Would I be paid extra for joining someone at his table? I had nowhere to put the six CN, so I folded the bills into a cube I tucked in my palm, made a fist. Suddenly, Aili was next to me, her hand out, jiggling as if to say, "Coins." She tapped her chest and held her hand out, open. Did she mean I should give her my money? I handed the cube to her, then followed Madame Su. Aili pointed at the locker room, me, herself. I was to find her there? I nodded and began praying that she would return the money to me. What if she took it? Maybe Wei had told her why he'd lost his job. Maybe Aili had told Wei that I worked here, something I didn't want him to know, even though she worked here, too. The money was enough for a jin of rice, vegetables, bean curd, sugarcane, soy sauce, oil, eggs, and flour. Maybe even a ticket someday to the other kind of dance, an enchanted one where Rebecca and Sally kissed boys from school like Benjamin and Abraham.

Madame Su pushed me toward a table of men, and I glanced back to see Aili walking onto the stage, standing directly under the spotlight, and looking out as she began to dance, as if inviting eye contact, daring everyone to watch, watch closer. Could I watch her and not be among those watching her? Her brows were arched, and she looked ferocious.

"Alenka!" Madame Su hissed, and I twisted back fast toward her and the table, around which six men—two in military jackets, the others in suits—were seated. "Do you think you're here to be entertained?"

"No, no," I said. "I'm sorry. I—"

Her voice cooled into something that sounded expensive. "Mr. Takati, this is Alenka, one of our European beauties. She danced in a troupe in Europe before arriving here in Shanghai."

I looked at Madame Su. Did she believe this? Mr. Takati said, "No wonder she's such an accomplished performer," and then, "Please sit." Madame Su vanished, and I sat in the softest chair since Warsaw, feeling abandoned.

Mr. Takati poured thick wine into a glass in front of me. It looked like blood. I had tasted wine at Passover at Babcia's, sweet and safe like grape juice. Now I was afraid, but I took a sip: coins, dirt, something rubbery. The color of it coated my throat and empty stomach. I must have made a face, because Mr. Takati laughed.

"Maybe your taste is more expensive than this red?"

I didn't know what that meant, so I smiled down at the table.

"Where are you from?" he asked.

I said, "Warsaw," wondering if he would find this disgusting, the way the first man I'd met at Magnifique had, but Mr. Takati only nodded, as if this meant something we both understood.

He said, "How fortunate you're here," and I tried not to look around the room, not to reveal my desire to run again.

I took another thick sip, remembered, be polite. "Where are you from, sir?"

"I am from Hiroshima. Perhaps someday you will visit."

"Oh," I said.

"We can prepare you. Start with konbanwa. *Good evening.*"

I said it, "Konbanwa," and a stab of unhappiness pierced me. What if Wei saw me speaking Japanese with this man? How could I leave, and where was Aili? Was she watching? Would she tell Wei?

"Are you hungry?" Mr. Takati asked, and my mood changed instantly, excitement coursing through me, warming my limbs. Should I deny how hungry I was? Had he seen it? Had I drunk the wine too fast, as if it were soup? I was terribly hungry. Madame Su wouldn't want me to say so. But if he could get me food, any humiliation was worth it. "Yes," I said plainly.

He laughed. "Oh. A woman who speaks frankly," he said. "Then let's order something for you to eat?" I realized then that his question was an offer, that "are you hungry" for some people still meant polite talk, meant rules, meant something social. I worked not to grind my teeth or let my stomach roar above my voice. I wondered: Was I a woman? One who spoke frankly?

"That would be lovely, sir, yes." At this, he tipped his head back and laughed more.

"No need to call me sir," he said, "We can be more informal than that. Call me Oue."

I would never call him by name at all. I had made this childish but reasonable decision with some of my friends' parents at home, too, the ones who said not to call them Pan or Pani, *Mr.* or *Mrs.*, but didn't mean it and therefore made it impossible to call them anything. Kassia's parents I had always been allowed to call Ana and Nacek, because they loved and respected children and were an extension of my family, the circus.

Mr. Takati beckoned the waitress over, and she glared at me while he ran his finger down a page. Then he pointed as she nodded, smiling. "Of course, Mr. Takati, sir." He did not tell her to call him Oue. She glided away as if on wheels.

I tried to ask questions that might sound adult and correct: what his hometown of Hiroshima was like, *the largest and most beautiful island in Japan*, how he liked Shanghai, *well enough*, how long he had been here, *long enough*, and then what he did in Shanghai, *I work*.

Finally, maybe tired of me, he raised his eyebrows and said, "Watch the show. Relax."

I turned back to the stage, worried I had asked too much, or asked wrong. A girl I didn't know was on stage, twisting her body as if it hurt to dance, and I looked at my hands, longed to chew them. I tried not to watch her, not to see or think anything at all.

The waitress returned carrying a heavy platter, covered by an upside-down silver bowl she lifted. The smell of meat rose, so delicious I swallowed, thought, *Lillia! Stay upright!* I worked not to fall forward onto the food. If I could just behave, just do a good job at this dinner and make Mr. Takati like me, maybe there would be more meat.

"It's pork," he said, in his voice a little laughter, thick and difficult, like the wine.

"It's fine for me to eat it," I said, thinking of Babcia's kosher kitchen, my beautiful babcia herself, her parrot, her painted ceiling, braided silver hair, English books, the chair up her stair-case, soft bedrooms on the second floor. Where was she? What was she eating? She would want me to have meat, even pork. I tried to go slow, not to lick juice from the plate, scrape the fork, gnash my bony teeth or starving mouth. All impossible. I drank every bit left of wilted green vegetable, butter flooding my body with hope.

"You enjoyed that," Mr. Takati said. I looked up with a white shock of loss. My plate was empty.

"Yes," I remembered to say, "thank you."

Maybe now he would say something that scared me, or touch my arm or leg, or lean in close, maybe even put his mouth on my cheek or lips. Would an old and unfamiliar man be the first to kiss me? I imagined telling Rebecca, the way she had told me, giggling, about Abraham. But Mr. Takati cleared his throat. "I hope you will dine with me again."

Out of my sideways eye I saw Madame Su gesture angrily. I hadn't done a good enough job, or I was to do something else now, but what? Mr. Takati stood and so did I. I walked to the door, where Mr. Takati turned and said good night. Confused, I returned to the dressing room, peeled my red silk skin, and wrapped back up in rags. I focused on the feeling of my full belly, food sending strength to my arms, legs, eyes, and mind. My thinking cleared. I loved Papa and Naomi, couldn't wait to get to 54 Ward and see them, to buy the food that would keep them fed, too. I was feeling this joy, hoping Aili would come with my money when I realized the skinny-necked girl was standing close to me again, staring. I hadn't noticed her come in. My happiness evaporated. We watched each other. She was striking and childish, blotchy cheeks, milk teeth streaked with lipstick I saw when she flashed a sudden, artificial smile. "Ni-hao, Alenka."

I sputtered in English, "Your name?"

"Fu," she said. A word I knew. *Fortune.*

I pointed at myself. "Not Alenka," I said, "Lillia." It was the first time I'd said my real name at Magnifique. I didn't know why I wanted to tell her. "Hua," I added, *Flower.*

"Nide jia?" she asked, *your home?*

I said, "Meiyou." *Don't have one.* I felt suddenly too tired to continue doing anything at all, standing, speaking, even thinking. But she didn't say anything, and I thought she hadn't understood. I wanted her to understand me. "Ni ne?" I asked. *You?*

She blinked hard, doll-eyed. "Wo ye meiyou," *I also don't have one.* So maybe she had understood.

Then she asked, "Duo shao?" *How much?*

"How much what?" I asked in English.

She made the coin gesture Aili had made. I looked around, hoping again to see Aili. If she stole my money, would I tell Wei? Fu said, "Takati xiansheng." *Mr. Takati.* She made the coin gesture again. "Duo shao?" *How much?*

I shook my head. He hadn't given me money. Maybe I had failed at something. She shrugged and then her mouth opened and some laughing sounds came out. I asked, "Ni xiao shenma?"

You're laughing at what? But her expression and her mouth both closed, went dark.

I turned: Madame Su.

"Unless you're working, *you* girls will pay *me*. Alenka, Mr. Takati requested that you come early next Saturday, so you can sit with him."

I did not look back at Fu, who would envy this news. I just walked out, desperate to find Aili. Someone brushed my arm. "Aili!"

"Li-li-ah," she said, her pronunciation like Naomi's, like Wei's.

She handed me bills, more than there had been before, too many, nine CN. I said, "Liu," *six*, and pointed at myself. But she shook her head. She pointed back at herself and said, "Shi'er" *twelve*. She had made twelve CN! Then she pointed at me, raised her hand, and slashed it from up to down. We would split what we made in half. This made me want to make more money even than before. How had she made twelve CN in one night? I heard her sing something under her breath when she saw Fu, and I heard Fu scream at her. The only words I could make out from the song were *country*, *city*, and *girl*. Was she making fun of Fu? And if so, why was she kind to me?

— ▣ —

Rosh Hashanah. Leo came into the kitchen humming, carrying an apple. My eyes followed the fruit as if it were a jewel I might steal, red in our gray concrete kingdom, where coal smoke and dirt ruled. I would leap onto the table and kick the apple from Leo's hands; it would fly up, peel twirling as I tipped my head back and opened my mouth, full of pearly teeth. An apple! We were forbidden to eat anything uncooked.

"Good morning, Lillia," Leo said. "Are you off to school?"

Apple. Apple. "Not yet. They're not finished moving yet. We start in winter."

"Would you like some apple?"

"Oh! Yes, please."

"It's safe?" Papa asked.

"Peeled," Leo said. "Should be good! A Yeshiva boy gave it to Talia, and she saved it."

"Yes, please," I said again, in case he had forgotten, and he cut the apple slowly. I imagined a fan of a thousand thin, skinless slices instead of the five actual ones. Leo would hand Naomi and me hundreds each. I slid a slice onto my tongue, feeling the tart fruit melt, willing myself, *Don't chew*. It was my first taste of fresh fruit since the ship. I counted my slices, tried to taste and appreciate each one, Wei's voice in my mind: yi, er, san. There were really only three. Leo had given me three, and Naomi two.

The Song sisters came then, singing into the kitchen: "Liang zhi laohu. Liang zhi laohu, pao de kuai!" Naomi clapped and shouted, "Lee Ang Jeh Hoo Hoo!" And lifted her arms. The eldest Song sister, Mei-Mei, picked up my sister. "Liang zhi laohu," she sang to Naomi.

"She's singing," I realized. "That's what lee ang is—she's been singing—it's a song about tigers." I told Papa and Leo the words: *two tigers, two tigers, run very fast, run very fast. One has no ears, one has no tail.*

I sang the last line, "Zhen qiguai, zhen qiguai," *How strange, how strange.* Naomi was clapping, but a flicker of sorrow crossed Papa's face. He was missing her first sentences and songs, and so was Mama. Her words, other than my name, were in a language he didn't know. I was sad for him, but to me, Naomi's choice made sense. Why pretend we had ever lived—or would ever live—anywhere but here?

— ◙ —

I took Naomi to temple for the high holidays, because Babcia and Mama would have liked it, because I was worried God couldn't hear anything but my worst thoughts, and because I was afraid of myself at Magnifique. I walked to Ohel Moshe carrying Naomi, singing *apple, apple* in English, singing *ping-guo* in Chinese. We sang the song about tigers, my favorite line the refrain at the end: *How strange. How strange.* Shanghai still felt strange, even autumn itself unfamiliar, leaves turning, the months falling into piles at our feet.

The temple smelled like wood and pages, dusty, lovely Warsaw before the war. Those from the Heime and shops arrived. There were no soldiers. Nobody walked with her head bent so low that her shoulders appeared broken. The Aron Kodesh on the eastern wall was intact, an unburnt Torah inside of it, safe pages of Hebrew. I thought of our temple at home, our rabbi's sweet voice speaking its too-little warning: "Things may get worse."

Rabbi Mer Ashkanazi's Birchot HaShachar, welcoming us and thanking God for our lives, sent me straight to Babcia's house, all its rooms still in my mind. Every Friday evening, Mama and Babcia were in the kitchen, braiding challah, roasting chicken. I was lying on the living room carpet on my stomach, drawing, wearing a clean dress, my long hair braided. Mama came to find me, bent to kiss me, laughed a strand of notes, and asked me to set the table. I remembered cloth napkins, crystal glasses, cream candles in golden holders. Smoke. But suddenly everything was gone except for *real*: the smoke at Magnifique on Saturday nights, my hunger, my hungry sister sleeping in my numb arms, Rabbi Mer Ashkanazi's Baruch She'amar v'hayah ha'olam, *Blessed is the One who spoke and the world came into being*.

I thought of the world coming into being and changing. How little of the world I'd seen or would see, even though I'd traveled all the way to Shanghai. Somewhere, some point at the core of the planet was equidistant between home and here, a spot—of what? Dirt? Lava? Water? It was another place I'd never see. Was she closer to Warsaw or Shanghai? Was she anywhere at all? And what did it mean or feel like to be nowhere? Loneliness rose on either side of me like panes of glass, pressing me flat. I could see through them but couldn't reach, touch, or know anyone. I was supremely, impossibly alone, holding

Naomi tight through the *Amidah*, the cantor's repetitive echo a shadow at my back.

The men sat in their separate space, below us. Gabriel had the honor of opening the ark; he carried himself with the calm confidence of a Japanese soldier. Our voices rose in a chorus of the "Song of the Day" and for a moment the room glowed. I retreated, tried to find a way back to Babcia's house, but the path to that memory was no longer there. I saw instead my mama that last night in Warsaw, heard her screaming, felt Papa grabbing Naomi and me, running.

We walked home in the dark, a bite of winter already in the night air. I struggled under Naomi, whose weight doubled when she slept. Suddenly, Gabriel was at my side. "Rabbi Mer Ashkenazi is the finest rabbi I have known," he said, as if I were an adult. "In this respect and others, Shanghai isn't so bad after all. Wouldn't you agree, Lillia?"

Low-hanging trees lined the lilong, *alleys* off the rows of attached houses where children played, even in the cold dark. I didn't want to agree with Gabriel, didn't want to answer him. I said, "Each alley is a whole world. All these people count as much as we do."

"Of course," he said, as if this were a stupid idea.

"Our lives aren't important," I clarified. A cluster of red-mouthed women appeared in front of us. I didn't want Gabriel to see them, didn't want to see them myself when I was with him. I looked across the street at a strip bright with light from businesses and automobiles. If he noticed the women,

Gabriel didn't show it. He seemed surprised by what I'd said, offended even.

"Each life is precious," he argued. "That there are many lives doesn't diminish the value."

"Yes it does. My mother matters to me, but every person in the world feels about someone the way I feel about her. How can God help us all?"

"We can help God help us. Think of Miriam," Gabriel said. "A prophet, able to lead the other women in dance in spite of her suffering. It was the strength God granted her that allowed that, not her singing, not her tambourine, not even the dancing itself."

Did he know something about my secret life? I didn't speak, lest I reveal anything else.

He continued, "Maybe your mother is doing work like Miriam, who shapes the entire Exodus narrative." I tried to pick up speed, but Gabriel kept up. "May I carry Naomi for you?"

Too relieved to say no, I handed my sister over, and Gabriel held her tight, carried her carefully. I felt a terrible mix of gratitude and unhappiness. "Doesn't Miriam's name mean bitterness?" I asked.

"Well, her context is bitter," Gabriel told me. "But she becomes a prophetess and uses her visionary power to save her brother and other Jewish babies, even though she is born into slavery. And she's also called Puah, or *Whisperer*."

"But what if she had no power and couldn't make anything better?"

"But you," Gabriel said, "*are* making things better. By being a good daughter and sister."

"I didn't mean me," I lied.

At home, Taube had tried to make pirogues from rice she'd pounded into paste. Talia played the violin while Leo swayed next to her, smiling with his giant teeth, and I thought we might be okay. We might study languages and Torah, wear shirts with Kadoorie insignias, teach our sisters to sing in Chinese. We might learn to be like Miriam, to save ourselves and each other. I drank hot soup, helped Naomi drum on overturned bowls, let her stand on my feet, hold my hands and walk. Taube surprised us with an extra bread she'd traded for a hat. She had even found honey on the black market at Wayside Park, since there was none at Abraham's Dry Goods. Three apples Talia had brought decorated the cots we pushed together into a table. We were alive, and that night in my cot, overrun by small biting bugs, I thanked God for everything left: Papa; Naomi; Wei; Aili; Taube; Leo; Talia; Rebecca; Dr. Hao; Dr. Rosen; the Song girls, bright-eyed, rambunctious playmates for Naomi. For Gabriel's compliment, Miriam's example. For Shanghai. When I was done with English, I repeated my prayers in Polish, dzieki ci, boże, and Chinese, ganxie shangdi, *thank you, God.*

Once everyone else was asleep, I moved my pitiful puppet parts across my cot in the dark, telling myself a story in which some of the puppets were murdered, some died of typhus, but others escaped on a ship made of paper. A brown-and-green tangle of banyan branches and floodwater ran underneath them. The woman who had jumped over the railing of the *Conte Rosso* tried to leap, but I offered her a tiny ladder made of twigs. The real woman was still in the sea, had not arrived in Shanghai, stayed caught in that moment forever. But I hadn't jumped, and now I was this Lillia. Papa was here, alive, working until his bones popped. If he had jumped, I would never have seen him dance with Naomi after she spoke her first word, or listen to Rebecca play piano, or walk me to school those first days. I put the Papa puppet with the lucky ones, let them find their wives and mothers at the foot of my cot. There were many ways for a story to end. I wanted to turn myself into Miriam, a whisperer who knew what was coming and made it better, made it matter. I assembled and reassembled bodies, my only constants hunger and wonder.

CHAPTER THIRTEEN

饥饿, Ji'e, *Hunger*

I sat with Mr. Takati the third Saturday night in October, hoping
he would order pork. When he did, I confused my hunger for
it with a more general hunger. I wanted to do anything in my
power to make sure he wouldn't stop inviting me, feeding me. I
didn't know what I wanted. Mr. Takati's friend, Mr. Otani, was
seated with us, and Fu, who hated me. I cast quick glances at
her, to see if she was mocking me. She was busy talking to Mr.
Otani, but he had ordered no food for her, and I could feel her
staring at my plate.

"What is your business?" I asked Mr. Takati, looking away from Fu.

Mr. Takati looked like he might laugh, but when he didn't, I thought I had narrowly passed a test. "Import and export," he said, and he could tell I didn't know what this meant, so he added, "I buy beautiful things here and take them to those who wish to buy them in Japan."

I asked what things.

"Porcelain," he said, "vases, shards, urns. And fabrics, sometimes silks." I nodded, as if I could imagine buying such luxuries myself. Then Mr. Takati did laugh, although I wasn't sure why. "I like delicate things," he said. "It gives me pleasure to move them from place to place without allowing harm to come to them."

He touched my cheek then and his fingers on my skin caused needles to prickle me, injecting points of heat. Madame Su appeared, smiling her wide client smile. "Is everyone happy here?" Her voice was warm oil. "Can I get anyone anything, Mr. Takati? Mr. Otani?"

"We are doing just fine, thank you," Mr. Takati said, sliding his fingers down my chin and off, as if they'd fallen. "Just hoping to see Alenka dance as soon as we can."

"Ah," Madame Su said, her top lip pulling slightly off of her teeth, an expression of displeasure Fu and I recognized but maybe the men did not. "Your wish is our command, of course, Takati-san." Now she looked down in a way that made me think she'd once been young.

But Mr. Takati didn't seem to notice. He turned back to me. "Let me hear you count," he said. He meant in Japanese, so I worked the round, quiet sounds out of my mouth, payment for the meat I'd eaten: "Ichi, ni, san, shi, go, roku, shichi, hachi, kyuu, juu."

"You do that almost as well as you dance," Mr. Takati said.

"Thank you."

"In Japan, we cherish women who are committed to the arts. Our best and most respected entertainers are women."

I tried to look like I understood, nodded seriously, wished for my mother or Taube.

"Patrons have genuine and meaningful relationships with performers," Mr. Takati said. Did he want a relationship with me? I couldn't tell whether he meant this in contrast to here or because he was reminded by me of the women who performed in Japan. Maybe this was why he came to Magnifique? "They're called geishas," he said. "It means 'artful ones.' Our artful ones dance and sing, and some recite poetry."

"I know a poem," I said. "One from school in Poland."

This made Mr. Takati smile, but he didn't ask to hear the poem. Instead, he watched me with a care that made me nervous. "Alenka, if you don't mind my asking, how old are you?"

I said, "Nineteen," and looked away, because I didn't want to know whether he believed me or not. I caught Fu's eye, shooting me furious beams, maybe because Mr. Otani seemed so bored. But before Mr. Takati could ask how old I really was, or

Fu could embarrass me, Madame Su came close with a crooked finger, calling me over.

She pointed at the stage, so I climbed onto it and this time lay flat, facing the audience. I looked at no one in particular, afraid to single Mr. Takati out, afraid not to. I bent my back and brought my feet to my shoulders, reaching to hold them, hearing my already torn dress rip further, but pulling my feet forward anyway, making my body a moon before stretching out again, rising into a handstand, toes pointed, dress torn but too tight to fall. I turned then, completed a circle upside down. The rotation of a Shanghai day. Or year. My hair was just long enough to fall over part of my face. No one could see my mouth shaping the words of the poem Mr. Takati hadn't asked me to recite, the same one I hadn't finished at Rebecca's: "Where are you sorceress, goddess, queen? Life-making, crazy, homicidal water spirit. You, wonder-working, immortal Hydra from Lyrna, are a Siren, calling me to Scylla, singing the graves."

I came out of the handstand and turned six clean flips across the stage, ripping the dress entirely, Alenka's leotard protecting me underneath. I twirled, rose up on my toes, and danced gracefully, reminded myself I was an acrobat and a dancer, that it was possible to be more than one girl. I whispered, "Mama," and bent at the elbows as she'd taught me, as I'd practiced, and I took the stairs on my hands, a fifty-six second handstand. The audience thundered, when I reached the bottom. I stood and straightened, curtsied toward Mr. Takati.

Now he would not think the performers in Japan were

better than we were here. Now he, and hopefully Madame Su, would be reminded of my talent and would let me keep working here, not make me take private visits in the back rooms. But had all those mornings of practicing holding her handstands, been for Magnifique, for this? Madame Su met me at the bottom of the stairs. "You'll have to fix that." She pointed to the ruined fabric.

"It will only rip again," I said.

She laughed deeply, as if drinking something delicious. Then she narrowed her eyes at me. "That's the best part of your dance. But you knew that, of course."

When I said good night to Mr. Takati, he patted me on the head. "You're a sweet girl, Alenka," he said, and I thanked him before making my confused way to the dressing room, where Fu found me fighting my way out of the dress. Did Mr. Takati think I was a child? And was I one? What sweet girl worked here? Fu and I stood side by side, transforming. She looked as sad as I felt, and this time, instead of anything mean, she whispered, "Do you know why Madame Su is the boss?"

I shook my head.

"A rich man gave Magnifique to her," Fu said, "when he loved her."

I didn't ask anything else, because I didn't want to know more than I had to about Madame Su. Or rich men. Or what any of it had to do with me.

Then Fu said, "Here." She held a needle and thread, and pointed at my torn dress. "You must"—she made a sewing motion—"or mafan." Or *trouble*. I was still thinking about this small kindness the next day, when we had disappeared into our other, Sunday selves, invisible at Magnifique.

— ⊠ —

Kadoorie reopened the last week of October. I told Papa I was going, washed, dressed, and packed my school bag. But I walked into the dawn light of Ward Road and went to Chusan Road instead of the new school building on East Yuhung. I knocked hard on Wei and Aili's door, and he surprised me by answering, his eyes puffed almost shut. He just looked out at me, didn't speak. I didn't deserve to go to school anymore if Wei wasn't allowed to work there.

"Wei, I'm sorry," I told him. "Please."

Nothing.

I asked, "Can we talk? Did you find a new job?"

Still, nothing. But he didn't walk back into the hallway behind him, didn't close his eyes completely, didn't wave me away. We stood there. His hands were black, maybe from ink or paint. I wanted to know what he did now, what had happened.

I whispered, "Please forgive me. I'm working now, too, not studying anymore."

This lit something in his face, made him twitch.

"Please," I said again. "Tell me something, anything. Talk to me, please?" Now he would never overhear lessons at Kadoorie again, or work on his English in the school building. He had loved being there. It had made him feel like a student. We waited.

"Have you found work, too?" I asked, talking too much, for too long, looping, my voice unnaturally loud. "I heard that at Kadoorie they will make the students learn Japanese this year." I hoped this would make him not want to be near Kadoorie anyway, that he'd feel better about not being allowed to work there.

At this, he spoke immediately, as if he hadn't been silent for months. "You say no," he said, in cubes of English. I felt as if ice had been thrown over me.

He held his hand palm out like a policeman and switched languages, but kept talking. I wanted him to talk more, no matter what he said.

"Youtai ren keyi shuo bu," *Jewish people can say no.*

How could I respond without making him shuttle back into silence forever? I tried to sound obedient when I repeated his words: "Say no?" I asked. "How?"

He stared. "Shuo bu," he repeated plainly, *say no.*

I stared back. No? Fine, then, no. No to the war. To losing my life, my mama, my house, Piotr, Kassia, Janusz, Papa as Papa, everything I'd been and known and loved. No, thank you. No to dancing in front of Mr. Takati, to the blazing confusion of how I felt around him, his voice, language, the food he alone could feed me. No to the warm, painful burn of the attention he paid me. No. A fast and miserable rage caught inside me, similar to what I felt when I loved and needed Papa most.

Wei raised his eyebrows. "Zhongguo ren shuo bu?" *Chinese people say no?* He drew his hand across his throat, a bayonet. His gesture and the way his face tightened gave me a wet, choking feeling.

Now I couldn't stop, even if he never spoke to me again. "Youtai ren!" *Jews!* I shouted the word, because it was true of us, too. I pulled a blade made of my hand across my own neck. "If we say no, we'll be killed, too. That's why we're here—that's why we—"

"Bu," he cut me off. "No. Riben ren xihuan youtai ren," *Japanese like Jews.*

I understood. Aili had told him. That I sat with Mr. Takati, licking pork from my fingers, speaking his numbers in Japanese, in my softest voice, music and smoke playing behind us. That I contorted myself into pleasing shapes for Mr. Takati. Wei had stopped speaking to me for more reasons than just my stupid thieving at Kadoorie and his lost job. I sat down on the dirty ground then, wrapped my arms around my knees, and said the sentence I'd practiced: "Wo yao biaoyan," *I want to perform.* "Gen ni he Aili," *with you and Aili.* "Can I show you, please?"

I didn't wait for him to say yes or no, just pushed myself up, out of my own sorrow and embarrassment, past him into his house, without asking. At the end of a dark, oily hallway I found an open door, and turned—this was their room? Wei stood behind me, nodding. It was a closet off the kitchen, a tangle of bedding on the floor. I tried to imagine him and Aili living here and continued to a cement room in which I found two chairs to drag back to back.

I slowly put a hand on each chair, shook, checked my arms, bent, and began to lift myself, straightening, trying to fly above that blank cement space, as I brought my legs over my shoulders. I wanted to show Wei I could be someone else, someone better, maybe even magical, but I had no words for what I needed to say, had only this. He watched in silence as I unfolded.

I was hoping for amazement, joy, even just understanding, some sign he might forgive me. Finally, he took pity. "Biaoyan," he said softly, *performance*, "is bad life."

I didn't respond, because I didn't know how.

He said, "Hurt," meaning my act.

"It's not real pain," I said. I could not ask him to be in my show, could not say or give or make anything else. I couldn't be alone or be with anyone or return to school or move.

"Can we go outside?" I whispered, and maybe he felt how trapped I was, because he helped me up. We made our slow way out and through the streets as the city's light changed from dim and early to mid-morning bright. We walked for a long time without talking, until Wei asked, "Wei shenma?" *Why?* He tipped his head down, showing me myself, asking why I watched the ground.

"Wo pa bingrende lian," I said, hopeful because he'd asked me anything. *I'm afraid of the soldiers' faces.*

"Zheyang ye haipa," he said, and I saw the words one at a time: *this way, also, can, fear.* "You are Jewish," he continued, but this time he said it gently, as if he meant to comfort me. He did not say again that the Japanese liked me but would kill him. And I did not tell him I was afraid in a way he didn't have to be, because I was a girl.

When Shanse Road crossed Fokien Road, I saw a temple on the corner, people pouring in. "What's that?" I pointed.

"Hong Miao," Wei said. I knew half of this word, the Hong meant *rainbow*. Maybe Miao was *temple*, making this the temple of the rainbow.

"Wo yao qu," I said, *I want to go.*

"To Hong Miao?" He looked confused.

"Yes."

"Xing," *okay.*

We wandered in. The air was thick with incense and choking hope that reminded me of the Heime, of mosquito coils we had burned our first summer here, disappearing into curls of smoke and engulfing the insects that devoured us anyway.

I turned to Wei. "Nide fumu zai nali?" *Where are your parents?*

"Wode baba," he said, *my father.* He tapped on his chest, then crossed his hands over each other through the air to indicate the end of something. I didn't know the Chinese. I thought of Aili gesturing to me at Magnifique, crossing her arms. "His heart?"

"Ta de xin," he said, *his heart,* and then, "Wo baba bu zai le." *My father's not here anymore.*

"Ni mama?" I asked, *your mother?*

"Yes. Ta ye bu zai le," he said, *she's also gone.* "Wo chusheng de shihou," *when I was born,* "Xianzai, wo"—he pointed back at himself—"he Aili," *now it's just me and Aili.*

He was an orphan, like the boy in Rebecca's book, *Oliver Twist.*

"Wo mama," I said, *my mother,* "ye bu zai le," *is gone, too.* I lifted my arms above my head, wound my hands together, and turned a circle, maybe to escape what I'd said, to return to my body from the terror of my mind. Wei was watching me. I raised my right leg high enough to catch it with my hand and hold it like a fluttering bird. I said, "Wode Mama tiaowu," *my mother was a dancer,* "gen Aili yiyang," *like Aili.*

Wei said in a soft voice, "Gen ni yiyang," *like you.* Did he mean to be kind or cruel? I didn't know, just wanted him to keep talking to me, not to take all the words away again. We walked toward a stone Buddha gazing from a forest of incense that bloomed around its sandy base. Each dot of fiery light was a wish for someone's mother, father, sister, home. Maybe a God who allowed war wanted us to doubt him. I pulled someone else's incense out, then stuck it back into the sand elsewhere and said, out loud, "Please let my mother be okay. Please let her come here." I imagined her rising from the sand, in instant response to my prayer, dancing with me. I took another piece of incense, licked my finger and thumb, and pressed out the lit tip before tucking the incense into my waistband. Then I saw the dish of coins, people's offerings, and I moved quickly, as if to put the rest of my incense down, sweeping my hand across the coin dish and skimming as many coins as I could. Four stuck in my palm. I made a fist, wove my way fast back toward the entrance. I didn't deserve Wei, didn't deserve anything. As soon as I got to the door, I ran.

"Lillia! Hua!" Wei called after me. "Deng wo ba," *wait for me.* I kept moving but so did he, and he caught up, running. Twice, his hand brushed mine. My heart rattled and clapped. He said, "Slower." I slowed down and our hands kept brushing. Mine held the burning coins, stolen straight from God. I used them to buy four steamed buns at a stand, and Wei let me. He didn't criticize, didn't ask, didn't tell me what was right or wrong. I handed him one of the buns and tore one open for myself.

Heat from the filling smelled like pork, like Magnifique. We bit into the sticky, sweet, salty bread, flavor everywhere, turning my mind into a rainbow of colors and numbers: red, orange, yellow, green, blue, indigo, violet, yi, er, san, si, wu, liu, qi. I realized, eating, that the Chinese numbers one and seven, yi and qi, rhyme. I told Wei this, as if he didn't know Chinese better than I did, and one of us started laughing, and then we were standing so close together, eating and counting in Chinese, rhyming digits, and I thought someday we might be older, still laughing for no reason, or for a reason we both knew but didn't have to say. Maybe we would have spent years eating and laughing together.

I saved the other two steamed buns for Papa and Naomi, who ate them cold, so grateful I shuddered. Naomi shouted,

"Yao! Yao!" *Want, want.* Papa kissed my head as Naomi tipped her sweet face back, laughing.

Papa said, "Thank you so much for those buns. How was school today?"

I said, "I learned a lot."

Naomi amplified my half-lie: "A yot a yot a yot," she sang.

— ◙ —

Magnifique, Magnifique. Two equally powerful parts of myself pulled me apart, one hoping Mr. Takati would be there to feed me, teach me, appreciate me, see me, that I'd be picked from all the angry, hopeful girls, while the other prayed he would never be back from his trip to Japan. Please, that half begged, let no one invite me to his table, lean so close he might lunge or put his fingers on my face, trace my neck. I didn't dare ask Madame Su when or whether Mr. Takati would return. The whereabouts of someone important was not my business. I made less money, danced less often, stood at the hostess stand. I waited in a shadow for Aili. I had only four CN, and I gave her two. She'd made ten CN and gave me five. "Thank you," I said, and wanting to be kind, to give her something but having nothing to give, I added, "Ni de gege hen hao," *your brother is very good.* The five words lined up, came out true. I felt better.

Aili's eyes were even wider up close. "Ta ye xihuan ni," *he likes you, too.*

Winged acrobats climbed my spine, and music played in my mind. I wanted to ask how much, if love, what she knew. I wanted to say that maybe I loved him, he was my real friend, the only one in Shanghai other than Naomi who made me feel less lonely. But all I managed was "I'm glad. I'm not—as kind—as he is."

She said, "Wo ting bu dong yingyu," *I don't speak English.*

I wanted something so powerfully then I didn't know how to tell her, what to say or do.

"Wo yao biaoyan," I tried, as I had with Wei, *I want to perform.*

When she didn't respond, I repeated it and added "gen ni," *with you,* and "bu zai zher," *not here.* I hardly breathed, just waited, desperate for her to understand, to say yes, to help me make something other than sorrow, dirty rice, rat habitats, and humiliating hope. But she stayed still. So I tried harder, tried a new way, held imaginary strings, first below me, making a puppet move, and then above me so I became the puppet. I pointed at myself and her.

"Yes?" I asked her. "Ni?" *You?* "Please?"

When she still didn't respond, I began to dance, this time bending into a bridge, flipping, standing on my hands and landing. I asked again, "Biaoyan?" *Perform?*

She said, "Wei gaosu wo le," *Wei told me.*

She had let me keep on, a patient parent applauding her child? I was unhappy until she lifted her arm above her, created her own strings, became a puppet, too. She pointed one leg into a straight, beautiful kick and then followed with the other. She was saying yes. This dance was for me, and I almost drowned in my own hope.

I clapped as she told a story, dancing and sprinkling words—English and Chinese—over me like the snowflakes my mother used to send floating into the ring. I sat, ready to be Aili's audience forever. First, she said, "Man," and became one, hulking and strong. Then a parade of animals came. When she bent and swung, an elephant, Kassia appeared in my mind so vividly I reached out and tried to touch her, as if Aili's elephant had opened a door between here and there, now and then, Kassia pretending to be an elephant in our courtyard when we were children and Aili dancing the part of one here. My hand found only air, and the image of Kassia transformed back into the reality of Aili, lying down now, hands over her heart.

Someone in her story was dying, I didn't know whether an animal or the man. Then Aili stood and carried a coffin above her, hands up, palms flat. Then she died again and again: the elephant, bird, tiger. I didn't know why, didn't understand her story. I thought she was afraid, though, that she wanted to warn me as Wei had.

So I tried to say that only people who loved us would watch our show. I said, "Kadoorie"; said, "No animals"; said, "For Wei, for my mama, for us." I said, "Zhiyou women," *only us.* I bent and made a trunk out of my arm. Aili finally smiled, entwining her trunk in mine.

"Xing," she said. "*Okay*."

Our show was alive.

— ▣ —

The whole first week of November, I worked on my puppets until my eyes spiraled. I did not return to school, although I kept pretending I was attending. Papa hardly checked. Sometimes the puppets spoke like characters in *The Great Gatsby*, who believed they had troubles but actually lived in luxurious America. Daisy, Jay, and Nick were free, such lucky puppets. I tucked them away, talking of parties, money, and love. They stayed safe under my cot while wind howled up Ward Road, our windows rattled and the river tantrumed: another flood. Tomorrow I'd make my puppets orphans from *Oliver Twist*. Like Wei and Aili. I thought of the refrain of begging children in the streets: *No mama, no papa, no whiskey soda*. My puppets sang it. When I slept, I dreamed their stories, the show we would make for my mother when she arrived.

Taube woke me, carrying a piece of broken glass. I told her Wei and Aili were going to help me make a show, that I was working on acts and puppets. I wanted her there.

"I would love to come," she said, "but let me help, too. Maybe I can make costumes?"

"Yes, please."

"I brought you something." She held the piece of glass up in front of me. "It's not a lovely thing, obviously, but it's close to a mirror. It's sad you can't see yourself."

My face was sharp, light reflecting off its angles as if I were made of something flat. My eyes and wild hair were Alenka's. And here came my sister, dismal, skinny, impoverished, but smiling up at me, singing. Pulling herself along the floor, pulling herself up to standing at the sides of things, trying, working, changing.

"Thank you for the mirror," I said.

"Lillia?" Taube said. Her hand was on my hand. Her eyes were dark and solid, more intense than usual.

"Yes?"

"It's wonderful you've made friends, and that you spend time out and about with your Girl Guide group. But you do know that you don't have to do anything that's dangerous to you, yes? Not for any reason, even helping your papa and sister."

I couldn't breathe. "Yes," I lied, "I know."

"You're gone so much, darling, sometimes so late. You— well, you deserve to be young. Look at your beautiful self, here—" She propped the glass up, and I saw both of us, blurred, close, almost as if we were one person, changing from me to her, a girl to a woman. My eyes hurt. Taube said, "You have to take as loving care of yourself as you do of your papa and Naomi, Lillia. You're a child, too. I just—Be careful."

I thought, but did not say, that she was not my mother. I said nothing, just sat still and pretended to understand her warning in only a general way. I thought how it was November, how 1941 was almost gone, how it was now a year and a half since we'd arrived. I hadn't been to school in five months, not since the beginning of summer. I thought how Taube knew I might be turning bad, might be in trouble. In Europe, the war raged. Hitler's army spread like disease across the map. Gabriel's radio said in Moscow the temperature had dropped to negative twelve degrees and Soviet soldiers had launched ski attacks on German troops. Gabriel had cheered when we heard this, and also when the radio told us that Stalin gave a speech to say four and a half million German soldiers had been killed. Papa and Leo were quiet. I sat drawing while I listened, soldiers flying down white cliffs, holding poles and guns, shooting at soldiers who shot back at them. Each small soldier I made stood for a thousand boys like Wei, or Janusz, or the man who grabbed me in line for the train from Lithuania to Italy.

It was November, and in March I would be seventeen, my rainy spring birthday likely unmarked even by me, my actual age as unreal as my artificial Magnifique age, nineteen, or would I be twenty now if I had been telling the truth? What difference did it make how old I was? No one asked again.

Naomi had turned three in August, while she still had fever. I didn't know if she even remembered that birthdays were something people celebrated elsewhere. Or that *elsewhere*, where our mama now resided, existed at all.

— ◧ —

Leo's girlfriend Talia lived in the International Settlement. She brought us cheese from Abraham's Dry Goods, in stock for the holidays. She also made Mandelbrot at her parents' house one night, and Papa contributed bread and three eggs, which we all shared, breaking small pieces of food into smaller pieces of food, until we were dining on delicious crumbs.

"You're a little mouse," I told Naomi. She licked her Mandelbrot bite from her fingers.

"Mo," she told me.

"Yes!"

"Mo!" she said angrily, and began to cry.

"I want more, too," I said. "More than this. Is that what you mean?" It was then that she said, "Mama." But who did she mean? Maybe me. I didn't think she could remember our mama. I didn't want to be her mama, didn't want her to mistake me for ours. I said, "Yes. I want Mama, too," and went to lie down. Naomi followed me, crawling, and then lifted herself at the edge of my cot and stood, looking at me. "Do you want to get in with me?" I asked.

"Yao," she said, *want*. I pulled her aboard. But when she pointed underneath us, wanting a story, I said no. And she cried until she fell asleep. I listened for a long time to her breathing but couldn't sleep myself, had the feeling of something wrong, a vibration in the house. I slipped out of bed to find Papa, and couldn't, so I went upstairs and knocked on Taube's door.

Mr. Michener came to the door, but he said, "Taube's not feeling well, Lillia. You'll have to come back in the morning."

"Not feeling well? Can I see her?"

"I'm afraid not," he said. "She has fever and I don't want you to catch it."

"I don't care," I said. "It's okay if I catch it, please, let me in to see if she's okay."

"She'll be okay," he said. "She would never forgive herself if she made you sick."

"Tell her I came?"

He reached out and patted me awkwardly, on the head, like a pet. "Of course," he said.

— ◘ —

I missed work the first Saturday in November, because Taube was too sick to watch Naomi and Papa wasn't home. Mr. Takati had been traveling at the end of October, so I thought he wouldn't be there anyway. Maybe no one would notice my absence. But the second Saturday, Taube was still sick and I told Talia and Leo I had a school meeting. They offered to watch Naomi and I rushed across the bridge.

Madame Su was furious. "You think you can miss last Saturday for no reason? That you're free to come and go as you like? Just because you're so pale?"

"It's not because—"

"Hush," she said. "I don't care for your excuses."

"But my father and sister were ill," I lied. It seemed not enough to say that Taube was sick, or to try to impress Madame Su with the fact that I hadn't missed any work when Papa and Naomi were actually feverish.

She stared at me, though, didn't seem to care.

I kept talking, desperate. "They had fever," I said, and since that still didn't seem enough, I added, "and then it was our holiday, and now our neighbor who helps care for my sister is sick, so I had to—"

"Is it typhus?" She made it sound filthy, and I wasn't certain what it was, but I nodded, thinking she would take pity, understand it had been grave. "Go home," she said. "You're contagious."

"No, no. They're better now. I never had it— It was— Please. I can't go home. I must work. I need the—"

"I already told Mr. Takati that you are ill. Go home. We're not exposing our best clients to deadly disease."

"Is he back? I didn't know he was—"

"You were gone, so I explained you must be sick." She walked away.

"Please. Madame Su. I don't have— I need—"

She was gone. I ran to the dressing room and grabbed someone else's dress, dragonless, only yellow birds of delicate stitches fluttering up its fabric. I remembered the men swinging birds in cages when we first arrived, Papa saying it felt like flying. In the dining room I moved fast, my skin under the leotard and bird dress itching. I wanted to find Mr. Takati before Madame Su found me, but from the middle of the room she was coming toward me, squeezing her squat boxy body between tables and chairs. She moved surprisingly efficiently, and I looked from side to side, about to be caught and devoured.

I saw my only escape—the stairs I had once been afraid to climb. I ran up them. There was no one on stage, no spotlight lit me, but I looked out into the audience anyway, the way I'd seen Aili look. I stared right at Mr. Takati and smiled slowly. I saw, across the dining room, Mr. Takati smile back. Madame Su froze in place, arms crossed, gaze livid. I danced across the stage, turning a line of łańcuch, *pirouettes*, my ballet teacher behind me in my mind, my weight moving invisibly from one foot to the other, my body spinning, lifting. Then I slowed, looked again at Mr. Takati, and did two jetés, turning each into an entrechat, landing softly. I would be elegant, innocent, blameless. I would be a ribbon like the ones hanging from the circus ring, a snake, a rope, a banyan branch for the birds on my dress. I would be anyone but myself.

I danced until music started and a spotlight shone on me. A Lillia with no connection to Lillia Kaczka, but instead a girl who could disappear by appearing as someone else. I thought of Biata, once so unlucky, now maybe a Girl Guide, paying her dues, camping and dancing, living in the International Settlement, her parents running a bar with endless food. Did Biata have meat, fruit, and vegetables every day? She never, I was sure, had to sit with a man other than her father or some sweet boy from school. Was she smiling at Benjamin right as I used jetés I'd learned as a child to try to keep Mr. Takati's attention and avoid Madame Su's wrath?

Fu danced onto the stage, dispatched by Madame Su to end my act. I rushed toward Mr. Takati's table, not even stopping when Madame Su intercepted me. "So it turns out you have a mind of your own," she said.

"I'm sorry, Madame Su, but I couldn't leave. I need—" I kept walking, pushing my way toward his table, but another man was suddenly in front of me, as if produced by the smoke.

"General Barbeaux," Madame Su said. "Greetings. This is Alenka."

He said, "Hello," in thick English. His voice was deep, with something wet in it. He wore a velvet jacket and a tie that gleamed under the fantastic light of Magnifique's crystal chandelier. I had never seen a man in velvet, except at the circus. He put his hand on my arm, and I imagined it like an animal paw, covered with a pelt of fur and hiding claws. Other people were watching us. Madame Su walked away, leaving me alone with General Barbeaux.

"Welcome to Magnifique," I said, pressing my arms down, wanting to pin the dress to myself, to erase the feeling of his blunt hand.

"Alenka? What kind of name is that? Where are you from?"

I paused, wanting to name a place as far away from me as possible.

"Don't be coy," he said.

I spoke quickly. "My name is not Alenka. It's Hua." *Flower*. Wei's name for me.

The man barked a hard short laugh. "You are Chinese, then, what a pleasant surprise." He put his other hand on me, this one on my hip, and I shuddered when he squeezed my flesh unpleasantly. I tried to breathe evenly. He asked me, "Where did you learn to dance like that?"

"My parents were in the circus," I whispered, hoping a mention of them might make him release me. But he held on, and I baked under the gaze of the others in his group, as well as the girls I knew were watching. Was Aili among them? Had she felt hands like this? Had Fu, who was now dancing on stage? Natasha, who hadn't been back for weeks? Even Madame Su flitted through my panicked mind. What else had the women I knew here endured? And why, even when we were all here, seen only by each other and those who put us in this position, did we still feel such shame?

Maybe everyone watching thought I was among the girls who had no choice but to say yes to private visits in the back room, girls who weren't lovely dancers, who had no clients inviting them to tables, who were never requested on stage. The hand on my hip moved lower, tried to push into the seam on the side of my miserable silk dress. I started walking, trying to shake free, but his hand found its way inside the cloth, on my right thigh, tearing another Magnifique dress. The red dress I'd stitched back together with Fu's thread after ripping it myself, flipping. This one I would not fix. The lights were flickering. I tried to move faster, to arrive as quickly as possible at a table. I wanted to push him into a booth, to hurt him, but he was hurting me instead, touching my skin. His hand was hot and hard, as if covered with thorns, and I suddenly felt all of everything—the war, my lost mother and babcia and self, moving toward me as if it were a train and I was standing willingly waiting to be smashed. If I could have been brave, I would have reached down and broken that brutal hand off its furred wrist, listened to it crack, made a wish.

But as usual, in my moments of wanting the most violence, I enacted the least. I didn't make a sound, just stopped moving and stood, stunned as he laughed into my ear and neck. With the hand he wasn't using to hurt me, he reached into his pocket and extracted a cluster of bills, waved them like a fan.

"Meet me in the back and this is yours," he began, and something dangerous rose up in me.

"General Barbeaux," a loud voice said then, "how good to see you. Won't you join me for a drink at my table?" Mr. Takati was standing close to the general, who gave an angry nod, as Mr. Takati took the money from him. The general removed his hand from inside my dress.

"That was a most impressive performance, Alenka," Mr. Takati said. "How generous the general is to celebrate it." He handed the bills to me and led General Barbeaux away.

I rushed to the dressing room and tore the dress off before Madame Su could stop me. Before anything else could happen, I had my own rags back on, and was handing Aili twenty CN, the most money we'd ever made. I had noticed she no longer wore her light green bracelet or necklace, and thought she must have had to sell them. I hoped this would help her retrieve at least one. I kept twenty CN for myself, enough to buy medicine from Dr. Hao for Taube, potatoes and buns and flour for Papa and

Naomi, extra tokens for water, extra bread, rice, maybe even meat. Maybe some fabric so we could sew something new for each of us, once Taube was well. Aili and I stepped toward each other as if we were going to dance or hug, so relieved to have that money, celebrating this merciful beauty. Someone shouted: "Aili!"

Aili's head snapped up and her eyes fixed on Madame Su's owl face. "Barbeaux Shenshang yao gen ni shuo hua," Madame Su said. *Mr. Barbeaux wants to talk with you.*

"Shenme shihou?" Aili asked, *when?* I heard her voice as if it were mine, breaking, falling, full of fear. The words felt like they came from inside me even though she was the one speaking them, just as afraid and ashamed as I was.

"Xianzai," Madame Su told her, *now.*

Aili backed away then, her eyes on the floor. It was the first time I'd ever seen her look down, Aili, who gazed so bravely out from the stage. She walked out of the room without lifting her eyes, as if we were all soldiers she didn't dare look at.

— ◙ —

Talia was with Naomi when I got home. "Your father is upstairs," she whispered, because Naomi was sleeping. Fear seared me. Would Papa be furious that I had been out? Would he demand to know where?

"I'm afraid Taube isn't doing well," Talia said. "Your friend's father was here but—"

I had already started running and was up the stairs to Taube's, pushing the door, not caring what Mr. Michener said. But he said nothing. He and Leo and my father and Gabriel were gathered at the side of the bed. Mr. Michener was crying, his once plump face a gaunt and lavender shadow. I remembered his tears over the news on the radio that a thousand French soldiers had been killed by the British, trying to prevent the French navy from being taken over by Germany. Mr. Michener had put his big hands over his face, and tears had poured through them. That seemed a hundred years ago—how many more lives had been lost since?

I pushed my way to Taube's bed, leaned down, and put my face next to hers, "You're okay!" I said, because she was looking up at me, her eyes glazed and gleaming. If Papa noticed I was late, or had been out, or was putting my face into the face of someone possibly contagious with typhus, he didn't say anything.

Taube spoke. "Lillia, I'm so happy . . ." but her eyes closed, four words enough to exhaust her. When they opened again, she looked confused, foggy with illness. I folded then, into my smallest self, resting my head on her chest. She was as hot as Shanghai summer, burning like the day we climbed off the ship. In six months it would be summer again, two years since we had arrived, no matter where Taube was, no matter where I was. The world was relentless.

I felt the rise and fall of her chest, each rattling breath she worked to take, fever coursing through her, poison. Her pajamas were soaked with sweat, and I wept into them, felt her hand in my hair, combing through it with her fingers. I thought how in the whole time we'd lived at 54 Ward, I had never seen Taube in pajamas and she wouldn't like to be seen this way.

I remembered what Dr. Rosen had said about Naomi and Papa, that there was one night when the fever peaked. If a patient made it through that night, she would survive. I knew, without asking, that this was that night for Taube. And I knew better than to ask if she was likely to make it. I told myself I didn't want her to hear the question and think I doubted her, but really I knew the answer was one I couldn't bear to hear.

"I'll go to Dr. Hao's in the morning," I said into Taube's shoulder. "To get medicine—the kind we boiled—the roots." I looked up, kept talking. "I have money. Papa, you can come with me to Dr. Hao's—he can help. He can help. He can help." I felt I was falling, even though I was already on my knees.

That's when Papa picked me up and carried me away from Taube, down the stairs, into our room. He put me in my cot, as he had that night Mama didn't return. But this time he tucked me in and stayed until I fell asleep. He didn't ask where I'd been.

In the morning, Mr. Michener came downstairs before the sun rose, and stood at the side of my cot. I didn't need to hear his words to know what they were, to know Naomi and I would never see Taube again. The vegetable merchant wouldn't call, "Tou-bah," up to our second-floor window. No one would sew hats and pillows, or pound rice paste into kugel. No one would wish to be our mother, except our mama, gone, too. The taste of the brisket Taube had made us came back to me. How angry and happy I'd been, eating that dinner Taube fed us, even as she cried over her own mother. I remembered the first noodles she'd bought us, how I'd hurt her when she called Naomi *Lalka*, the broken mirror she'd made sure I had. I had thought only of myself. When I looked in that glass, I saw the image of myself Taube gave me. I gave Mr. Michener the lipstick Rebecca had given me, asked him please to put it with Taube, in her pocket, or her hand, so she could feel beautiful. He wrapped it in his hand as if I'd given him a diamond.

On November 28, two days after Taube died, we hired rickshaws to carry us and the pine box that held her to Wayside Park. I rode, in spite of my idea that I would never sit in a cart carried by a human being, never break another person with my own weight—what was one more lost promise? Most who started out thinking we wouldn't be carried by anyone without shame ended up closing our eyes in the backs of rickshaws, feeling a rare breeze across us, leaning into the freedom and relief of being carried by someone else. Forgetting that he, too, was a person who would prefer to be carried rather than to carry.

Taube's was only the second funeral I'd been to, so simple it felt unreal. It was too fast, too sad, too little. When my grandfather died in Warsaw, Babcia and Mama held his funeral at our synagogue, a warm, important ceremony, his coffin a castle we planted, one he would preside over forever. Not so for Taube. Here, Mr. Michener was lucky to have managed a box and a spot at Wayside Cemetery. I helped pay, unfolding General Barbeaux's dollars, the withered bills for which I'd had such plans. No one asked where I'd gotten them.

Mr. Michener stood at the gaping grave. My father put an arm on him. Naomi laughed, nervous or wishing to console me. She knew to whisper, her laughter soft and quiet, her small voice calling my name and other words carried off by a cold, stiff breeze: *Tou-bah*, *Papa*, *yao*, *mouse*, *noodle*. She asked for the Song girls, *Mei-Mei* and *Xiao Su*, and spoke a refrain of her own name, *Naomi*, *Naomi*, *Naomi*. Rabbi Mer Ashkenazi came and said the Kaddish. Cracked leaves fell from trees. Everything was dying again and again. We all bowed and rocked on our feet, Naomi on mine, reaching up, holding my hands. Papa's hand never left Mr. Michener's arm. Taube would have been proud of Naomi, so quiet at her service. Someday, maybe I would take Naomi to Kadoorie. Maybe she'd be okay eventually, but neither our mama nor Taube would ever know. We each put a shovelful of Shanghai dirt over Taube's coffin.

Maybe God was furious, had taken Taube as a punishment for the person I was becoming, but I went back to Magnifique the following night anyway, Saturday, November 29, because I was furious, too. And because I had no choice. We needed the money. I needed Mr. Takati.

Fu was already seated, giggling as I approached. Mr. Takati was leaning in, saying something into her ear, and I felt my throat tighten. Maybe he would order food for her instead of me from now on, ask for her dances, rescue her from generals, and forget me.

Fu's eyes rose and fixed on my face, her mouth moving. Mr. Takati stood and pulled a chair out. I sat, Fu's words coming into focus as if I saw them, rather than heard them: *six, seven, eight, nine, ten.* She was counting. Then she said to another man at the table, someone new, "Now you say, yi, er, san, si, wu, liu," I hadn't thought to teach Mr. Takati to count in Polish and didn't want to. He poured from a bottle into my glass and I sipped, coughed, clear wine with bubbles in it, sharp down my throat.

"How are you, Alenka?" he asked. I almost told him about Taube, almost said we had pooled all we had, peeled General Barbeaux's dirty bills apart to help pay to bury our beloved friend instead of letting the cart take her body, instead of watching the river overwhelm her. I almost said my papa didn't know me anymore, hadn't asked where I'd been or where my money came from.

But what I said was "I'm very well, thank you."

"Mrs. Su told me your family was ill. Are they cured then?"

"Yes, thank you." I swallowed a gray feeling rising in my throat, wondered if Taube was now a ghost, able to see me here. I told myself she would forgive me, but I couldn't believe it. I tried telling myself she wasn't gone, would be at 54 Ward when I got there, would come in the morning again, with hats, bread, and ideas, would scoop Naomi up. I could pretend as hard as I wanted, whenever I wanted. Even now.

"Will you dance tonight?" Mr. Takati was looking into my eyes. Did he see something inside me? Or a reflection of himself?

"If you ask Madame Su, I'm sure she'll let me," I told him, trying to meet his gaze, grateful for the flickering, vague light. He was old, loose around the neck as if wearing a scarf of skin. His teeth were mismatched, his nose crooked, maybe broken and never set right. His hair was sleek as an illustration, wet combed. "How have you been, sir?"

"I'm well, thank you, but no need to call me sir, Alenka," he reminded me. "Call me Oue, please."

I could not. "Of course. Have you been well?" I felt I was dancing in a foaming circle like a sick dog. Maybe I would bark the same question out all night, and Mr. Takati would realize I was crazy with loss. But he laughed, as if I'd meant to be charming. "I'm just back from a trip to Hiroshima," he said. "Business is excellent."

I sat with him for the rest of that night and danced twice. First I stayed with ballet, but then someone requested my contortion act. I didn't think it was Mr. Takati who had asked, believed he preferred me more elegant without knowing how I knew. He said nothing about either dance. When I crossed the bridge back to Hongkou, men whistled and I felt the cold stares of soldiers.

Inside our front door, I found Talia sitting on the stairs. The sight of her set alive in me the howling feeling of missing Taube. Why hadn't someone else died instead? I tried not to think this, not to wish it had been Talia. "You scared me," I said. "What are you doing?"

"I'm waiting for Leo to get back from the distillery," she said, "And for you, Lillia. I wanted to talk." She patted the stair next to her, but I continued to stand. She stood then and put her hands on my shoulders. "You made Taube's life here so much happier," she said. "You and Naomi. She felt like you were almost her daughters."

I set my top teeth on the shelf of my bottom ones, hard. My face ached, and my neck and arms. I wanted Talia to love me, but I couldn't be lovable. Talia tilted her head and curls tumbled down her shoulder. "Where are you so late on Saturday nights, Lillia?"

I still didn't speak. I had a surge of the powerful knowledge that I could outwait her for the rest of time, that nothing would ever make me tell soft, violin-playing, music-making, Leo-loving Talia of the International Settlement, of the two parents and gemstone eyes, where I had been or why. I stared at her, loving her, hating her, wanting to be her. Wanting Taube. Wanting my mother. Wanting so many things I couldn't have. Wanting to learn to want nothing. I thought of Naomi's little voice, her perfect, lilting Chinese: yao, yao, yao, *want, want, want.*

"It's none of my business, Lillia, but I just want to say that you don't have to do the sort of work that makes you—"

My voice was a whisper. "Makes me what?"

"Sad, or afraid."

I said, "I'm doing what I have to in order to survive."

"You don't have to put yourself in danger."

I thought she had talked to Taube about me, a betrayal.

"All I do is dance," I said evenly.

"Of course," she said. "I don't mean to criticize, just to help."

"Please don't," I said. "Don't ask. Don't help. I don't want help."

"We all need help here, Lillia. Taube knew that. . . . That's why she— Well, no one in this house is alone, that's all."

I didn't want to know what she was going to say about Taube. I felt she was using Taube as if she contained more Taube than I did.

"Lillia," she said, and I felt she was going to put her hand on me. I moved away, out of her reach. "Leo and I have decided to get married. We hope you'll be a part of whatever wedding we manage to have here. A part of our family, our life."

Talia laughed lightly then, notes of happiness rising, ringing. I imagined slamming her into a circus trunk, Papa and a gang of clowns carrying it away. When they brought it back in, I would emerge instead, a lacy bride draped in white clouds. The klezmers would play as my two parents, who lived in the International Settlement, floated me down the aisle. Taube, too, holding hands with my mother. They would all be so proud of me. I couldn't get a single word out, not *thank you*—for watching my sister, for guessing my secret and caring, for advice, for forgiveness. Not even *congratulations*, which rose and caught in my throat. I slipped by silent, choking into our room like a demon.

CHAPTER FOURTEEN

珍珠港, Zhenzhu Gang, *Pearl Harbor*

I returned to Kadoorie on Monday, December 1, 1941. Not because Talia had told me to quit Magnifique, and not for God
or Wei or even myself. In case Taube was watching. I would
be good again, study, be friends with girls Taube would have
loved. I wore the sash, some stars torn, others transparent, and
walked into the new building on East Yuhung Road, feeling no
longer young. Biata saw me before I saw her. "You're back! How
are you? What happened? Where have you been?" She had run
up to me and was out of breath.

"Working," I said. "I had to work for a while."

Biata looked plump and pleased, her stringy hair pulled away from her face. I thought she was giving me a knowing glance. I looked away.

"Did you hear that Sally has gone?" she asked, in a conspiratorial whisper.

"Gone where?"

"Singapore. And from there they'll go to Palestine. They escaped!" She lowered her voice. "It's not safe for Americans here anymore."

"What about Rebecca?" I asked. I remembered Renia Antol fleeing Warsaw, my mama vanishing from the ring in blackness, Taube disappearing entirely. Rebecca came up to us then. She hugged me. I was wearing her pink dress. "You're still here!" I said.

She smiled sadly, "Are you hoping to get rid of me so easily?"

"Of course not."

Biata linked arms with Rebecca, as if they'd been best friends all fall and winter.

"My father insists on staying to help at the hospital, just for another six months or so, but he can't bear to leave when so many people are ill and need help. And of course my mother is much happier now that she's busy working with Laura, who runs the soup kitchens for the JDC."

I said, "The JDC replaced Papa when he was sick. They didn't take him back."

"That's terrible," Rebecca said. "I'm sorry. And I'm sorry about Taube, Lillia. My father told me."

"Thank you," I said. "How is Abraham?"

"Good," she said, blushing. "He's graduated and is working at the bookshop on Henan Road. My mother and I are going a week from Saturday, on the thirteenth? Why don't you come with us?"

I didn't hesitate. "Yes, please." A few scraps of Magnifique money remained in my mattress, and the promise of even a moment in Rebecca's life felt irresistible. Maybe I could bring enough to buy her a book. I had never returned *The Great Gatsby* or *Oliver Twist* or *The Good Earth*. I told myself I still meant to.

"If you leave after six months like your father said," I asked, "where will you go?"

"Probably first Singapore, too," she said. "That's our best choice until the war ends. Then, back to America or to Palestine like Sally. . . . What about you?"

"Oh. We won't go anywhere until my mother joins us. She knows we're here, so we have to wait here until she arrives. We left detailed instructions."

Rebecca smiled gently, but Biata looked me over as if I were a sick infant or starving kitten, said, "I didn't realize there was a chance your mother was still coming. . . . I thought . . ."

Rebecca and I waited. Was Biata going to say it? Maybe she had replaced Sally now that Sally was gone. I wondered whether I'd have been unkind if I could have been. Maybe. But then Rebecca cut Biata off. "When your mother comes, we'll tell her how you saved Naomi and your father."

She didn't believe me, either, and her voice took on an artificial pitch. Maybe her mother had told her my mother was dead. I remembered telling myself her mother knew nothing about my family, telling myself she hadn't seen me steal sugar to feed Naomi. Of course she had. Everyone had. I had no mother, and my family was hungry, and everyone knew everything.

"Actually your father saved mine," I said, the true words metallic as a Japanese plane slicing open the sky. Both Biata and Rebecca leaned back. Our new teacher, Mrs. Katz, walked in and asked us to be quiet. She was made of something sharp, and all I could think each time I saw her was how unfair it was that Taube had never gotten to be a teacher here.

But I worked on every subject, even Japanese, maybe especially Japanese. I had promised myself I wouldn't go back to Magnifique, but what if I saw Mr. Takati again anyway? I was ahead with my numbers and polite talk, so I'd have some shiny new vocabulary to say in my soft Saturday night voice if I needed to.

Five days after I returned to Kadoorie, on Friday of my first week back, I went to find Mrs. Aarons and ask if I could borrow the lunchroom for a performance.

"A performance?" She said the word as if she were learning it for the first time. "Of what?"

"Puppets," I told her, and then added, "With my father. He was a circus performer at home."

At the mention of him, she said yes we could use the room.

That night, I whispered good night to Taube before I fell asleep. I told her my plans, that I was going to go to Kadoorie again like a regular girl, and I had a plan for a week from tomorrow, to go with Rebecca to a bookstore. I would ask Rebecca to be in our show, too, invite her over, buy her a book, whatever book she most wanted. I had enough money saved up to buy one for Naomi as well. I told Taube I was going to borrow a room at school and put on a small Shanghai circus. I hoped Taube would be proud. Mama, too.

— ⊠ —

But before our bookstore date could happen, seven days into December, I was bending backward off my cot into a flip when I heard a sound so loud I thought something had blown my ears from my head. The house shook and there was shrieking outside. I dropped to the floor, scrambling to find Naomi and also keep my hands over my ears, keep the sound out, but it stopped for a moment and then came again: an explosion of sound, the loudest drum vibrating our entire house. It stopped. The house shivered and I tried to balance myself as Leo came roaring into our room and grabbed us—both Naomi and me—the way Papa had in Warsaw. Holding my hand and carrying Naomi under his arm, Leo plunged down the stairs to Gabriel's. Mr. Song came, too, running with Mei-Mei and Xiao Su. The little girls were sobbing. I had never seen Mr. Song move quickly, but now he was tumbling forward down the stairs, trying to use his body to protect the girls when they fell, too.

And then the shaking and rattling and screaming stopped, and a silence lasted long enough that we began to believe it. Mr. Song and the girls stood up. We crawled out from under and over each other. The front door opened and Papa flew down the stairs, in the worst despair I'd ever seen. He dropped to his knees in front of Naomi and me, and I remembered he used to kneel when I was small. "You're too tall!" he would say, placing shoes in front of his knees so they looked like feet, so he was short, like me. Now he hugged my waist. He was crying.

Mr. Song spoke: "Radio?" We all looked up, caught. He could have Gabriel—maybe all the men—arrested. But he pointed to his ear. "Radio, okay!" he said. He wanted to listen. Leo pulled the radio from under Gabriel's cot and its bodiless voices said Japan had attacked an American naval base at Pearl Harbor in Hawaii and declared war on Britain and America. It was Gabriel himself who told us, moments later, shouting down the stairs, that our harbor was under attack, too. "The Japanese have attacked the American and British ships! They're firing from warships and shore batteries—the harbor is on fire. Men are dying! The Japanese army is everywhere!" He seemed to realize where he was only after this outburst. He looked from the radio to Mr. Song, who nodded. Gabriel took this in, per-mission.

"The Japanese are burning the *Peteral* and the *Wake*." He was breathing as if the fire were inside him. I felt it in me, too.

"What was that noise? Why was everything shaking?" I asked.

"Cannon fire from the shore batteries. But the British general aboard the *Peteral* is refusing to surrender the ship—he's resisting. He's either very courageous or very crazy."

"What about the Americans who are still here?" I felt something howling in my chest.

"Japanese soldiers are rounding people up. They're driving tanks through the city right now. Now that they're at war with the Americans, they're taking over the settlements."

I said, "Today?"

And Gabriel said, "Right now."

"What do you mean rounding up?" I was screaming. I turned to Papa. "Rebecca is still here!" I cried. "She hasn't gone! Her father stayed to help at the hospital." Dr. Rosen with his shiny head and beard, his missing finger, shots of medicine, his food and clean towels. Dr. Rosen, who had hugged me like I was Rebecca, someone's daughter, a good girl. And Mrs. Rosen with all the books she'd lent me, with her tea and cubes of sugar. What about Rebecca's little brother and sister?

Papa had no choice but to go outside to wait for rice and boiled water—no matter how upside down the world went, we still lined up to eat—and I left immediately. I handed my sister to Leo and Gabriel, who tried to prevent me from leaving, who called after me, "It's not safe, Lillia. It's not safe!"

"What's safe? When were we last safe?" I yelled. I leapt up the stairs and went straight outside to see parades of Japanese military vehicles rolling across the bridge and into the streets of the International Settlement. How fast this had happened. I moved in a crushing crowd, wild and violent with panic. From windows and archways, clothing hung stiff like half-frozen surrender flags. It seemed unreal that we'd ever washed or hung our clothes, now that the harbor was on fire.

The sampans, jetties, and military boats were in an extravagant jumble of chaos, smoke ballooning up and hanging in the sky while pieces of machinery fell from ships: metal, wood, and glass sizzling as it sunk. The fish market, usually lively with shouting and sawing and selling, seemed never to have existed. Instead of vendors or fish, dazed men emerged from trenches as if they had originated in the river's black mud, and were dragging their tails, choking through gills. I crossed the bridge, glad I had nothing for anyone to steal from my pocket or bag. Gabriel's wallet had been taken the week before, and although his money and notes from some of the Yeshiva men were gone forever, miraculously, his ID cards had been returned to the Embankment Building. Having nothing prevented me from losing anything.

I walked until my legs were numb, my heart trying to escape my body, all the way to Bubbling Well Road. All the driveways were full of tanks, and on doors and gates hung Japanese banners. They had taken over so quickly, I thought they must have been waiting to do so, must have been perched, stalking the city. When I arrived outside Rebecca's house, I saw that her gate, the one from which her mother had hung ribbons to welcome the Girl Guides, now held a Japanese flag and a piece of paper printed with Japanese characters. Soldiers stood in groups in her circular driveway, next to trucks and a tank. I ducked behind the bushes to watch soldiers enter and exit her house. How fast they had come! Had her parents still been home when the soldiers arrived? Had they left willingly or been dragged away? And why had they stubbornly stayed? I wished it had been Sally whose family remained and Rebecca's who had left for Singapore already.

I imagined soldiers inside, sitting at Rebecca's piano or raiding the bookshelves and teacups. I heard Rebecca singing the word *somewhere*, from the American rainbow song, saw her joyful construction of our tent at Holt's Wharf. I had never returned her books or bought her a new one. I had worn her pink dress until it was more mine than anything I'd ever owned. I longed to sneak inside and retrieve her Girl Guide diaries, records of when our lives were better than we realized. Even mine. But getting any closer to her house was too dangerous, and I landed suddenly on a hard and selfish thought: now even if I could have paid the dues, I'd still never be a Girl Guide. It cost more to be innocent here than we could make or save.

I backed away. My feet walked me toward Hongkou, wind tearing at my skin. To my right was a cluster of men whose bayonets looked as natural as limbs. My legs were soft with exhaustion, but I arrived back at the bridge, its metal *X*s now resembling sinister blades.

"You!" I looked. The soldier manning the hut made a bowing motion and pointed at me. I dropped my head forward on my neck and bent my body into a deep, nauseating bow. Wei and Aili had been bowing all along. So had the Song family—Mr. Song and even the little girls Mei-Mei and Xiao Su. Now we would bow, too. When I came back up, lights flashed in my vision. I didn't know whether they were real or coming from my mind. I never used to get dizzy, no matter how long I spun or how many times I flipped. The soldier pointed. Now that humiliation might melt me, I was allowed to cross.

Suzhou Creek was still crawling with mud-men, and I looked back at the burnt boats. What incinerated ship could bring my nonexistent mother across the ocean now? I kept on, past the movie theater, a picture of the star from the Heime poster smiling out, untouched. I passed the sentry boxes, where soldiers stacked heavy bags—of sand, maybe—and plates of steel. Armor, I guessed, to protect themselves. But from what? They were the danger.

Up ahead, a fury of movement broke out and I began to back up. A group of soldiers was beating and kicking something, and the giant mass of moving people knew how to part. No one intervened, even though we all knew what they were kicking was a person. My own bones told me the sounds I heard were bones being broken. I made myself look: a gap between the soldiers revealed two bare feet. The person's skin must have been frozen, but he didn't scream, and the absence of his voice echoed through the lane. I thought I would never go outside again.

Inside 54 Ward, my body chattered like a mouthful of loose teeth. I pushed into our room and sat on the floor. Papa ran toward me. "Lillia, where were you? Gabriel said he warned you—"

I looked up. Past Papa I saw a Chinese woman with a round face and high shiny forehead hunched on my cot. Only when she stood did I notice the baby, tucked under the fabric of her shirt. "Nihao," she said.

"Nihao!" Naomi said. "Lillia!"

"Lillia. Tell me what happened." Papa was holding my shoulders.

Naomi said, "Lillia! Xiexie, xiexie," *thank you, thank you.*

"You're welcome," I told my sister in English. But I was staring at the woman, wisps of slick black hair falling into her eyes, her baby gulping. He was nursing. Papa said, "This is Shan. We met when I was at the JDC. She works in the factory next door. She and Ping are having some trouble and need a place to stay. I told her they are welcome here with us. Of course."

I didn't know the rules or even what I felt. What could it mean that a woman and her baby had come to stay with us? Or that Papa knew people I didn't know, had a life taking place away from mine, Naomi's, our family's. Or that I did, too.

I said, "I went to find Rebecca, but soldiers are in her house. And I saw them beating a man in the street. I saw his feet.... They were—"

"You went across the bridge? It's not safe, Lillia. You mustn't go out," Papa said.

The woman looked like she was trying to understand something by sight that she could not make out by language. Maybe she didn't speak English. Papa had let Leo stay; would I object to his taking this woman and her baby in? Maybe the man whose feet I had just seen was her husband. My chest tightened. That man belonged to someone, so maybe this baby's father had been beaten to death. Maybe my mother, too, and Babcia. The baby sat up and looked around cheerfully, thin milk spilling down his chin. He didn't know enough yet to be heartbroken. He was naked except for a makeshift diaper and must have been cold. Naomi pulled herself over to me, and tried to climb into my lap. In her movement I saw the men emerging from mud, bleeding and crawling. I made myself say, "Huanying," *welcome*, to Shan and Ping.

Naomi, once on my lap, laughed and pointed at Ping. "Baby," she told me, another new word, this one in English. Papa's face was strange then, like in a photograph, between expressions. Naomi smelled sharp. I hadn't washed her in days.

I bathed her in the bucket, and Shan asked quietly, in Chinese, if she could use the water afterward for Ping. I tried to wring the towel out well. Shan bathed her baby in Naomi's dirty bath, and I carried my sister down to Gabriel's, where we listened to our radio, clinging to news, all of us limp as if we'd been fished from the river and gutted, listening: while ships were burning in Shanghai's harbor and Rebecca's house was filling with Japanese soldiers, a synagogue was burned in Bialystok, full of Jewish men. I put my hands over Naomi's ears, but she struggled against me. Every single man in the temple in Bialystok had been reduced to ash. Not one survived. An animal sound of screaming came down then, so loud it disoriented me. Did it originate from the radio? From burning men or their wives and daughters? But it was Leo who reeled down the stairs. The sound was Leo, everything about him reversed. No laughing, singing, running the bow over the violin's strings, just sobbing, the word inside his screams taking sudden shape: "Talia, Talia."

She had been standing in the doorway of a building on the harbor with another girl when a storm of bricks exploded out from the wall and part of a ceiling beam fell from above. Both girls were crushed. Naomi echoed, "Talia, Talia," like a small bird that repeats, reaching out to pat me, as if this sorrow, too, were ours.

— ▣ —

Shan and Ping slept on Papa's cot, Papa on the floor. I wanted to climb straight out of myself to escape. There was no space, no air, not enough water even though we scrounged for bamboo tokens to trade at the water stations. There was no quiet. My puppets hid. Shan never slept, because she worked at an artificial silk factory across from 657 Amherst all day and then stayed awake comforting Ping. Ping's crying I didn't mind. He spoke for me, for all of us, sobbing into the dark. No one ever mentioned his father.

One night, Ping finally slept and it was Papa's voice that

came at me in the dark: "Have you been able to find anything out about Rebecca?"

I said, "No."

"I'm so sorry. I have asked, too, at the Heime and the JDC."

I sat up. "And?"

"The Americans were taken to a camp. Somewhere outside the city. Near the airfield."

"Can refugees still come here?"

I heard him turn over on the floor, imagined his cold bones rattling. "Why would they want to?" It was the most hopeless thing he'd ever said.

I thought for a moment. "Other people decide if we die. If we burn, lose our heads. They say who we are."

He seemed surprised out of his sorrow. "No one says who anyone else is."

But he was wrong. The papers had closed, as they had in Warsaw, and news was made of rumors: the Germans, who were pressuring the Japanese to kill us, had sent a man named Meisinger. Some believed he was here already, had already conveniently consolidated us for easier killing. Some said every Jewish person would soon be forced to move into the smallest area of the city, all of us into one corner of Hongkou.

"But we'll never be our other, real selves again," I whispered. I wanted to tell him about Magnifique, to say I had danced on Saturday nights for drunk men until this December, had pushed chairs together and flew, disgracing myself and my act, that I had sat each week for months with a Japanese man and begged for pork. What if I told my father that I knew girls who went with men into back rooms, including Natasha? That if I was asked, I wasn't certain I could refuse. That I'd only stopped since the harbor burned because I'd heard Magnifique wasn't open.

"*You* get to be your real self however you choose to," he was saying, his voice rising with panic or anger. "You decide who you are, Lillia. Every day you decide that, many times. Who you are is determined by how *you* act, not how you're acted upon."

Where did Papa think I'd gotten money for the medicine that maybe saved him and Naomi, but also maybe made no difference? How did he think I had helped buy rice, bread, potatoes, helped bury Taube? He didn't want to know who I had been, who I was. I was angry, too. "But how we act *is* determined by how we're acted upon. I wouldn't have acted in the ways I've had to act here except—"

"I mean how we treat each other, Lillia. How we love and continue to make our lives, what we say and do. Those choices add up to a life—to who a person is or has been."

"You and I are different from who we were before, Bercik. We are strangers," I said. It was the first time I had ever called him anything other than Papa. I felt powerful and cruel.

He flinched, but didn't acknowledge his new, old name, just said, "That might be true even if the war hadn't happened. Everyone changes all the time."

"I don't want to change," I said.

"No one stays the same forever," Bercik said. "That's not

how— I'm sorry." He paused, gathered himself. "I miss your mother unimaginably. Sometimes it's unbearable. But the solution isn't to stop changing. You can't hope for it, because that's hoping for death."

I felt he had used the word to punish me. "Is that why you let Shan and Ping move in? As if we could just replace her with a new family?"

"Stop," he said. "Don't say what you don't mean. I'm trying to live, Lillia, and to keep you and Naomi safe. I can't do any of that without you. I'm sorry our life here is so difficult, and grateful for all you've done."

I said, "I know," softly. "I'm sorry, Papa." I lay back down.

He said, "I'm not happy without Alenka, if that's what you fear."

Pain shot straight through me. "I want you to be happy," I cried. And it was true and a lie. I felt opposing parts of myself tear away from each other.

The next day I stayed as still as Leo, who now spent his days staring at the low, cold ceiling, his face gray plaster, expression erased. He was as scary as Mrs. Lipner, another adult both here and vanished. I tried lying on my back for many hours. Only when Naomi wanted a story, did I sit up. Rosy Mischa played Miriam, but I called her Lillia. She led our family home on a boat that was an upside-down bucket. Naomi clapped joyfully, knowing it was a happy story if we escaped.

The parade of days that followed were indistinct from the nights, because we were barely allowed out, and had almost no food, except what was left of our rice, and a few potatoes. It became impossible to tell who was watching whom. Some refugees had become police. Jewish families were no longer welcome. Now we needed visas to arrive, papers to stay, money no refugee could possibly have. Now, to cross the bridge, we needed not only to bow but also to beg for permission from a man named Goya, a Japanese official who called himself King of the Jews, and beat, tormented, sometimes even tortured refugees. He humiliated those who most needed to cross the bridge and denied them passes to leave Hongkou.

I was lucky. Since Kadoorie had moved to East Yuhung Road, students were allowed to cross the bridge. I guarded my pass like a jewel, even though I had not returned to school or Magnifique. Mostly I stayed home watching Papa, as he watched me. We were each afraid of the other becoming like Leo and Mrs. Lipner, more live ghosts.

— ◙ —

But sometimes he had to leave to find food, and on December 27, twenty days after Pearl Harbor, Papa hurtled toward us from outside, shouting. I knew it had happened. He had become Leo, crying Talia's name, had come to tell Naomi and me the worst news. All of our hoping was over.

I began screaming, "No! No! No! No!" until I couldn't feel the screams coming from me, could only hear them, trying to fill the air so he couldn't tell me, so I wouldn't hear it. I held my hands out to keep him away. But he shook me, tears flying from him as if from an overfilled glass tipping and splashing.

And he held something out: a card, a hard post card, some black ink, ten words: Żywy. Trans Syberyjski. Kobe, Japonia. Potrzebujesz wizy docelowej. Proszę pomóż. *Alive. Trans Siberian. Kobe, Japan. Need destination visa. Please help.*

It was her writing. The stamp was from Japan. I dug a broken fingernail into the skin on the inside of my arm and felt it, was here, awake, conscious. I wasn't dreaming. My mother was alive. She had written, was as close as Japan, needed only a visa to get to me.

Naomi, maybe because I'd been screaming, or maybe because I'd stopped, began to sing the tiger song: "One has no ears, one has no tail, how strange, how strange."

Her voice, lining Chinese words up as neatly as the notes, prevented me from fainting.

CHAPTER FIFTEEN

然后, Ran Hou, *After*

I went straight to Madame Su in the morning the freezing first day of January. I didn't know if she, or even the place, would be there, or if she was, how furious at me she might be. I couldn't imagine Magnifique outside the smoky dark of Saturday nights.

The red double doors were locked, their lion knockers powerless. I went to the back of the building, made brave by desperate need. No one prevented me from pushing open a door that led to a series of darkened hallways, internal parts of a body more beautiful on the outside: trachea, capillaries, veins, lungs, heart. All those lists I'd made for school! I wound through a kitchen and a cluster of offices, peering into each until I found Madame Su. I held myself straight as I walked into the office where she sat. I knew I must not appear weak.

"What are you doing here?" She was at a desk, her posture suggesting work, but no pen or paper before her. Two windows on the left wall were shattered, and shards of light lit Madame Su's face. I had never seen her during the day. Gray hair made stripes at her temples, and deep creases outlined her eyes and mouth.

"Madame Su, I'm sorry to bother you. I need help."

"Ask me how I am."

"How are you?"

"I'm finished! Look what they've done to my place!" She flung her hands up in a surprisingly graceful gesture, toward tape pasted across the cracked glass, limp edges hanging where it no longer stuck. Those fluttering ends made me inexplicably sad. "Everyone with money is getting out. And those are the ones who pay for entertainment, so as you can see, I'm not well. We're closed for now."

I didn't know how to respond to this. "I'm sorry?"

"It's not your fault, Alenka," she said.

We looked at each other, and she waited.

"Madame Su, my mother is in Japan. She's alive."

"And?"

"I thought she was—um, dead," I said. "She was supposed

to come with us to Shanghai, but she disappeared the week we were to leave."

"And you left anyway," Madame Su prompted, her voice a hiss. She wanted to fight, so that I would leave and she wouldn't have to help me. I couldn't let that happen, so I nodded like an obedient doll. I would do anything, take anything, and maybe seeing this made her fold faster.

"Well, people will do what they must to survive." The lines in her face darkened, as if I were going over each with a fat black marker. Once I asked Babcia where wrinkles came from, and she said, "Mine? They're from laughing, like a record of love."

Of what were Madame Su's wrinkles a record? What might mine someday be? I wished I weren't young. I begged her then, "Can you please help me get my mother's visa?"

She sighed. "I can't do anything, Alenka. I have no power. I'm just a leftover woman. Use your beauty. If I hadn't been beautiful when I was young—" She coughed up a laugh. "Go ask Takati for help. He's powerful and rich. I'm sure he'd love nothing more than to assist you."

I tried to look ashamed. "Do you know where I might find him?"

She stared at me before reaching in a drawer for paper and a pen. She wrote on a shred she shoved across the desk. "Thank you," I said, grabbing it. I might never see her again. My relief was delicious. Guilty for such luck at not being her, I lied, "When Magnifique reopens—"

But she cut me off, holding her hand up like a soldier,

about to inspect my passport. "No," she said quietly. "You won't work here again, Alenka."

I went straight from her office to the dressing room, where I collected two of the dresses we'd had to wear, and walked out holding my face up, daring anyone to stop me from taking them, to arrest me for the thief I was. But there was no one there, and the dresses belonged to me as much as anyone.

I left through the back doors of Magnifique with those thick silk torments under my arm and in my pocket, Mr. Takati's address.

— ◙ —

I washed myself and Rebecca's dress, which had begun to resemble tissue. When the translucent fabric was dry, I put it on carefully. Along the Garden Bridge was a writhing line of refugees, bowing one at a time to soldiers. I lined up, freezing, until it was my turn to show my Kadoorie pass, and dip my head down. They let me by, a puppet with a bent neck, my head heavy.

The address became a house on Foch Road, four tall stone stories, no gate. I rang the bell and watched through a frosted window. Time slowed. He wasn't there, wouldn't help. I would never see him again, and I began to panic, to feel starving, fear and hunger joining to topple me. I had no plan past begging Mr. Takati, no ideas, no official to ask, no one else who might find my mother, help me get her here. I was shaking when the door opened so slowly I saw myself and the woman looking out at me as if we were both floating, outside time.

I tried to stop rattling, to keep the tears from coming, to see her, her hair a silver-streaked bun, her face slim, chin the dot of an exclamation point. She wore white-framed glasses, a white blouse, and a white skirt. On her feet were clean cloth slippers. I stared, my heart low, somewhere near my stomach and falling. Was she his wife?

I whispered, "Hello?"

She did not respond. Maybe she didn't speak English. "Takati-san zai ma?" I asked, and flushed, the mix of words toxic, his name, *Mr.* in Japanese, *here* in Chinese.

Her English was as clear and measured as Mr. Takati's. "Who are you?"

"I'm Lillia—just a—just— We heard he might be able to help find my mother. Are you Mrs. Takati? I'm sorry to trouble you. My father said Mr. Takati might be able to help?" I lied in Sally's voice, my question marks apologies. "My mother is in Japan and needs to get here?"

"Your father knows Mr. Takati?"

I nodded.

"And your mother is in Japan?"

She didn't believe me. But what did she believe, and what was true? Had I met Mr. Takati at Magnifique, and if so, what did that mean to her, to me? I reached out and touched her hand. I don't know which of us this surprised more, but I was ready to kneel, to fall onto her doorstep. I held on to

Mrs. Takati's hand. "Please," I said. "Please. My mother disappeared just before we had to leave home. We didn't know if she was—but now she's in Kobe—she needs to get here, doesn't have papers—we don't have— I don't know who to ask or how to—"

She changed then, maybe because I was telling the truth, or because I was looking for my mother. I saw her see me, slow down, take something in. But then I heard footsteps. Mr. Takati was on the stairs coming toward us, his face and eyes tight. He wore slippers, too, and glasses I had never seen. She turned to him and spoke in Japanese. He asked me for my mother's name.

"Alenka," I said, the name I'd told him was mine. Everything in me caught fire.

"I see," Mr. Takati said. "And what is your name?"

"Lillia." I swallowed flames, an orange taste spreading to the back of my mouth and down my throat at the whisper of my actual self, the reveal of another lie. "Lillia Kaczka-Varsh."

"Who do you stay with in Shanghai?" Mrs. Takati asked.

I said, "My father and my sister."

"Come in," Mrs. Takati said. Behind her were shadows of servants in the kitchen. A living room to the left: couches, pillows, lamps with tassels, books with characters climbing their spines. On the wall of the hallway she led me down were three photos: first, a baby in a gown, second, a teenage boy with big features and a small face. The boy had an uneven smile, one side slight, the other open, as if his face were in a disagreement with itself, only half willing to show joy. The final photo was of a soldier with the same strange, half-shy smile.

I stared. "Is that your son?"

Mrs. Takati's head jolted back as if she'd been hit or shocked. Mr. Takati pivoted so sharply he might have been me at Magnifique, exiting the stage in fear. He went up the stairs. "Leave your address with Mrs. Takati, please," he said. "She will write if we can help."

I began to back away, stumbling. "Thank you. I'm sorry to interrupt you."

Now I felt Mrs. Takati's hand on my arm. "Please stay," she said, and then, "He passed away." I stopped, the heat of her hand both comforting and terrifying. "Our son," she added, as if I hadn't heard or understood. "Our son passed away."

Maybe she was saying it to herself, trying to believe it. Or not to. "I'm sorry," I repeated, trying still to leave. I wanted to escape her suffering, Mr. Takati's life, their haunted house.

But she said it again: "Please stay," and so I drifted back in, looking down lest my eyes fall upon the photo of their son again.

I followed her to an immaculate kitchen and sat across a table from her, from Mr. Takati's wife. We drank warm tea that tasted of smoke, wood, and flowers, and we hardly spoke until she asked, "Do you go to school?"

I weighed possible lies. "I went, before—it was important to my father, but then when he got sick I had to work, and take care of my sister, who is . . ." I wanted to tell Mrs. Takati the truth, but I didn't know how. I had never talked about Naomi, didn't know how to describe her, couldn't compare her to other babies, other people's sisters.

"Well, she needed me," I said.

"Where did you find work? It's so difficult here," she said.

I looked down at my shattered fingernails, an ever-present black crescent beneath each. I whispered, "I tried to dance, at a restaurant, but I . . . "

She waited, so I started over. "My parents were dancers, acrobats at a circus at home, and I thought I could perform here. But this was different. It was bad, a bad kind of work for me. It was . . ." I pushed tears back down inside me again and again.

"Akio doesn't like to read," she said, like Mrs. Lipner, another mother with her children lost, but their ages in her mind present tense. Mrs. Lipner had been in bed for two years, weeping for them, Shanghai closing in on her. Now Leo was lying in the drained tomb of Gabriel's room.

Mrs. Takati's eyes went wide and blank, as she continued, "He loves science and to make fires. He's a very curious boy." She finished her tea and set the empty cup in front of her, staring into it as if at its edge herself.

"He sounds nice," I said limply.

She looked up then, surprised to find me there. "You should go back to school," she said, like Taube, like Talia, like Papa would say if he knew anything about me.

"If my mama gets here, maybe I can," I said.

When I left the Takatis' house, Mrs. Takati touched my arm again, trying to touch her son through me, the way I had tried to see my mother in her.

"We will help your mother if we can," she said, and closed the door after me. I had begun the numb walk home and was three streets away when I heard his voice: "Alenka."

I turned. Mr. Takati was walking behind me, and I stopped moving.

"Can we meet at the Nanjing Theater on Sunday at two?"

"The movie theater?"

"Yes."

And that was all. He turned toward home. Returning to Hongkou, I felt ancient and powerless, looking back at my own life. Would Mr. Takati make me pay? And if so for what and with what?

That's when I saw it. After meeting Mr. Takati's wife. After the explosions and smoking ships, our house shaking, Talia crushed. After the soldiers marching into the International Settlement and taking the hospitals, the Cathay Hotel, the Sassoon offices, all the buildings. After the Japanese flags, flying like taunting laundry. After Rebecca being stolen, just as my mother and Babcia had been. It was bobbing above the street, its hair moving as if the head were still attached to a walking body. The neck, although a spear remained embedded in it, wasn't bleeding. A soldier held it high. It was somebody's head, a Chinese man's or boy's, maybe someone like Wei. Someone like Ping. The head resembled slaughtered meat, but still had human eyes, both open, frost on its intact lashes.

The street was quiet, freezing. I had never heard any part of Shanghai quiet until I saw that silenced head. I had not been surprised by the bodies, which were now so commonplace that some of the smallest children at Kadoorie kept competitive tallies. But I knew the head would stay with me forever.

— ◉ —

Later I sneaked out anyway, past Naomi and my father sleeping, past Shan, who would not tell, wouldn't dare contradict me even though she was awake. I carried my pass and my identification card, showing them to soldiers who stopped me, who had multiplied like termites, come to devour everything.

I made it to Wei's, wedged myself into the dark box of a room where he and Aili lived, and took out the card from my mother, which I read to him in Polish. "She's alive," I explained. "She's in Kobe, trying to get here. But the card was from *san ge yue*. *Three months* *ago*. Maybe she got to Kobe but then—"

"Bu," he said, *no*. "Ta mashang jiu lai Shanghai." *She will come to Shanghai immediately*. He had taught me this word for *immediately*, *mashang*, its characters *ma* and *shang* meaning "on horseback." I saw my mother galloping on a water-walking horse, jumping over waves. He asked if she had papers, stamping his hand.

"Not yet. I asked for help," I said, and he did not ask from whom. I told him about Shan, how my father had let her live with us. Wei listened. I was glad, telling Wei about Shan and Ping, that they were Chinese. If Papa had invited a Japanese woman and her baby to live in our room I could not have told Wei. Such were the stupidities of war.

I felt some of my fear sliding off me as we talked about the harbor, the burnt ships, and Rebecca. We knew now that one of the camps where Americans were being held was near the airfield at Hongjiao. We knew there was too little food and water there. Americans were dying.

I felt brave because Wei and I were talking. I said, "We should go. Let's take Rebecca something—food. Let's find her, and at least tell her we know she's there."

Wei looked at me for a long time, trying to tell whether I was crazy. "Sorry, Lillia," he finally said. "Tai weixian le," *too dangerous*, and "Zhao bu dao," *we can't find it.*

I sat still, said, "We can imagine it." I didn't know *imagine* in Chinese, so I used, zuo mengxiang ba, *let's dream it*, and then imagined, out loud, how we would rescue Rebecca. "We'll arrive at Hongjiao at night," I whispered. I closed my eyes, reached for Wei's hand, and when he held my hand back, waves of unlonely energy shot up my arm. I felt the city was gone, that we were elsewhere, where the ground was a tangle of weeds, wild as Holt's Wharf, dark as the sky there had been. "Hongjiao," I said out loud. "We're nearing the camp at Hongjiao." Then nettles were scratching our ankles as we fought our way toward the camp where the Americans were. Wei listened as we found a path of rocks and gravel, slightly lit by a cold moon. He was moving his fingers against mine, sliding a finger down my wrist.

I told him, "There's so much space near the camp. There's grass, there are stars, there's room to move, and moonlight. Then we find her and feed her meat we've brought, hot soup, roasted potatoes, and noodles."

But how did we get her out? Suddenly, the camp came alive so vividly inside me that I shook at the question of what kept Rebecca in: Wires? Razor? Soldiers? Guns? Guards with bayonets? Cages. Did metal cages hold Rebecca, Mama, Babcia? Babcia's delicate fingers came at me through sharp bars in my mind, pleading, reaching. Rebecca's fingers moved on piano keys, and my mama's combed through my hair.

I stopped, lost my words, scared myself back into what was real. I found myself crying and let go of Wei's hand to reach up and wipe my face. I knew then that the good parts were lies. We would never go to the camp or feed Rebecca. We couldn't help anyone, not even ourselves.

"It's a good story," Wei said. His hand looked sad on his lap.

"I can't finish it," I told him.

"I know," he said, "because—" He slashed his chest, heartbreak.

"Everything feels impossible," I said.

And then he asked what he had never asked before, what we had never acknowledged: "What is it like where Aili worked?"

A taste of metal spread through me as if I'd licked a bloody knife. He'd been waiting to ask this, I thought, afraid of the answer. Aili's bangs always fell across her face when she danced, when she looked straight at the audience. When we split our money. That splitting had evened out, turning quietly into the answer to my questions about Aili. She had known I needed help when we started and been willing to help me, knowing that someday she, too, might need help. She'd been right, and in this way we had helped each other, made a tiny alliance. That had transformed into something bigger, into an agreement not to be completely alone, even at Magnifique. I imagined her now, looking down, walking from me to General Barbeaux.

"It's fine where we worked," I lied. She had gone to the back room that night, I knew. "Aili is the best dancer," I said. *Imagine*, I thought to myself, *imagine a better story*. Wei said nothing, maybe because he knew I was lying, because nothing was okay at Magnifique, not for me and certainly not for Aili. Wei's silence was always my worst punishment, and so I rambled on.

"I'm not as good." I saw myself twisting my legs over my head, standing on shaking hands, every jeté I'd done across the stage in my mother's leotard. I tried both to remember and to forget who I'd been at Magnifique, and in my confusion, admitted: "I'm so afraid there."

Now he spoke. "Aili is so afraid there, too," he said.

"I know. I'm sorry. I think she's sorry for me, too."

I put my arm around him then, bony and awkward, felt the width of his wingspan, leaned into his body. My teeth stopped clacking against each other, and my body hurt less. A bit of the blue glow Papa used to have around him rose around me, like a shield, and I could hear Wei breathing, feel his pulse where my face touched his shoulder.

For a few minutes, Wei stayed there, holding on, safe inside the blue with me. It lingered over both of us like all the time we needed, all the hope.

CHAPTER SIXTEEN

见面, Jianmian, *Meeting*

I was at the Nanjing Theater before 2 p.m., handing over a final withered bill from Magnifique, trading entertainment for entertainment. Inside I sat in perfect dark, hoping Mr. Takati would find me, hoping—what was I hoping? Why had he asked me here? To help, punish, or forgive me?

The dark was so complete I didn't know whether my eyes were open or closed. The theater stayed empty, and I sat still enough to disappear. Then the screen lit up with English words: *Street Angel*. Zhou Xuan, the woman from the poster at the Heime emerged. I reached my fingers toward the screen, wanting her to be real, there with me. Then I lost myself watching two sisters escape war, one selling her body, the other her voice. The luckier sister became a singer in a teahouse, and the teahouse felt like Magnifique, each sister felt like me, on stage, dancing, selling something I couldn't hold on to myself. When Chinese names rolled by like clouds, loss washed over me. I wished the movie would not end, that I could continue to live in someone else's story. But even the words on the screen stopped, my throat tingled, as if I were waiting for Mr. Takati to kiss me, rather than to arrive and say whether he and his wife had helped my mother get papers. He didn't arrive and didn't arrive, and still I sat, imagining his hands, imagining him extracting from me anything he wanted, in exchange for her life, for that part of me back. I closed my eyes, tried not to think about Mr. Takati or Wei holding my hand, the drumbeat of his heart I'd felt in his wrist. I tried turning my thoughts off.

"Lillia."

I turned fast in the dark. "Mr. Takati."

Notes of hope and fear in my voice clanged like stupid chimes. He flinched but did not tell me to call him Oue, just slid sideways into the row and sat.

"You came to my house," he said.

"I'm very sorry. I needed—"

"My wife was taken with you. She wants to help."

"Please thank her."

We were quiet for so long that time spun, dizzying me. I

longed to feel real again, grounded, anything other than the sickening spin of our silence.

I got the sentence out: "Could you help my mama?"

Mr. Takati cleared his throat. "Mrs. Takati has sent a letter."

"How did she know who to write to?" My words knocked into each other like frantic people in the street, the question wrong, impolite. I should ask nothing of him. What if my asking made him want to take the favor back—or worse, led me to discover he was lying, that they hadn't helped and she wouldn't come.

He said, "She has friends everywhere."

I said what I knew I should: "Thank you, Mr. Takati."

"Your gratitude is owed to Mrs. Takati, not to me." From the formal way he spoke, I understood we were no longer friends, but he leaned in so our faces almost touched. We had never been friends. What had we been? What were we? "Lillia. I will leave for Hiroshima in three weeks. I won't— I asked you here because we won't—" I felt the heat from his words on my own lips. He didn't finish his sentence, but I didn't know why he'd stopped. We won't what? Have Saturday night dinners? Love each other? Be father and child? Eat pork from white plates?

"We won't see each other again," he said simply, as if he'd heard my childish list. "I asked you here so we could say a proper good-bye."

I saw us then, as we were, in the theater, far from Magnifique's Saturday nights, yet in an artificial daytime dark. And I thought that what Mr. Takati had loved were the performances, that we were alike, wanting pretend lives instead of the real ones in which his son died, my mother vanished, in which—what? I was consumed by my own confusion and by being too young to know anything, which filled me with anger. I didn't know anything about Mr. Takati's life or what he felt or wanted from me. Now he was leaving Shanghai, would be gone from both my real and pretend lives. I shrugged and said, "Good-bye," like I didn't care.

He stood then, having decided something that made his voice different now, final, grown-up, like my father's: "Good-bye, Alenka-Lillia."

Mr. Takati slid smoothly down the aisle, and I wanted terribly to follow him, to call him back, to dance like a shadow puppet against the background of the movie screen, to reverse whatever truth he'd suddenly seen at his house or because Magnifique closed, that I was a real girl, not a dream. No one he could love.

But Mr. Takati was gone. The projector started spinning again and lights on the screen came alive. I slumped low in my seat and closed my eyes, took a look inside my dark, secret heart. There, Mr. Takati was my husband, taking care of me, feeding me forever. Or he was my father, taking care of me and feeding me. There, he loved me. Had his wife tried to help my mother get to Shanghai? Maybe. Or maybe she and Mr. Takati had only pretended to want to help, showing each other their kindness. I might never know. I wanted to ask my mother what made people behave in the ways we did. My unsureness was surging back. I didn't know who I was. Maybe what I had wanted from Mr. Takati, in addition to food, money for medicine, and help with my mama, was to be told a story about myself, one that wasn't terrible.

I watched the movie again, tasting the meals Mr. Takati had fed me, mixed with words he'd taught me, my own halting Japanese. And feeling, the whole time, the absence of his hands, never touching me, never making me pay.

— ◙ —

All February we waited. I did not return to school. March arrived, and on the evening when Japanese cruisers *Atago* and *Takao* sunk an American ship called *Pillsbury*, I was standing in the alley outside Wei and Aili's house. Wei had saved enough money from his job at the printshop to rent a rickshaw at night, when its other drivers were sleeping and he was not yet required at the printer's. He carried soldiers from place to place, Astor House to Nanking Road, the port to the settlement, the settlement to the French concession. His body had diminished into an outline, but he was proud of the work and told me he could make more than 1.50 CN every day, forty CN a month.

"It's as much as a teacher," he told me, and I wanted to ask why he didn't try to be a teacher instead, but I couldn't. It was my fault he would never be in the Kadoorie building again. This would always be between us, no matter what else was. "If I work enough," he continued, "I could buy this. Then another man can pay me to rent it, and I can be laoban," *boss*.

I thought of the hours Wei would have to work his muscles and bones to be the boss of this single rickshaw. He was the youngest driver of the six who used it. One man had lost a hand but still drove, tying a rope to his shoulder and pulling the handle with it. When Wei told me this, he bent and tied an imaginary cord to himself.

I tried to smile. "Maybe you can get another job someday. I think you'd be a very good teacher."

Wei said, "Well, I am not a pretty girl, so I can't thief coins and tools."

He was smiling, so I smiled back, instead of fighting. "Will you let me drive the rickshaw?" I asked.

He thought I was joking. "What?"

"Let me give you a ride, please?"

Wei raised an eyebrow at me, curious. "Keyi," he said, *you can*.

So I put my body between the two plank-handles sticking out of the rickshaw's front.

Wei gamely climbed into the seat, and I heaved the cart and his body up by lifting the handles, then tipped the rickshaw back and felt some of the weight transfer from me onto the wheels of the machine. I began to walk.

"Faster, sir!" Wei called, and I started laughing, tried to run. The ground was uneven, and as soon as we were out of the alley behind Wei's house, there were crowds. People stopped to stare, point, laugh—a foreign girl pulling a Chinese boy in a rickshaw—it was unthinkable. I went as fast as I could, Wei in the rickshaw bouncing behind me, both of us laughing, too. I didn't know how to turn the rickshaw around, so as soon as we reached the corner of Chusan and Tangshan Roads, Wei hopped out, turned us around, and walked the rickshaw home with me. In his alley, I stood on my toes and put my arms around his neck, pressed myself to him, hugging as hard as I could. He felt the way I'd imagined he would, skinny, familiar, his warm neck lovelier than any place I'd been. He put his arms around me, too, before we broke away from each other and looked down, too embarrassed to bear. I held my breath, reached up with my finger to his mouth, touched the sharp edge of his broken tooth. He kept looking at me.

"What happened to it?"

"I fell," he said. "I was small." He held his hands as if on handlebars and grinned, turned an imaginary bike. For some reason, this idea, that he'd been a child once, with a bike, made me think I might cry.

"Did it hurt?"

He said, "Not now." I didn't know if he meant because we could grow up past pain or because I'd fixed a bit of his.

— ◩ —

When the American and British government loaned the Chinese government millions of dollars to help fight the Japanese, it was Wei who told me. In March I learned the names of ships and places from Papa and Gabriel: the Japanese now occupied the Andaman Islands and Sumatra, an island called Christmas. These words I whispered to Wei, who didn't have a radio, a Papa, or a Gabriel. Wei told me that the Japanese army was formalizing what Papa had feared they would: every Jewish person in Shanghai was being forced to move to Hongkou. Thousands more families moved into our neighborhood. Now hunger deepened into starvation.

Papa got rice when he could. There was no more fruit, meat, or flour. No one had money. I went to ask at the pawn shop if Mama's ring was still there, even though I couldn't have bought it back. I wanted just to visit it. But the man was gone, replaced by another man who stared when I said, "Star," whose teeth shut when I said, "Ring," who didn't look up when I left.

I returned to my puppets, showed them to Aili, said we had to make something that mattered. People would watch our show and it would change them and us, make our lives better. She didn't believe me and neither did I, but we worked together, making garlands from banyan leaves, placing them on the puppets' heads. We told stories, using the puppets and as little language as we could. I started with Babcia's favorite fairy tale, about three gifts. Rosy Mischa played the mother, who loves her daughter but hates and neglects her stepdaughter. My Biata puppet got to be the lucky daughter. The Rebecca puppet was the tragic stepdaughter who meets a magical man in the garden. For him, I took out the Wei puppet; said, "Magic"; said, "Spell." He casts a spell for the sad girl, turning her tears into pearls. I streaked my own cheeks to say *tears*, and for *pearls*, gestured a necklace. Roses fall when she laughs. I knew the word meigui for *rose*. When the girl touches water, golden fish dance up. I had in Chinese *touch*, *water*, *gold*, and *fish*. Aili watched closely. The girl weeps, because the mother she has doesn't love her. Pearls fall from her eyes and the mother scavenges them greedily, then sends her own spoiled daughter to the garden to get a magic spell, too, but she comes back with toads for tears. Lizards crawl from her mouth when she speaks, and whatever water she touches elicits serpents. Whether she understood the story or not, Aili watched with her eyes sparkling and clapped when it ended.

I took the puppets to Wei and Aili's, often bringing Naomi with me. We went outside, into the alley, where there was more space, and Aili danced with me. Sometimes neighbors gathered to watch and laugh, and we let them. This became our work, to imagine. To show each other what we saw inside our minds. To teach Naomi more words, more steps while Papa was gone all the time, frantic with trying to find news of my mother and trying to find a day's worth of work each day, sometimes helping translate papers for friends who had businesses, other times helping build or clean, still other days finding nothing. When we had nothing at all, he returned to the Heime for bread.

One night while Papa was out, Aili cut characters from paper and cast their shadows on the wall of our room with the flame of a candle we borrowed from Mr. Michener. Naomi shrieked with joy and waved her arms, wanting to touch the puppets. I couldn't bring myself to tell her they were nothing but shadows. Afterward, I dreamed that Wei was cut from paper, the rickshaw having caused his flesh to vanish. Then he became a paper instrument across which Talia moved a bow of bone. Hollow notes rose over Shanghai, and the puppets came alive.

I woke cold with fear, bundled Naomi and ran, arriving at their room so early that both Wei and Aili were home. I tried to explain my dream and also what I'd heard from the radio's tormenting crackle: sixty-two children and one hundred and eleven adults had died in a subway station in London, panicking during an air raid drill. All it took, the announcer had said, was one woman tripping down the stairs, and an old man falling over her body. Hundreds of others followed. I didn't have all the words I needed, so I tried to show this part, first tripping, then falling, then tripping and falling again and again. Aili stood behind me and fell, too, while Wei watched us. We all spent a moment imagining what it had felt like for those people, what the fear must have been.

Then Wei said, "In our circus, we can show it."

"Show what?"

"A city." He crashed his hands together, showed a city crushed. "But then . . ." He built it back up, his fingers moving up, smoothing.

"That's perfect," I said. "We'll show Shanghai collapsing

and then all of us working to put it back together again." He translated for Aili, and we went to work, even Naomi.

— ▣ —

Gabriel switched the radio off when we heard someone on the stairs. I looked up, Talia's parents were in the drained tomb of Gabriel's room, where Leo lay all day, hardly eating.

"Leo, darling," Talia's mother said. "We hope you can help us."

"With what?" Leo asked. I was surprised to hear him; he'd spoken almost no words since screaming Talia's name.

"They are making us move, saying we are stateless," Talia's mother said. "But we're not stateless, and we cannot move to Hongkou. Can you help us write a letter?"

I knew then. They didn't need his help, just hoped to revive him by pretending. I didn't think Talia's mother would insult Hongkou in front of those of us who had lived here since we'd come. They thought if Leo had a purpose—something connected to Talia—he might wake up. Naomi was on my lap, twisting my hair into springs. "Here is what we've written so far, can you help us?" Talia's mother asked. "And write one for yourself, too, so you may come stay with us, now that Talia . . . You could—" Her voice broke off. She turned and I caught her eye, beautiful like her lost daughter's, the same lashes casting black patterns on her cheeks. "Hi, Lillia, darling."

Talia's father began to read then, a monologue with which

he must have hoped to rouse Leo: "'I, the undersigned, with my family, wish to have the confirmation of the fact that I am not subject to the Proclamation about the stateless refugees, and therefore I am allowed to live outside of the designated area. I am a Russian citizen and have lived in Shanghai since January, 1939. Yours faithfully, Aleksander Vladov.'" He looked up at Leo. "We will say you are our son. We have a copy of the membership book from the Anti-Communist Committee of Russian Immigrants in Tientsin, and a letter from an official testifying to our characters."

I understood, like an adult, that this letter wouldn't work, that there was no sense in Leo's writing one. We all lived here already, and life in Hongkou was about to become worse, as well as mandatory—for all Jewish refugees.

But I agreed that Leo should write anyway, because such a letter could be his purpose, his circus. Just as the fragile show I was building with Wei and Aili was mine.

CHAPTER SEVENTEEN

阿兰卡, A-lan-ka, *Alenka*

Summer again, July again, two years after we fled Warsaw, and I was inside the moments of my regular routine: bugs, glass, shards to pick from rice with my tired fingers, not quite enough water traded for tokens, the same blankets soaked again with sweat, more fear over how I'd wash Naomi and our clothes, feed us without food. But hope, too, because Naomi was talking, standing up alone, balancing with her arms out, walking two, sometimes three steps on her own before toppling, singing entire Chinese songs. Because I had her, had Papa, had puppets, had Wei and Aili. I had a place to go sometimes—their room—had the show we were all making.

Papa was still gone all the time, searching out single days of work, sometimes in Hongkou, others outside the neighborhood, forcing him to rely on the mercy of Goya for a pass across the bridge. Shan worked thirteen hours every day, taking Ping with her, returning after dark, Ping asleep and tied to her body. Naomi cried for Ping during the day but was asleep by the time he came home, before he woke, crying, too. I didn't know for whom Ping cried.

Papa discovered an acrobat troupe and went several times to beg for work but never mentioned it again, so I knew they'd refused him. Were they the ones Sally had mentioned, who flew? Poor Papa. He wasn't in shape to perform, although this we did not say, of course. The rejection broke him further, bending his spine into a question mark. Everything was an ask or a plea.

He had been gone since before we woke one day when I was washing Naomi's sticky neck and singing, "Two tigers, two tigers," and we heard shuffling outside. Something like fear pulled me up, ran me forward toward the door, my hands still dripping, Naomi naked on our floor, our rag of a towel underneath her. What made me move so fast? The rhythm, maybe, of those steps, light clacking mixed with a heavier gait—a Warsaw sound, my parents returning from a night out, coming to kiss us, my mama whispering: "We're home."

I saw her.

She was standing there, here, behind Bercik, leaning forward into him as if she might fall. She was standing with Papa in the doorway of 54 Ward: my mother, Alenka Varsh.

She was coming toward me. Too afraid to move, I kept my eyes on her.

She was smaller than I remembered. Sharper, lighter, and yet instantly herself, even with her hair invisible. The cap she wore made her face so angular that when she came toward me, I thought, *Paper*. Other words came, too: *mother, Warsaw, metal, dead. Cats, goddess, bridge, eyes.* So many *eyes* rolled toward me, then came my Chinese name, *Li-li-ah, Flower, Shanghai*, and images, the ship *Conte Rosso*, Papa's eyes red with fever, Wei's skin and pulse and tooth. I felt everything inside me boil: screams, sobs, laughter, words in the languages I knew and didn't, a billion syllables I hadn't learned, or had yet to learn. And then, nothing happened.

Everything drained to numbness so complete that I floated above us and watched myself fly toward her, saw her arms wrap around me and smother the sickening sense that had been with me for so long. That she was dead. No matter what else happened to me for the rest of my life, the worst thing hadn't happened. The city spun around us and we didn't move, just stood in the doorway of 54 Ward. Naomi pulled herself over, still naked from her bath. I smelled Mama, her skin that used to have Warsaw on it when she'd come home to our apartment. She had always carried the city in with her, but now she smelled unfamiliar, of dust, or ash, almost like the box I'd pulled from under Papa's cot.

I said, "Witaj, Mama. Tesknjliśmy za toba," *welçome, Mama. We missed you.*

She didn't speak, pulled away to look at me, and I bent to pick up my sister.

"We were very worried," I whispered, in English.

I watched her as she watched me, and she changed when I blinked—from Mama into a stranger. She was wrapping both of us now, Naomi and me, into her sharp, familiar, unfamiliar arms and holding us for so long Naomi squirmed and I couldn't have said whether hours or days passed as we stood clutching each other, not speaking, gasping, crying, laughing—were we laughing? Time dropped from underneath us again and again.

Naomi cried and clutched me. "Li-li-ah? Li-li-ah?"

"It's okay," I told her. "It's Mama."

But she struggled away. I felt panicked suddenly by her nakedness, as if Papa and I hadn't managed all this time even to get Naomi's clothing on her. As if we'd done a bad job. But Mama didn't seem to notice.

"Come. Let's go inside our room," Papa said. Maybe he felt bad, too.

We shuffled, holding onto each other, and I wrapped Naomi in one of the towels Dr. Rosen had brought while Papa sat Alenka on his cot. She had nothing with her, not even a bag.

Alenka. Sitting, breathing, speaking. Naomi, wrapped up on my lap, stared at our mother and then at me, moving her little face, blotchy and red, back and forth, speaking her words: "Lillia, Mo, More, Mouse, Nihao, Zaijian, liang zhi laohu, la, la, toe, toe, ba, ba, Tou-bah." She had words for Taube but no idea who our mama was.

I said, "She doesn't really speak so much English yet," thinking this would help.

Mama asked, "Polish?"

I shook my head, worried this would upset her, but also wanting her to think Naomi knew her but just didn't have the right language. "Most of her words are in Chinese."

"Oh," Mama said. "I'll have to . . ." But she trailed off.

"It's harder for those of us who are old, of course," Papa said. He was trying to be kind, but a light in Mama's eyes dimmed. She shook her head, as if getting rid of a thought, and began speaking quickly, half in English, half in Polish, telling someone—was it Papa? Me? Both of us? All three of us?—what had happened. Did she know that Naomi could understand?

Even in the first moments of hearing it, I realized her story would take me the rest of my life to know and un-know. Papa, suddenly protective again, kept looking over at me, trying to signal Mama, but what, not to tell us?

Mama was holding me, Papa was holding her, and I was holding Naomi, who was chattering and squirming and occasionally shouting for Ping. Shan was at work. I wondered whether they would stay now that Mama was here. Naomi slid off my lap and began to propel herself back and forth on the floor. My hands, no longer numb, now shook. I wondered if Papa would lie to Alenka about Shan and Ping, and if he told her the truth, what it was. Did he love Shan? Did it matter?

My disbelief was so intense it felt as if I were imagining my own hands and Alenka's, that we were puppets under my cot. I checked Papa, who had been real all along. And there he was, yes, his eyes almost lidless. He was afraid to blink, too.

I turned to her. "Jesteśmy tutaj, w Szanghaju. To jest moja Mama. Mama?" *We are here, in Shanghai. That is my mama. Mama?*

It was her voice that said back, "Tak, Słodkie Lillia," *yes, Sweet Lillia.*

"Lillia, Lillia," Naomi said.

When our mother went back to speaking, a rushing sound ruined my hearing, blood maybe, the Huangpu River, the ocean, the train she said she had taken, Trans-Siberian, across the world to us, whatever boat she'd boarded from Kobe. I began rocking as her voice came in and out: "... yes, and yet, if not, I would have gone to the chambers." She used Polish, and between her sentences I heard the air coming into and leaving my father's lungs. My senses crowded and crossed, and I couldn't concentrate on her words. She said, "Like so many who were sent there."

I made my own voice ask, "Chambers?"

I worked to hear clearly again, to understand something about what had happened, what was happening. But now my mother seemed not to want to answer. Had she only just remembered I was her child?

I whispered, "I am seventeen," all the time we had spent apart opening between us. Maybe she had not been able to hear my thoughts, after all, knew nothing of what had happened to me, just as I knew nothing of what had happened to her. Something. Two years of something had happened to her and now she nodded. "Yes," she said, "I counted every day—"

She turned the corners of her mouth up into a twitching smile. I thought of Papa's clown makeup, how my mother had always worn only her own face. How beautiful she had been. Was she still beautiful? I couldn't say. She was a negative now, a shadowy Rosy Mischa puppet of a person, but here she was, herself. I couldn't stop touching her arm, her hands, even though I felt shy. She still understood me, because she said, "You and I will get to know each other again."

And then she turned. "Sergo kept me just outside Warsaw," she said. She kept her face still, but Papa began to cry. Sergo. Their boss at the Stanislav Circus. He had kept her. I both knew and didn't know what this meant. And just outside Warsaw— we had abandoned her.

Papa was staring at her with a look of horror so vast that when he noticed me watching him, he tried to reorganize his face into some other shape. He cleared his throat, and I heard the two cities and the fever he'd survived, how he'd caught me when the soldier threw me as we boarded the train. I felt him carry me downstairs the night Taube was sick and I couldn't stand. I saw him everywhere, a crowd of Papas. How strong he had been so many times, even when I'd thought he was failing.

Maybe he had known all along about Sergo, agreed to leave her, to save me and Naomi. Maybe he had known as little as I had. I couldn't guess which truth would have made him cry more. I would never know, never ask, try not to allow myself to wonder.

"You couldn't have found me there," Mama said, her hand on my father's face, holding his chin. But I had the sense that she was telling *me* what he already knew. "I was in a shed . . . and I . . . Well, there were trains."

Alenka's right eye flickered as she spoke. "I saw so many go by every day, so many trains, so many human beings, in cars meant to hold cargo, or cattle. I thought—Sergo said—they were being brought to work, to a camp where they would build a new town. He said Warsaw was expanding—that they were arriving to create a new society, but no one ever left. More and more were brought. I would have known something of the chambers even if Sergo had not mentioned them to me one night when I—"

She stopped speaking and looked confused, began to shudder. I wondered suddenly where everyone was, what our odd family would now be. Missing Taube pierced my side with grief, and I clutched it. Had God wanted me to give up something in exchange for my mother, making Taube a trade? I watched my mama sip water I'd boiled. I was actually going to have her back and Papa here, too. I couldn't allow myself to miss anyone else ever again. This was what I had hoped for, dreamed of, needed, prayed for—every minute of the last two years. But she was talking about smoke, a smell of burning.

". . . hair, Bercik, hair and flesh—they are killing people."

Her voice hit a strange register. "They're not just working them as they are saying . . . The camps are . . . The trains are . . . Ana and Nacek—" Here she looked over at me, and then shook her head as if she were mad, trying to fling out thoughts. But she kept talking. "People are being slaughtered like animals. It's . . . I know, because it's bodies they are burning. Maybe they have no space, so they burn corpses? Or maybe people are still alive. It was only when Sergo died that— Oh, Bercik. A child lived near the farm and saw me all those months and never told. Just a boy of maybe thirteen, but he managed to get my note, which had written on it only where I was, my name, and the Kozaks' address. That was all. And they found me. Nacek found me, Bercik. He came and—well, he found me. They befriended Sergo's family while they tried to rescue me. I knew they had found me because Nacek began appearing at the farm. The first time I saw him walk by the place I was kept, I had to bite my hand not to shout or pound. Nacek! I was shut up all the time. Sergo said for my own safety. Maybe that was true." Mama's eyes flashed. "The space was just long enough to lie down in. It had—I will always be grateful for this—small cracks in the boards that allowed light during the day and let me watch the nearest road, behind it was the train track. So I saw people being carted, always only in one direction. And smoke, so much oily smoke. If Nacek hadn't found me, hadn't learned of Sergo's death and come to rescue me, I'd still be . . . I'd still . . . No one would have brought food anymore, or—"

I had the falling feeling and took a sip of her water, which flooded me unpleasantly. I could never know again what was true, who among us was crazy. What if her body was back with us, but her mind was lost? Could the story she was telling be true? Had Sergo died? Were they killing people? Burning bodies? I thought it couldn't be.

She reached out to pick up Naomi, but my sister kicked away. "Lillia!"

Our mother's speech started speeding. It was as if she had to get the entire story out immediately or live with it inside her. She stood, picked Naomi up again and bounced her on her hip as she talked, as if reciting a horrible fairy tale to a baby. This time, Naomi stayed put, watching her.

"When Sergo died, Nacek convinced Sergo's family that he deserved a grand funeral and helped arrange the hearse. With all those bodies burning nearby. They prepared Sergo's body in a coffin, and Nacek snuck mine out beneath his. I had only learned the night before that he was dead, that I would be . . . carried out in his coffin . . . with him to the end."

Her eyes glittered, and she coughed, and I thought again she might be mad, that we would have to save her. I had no idea how such a rescue might be accomplished. From how many horrors would we have to save each other and ourselves? Would we fail her again? Was her nightmare real? Spirited away in a coffin, with Sergo's body?

"It was Nacek who saved me, who found me, who—" She looked at me over Naomi's curls. "They were ruined already when I found my way to them, but they sacrificed everything they had," she said. "I escaped to Vilna and from there to Kobe. But everyone had already gone. It was very difficult to get papers, but then I wrote and waited and waited until papers came—as if by magic. Someone wrote on my behalf; they let me board the ship. They let me—"

I closed my eyes and thanked God for the Takatis, for my mama, for Vilna and Kobe and Shanghai.

But her eyes clouded again. "I've had no news of my mother. The Kozaks were arrested, and I suspect they were taken to a camp, too. I don't know which one."

Naomi was staring at Mama, curious.

"They were arrested for helping so many Jews," Mama said. "Disabled people, too. Gypsies. They thought everyone deserved to live. I wish I had been able to help them."

I wished she would go back to sparing us, that she would fear Naomi's understanding, but I didn't know how to ask for anything other than having her here.

"The only reason I'm alive is that Sergo kept me alive—for himself. I'm the last one—"

I stood then, and maybe Naomi felt my fear because she reached out for me, shrieking my name. Mama nodded, so I took my sister. She clung to my neck. When Mama stopped talking, we all stopped. We sat, staring at each other, not knowing what to do or how to do it. Papa boiled more water, picked rocks from the rice, fed us. He and Mama shared a single bowl.

When she took her shirt off to wash her body with our rag and bucket, I saw her skin—her arms, back, stomach, and sides, all the way up to her shoulders and down to her hips, covered with slivers, cuts, some new, some healing, some scars, layers of them and I cried out.

"What is that? Who did that to you?"

She looked over at me, as if taking a moment to remember who I was. She touched a cluster of cuts on her arm. "These? They were my calendar of time without you. Don't worry, Słodkie Lillia, they don't hurt."

Naomi was already asleep in my cot when I heard Mama weeping, and Papa trying to soothe her. Before I put my fingers inside my ears, she asked him to get rid of the broken piece of mirror Taube had given me, which I had propped against the wall after Taube died.

"I can't bear to see my face, Bercik," she said. "It looks like the ones in the windows of those trains."

I heard him whisper to her then, "Imagine."

But Mama, unrecognizable, whispered back, "Nie," *no*.

When they were asleep, I hid Taube's mirror under my cot with the puppets.

— ▣ —

When my mother met Wei, I thought she would know him somehow, from being in my mind all the time. Bercik had met him in passing, at school, once at our door, but he hadn't seemed to make much of it. I worried Mama would be unhappy, though. How could she feel about a Chinese boy? About a boy who was anything but Jewish? Would she be angry? Would she guess I loved him, even though Papa hadn't seemed to notice? Were we past concern over such matters as who belonged to what history, even though that distinction had meant every possible hope or horror at home?

No recognition flickered when she watched Wei come into our room; her gaze remained strangely blank even when I said, "Mama, this is Wei." I said it again: "My best friend, Wei. Wei, this is my mama, Alenka." The taste of the word *mama* was sharp in my mouth, the taste of his name a relief. I felt as if she were still gone, as if I'd never have her back, but apologized to God even before the feeling faded. Could she disappear for real again? And what was more real, our bodies or our minds?

Wei cleared his throat, politely, as if he were an adult about to make a speech. He had dressed in his best clothes, clean and sweet to meet my mother. He looked to me like a beautiful escape. I longed to hold his hand, ride a train somewhere safe, eat a real meal with him and my family around a table. Alenka didn't speak. She closed her eyes and leaned back, and I thought maybe she didn't know what language to use. Did she dislike that he was Chinese, after all? Wei said nothing, maybe because he didn't have the right words, either. He and I looked at each other's hungry, afraid faces and smiled. Then we started laughing quietly, as we always did in joint embarrassment. I saw his front tooth, with the piece knocked out, and thought I loved him.

When Alenka heard us, she opened her eyes and tried

to laugh, too, because she wanted to be with us, in Shanghai, in now, our same world and life. But the smile she managed looked as if she had sliced it open across her face with a knife.

That night I went and got the cleaver we all shared. I propped the mirror she'd turned away from up on the tiny table in our kitchen. I twisted my hair, long again, down past my ears, soft against my neck, into a single braid. Then I leaned down, put the neat strand on the table, and sawed it off like a live snake. I put the braid under my cot, too.

When I looked in the secret mirror of Taube's I would keep forever, I had only a shock of cut hair left. I looked like a boy again, like I'd looked on the ship here, and also like Mama, the way she looked now.

CHAPTER EIGHTEEN

开始, Kaishi, *Beginning*

In Shanghai, Alenka liked to stay inside. For all of July and half of August, she never left 54 Ward, was shiveringly afraid. I hardly left either, because I was terrified to be away from her, and because Papa asked me to be at home. We didn't say so, but he wanted me to watch her. I didn't know what to make of this. She wasn't in danger, as long as she was in the house, and sometimes I longed to escape. Shan and Ping moved to Mr. Michener's room. He said Taube would have been glad to have them and so was he. Everything he said he prefaced with Taube, as if he'd consumed her, become both of them. The way Papa had tried to be Mama as well while she was gone.

I was free to leave to trade tokens for rations of boiled water, and one day at the end of June, I walked quickly to the building in Hongkou where I had heard Biata lived. They had been forced to move from the International Settlement. She came to the door and led me into a dark, wet-smelling room.

"We share this horrid place with nine families," she said, with none of the pride she'd once had. "We had to trade our new apartment with a Chinese family allowed to live across the bridge. They took our place, and this place costs the same!" She was almost screaming.

"That's unfair," I said. "I'm sorry."

"They took my parents' bar, too. We have no work, no money. We have nothing left."

I remembered Natasha, on the ship, crying over their manager taking the family's toy store in Moscow, and how much worse I thought it had gotten for her. What was she doing now with Magnifique closed? Something better? Worse? Why had she stopped coming even before Pearl Harbor? What had happened to her? Had the boys ever gone to school? I knew better than to hope they had.

I reached out and took Biata's hand, but she drew hers back.

"I'm sorry," I said again.

"It was ours . . . My parents worked so hard to . . . It's just like in Poland now. The soldiers can take whatever they want. Nothing can be—"

I said, "I know," and then, "My mother came. She's here now."

We looked at each other, neither of us knowing what to say. I thought how easy talk had been at Kadoorie. I hadn't appreciated it. "I want to find Rebecca," I said.

Now she was interested. "What?"

I shook my head. "I want to find the camp where they're keeping her and help Rebecca."

"You're crazy! It's dangerous!" Biata said, "You could be killed."

I shrugged. "I didn't say I'd do it, Biata, just that I wish we could."

"Well, we can't."

We both waited, until I said, "Wei and Aili and I are doing a show. For my mother and whoever else wants to see a show. Do you want to be in it with us?"

She arched one of her skinny eyebrows, didn't answer me, just said, "I want to show you something."

This felt like a test. I didn't like to be away from my mother for so long, but I said yes, curious and also hopeful that Biata would agree to be in our circus. She led me to Shajing Road. It was turning fall again, the city cooling, leaves shedding from trees along the streets. The air smelled confusing, pavement still smoking from another Shanghai summer, and yet a cool smell, too. Soon a stone building rose before us, gray circles across it resembling bubbles without buoyancy, hard and heavy.

"What is this place?"

"Shhhh," she said. "Come."

She pulled me around to the side of the building, to a stone ramp. The ground was engraved with the Shanghai Municipal Council's initials, SMC 1933. A truck had backed up against the ramp and was open, a crowd of men shouting and leading something from the truck onto the ramp. The smell rose from my nose up and made my eyes and head ache. I clamped my mouth shut, so none would get in my mouth, tried to hold my breath. I remembered the words the soldier in Lithuania had spoken into my mouth and nose. Now, muffled sounds came from the things they were leading, animals. Cows. The sound was the lowing, sorrowful song of cows, hoods over their heads, disoriented, on their way to die.

I turned to Biata. "Why are you showing me this?"

"Because," she said. "Look up."

I looked up and saw that the building was curled, a spring of ramps leading up four stories, the center open, ribbons of red flowing through grooves carved out of the floor. The red poured into drains as it moved, but there was so much of it and it flowed so quickly that it collected force and weight and splashed over the sides as it made its way to the ground floor.

A thick pool bubbled on the ground near where we stood.

"That's blood," Biata said. "The noise is the cows, scream-ing when they get their heads cut off." Her shoulders were shaking, like she was the one being led up the stone ramps. She was crying, a broken girl, too, so sad for the cows she couldn't bear it, needed me to bear it with her, I thought, watching misery because it made her own more manageable. Someone who needed to see suffering as awful as what she felt.

I put my arms around her, the way Rebecca had once put her arms around me. The way I knew Taube would have if someone had brought her to a slaughterhouse to weep. I whispered, "I feel bad for them, but I'd eat them if I could. With a little cooking and some salt? Yes, please."

Biata laughed in a shocked way, and I laughed, too, and we stood, shaking with laughter together in that hideous place.

When we stopped, she said, "Thank you for inviting me to be in your show."

"Will you?"

She said yes.

— ◙ —

The letters Talia's parents sent claiming they weren't stateless came back stamped DENIED. None of us was from anywhere that would have us. We weren't Polish, Russian, or German, and we didn't get to be Chinese, either. Mama was here, so this nothingness mattered less to me. I could be from nowhere as long as my family was here, intact. Maybe Shanghai would keep us safe until the war ended and then we'd be able to name ourselves again, to be from somewhere.

Kadoorie reopened at the end of the summer, without our British and American friends. They taught us to hide under our desks in case bombs fell on the city, and when we practiced drills, they made the smallest children close their eyes as they walked outside in lines, as if anyone could be protected from bodies littering the streets. We all knew this was a joke.

I went to school because I needed to escape 54 Ward sometimes, and because I wanted to be able to use the lunchroom for our show. I asked Mrs. Aarons again, and this time, she was so distracted she didn't seem to remember that I had asked her last spring and she'd said yes. She didn't even really seem to know who I was or what I was asking, but she nodded.

One afternoon during the first weeks of school, I got home from school to find Mama holding Rebecca's *The Great Gatsby*, and smiling at me strangely. "I don't know why he makes such a fuss over the nose hair of the Jewish man," she said.

I was glad she'd said this, odd though it was, because it was something about a book, a conversation she was starting that wasn't full of the burning smell, the trains, Sergo, or Poland. I thought, *Well, I'll tell her about my day at school. We'll be a mother and a daughter talking about my day at school, just like in Warsaw.*

But before I could think of what mattered enough to start with, a sound like the burning of the harbor came down on us, so wide and incredible that it seemed to originate from everywhere at once, to be on top of us, to smash the boundaries between us and our objects. Then silence. Then it happened again.

The house shook and broke, wood splintering from the sills of our suddenly shattered windows, rainbows of glass. I saw Papa holding Naomi, falling or lying down. Someone yanked me under a cot, Mama, screaming, "Down! Get down!"

There was another round of noise, another shaking so violent we were shards, too, tiny in a pile of splinters and then silence again, this time so absolute it was its own horrific noise. Whatever had happened was over, but I knew it would never be over, was a kind of violence that existed all the time, underneath whatever calm moments took place between outbursts. Even so, we crawled from under our cots into the quiet. The windows were gone, nothing between us and the street anymore, between us and the chaos and creek.

Outside, bricks and part of a tree branch had fallen into our concrete sink, wrecking the pipes. We would have no water, yet under my cot, where I'd hidden, my puppets and I remained okay. God made arbitrary choices. We were being bombed, which we knew before the radio told us, but the surprise was that the bombs weren't Japanese. They were American bombs, sent to drive out the Japanese.

I began shouting when I heard this. "No! They can't!" I felt wild, like I might lose control of my voice, my arms, my thoughts: "How dare America? When Rebecca . . . when . . . no!"

We were in Gabriel's room—Mama, Naomi, Gabriel, and I—and when I started yelling, he put his hands on my shoulders. "The Americans mean well," he said. "They are on our side."

I twisted away from him. "No. Bombs hit everyone—everything—they can't mean well!"

"Now, Lillia," he soothed. "The Americans know we are here. They know their own citizens are in camps nearby. They will aim carefully."

"They'll aim at Wei then, you mean. And Shan. And Ping."

"Ping!" said Naomi. "Baby."

Now Gabriel raised an angry eyebrow. "They're aiming at the Japanese. And hopefully the Chinese among us will benefit from the protection we can offer them."

I said, "We owe our lives to the protection the Chinese have offered us."

As if I had conjured her, Shan came down the stairs then, strangely, half falling, covered with dust, blood pouring from her pant leg to her ankle, where the fabric had been torn away. I heard shrieking then, metallic and sharp. It was only when someone slapped me that I realized the sounds were coming from my throat. Mama's hand had hit my face, and now she was holding it out again, ready to slap me again.

"Lillia! Calm down."

Naomi was holding Shan's good leg, as my mother gathered Shan up.

"Lillia! Lillia! Ping!" Naomi cried.

"Where is Ping?" I echoed.

"Słodkie Lillia, go get water," Mama said. It was the first time she'd told me what to do since coming back to us. "Gabriel," she said, "go outside and look for Ping."

I went upstairs and found a blanket, but no water came from our wrecked sink. We bandaged Shan's wounds without washing them and asked her what had happened, but all she could do was cry for Ping.

"Gabriel went to get him," Mama said. "He'll be okay." She stroked Shan's hair. Mama alone remained in the habit of pretending to know what couldn't be known. Papa and I had stopped lying to each other. Maybe she would reteach us how to tell the untruths we needed.

I carried Naomi outside to search for Ping, where rubble was piled around our house. But we had only stood a moment when Gabriel emerged from the south side of Ward Road, carrying Ping. Naomi held her arms out, and Gabriel brought Ping up close to her. They grabbed each other and began—to my amazement and maybe Gabriel's—laughing. Ping was dirty but unharmed.

"He was crawling into the street when I . . . One more second and he—" Gabriel began shaking. "One more second and I . . . Oh, God . . . he . . ."

I had never heard Gabriel lose words. I put my hand on his arm. "He loves trucks," I said.

— ◙ —

Forty Jewish refugees were killed in the American air raid, seven of them Polish.

I asked Papa, "How many Chinese were killed?"

He said in a low voice, "Hundreds."

I waited and prayed for Wei. Mama sat by Shan all day, sending me to the water coolies to get boiled water so she could clean the two deep parallel cuts along Shan's right cheek bone, a lip so swollen it looked like another nose, and her leg. If Mama wondered whether Papa loved Shan, she hid it. And she seemed more herself suddenly, calmer, saner, whole again. Maybe she just needed someone to need her, someone to take care of now that I was grown up and Naomi was no longer hers.

When Wei came, he was with Aili, and the three of us held onto each other in the doorway of my house like we would never be brave enough again to let go. And while they were at 54 Ward, safe and alive, I invited my parents to our show. I did so shyly, knowing that nothing could be important anymore when the city was crumbing and bombs might fall at any moment. But I had to. "It's the first show I've ever made myself," I said. "But not myself, I mean, with Wei and Aili." They nodded.

"Oh," Mama said, looking at us. "Is that what you've been working on?"

"Yes. It's nothing big, but we will only be able to do it one time."

Her eyes clouded. If she agreed, it would be the first time she had left 54 Ward since arriving. She hadn't gone outside once, and her skin, lavender already, was almost translucent.

We scheduled the show three Saturdays away, hoping Shan would be walking. I returned to Kadoorie and reminded

Mrs. Aarons that we were making a show for our parents. This time, she seemed to remember.

It was Papa and Shan who finally convinced my mama that she should not miss our show. She stayed awake the entire week before, twitching and asking Papa if it was safe to apply for passes, to walk outside, to cross the bridge. What if American bombs fell while we weren't inside? He whispered the refrain of a dreadful song: "It's safe, yes, safe. It's okay, will be fine. We should explore, watch Lillia's show. It's safe, yes."

In order to bring them to the school building, Papa applied for passes for himself, Mama, and Naomi. I had my student pass. I went with my parents for their interview, thinking how strange it was that Mama would walk right by Magnifique. Only Aili, Madame Su, Mr. Takati, and I knew how many nights I'd spent there. Now the club was gone, so could I erase it from my history and memory? Warsaw, too? Maybe all that mattered was what I chose to remember and make. Or maybe it was the opposite: Had the Magnifique Lillia been more real than the daytime one? And did Alenka wonder about Sergo the way I did about Mr. Takati?

We had to beg Goya for passes to cross the bridge, so we dressed in our best clothing, scrubbed until it had almost dissolved, and went to line up. Papa carried Naomi. We waited for three hours. I worried my mother wouldn't last, would return to 54 Ward and never leave again.

When it was our turn, we approached Goya, displaying the kind of patience that can only be faked, smiling, but not brightly. Working to be respectful, but not so fearful he'd pounce. His face was tight with roping, healed wounds. His eyes, slight and lively with an unpredictable shine, were pushed in among the scars like black buttons into dough. "Why is she with you?"

We all knew he meant me. I kept my eyes at the point where the asphalt met the blade of the bayonet held by a soldier guarding Goya. The severed head, with its gaping eyes and neck, came into my mind, impaled on every knife I'd see forever. "Answer the question!"

"I have a pass, sir," I said, and showed him my school pass. "I came to—"

"She is our daughter," Papa said. I could hear my mother crying as Mr. Goya climbed onto his desk and towered over us, almost ludicrous, except that we had heard he sometimes beat people raw and unconscious.

"We need our daughter's help at the JDC office." Papa's voice remained calm, but I was afraid my mother would faint, or say something terrible. I was terrified of not knowing her. As Goya shouted at my parents, I thought about how Mr. Takati could have done whatever he wanted to and had never hurt me. What makes a man act the way he does or doesn't?

My father pleaded. "We are helping record ID numbers of all the Jews here. Our daughter types. She is registering people, creating lists for the army."

Then Goya turned his vicious attention to me, his look a combination of revulsion and something else, fury, maybe, or desire. "What's wrong with her?" He was pointing at Naomi, but when he lunged as if he were going to touch me or her, Papa moved between him and us. A rock of anger rose, visible in Papa's neck. "There's nothing wrong with her," he said. "Let us pass."

At this, Goya seemed to lose interest. Strangely, he waved us on, looking at those next in line. "I'm so sorry, Mama," I said.

She had stopped crying, but her eyes had the gone look. "Sorry about what?"

"Everything's fine, Lillia. We're all fine," Papa said. "And now we can show your mama Shanghai, as we've always planned to. And see your show."

Our show. I remembered a poster I'd had at home in Warsaw, of Anita the Living Doll, how Mama hadn't approved, because Anita was famous just for being tiny. My parents said to be a star you had to have a real act, that it was inhumane, the opposite of art, to display people just because their bodies looked different. To put needles into your flesh or twist yourself boneless. They didn't applaud the eaters, either, Moyshe Fayershteyn, swallowing frogs and mice, or Mac Norton, spitting streams across rooms, sometimes with fish alive in the water. What would they think of our pitiful show here? Could it matter to my parents, to anyone?

Papa set Naomi down, holding her hand on one side and Mama's on the other. The three of them stood, Naomi wobbling but standing, holding Papa's hand as if she might use it to save herself. Mama squinted. I saw the haze on her face lift and drop, saw Papa, their anchor, see it, too. Maybe the smoke she had breathed, made of bodies, skin, and hair, had filled her head. She was working to clear it.

⬛ ⸺

We gathered at Kadoorie, moved chairs, switched off lights, set up. We had made a sign on stolen Kadoorie paper, drawn with ink I'd taken, too. It read: SHANGHAI TENDERFOOT CYRK. Beneath the words, Biata had drawn figures dancing, lines to make them move. I had added, in the bottom right corner, Anita the Living Doll. And in the left, Naomi.

When people began to arrive—Biata's parents, my parents, teachers, members of Ohel Moshe, some from the Heime, Joshua Michener, Gabriel, even Leo and Talia's parents, even the Lipners—Aili and I greeted them at the door, in dresses we had made, adding plain fabric to the dresses I'd taken from Magnifique, widening the skirts, closing the seams. I wore my mother's tights underneath my homemade gown, was a trapped snake transformed into a peacock, fanning my feathers out, unashamed.

Entry cost anything anyone was willing to pay. If nothing, nothing was okay. Some refugees gave no money because they had no money to give. Others placed coins in a hat Aili held. A few families put CN bills in. Our teacher, Mrs. Katz, was one of them. The principal, Mrs. Aarons, was another. Gabriel put in bills as well.

Everyone was seated and the room settled. Aili turned the

⚜ 335 ⚜

lights off and then back on, and I raised our curtain, a ratty collage of scraps: fabric napkins from Magnifique, some navy from the sash Taube had made me, a square of the wedding dress Talia had been sewing for herself, a tiny square of Ping's outgrown cloth diaper.

We danced out in a line, singing Rebecca's now forbidden favorite American song, "Somewhere Over the Rainbow." People turned to look behind them, because American and British songs had been outlawed by the Japanese. We defied the rule and honored Rebecca with our loud and chaotic singing. No one arrested us, and over the final "Why then, oh, why can't I?" I turned six crisp flips across our stage, landed standing, and grabbed the ribbons I'd taken from Rebecca's gate. I twisted them above me into a storm. Wei and Biata prepared the puppets, who, when I danced off stage, sat at a table we'd built from two planks and twelve broken bricks.

Wei and Biata moved their puppets' hands in the smallest gestures, in sync to rhythmic sounds I made with my mouth, chopsticks clicking. The puppets were eating while they talked.

"Friend," Biata's puppet said to Wei's, "pengyou," the first word of our circus, in English and then Chinese. "We must prepare our city."

"Yes," said Wei's puppet. Wei and Biata were visible, holding the puppets, making them talk while moving their own mouths, but to me, on the side of the stage, even knowing everything about our small, poor circus, the puppets seemed alive, separate from us, almost real.

And as they stood up from the table, Wei and Biata disappeared into shadows Aili cast: buildings and rickshaws cut from paper. She made Shanghai rise on the back wall, bund, river, bridge. Biata's and my puppets hauled rocks, rebuilding a city, then slumping, drooping and exhausted, sleeping.

When Aili turned the lights back on, Wei held our masterpiece, the puppet we'd dressed in a clown costume, a blue hat of Taube's with a feather poking out from its brim. Onto his small face Wei and I had painted one tear and glued to his hand was the shard of pencil the beggar girl had given me. He was Papa. I heard Bercik clear his throat in the audience.

Wei wandered the puppet uncertainly through the city, then turned and gestured behind him, said in English to someone behind him: "Come! Shanghai is safe!"

I entered. Aili held a flashlight on my puppet's touched-up eyes, lips, and fiery hair.

"Rosy Mischa," Wei's puppet said to my puppet, "we are here. We are safe."

"Where are we?" Rosy asked. I had always imagined her as Alenka, but now her voice was mine.

"Shanghai," said Wei's puppet. He took out the ladder of sticks and began to climb.

Rosy watched this, and then, as I had, miserably at Magnifique, and now hopefully, I began to dance. I saw Mama in the audience, watching, her face still but not absent. Her eyes were on us. She was following. Shan was next to her, watching Alenka rather than the show. She had her arm over my mother's shoulder.

While Wei's puppet climbed, Rosy Mischa and I made slow, traditional moves like the old women in Wayside Park, in the courtyard at the Embankment Building, in the mornings along Suzhou Creek. A shadow of the banyan tree rose behind us on the wall.

Rosy Mischa stopped and crossed her arms. "You changed. How can I know you?"

Wei's puppet said, "Like this. Look. I'm still changing." He began to dance at the top of the ladder fast, then faster, pulling Rosy Mischa up with him. They spun until Aili played the shadow of a snake across the back wall.

"I have come for what's mine," said the snake. Biata spoke these lines in her lowest register and Aili turned the snake into a warplane that flew over the cowering puppets. The ladder fell, bringing Rosy Mischa and the Bercik puppet to the ground, all the cloth, rock, wood, and paper around them. The floor of the stage was a pile of debris, and the puppets stayed still. We stopped the music for a hundred seconds of real silence, Wei counting in Chinese, our cast under rubble and the audience wondering whether we would rise at all. I heard someone crying.

Then slowly, the music started again, and we moved, brought our puppets back to life. The ladder of sticks, turned onto its side, had become a cage. We imprisoned a puppet inside it, and Biata made her hold the bars, shake them, and cry to be let out. She asked, "Where is my family?" She begged, "Please free me, please."

The Bercik puppet and Rosy Mischa walked to the cage, carried by Wei and me, and lifted the ladder and threw it aside, freeing Rebecca. And then we fed her: our hands to her mouth, over and over, like a dance. Rosy Mischa led me, and I led the others, all of us collecting pieces of the city, putting our stage back together, boiling, cleaning, singing, "There's a land that I heard of once in a lullaby."

Then Aili lifted the shadows of the planes and Wei took over Rosy Mischa as I made my way to the two chairs we'd set up. I held onto their backs and rose, extending my legs into a handstand before bending them over my shoulders. I looked out at the audience, free, flying like a bluebird in my own safe dream, smiling out at my parents, Shan, Ping, and Naomi.

Aili, Biata, and Wei moved behind me, in unison, and Biata began her favorite Hanka Ordonówna song, "Miłość ci wszystko wybaczy," *Love Will Forgive You Anything*. On Biata's third verse, I unbent my body and danced into the audience. I nodded at Naomi and Shan, then picked Naomi up and walked her to the stage on my feet. Shan limped to the other side, with Ping.

We stood across the room from Shan and Ping. Shan crouched slowly and opened her arms as Ping jumped excitedly. Biata sang her final note, and I released Naomi, and said, "Go!"

Barefoot and solo, my sister walked toward Shan and Ping. Ping wiggled his toddler body like a champion, screaming with excitement as she made her way toward him. I danced slowly behind her, my tiny upright sister who walked and walked, wobbling but not toppling, and when she reached the edge of the stage, just before she held her arms up to be embraced by Shan and Ping, she turned to the audience. Maybe facing our mama in particular, Naomi smiled like a star.

The music stopped. I said, "Please give a hand for Naomi Kaczka-Varsh! Her first act is dedicated to our mama, Alenka; our papa, Bercik; and our friends Taube, Talia, and Shan."

I looked out to see Mama staring at us, her hand over her mouth, as if she were watching the greatest performance of all time.

— ▣ —

Alenka asked every morning whether the show had been reviewed. Even as we waited for more air raids, she was there, cross-legged on Papa's cot, disappointed that our show wasn't newsworthy. We didn't even get papers anymore, and our performance had been a few friends in the cafeteria, pretending bright lights, acts, magic, puppets made of twigs and rocks and paint. How could such a desperate circus be reviewed?

But one afternoon I came home from visiting Wei to find Alenka writing.

"A review," she said: "'Lillia Kazcka-Varsh, from Warsaw, Poland, with siblings Wei and Aili Liang, from Shanghai, China, in honor of interned members of the Girl Guides from the Shanghai Jewish Youth Association's Kadoorie School, performed an acrobatic, dance, and puppet show at the school on Saturday, one that transformed our community's collective grief into an hour of joy and spectacle, even catharsis. Lillia, the daughter of former performers from Warsaw's Stanislav Circus, created a love story about Jewish refugee children—including Lillia herself and her little sister, Naomi, who manage to pick themselves up and keep moving after the sky literally falls on them."

Here, Mama stopped. She set the pen down and looked at me with her newly strange and sideways smile. "It counts, even though I wrote it," she said.

I said, "It counts more."

Encore

Someday I'll be twenty. It will be 1945, and I'll be awake, so I'll know it's not a dream. Maybe the war will have ended. Maybe Bercik, Alenka, Naomi, and I will walk out of 54 Ward into a glittering, different, prosperous city. Or into the same Shanghai we know, but free of war, no more bodies in the streets, no more children imprisoned, no more parents or babies missing, lost, or dead. No more this.

Maybe Shan, Ping, Wei, and Aili will walk with us to the dock. Ping will be six, a boy whose future we'll see in his face, the teenager and man he'll someday be. Naomi and Ping will hold hands, sister and brother, and skip, maybe, singing English and

Chinese songs. Chinese will be mine by then, too. Polish I'll have made into a memory, except for poems and circus stories I'll save for Naomi in that language alone. I will have stopped counting days, steps, stroke marks, pieces of broken puppets. I'll have assembled everything in my mind into something whole, no need to count parts.

It will be summer in Shanghai, sun everywhere, heat rising from the streets, smoke from the factories. Fishermen will line the banks, poles pulling delicious fish from the river, boats rocking on the water's surface, oil popping with fish and ginger, garlic, fresh vegetables, noodles in a tangle as endless as the city's lanes. Our belongings will be tucked in rickshaws we pull ourselves. Nobody will break under the burden of us.

I'll tightrope walk, each foot pointing the way for the other, my balance perfect. Wei will be next to me, on a parallel rope. He'll be strong, brown from so much working in the sun, smiling, his chipped tooth as familiar as my own name, as language, as sleep or breathing. We'll walk to the edge of Shanghai, looking out at the horizon where the Huangpu meets the sky. Wei will take my hand and Aili's. Then we'll close our eyes and lift our arms. Some magic force will allow us to fly.

Or maybe a ship's horn will sound and we'll cross a bridge where nobody bows, board a ship heading somewhere that's a beginning, instead of an end, a place we'll be allowed to land and call home. Maybe I'll rise higher than the ceiling of any circus ring, any stack of acrobats, ladder, or warplane. I'll have wings, be Wróżka, the fairy Lillia I once was, my arms around

Wei's neck. Maybe I'll kiss him, with millions of people and also ghosts watching. The universe will be our audience. Maybe someday we'll have a baby and name her Babcia, which won't be a word anymore but will be Babcia herself, come back to me in the only way she'll ever really return.

Maybe I won't learn for a decade what happened to Babcia, or Rebecca and her family, and when I do, the stories will be so brutal that I'll faint again for the first time since blacking out at the start of the war. I will never say the word *good-bye* in English for the rest of my life, only Chinese. Because zaijian means *see you again*, has hope built in.

Someday my second city will recede. Shanghai will transform from the giant world it has been for us back into a memory far away. The way Warsaw already has. The buildings towering over the bund and the crisscrossed metal of the Garden Bridge will shrink away. The lilong alleys will stay in Shanghai even once they vanish from my sight, as will the lines of graves in Wayside Park, Taube's and Talia's among them. Ohel Moshe will glow with its silent foyer and rows of benches. Its *Aron Kodesh* will continue to hold our Torah.

All the water in the world will be in front of us, and I'll dance on the deck of a glittering ship. I won't be feverish this time, or young. I will know a bright, sure happiness: I won't have to get married or have the babies I've already named in my mind without my mother there. I will not have to miss her the way I did when she was stolen. Even though I'll have to face how we are both transformed, have to mourn—together and alone—the women we might have been and the years and people we lost. We will write, carve, say their names forever: Babcia; Kassia; Janusz; Ana; and Nacek Kozak; Rebecca and her parents and sister, Ruthie, and brother, Jacob. Taube and Talia. We lost Leo to madness and grief, Gabriel to Leo's care. Maybe we'll learn numbers of those killed. How many will have been lost? How many Chinese people whose families will never see them again? How many Jewish lives?

There will be those whose futures unroll forward still. Maybe America will welcome us, coming into sight as a towering copper woman who holds a torch to light our arrival. Like the picture Rebecca showed me at Kadoorie of New York. I can see the woman's face, so serious under her crown that Wei will imitate it, making me laugh. I will turn to see Mama, looking not west but directly at me, her eyes half lively. I won't know what she sees. Maybe how alike we are. Or just that I'm grown up. I'll smile at her and Papa, my strong parents, then lean into Wei and close my eyes. Shan, Ping, and Aili will speak softly in Chinese, and looping through the music of their language will be Naomi's unique voice, her own sentences about whatever ends up being important to her: the ocean, the sky, the ship, Shanghai, Ping, Mama, maybe Rosy Mischa.

I bet she'll be in a state of hope and wonder about where we might land, what home will be. If my little sister asks me questions, I'll answer them honestly. I don't know who we'll be when the war ends, when we fly or sail elsewhere, when another new sun warms our always-changing family.

But I can imagine.

Author's Note

I wrote *Someday We Will Fly* because I was curious about something I happened upon in Shanghai. For me, wonder is the central engine of fiction; it inspires and allows writers to render the lives of characters whose experiences may be radically different from our own. Most novelists ask questions in and by way of our work; we explore toward a kind of truth best accessed by asking (rather than answering), by imagining the lives of other human beings. This sort of thinking, even before the writing begins, requires literary empathy. I don't mean empathy of the pop or therapeutic sort, but rather what Virginia Woolf means when she describes reading as "perpetual union" with another mind. There is no better way than by reading a novel to inhabit the interior life of someone else. Except maybe by writing a novel.

I was in Shanghai in 2011, working on a contemporary television project, when I visited the Shanghai Jewish Refugees Museum and saw two photographs that shaped my imagination suddenly and indelibly. The first was of a group of teenage boys, war refugees from Europe, like so many of the Jewish settlers who found themselves in Shanghai between 1939 and 1945. These boys were staring into the camera with the soulful, hollowed-out look of kids growing up in the deadening context of war. They also looked like boys anywhere, mischievous and sweet. Stunningly, they were dressed in polo shirts with school insignias and little tennis rackets printed on the chests. These were teenagers who had arrived in Shanghai having fled entire lives, and yet their grown-ups, on top of managing near-impossible survival strategies, had made a school, a table tennis team, and then, from there, shirts. Those tiny insignias made me cry; they seemed iconic of how human beings save each other and our children, not to mention the resilience refugees demonstrate—in ways both too small to be seen and too vast to be measured.

Next to that image was a second, this one of two toddlers, girls holding rag dolls. The girls were in rags themselves, but someone who loved them, their parents, maybe, or friends, or aunties, or Chinese neighbors, had sewn dolls for them, and painted on those dolls lovely, expressive faces.

The records of these children's lives, and the objects that revealed their community's devotion to them, inspired Lillia Kaczka-Varsh. Lillia let me ask, in as many and as complicated ways as possible, the horrifying question of how human beings survive the chaos of war. Who loves us enough to keep us safe in the face of staggering danger and violence, and how can children come of age in circumstances as unnurturing as those of occupied cities? How do we figure out how to live, to use languages both familiar and unfamiliar to tell stories that make our lives endurable? How do we manage to hold on to the possibility of hope, even when we feel the constant pulse of its twin force, dread?

For the wartime Shanghai Jewish refugees, survival itself relied on numerous converging factors, ranging from complex glitches in passport control to acts of stunning heroism and self-sacrifice by human beings (Japanese consuls, unsung Chinese citizens, European parents and children willing to take astronomical risks on each other's behalf). It also required and inspired the creation of impressive amounts of art, music, and literature.

The relationship of fact to fiction is tricky, and because I needed to read and feel the facts of 1940s Shanghai in order to imagine Lillia's life, I read dozens of books and articles, watched documentaries, and spent six summers in Shanghai, living in the Embankment Building. Historical fiction allows writers and readers to visit moments that aren't the ones we live in, and to create connections between then and now, them and us, our own histories, present tenses, and hopefully futures.

In blazing heat, I walked the streets Lillia would have walked, explored people's kitchens, climbed the staircases of houses almost unchanged since the war, and sat thinking in places from Wayside Park to the Bund to the skinny alleys and lanes for which the magnificent city is famous. To write the streets, bridges, and buildings, I ran along Suzhou Creek and over the Garden Bridge every morning for many months, looking up at the banks and hotels, imagining what Shanghai looked like to Lillia. I thought about bowing at the entrance to the bridge, what the requirement of such a humiliating gesture might have felt like.

The Embankment Building, where I rented an apartment, was built in 1932 by the Sassoon family, and served as the processing center and a shelter for Jewish refugees from the late 1930s until the mid-1940s. I wandered its halls all these decades later, mining artifacts and memories. Those Shanghai summers were a scavenger hunt for nouns: What boxes, puppets, jewels, coats, books, trunks, letters, and musical instruments did families bring or make or long for? What coal lit fires in the buckets over which they boiled water? Who baked bread, stirred soup, washed sheets, or hash-marked epic cycles of days and nights? What were Shanghai's economies—not only of actual trade, but also of emotion and hope? I visited the old slaughterhouse, a beautiful art building now with sleek photo studios and coffee shops, and envisioned Lillia and Biata watching cows being led down the ramps.

Back in the west, I spent a lovely parade of afternoons in the Chicago home of a doctor whose mother was a Shanghai Jew. She has her mother's book bag, photos, Girl Guide logbooks, and papers. From antique report cards, I gleaned the curriculum of the Kadoorie School from 1941 to 1947—lots of science, especially about the body, organs of respiration, and blood. From diaries, I read the inner life of a real, lived girlhood in wartime Shanghai. For this one courageous German Jewish girl, it seemed to me that science, maybe even facts themselves, kept her tethered to her own life, helped her feel safe. So I gave Lillia lists, Chinese characters, numbers, and letters that would keep their meaning no matter what else was lost.

I also talked with and read the books of Michael Blumenthal, the supremely generous former secretary of the U.S. treasury under President Jimmy Carter. Michael is a Shanghai Jew who grew up in Hongkou (the district where the Embankment Building is, which after 1943 became a ghetto—all Jewish refugees were forced to move there). He gave me a view of China and humanity both profound and intricately detailed. He remembered the boys walking in circles around Hongkou, like teenage boys anywhere, hoping for the notice of their crushes. And he described his childhood understanding that some adults rally while others disintegrate, and his curiosity about the powerful people he met while working in the White House—how would they have done in 1940s Shanghai dressed in flour sacks?

His wonder informed mine.

Lillia and the people around her are made up, but the Shanghai they inhabit is quite real, and in some ways, maybe not so different from the world we live in today. I changed certain historical details to make the story work, to get Lillia to China by water rather than land, to include the shelling of Shanghai by America, even though I had to condense the real-world timeline to do so. For the sake of clarity as well as for readers of Chinese and those learning Chinese, I used Mandarin and Romanized with Pinyin, a modern system of Romanization for Chinese characters, rather than relying on an older method. But the Embankment Building is real; the rickshaws are real; the white cushions in the private rickshaws were really white. Roots did hang from the ceilings of apothecaries; the Japanese Consul Chiune Sugihara did save thousands of lives by granting transit visas; America did turn a ship of 937 refugees away in 1939, and more than a quarter of those sent back to sea were then murdered in the Holocaust. These realities made Lillia and Naomi, who are fictional creatures, feel real to me as I wrote. The danger they face scared me, partly because the girls are composites of me, my own little ones, my niece, and other children I love and am watching grow up. I wanted to create characters who were at once of their own era and also recognizable to us as people who could live in ours. I gave Lillia both the tools she needed and also the sorrows and difficulties of potentially any human life: a missing mother, a baby sister struggling to fit the sometimes narrow definition of what we deem typical, and a heartbroken father doing the absolute most he can, both enough and not enough.

A final note on what's imagined: Lillia and Wei's friendship is of a sort I haven't found in the history books. I have been told by many who lived in Shanghai during the war that their connections to Chinese citizens were difficult to deepen, were transactional, and were limited by forces of bias and also circumstance (language, dress, diet, and countless other threads in the fabric of culture). But it was important to me to tell a modern story of love—love I saw and experienced when I lived much of my own young life in China. Love I am certain was happening somewhere, sometime, both during the war and after. Because love that defies danger and all the possible divides is more important and real to me than fact.

I take fiction to be the antidote to propaganda, cruelty, and ignorance because it asks rather than answers, complicates rather than simplifies, imagines rather than settles or accepts without question. Wonder drives this novel, not so much about what happened, but instead about why people do what we do, and what that says about who we are and who we must be. The books I read while working on this novel are a testament to the kind of resilience that inspired me to write. So I included my giant bibliography here to say thank you; to say there is so much reading that goes into writing; to say that writers have to do our homework, and I worked on mine. But even more, I hope to express how much it means and matters to me that people wrote careful accounts of this era and their lives. Even listening to recordings of the minutes of the Shanghai Municipal Council meetings from the 1940s gave me a sense of the texture of a kid's life in Shanghai then, including vocabulary she would have been working and struggling to understand.

The more we record—of both our lives and our imaginations—the more perspectives we get. Write your stories. And your parents' and grandparents' and fictional characters' stories. Make them yours and all of ours. Because reading offers a view not only of the events that define us but also of how to know, imagine, and feel for each other. If we can inhabit each other's lives and experiences, we have real hope of bringing the world a bit closer, of feeling the connection reading allows, one James Baldwin felt, "with all the people who were alive, or who ever had been alive."

—Rachel DeWoskin, 2018

Sources Consulted

Bacon, Ursula. *Shanghai Diary: A Young Girl's Journey from Hitler's Hate to War-Torn China*. Milwaukee: M Press, 2004.

Bartoszewski, Władysław. *The Warsaw Ghetto: A Christian's Testimony*. Boston: Beacon Press, 1987.

Bei, Gao. *Shanghai Sanctuary: Chinese and Japanese Policy toward European Jewish Refugees during World War II*. New York: Oxford University Press, 2013.

Chey, Jocelyn. "Xiangsheng." *Encyclopedia of Humor Studies*. Edited by. Salvatore Attardo, Thousand Oaks: SAGE Publications, Inc., 2014, vol. 2, pp. 808–810, *SAGE Knowledge*.

Coble, Parks M. *China's War Reporters: The Legacy of Resistance against Japan*. Cambridge: Harvard University Press, 2015.

Dolan, Thomas P. "World War II in Asia." *Berkshire Encyclopedia of China: Modern and Historic Views of the World's Newest and Oldest Global Power*. Edited by Linsun Cheng. Credo Reference. Great Barrington: Berkshire Publishing Group, 2009.

Eber, Irene. *Voices from Shanghai: Jewish Exiles in Wartime China*. Chicago: University of Chicago Press, 2008.

Epstein, Ira C. "Shanghai Sanctuary: A Story of Survival in the Midst of the Holocaust for Twenty-Five Thousand Jews Who Fled to Shanghai, China." UMI Number 1410050. Southern Connecticut State University, 2002. Ann Arbor: ProQuest.

Fu, Ch'i-feng. *Chinese Acrobatics through the Ages*. Beijing: Foreign Languages, 1985.

Glaser, Zhava Litvac. "Refugees and Relief: The American Jewish Joint Distribution Committee and European Jews in Cuba and Shanghai 1938–1943." Order No. 3672545. City University of New York Academic Works, 2015. Ann Arbor: ProQuest.

Goodman, David G. "Fugu Plan." *Antisemitism: A Historical Encyclopedia of Prejudice and Persecution.* Edited by Richard S. Levy. Santa Barbara: ABC-CLIO, 2005. Credo Reference.

Grebenschikoff, I. Betty. *Once My Name Was Sara.* Original Seven Pub Co, 1993.

Guang, Pan. "Shanghai: . . . a Haven for Holocaust Victims." *The Holocaust and the United Nations Outreach Programme: Discussion Papers Journal,* Volume II. New York: 2012. PDF.

Hannah, Norman B. "Vienna in Shanghai." *Asian Affairs,* vol. 2, no. 4, Mar–Apr 1975, pp. 246–263, www.jstor.org/stable/30171372.

Harris, Lane J. "Green Gang." *Berkshire Encyclopedia of China: Modern and Historic Views of the World's Newest and Oldest Global Power.* Edited by Linsun Cheng. Great Barrington: Berkshire Publishing Group, 2009. Credo Reference.

Henriot, Christian, and Wen-Hsin Yeh. *In the Shadow of the Rising Sun: Shanghai under Japanese Occupation.* Cambridge, UK: Cambridge University Press, 2004.

Heppner, Ernest G. *Shanghai Refuge: A Memoir of the World War II Jewish Ghetto.* Lincoln: University of Nebraska Press, 1995.

Ho, Wan-Li. "Judaism." *Berkshire Encyclopedia of China: Modern and Historic Views of the World's Newest and Oldest Global Power.* Edited by Linsun Cheng. Great Barrington: Berkshire Publishing Group, 2009. Credo Reference.

Irwy, Samuel. *To Wear the Dust of War: From Bialystok to Shanghai to the Promised Land—An Oral History.* Edited by L. J. H. Kelley. (Palgrave Studies in Oral History) New York: Palgrave Macmillan, 2004.

Kaplan, Vivian Jeanette. *Ten Green Bottles: The True Story of One Family's Journey from War-Torn Austria to the Ghettos of Shanghai.* New York: St. Martin's Press, 2004.

Kranzler, David. *Japanese, Nazis & Jews: The Jewish Refugee Community of Shanghai, 1938–1945*. New York: Yeshiva University Press, 1967.

Krasno, Renia. *Strangers Always: A Jewish Family in Wartime Shanghai*. Berkeley: Pacific View Press, 2000.

Lu, Hanchao. *Beyond the Neon Lights: Everyday Shanghai in the Early Twentieth Century*. Berkeley: University of California Press, 1999.

Mandelbaum, Lia. "The Jewish Refugees of Shanghai." *Jewish Journal*. N.p., 30 December 2013.

Mann, Amir, and Dana Janklowicz-Mann. *Shanghai Ghetto*. Docurama. January 2005.

Meyer, Maisie. "Shanghai, China." *Encyclopedia of Jews in the Islamic World*. Edited by Norman Stillman. Leiden: Brill, 2010. Credo Reference.

The Minutes of Shanghai Municipal Council. Vol. XXVII. Shanghai Classics Publishing House, 1936–1939. Archives Unbound.

The Minutes of Shanghai Municipal Council. Vol. XXVIII. Shanghai Classics Publishing House, 1940–1943. Archives Unbound.

Mitter, Rana. *Forgotten Ally: China's World War II, 1937–1945*. New York: Houghton Mifflin Harcourt, 2013.

Portnoy, Edward. "Entertainers." *The YIVO Encyclopedia of Jews in Eastern Europe*. 5 August 2010.

Portnoy, Edward. "Freaks, Geeks, and Strongmen: Warsaw Jews and Popular Performance, 1912–1930." *TDR: The Drama Review*, vol. 50, no. 2, pp. 117–135, Summer 2006.

Prażmowska, Anita J. *Poland: A Modern History*. New York: I. B. Tauris, 2010.

Ristaino, Marcia Reynders. *Port of Last Resort: The Diaspora Communities of Shanghai*. Stanford: Stanford University Press, 2003.

Ross, James R. *Escape to Shanghai: A Jewish Community in China*. New York: Free Press, 1993.

Schoppa, R. Keith. *The Columbia Guide to Modern Chinese History.* New York: Columbia University Press, 2000.

Stachura, Peter D. *Poland, 1918–1945: An Interpretive and Documentary History of the Second Republic.* New York: Routledge, 2004.

Tobias, Sigmund. *Strange Haven: A Jewish Childhood in Wartime Shanghai.* Urbana: University of Illinois, 1999.

Utz, Christian. "Cultural Accommodation and Exchange in the Refugee Experience: A German-Jewish Musician in Shanghai." *Ethnomusicology Forum,* vol. 13, no. 1, 2004, pp. 119–151.

Acknowledgments

So many people were essential to *Someday We Will Fly*, and I am very grateful. Thank you to the M Literary Residency in Shanghai for giving me the time and inspiration to begin this novel, and the MacDowell Colony for the space and quiet to finish it.

Jacqueline Pardo, whose mother, Karin A. Pardo (nee Zacharias) came of age in Shanghai, shared with me all the fears and aspirations of a lived girlhood. Michael Blumenthal's stories and books provided views of China and human nature both profound and detailed. Jill Grinberg, thank you for sixteen years of loyalty, hilarity, and co-strategizing. And thank you to my elegant, tenacious, and profound-thinking editor, Regina Hayes, and to Viking's empathetic powerhouse, Ken Wright, for steadfast belief in and help with this project. For your historians' brilliance, Patrick Cranley and Tina Kanagaratnam. For Shanghai in the first place and so many walks and talks, Michelle Garnaut. To this beloved army, for reading and helping in ways too numerous to list: Christine Jones, Julia Hollinger, Lara Phillips, Donna Eis, Erika Helms, Shanying Chen, Ally Sheedy, Rachel Cohen, Andre and Maria Jacquemetton, Dan Halsted, Dan Krassenstein, Kathy Boudin, Michelle Goldwin, Jay Kaufman, Kirun Kapur, Tamar Kotz, Nami Mun, Gus Rose, Sasha Hemon, Teri Boyd, Ilse Lehmeier (nee Cassel), Suzanne Buffam, Chicu Reddi, Vu Tran, Dan Raeburn, Thai Jones, Gabe Lyon, Rudi and Yenling VonMeister, Yuan-Qing Yu, Emily Rapp-Black, Fred Speers, and Cheryl Strayed. My writers group, for moral and poetic support: Gina Frangello, Zoe Zolbrod, Emily Tedrowe, Dika Lam, Thea Goodman, and Rebecca

Makkai. Thank you to Ruthie Williams and the historical fiction book group at the University of Chicago Lab Middle School, and to my students and colleagues at the University of Chicago.

To my family: you create me again and again, by way of experiences and the freedom, inspiration, and permission to write. I am inexpressibly indebted to my wildly generous and loving parents, Kenneth and Judith. I wrote this for their parents, Irv, Mary, Eleanor, Sig, and Lucy, and for my Great Aunt Naomi and Uncle Saul, who died just before it was finished but whose memories, songs, and Seders will always be part of me and every book I write. Thank you to my niece McKenna, who dances to the beat of her own unique mind, beautifully. And my nephew, Adam, always right behind her. To my charming brothers Jake and Aaron, and my beloved in-laws, Bill Ayers and Bernardine Dohrn.

Dalin and Lightie, you anchor me to the world and allow me to frolic in our collective imagination. You are empathetic and analytical readers of the first order, and I could not have made Lillia without you, your drawings, glorious back-talk, singing, playing, thinking and dazzling asking. You two let me believe not only that fiction is real, but also that it counts "more"; thank you, my sweet girls.

Zayd, how to write our thank-you's as the years stack and gather? You are the other half of my feeble, bisected brain, first and final reader, hot fox, keeper of the best secrets and edits, sharer of our daughters, love of my literary and entire life.